Deliver Me From Evil

Deliver Me From Evil

MARY MONROE

KENSINGTON BOOKS
http://www.kensingtonbooks.com

DAFINA BOOKS are published by

Kensington Publishing Corp.
850 Third Avenue
New York, NY 10022

All Kensington titles, imprints and distributed lines are available at special quantity discounts for bulk purchases for sales promotion, premiums, fund-raising, educational or institutional use.

Special book excerpts or customized printings can also be created to fit specific needs. For details, write or phone the office of the Kensington Special Sales Manager: Attn. Special Sales Department. Kensington Publishing Corp., 850 Third Avenue, New York, NY 10022. Phone: 1-800-221-2647.

Dafina and the Dafina logo Reg. U.S. Pat. & TM Off.

ISBN-13: 978-0-7582-1216-0
ISBN-10: 0-7582-1216-X

First Hardcover Printing: September 2007
First Trade Paperback Printing: August 2008
10   9   8   7   6   5   4   3   2

Printed in the United States of America

ACKNOWLEDGMENTS

My acknowledgments would be as long as this book if I thanked each person individually for my success. And even then I am sure I'd overlook somebody. The last time everybody except my ex-husband wanted to know why I didn't thank them for something. My mechanic pouted for days.

So to make everybody happy this time (I hope) I'd like to thank all of the following for helping me make it to the *New York Times* best-seller list: My relatives, friends, former co-workers, ex-boyfriends, former bosses, former teachers, neighbors, my dry cleaner, my paperboy, my cellmate during my "visit" to juvenile hall a gazzillion years ago, my former classmates, my eye doctor, my gynecologist, my bartender, my mailman, my pharmacist, the waitresses at Nellie's Soul Food restaurant in Oakland, my writer/sister Debra Phillips, and especially my mechanic.

To Andrew Stuart: You are a super literary agent! Without you I'd probably still be collecting rejection slips.

To Karen Thomas: Thank you for editing my previous books so well. You turned my ugly ducklings into swans.

To EVERYONE at Kensington Books: You all continue to make me feel special and appreciated. In some ways you feel more like family to me than my real family. (I know that a lot of my relatives are going to chastise me for saying this, but it is true.)

To L. Peggy Hicks at Tri-Com and all the wonderful folks who work with you: Thank you for arranging my fun-filled book tours, interviews and public appearances. I hope I don't sound greedy, but a few days in Hawaii on the next tour would be nice (hint, hint . . .).

To the book clubs and bookstores: Your support is sincerely appreciated. On last year's tour my flight from Houston to Dallas was several hours late, making me miss my reading/signing at Black Images Book Bazaar—or so I thought. When my driver took me to the bookstore anyway to sign stock, I was surprised and pleased beyond belief to see that the audience had waited all that time for me anyway. Support like that is priceless.

I would be remiss if I didn't mention some of my local bookstore supporters. Blanche Richardson at MarcusBooks in Oakland is one of the most important people in the business, and if you are lucky enough to have her in your corner, you are truly blessed! Jerry Thompson at Cody's Books in Berkeley is and has always been a very special person in my life. Bernard Henderson at Alexander Books in San Francisco is such a rich and colorful character, I'd like to be the one to write his biography.

Please visit my Web site at *www.Marymonroe.org* and sign my guestbook and/or send me a personal e-mail at *Authorauthor5409@aol.com*.

Peace and blessings,
Mary Monroe

CHAPTER 1

A crude tattoo on his right bicep told the world that his name was Wade. I recognized prison artwork when I saw it, but he didn't look like a thug. At least not like any of the ones I knew. There were no grills of tacky-looking gold teeth decorating his mouth like stale corn. There was no thick gold chain wrapped around his neck like a noose. With his neatly trimmed jet-black hair; smoky gray eyes; sharp, handsome features; and a thin T-shirt and tight jeans hugging his well-developed body, he looked like a low-income Lenny Kravitz.

Between sips from a can of Coors Light, he puffed on a thick blunt. A strong haze swirled around his head like a halo. It was some pretty good shit, too. I welcomed the immediate buzz I got from inhaling the secondhand smoke. I hadn't smelled weed this strong and sweet since I was a teenager, more than ten years ago. But within seconds that halo around his head turned into a dark cloud and was moving in my direction.

I swallowed a huge lump that was threatening to block my throat. Then I held my breath as he dialed the number to the video store that my husband owned and managed.

"Hello . . . Yes!" Wade said in a loud and gruff voice as soon as he got a response on the other end. It sounded like he had a huge lump in his throat, too. He coughed and cleared his throat, altering his voice this time. "I need to speak to Jesse Ray Thurman." He talked with the blunt dangling from the corner of his lips. "Put him on the phone. Put him on the phone right now," he ordered, a grimace on his face. "Dude, I ain't playing!" He even sounded like Lenny Kravitz.

The telephone, sitting in the lap of a wobbly bamboo chair, was so cheap looking, it resembled a child's toy. The Wal-Mart bag that he had removed it from lay on the floor, with the sales receipt peeking out like a white tongue. But the cheap telephone had a speaker feature, so I could hear my husband's response on the other end of the line from where I stood, a few feet away from Wade.

"You've reached Video-Drama located on Alcatraz near downtown Berkeley," my husband answered, sounding as cheerful and phony as a used-car salesman. "Please hold."

Wade's mouth dropped open so wide, the blunt fell to the floor, scorching the faded carpet. He immediately ground it out by stomping on it with the heels of his run-over, well-worn shoes, which he had probably picked up from Payless or Goodwill. It must have been hell for such a handsome man to be so broke in this day and age. I wondered where he'd gotten the money to buy the weed.

"This motherfucker put me on hold!" he hollered, looking at me with an incredulous look on his face. "What kind of dumb-ass motherfucker are you married to?" he yelled, shaking the beer can at me like it was a weapon.

"He doesn't know I've been kidnapped," I whimpered. My eyes were itching, and the insides of my nostrils felt like they were on fire. I held my breath again. I could barely feel my lips when I spoke again. "Give him time . . . He'll be with you in a minute. Please give him time."

"Fuck this shit! You better be right! I ain't got all day! They got another line I can call at that damn place?"

"They . . . they have two lines, but . . . but if you call the other one, you'll just get put on hold again," I managed, my words rolling out of my mouth like rocks. "Please give him time," I begged. The inside of my mouth was so dry, it felt like my tongue had stuck to the roof.

I closed my eyes and prayed that the man who was about to demand a half-million-dollar ransom for my release was not going to run out of patience. I knew from experience that a caller to my husband's business could be put on hold for one minute or much longer and left listening to an instrumental version of "Strangers in the

Night." That was why when I needed to call him up at work, I usually called him on his cellular phone.

"This is Video-Drama," my husband said after what seemed like an eternity. "We are located—"

"Shut the fuck up!" Wade roared, cutting my husband off in mid-sentence.

"Excuse me?" Jesse Ray said, still sounding cheerful and phony.

"I need to speak to Jesse Ray Thurman. Right now!" Wade glared at me with such an extreme sneer, it looked like his face had been turned inside out. He looked raw and more menacing than ever. Now he did look like some of the thugs I knew.

There was a pause before Jesse Ray responded. A pause that was long enough to make my blood pressure feel like it was about to go through the roof.

"Speaking. How can I help you today?" Jesse Ray continued, almost singing his words. "We are here to fill all of your video needs. We've got everything from the earliest to the latest Hollywood hits to—"

"I said shut the fuck up! I got a gun, and I know how to use it!"

My husband let out a gasp that was so loud, it made me jump. "What did you say?"

"You long-eared motherfucker, I know you ain't deaf. I know damn well you heard what I just said. But in case you didn't, I will say it again. I got a gun, and I know how to use it!" I hadn't seen a gun yet, and I hoped I wouldn't.

The hollow silence that followed for a few moments was almost unbearable. It seemed like every sound in the world had come to an end. My body had begun to let me down. It felt like spiders were crawling over every inch of my flesh.

Then there was a muffled hiss. Jesse Ray cleared his throat before he responded. "Who in the world is this?" His voice was almost as hollow as the silence I'd just endured.

Wade leaned his head to the side and sucked in a deep, loud breath. Then he spoke like he was reading a script. "Listen and listen good, motherfucker. Don't you say another goddamn word until I finish. Now, this is the score. *We got your wife!*" He paused, winked at me, and then lowered his voice. "I just wish she wasn't so damn pretty. It's hard to keep my eyes off a woman with such a nice, juicy petite body, such big brown eyes, cinnamon brown skin, and a head full of thick black hair falling across her shoulders. She looks like a film star." He sighed and moaned, sounding like the same obscene caller who had called me up one night a few years ago.

I didn't think that I was "so damn pretty," but I was attractive. The rest of his description was quite accurate. This situation was more about my husband's money than my looks, but it didn't matter. I was still nervous and frightened about how it was going to turn out.

Wade increased the volume on the speaker. Now I could even hear Jesse Ray breathing on the other end of the line. My husband was a healthy man, but by the way he was wheezing, coughing, and clearing his throat now, you would have thought that he was struggling to stay alive. And I guess in a way that was probably true. He worshipped the ground I walked on and had once told me that if I died before him, he didn't know how he'd be able to go on living.

There was another pause before Jesse Ray responded again. "You need to tell me who this is, and you need to tell me now," he said in an impatient and amused tone of voice.

"You'll find out soon enough. Like I just said, we got your wife. And what a fine piece of tail she is! If you want her back with her pussy in one piece, you'll do everything I tell you to do. Now, first thing is, you don't call no cops, and you don't tell nobody else about this. If you do, I'll know about it, and you can forget about ever seeing this sweet little woman of yours again. Any questions?"

Jesse Ray let out an impatient sigh. Then he laughed. *He laughed.* He cackled long and loud, like a hyena. My mouth dropped open, and I stared at the telephone. My life was at stake, and my husband was laughing!

"Man, what the fuck is wrong with you? Didn't you hear what I just said?"

"I heard you," Jesse Ray said, still laughing.

"You think I'm playing? You think this is funny?"

"Hell, yeah, this is funny," Jesse Ray said, mumbling profanities under his breath. "But I got work to do, so you have to call me back at a better time."

I sat there in slack-jawed amazement. I could not believe what I had just heard.

"Harvey, I know this is you. I've heard you use that same voice when you do your lame-ass impressions. I must say, you are beginning to sound more and more like the Godfather, so keep practicing," my husband said in a stern voice. "But don't practice on me. I'm a busy man."

"Shit! Look, I am not playing with you! Damn you to hell!"

The room got so quiet, I could hear the water dripping in the sink in the bathroom across the hall.

"Are you still there, motherfucker?" Wade shouted, kicking over a chair.

"Yes, I'm still here."

"I told you, I wasn't playing with you! Do you understand what I'm saying?"

"And I am not playing with you, either, Harvey. You are my only brother and I love you, but you are one sick-ass puppy, and you need some serious help! I begged you for years to get some therapy, and you didn't. Now look at what you are up to. Now let me get off this phone so I can get back to work."

Wade and I looked at each other at the same time. My mouth was hanging open wider than his. My husband had just hung up.

CHAPTER 2

Wade redialed the number to the video store, one of three that my husband owned and managed. Jesse Ray had worked hard to build his small empire, and he had taken me along for the ride. Not as an equal partner, but more like a paid companion. He never let me forget that it was *his* business, period.

"Woman, you are a lot more trouble than you are worth," Wade shouted at me, giving me a cold look. "You better pray that your old man comes through with that half a million bucks. All this drama I'm going through, I better get paid! What the hell kind of fool did you marry? What kind of man puts his wife's kidnapper on hold?"

"I told you, my husband doesn't know I've been kidnapped," I reminded.

"This is some . . . Hello? Yes, I need to speak to Jesse Ray Thurman," Wade yelled, tapping the top of the telephone with his finger.

"Herro. This is Vlideo dwama." The cute but heavily accented voice that answered this time belonged to Kim Loo, the twenty-two-year-old Korean woman who worked for my husband. Of all the people who worked for my husband, Kim was the most valuable. As his assistant manager in the main store, she was dependable, punctual, trustworthy, and smart. She even took care of all the accounting. Even though Kim was young and had some mysterious affiliations with the local Asian massage parlors, I didn't worry about her working alone with my husband. She looked like a sumo wrestler and had the face of a mule.

"I don't believe this," Wade hissed. He glared at the telephone like it was a pile of shit. He glanced at his watch as I sat there, with my heart beating about a mile a minute. "I said, put Mr. Thurman back on the telephone."

"Misser Turman busy," Kim Loo said. "I happy to assist you. We are located at—"

"Listen, bitch, I need to speak to your boss!"

"Misser Thurman very busy," Kim Loo answered in a shaky voice. In addition to the massage parlors, Kim had also run with one of the toughest Asian street gangs in the Bay Area. She was not a timid girl, but she sounded frightened now.

"Busy my ass. Look, china doll, you put that black-ass nigger back on this telephone right now, or I'm going to come over there and teach him, and you, a lesson you won't never forget!" Wade warned, still looking at the telephone with disgust.

"Misser Thurman reely busy talking to his brother on other telephone," Kim Loo explained. I was glad to hear that she no longer sounded frightened, but she did sound impatient. And under the circumstances, I didn't know which was worse.

My biggest fear was that she would put Wade on hold for ten minutes or hang up on him altogether. Like Jesse Ray, she was probably thinking that this call was a prank or some disgruntled customer. But if Jesse Ray was on the other line, talking to his brother, Harvey, he knew now that the caller he'd just hung up on was not his brother. That gave me some hope. I was almost as anxious to get this "incident" underway as Wade was.

"Shit! I'm going to stay on this phone. You let your boss know that!"

"Who I say is calling?"

"Just tell him this concerns his wife and her whereabouts and her safety," Wade answered with a smug look on his face. "You tell him that I'd like to make him an offer he can't refuse. For the right price, he can have his wife back."

There was some mumbling on my husband's end and, suddenly, a sharp, shrill yell. I couldn't tell if it was coming from Kim Loo or Jesse Ray. But the next voice I heard belonged to my husband. "This is Jesse Ray Thurman," my husband said, sounding more serious now. "Who are you, and what is this all about?"

"You alone? And you better tell me the truth, motherfucker, because I ain't playing," Wade said in a firm and threatening manner. He no longer bothered to disguise his voice.

"Uh, something like that," Jesse Ray replied.

"What the fuck does that mean? Are you alone or not?"

"Uh, my assistant manager is here . . . and a few customers," Jesse Ray muttered.

"Get rid of them motherfuckers. Every last one of them! That chink heifer assistant manager, too!" Wade demanded.

"Please hold on—"

"Hell, no! Hold my ass! This shit has gone on long enough! You put me on hold again, and you won't never see your wife again. It's time to get down to business! Do you understand me, asshole?"

"Yes, I . . . I do understand," Jesse Ray said in a hollow voice. He paused, and I heard Kim Loo mumbling in the background as Jesse Ray dismissed her.

"You get rid of your brother on that other line, too?"

"Yes, I did," Jesse Ray said, then sighed.

"What about them few customers?"

"My assistant is taking care of them," Jesse Ray said sharply, sucking in his breath. "Now who is this, and what is this all about?"

"This is about you getting your wife back and me getting paid."

"Listen, whoever the hell you are. I don't know what kind of scam you are trying to pull, but it won't work on me. Now, whoever the hell this is, if you call here again, I'm going to call the police. I don't have time to play games. Is that clear?"

"Motherfucker! You stop talking crazy! This is for real! We got your wife, and if you want her back, you'll do what I say!"

Jesse Ray let out an exasperated sigh. "My wife is at the beauty parlor. I dropped her off there myself a couple of hours ago."

I sat as still and stiff as a statue, looking from the telephone to Wade. At this point, Wade looked at me and pointed at me, then at the telephone.

"You know what to say," he whispered, shaking a fist and giving me a threatening look.

I cleared my throat and closed my eyes as I spoke. "J.R . . . honey, it's me," I whimpered. "I've been kidnapped, baby, and I'm . . . I'm so scared."

CHAPTER 3

"What the hell? Christine? Baby, what is this?" my husband asked in a low, steely voice. "Honey, where are you?" Jesse Ray was yelling now, and he sounded terrified. "Are you all right? Have you been harmed?" His voice was trembling so hard, I could almost feel it vibrating through the telephone.

"I'm fine . . . for now. Please do what they tell you to do," I pleaded, with a sob. "If you don't . . . they . . . they are going to kill me."

"*Shit!*" Jesse Ray roared.

"Baby, go into your office so you can have some privacy. I don't want Kim Loo to know what's going on." I didn't plan on it, but I let out a sharp sob and a loud sniff. My tongue felt like it had doubled in size, and it was flopping up and down in my mouth so hard, I could barely talk. "Baby, I'm so scared," I managed.

A few excruciating moments of silence passed, and I kept my eyes closed until I heard my husband's voice again.

"I'm in my office now," Jesse Ray said, breathing hard. He yelled for Kim Loo to hang up the other phone. Then I heard a door slam and a glass crash to the floor. "Baby, talk to me," he bleated.

"J.R., don't let anybody hear anything you say," I warned, scraping my tongue with my teeth.

"They won't. I'm alone in my office, with the door closed," Jesse Ray said in a guarded tone of voice. "Don't you worry about a thing, honey," he told me, his voice sounding tired and raspy now. I could imagine how hard he was sweating. Jesse Ray was the kind of man who got nervous real quick.

"J.R., don't call the cops. Don't tell anybody about this," I said, sounding as hysterical as one might expect a kidnapped woman to sound. "Please get me out of this mess. I . . . I want to come home—" Wade pushed me roughly to the side as he leaned toward the telephone.

"Satisfied? You believe me now? This sound like a game to you now?" Wade asked, screaming toward the phone so hard, spit flew out of both sides of his mouth.

"Yes, I . . . I believe you," Jesse Ray stuttered.

"And by the way, this juicy butt, big-legged woman of yours looks mighty delicious to me . . . yum-yum. If there's a bitch better than this one sitting in front of me now, God kept her for himself. I will do my best and try to be a good boy. Uh, I'll try to keep my hands to myself, but *I am a man.*"

"*Shit!* Don't you touch my wife!" Jesse Ray shouted.

"Then you better get me my money on time before I lose control. And I know, you know what I mean."

"Don't hurt my wife . . . Please don't hurt my wife," Jesse Ray said, this time in a weak, pleading voice.

"That's up to you. You do what I tell you to do, and everything will be all right."

"What do you want?" Jesse Ray asked, his voice trembling. "I'm not a rich man. . . . "

"Bullshit! And Santa Claus ain't got nothing to do with Christmas," Wade said, then laughed. "Brother, you rich enough for me! I got friends in all the right places, so I know just as much about your business as you do. I know what your black ass is worth!"

"How . . . much do you want?" my husband asked.

"Do you love your wife, my man?"

Jesse Ray hesitated before he answered. And that gave me something else to worry about. "Yes. I love my wife very much," he said finally. "I have always loved my wife, and I always will. She means the world to me." I breathed a sigh of relief.

"Then you'd be willing to pay to get her back." I couldn't tell if the sentence was a statement or a question, because Wade winked at me when he said it.

"I just told you, I am not a rich man. I don't care what you heard about me. I'm a working man," Jesse Ray said, raising his voice again. "I don't know why you decided to grab *my* wife of all people. Especially since the Bay Area is full of men with a lot more money than I'll ever have—and the women they love. Sean Penn's wife, Mick Jagger's daughter. Why my woman?"

"Well, I know about all them rich folks, but I ain't that greedy," Wade said, with a sinister chuckle. "And I don't want to put myself in no position that might attract a lot of attention. I ain't fool enough to snatch no famous person's woman."

"But you are fool enough to snatch mine?"

"Don't you get cute with me, motherfucker! I'm the one in charge here! And I just told you, I know what you worth. I done my homework. You want your wife back. I want my money. It's as simple as that. Do you understand me, motherfucker?"

"I understand," Jesse Ray mumbled.

"Good! Now just to show you that I ain't one of them greedy bastards you read about in the newspaper, all I want is half a million dollars." Wade was as cool as a block of ice. He could not have sounded more casual if he'd been ordering a glass of wine.

Jesse Ray gasped and started coughing. It took him almost a minute to compose himself. "*A half a million dollars?* Mister, you must be out of your goddamn mind! Who the hell do you think you are?"

"I'm the man with the gun and your wife. You'll get me my money, or you won't never see your wife alive again."

"I don't know who the fuck this is, but whoever you are, you are talking like you're crazy as hell!"

"No, brother. You are the one talking crazy."

"Look, be reasonable. This is not P. Diddy or Donald Trump or Bill Gates you're talking to!" Jesse Ray shouted. "I told you, I am just a working man. I live from payday to payday. I buy my suits from Penney's. I buy just about everything else from Wal-Mart. I don't have the kind of money you're talking about!"

I gasped myself because I knew Jesse Ray was lying! We had over two million dollars in the bank. Or I should say, Jesse Ray had over two million dollars in the bank. And that was just the money that I knew about. For a man who worshipped money the way he did, there was no doubt in my mind that he had another fortune stashed away somewhere. For one thing, he had made more than one mysterious trip to the Cayman Islands in the last couple of years. I knew that a lot of Americans hid money from Uncle Sam in island banks.

But I honestly didn't know what my husband was worth. In addition to the money that the video stores brought in, he had invested wisely over the years. He owned an apartment building in San Francisco, and he had made a lot of wise investments in the stock market over the years. These were just the things that I knew about. I was surprised and hurt that Jesse Ray would deny his wealth, knowing now that I was in such an ominous position.

"Well, if you ain't got it, you better get it. If you want to see your wife again. And just to show you I ain't all bad, I will give you till Friday to get me my money. Today is Monday, so you got enough time to do your thing. I will check in with you on . . . say, tomorrow morning, this same time, this same number. Don't you do nothing stupid, like call the cops. Or tell that big-mouthed sister of yours. What's her name? Yeah, Adele. She got a couple of cute kids, so we just might snatch one of them next if we have to."

"Don't you go near my family!" Jesse Ray shouted.

"Then you better do what I say," Wade warned, snorting like a bull. "Don't get your phone tapped, and don't have nobody up in that damn shop with you when I call you tomorrow. You can afford to close up shop for an hour or two. You understand me, motherfucker?"

The silence on Jesse Ray's end was disturbing. It was so complete, it seemed like he had left the telephone. I held my breath until he responded, which was a few more seconds later.

"I . . . I understand," Jesse Ray stammered.

"Like I said, if you call the cops, your bitch is dead. And . . . so is *your mama.* Bye." Wade unplugged the telephone and looked at his watch. "I can't believe it took all this time to get that stingy motherfucker you married to take me serious. I don't know what this world is coming to!" Wade said, with an incredulous look on his face. "You sure know how to pick 'em!"

"You didn't have to say that about his mama," I said, folding my arms. "Miss Rosetta is the sweetest woman I know. You didn't even have to drag her into this mess. You got me, and that ought to be enough," I insisted.

"Baby, I want this thing to work, don't you? If we want to make sure it works, we got to use every trick in the book."

"I hope it does work," I admitted. I moved the telephone from the wobbly chair, and then I flopped down into it. "I don't know what else to do."

"Look, there ain't nothing else for us to do! If he don't pay, you can't go back to him and pick up where you left off. You'd be a fool to go back to that stingy punk. Bottom line is, he'd better come through. You and me both are fucked in the asshole if he don't."

"But what if he doesn't?" I asked, wringing my hands, rotating my wedding ring.

"Then we go to Plan B," Wade said, with a heavy sigh. "I go on back to L.A., and you go with me, if you want to. Somehow we'll make it," he said, with a shrug and a tired look. "Being broke ain't the worst thing in the world."

"Oh," I muttered, looking around the cluttered room. "Wade, do you really love me? Do you love me enough to take me back to L.A. with you and take care of me?"

The tired look immediately disappeared from his face, and he replaced it with a smile, his tongue licking his lips. It was hard to believe that he was the same man who had looked and sounded so mean and angry a few moments ago. "Why don't we trot back upstairs to my bedroom and let me show you."

•

CHAPTER 4

Unlike the neat living room in Wade Eddie Fisher's mama's house, where Wade had just called my husband from, his bedroom was a mess. From the room's condition and smell, nobody would have believed that Wade was a mature man of thirty-three, and not some musty teenager who expected his mama to clean up behind his lazy ass.

All four of the walls and the low ceiling in the room were covered with posters of half-naked video vixens and various entertainers. Some I'd never even heard of. Like Eddie Fisher, the singer that Wade's mama had named him after. Madonna stared from a dog-eared album cover that had been tacked to the back of the only chair in the room.

Empty beer bottles and Pepsi cans were everywhere I looked, even on the windowsills. One window had a dingy pillowcase tacked across it. The other windows had curtains so thin, you could see through them. Clothes, jockstraps, and smelly socks were strewn all over the floor. Empty fast-food containers littered the top of his scarred, wobbly dresser. The bed, which was just a mattress in the middle of the floor, was unmade. Plates and saucers with half-eaten sandwiches sat on the windowsill.

Pork-chop bones, cookie crumbs, a fuzzy white ball that had once been an orange, and an apple core with a swarm of gnats rolled to the floor as soon as we flopped down onto the mattress. The only thing in the room that was remotely organized was a bookcase in a corner. All four shelves contained shabby paperback copies of urban fiction books with covers just as lurid as the posters of the video vixens on the walls.

"What time did you say your mama was coming back?" I asked, looking at my watch as I wiggled out of my panties and kicked off my shoes. Everything else except my blouse and bra were already on the floor. Wade had already slid off his jeans and wife-beater T-shirt. He looked downright comical standing in front of me, wearing nothing but a smile and his battered running shoes with mismatched shoelaces. I looked away. I didn't want to laugh, because I felt so sorry for him.

Life had not been kind to this man. He hadn't worked in three months and had lost his last job as a busboy in a Greek restaurant to his boss's teenage nephew. He was a failure everywhere except in the bedroom. But despite his good looks and a long, thick dick that looked like a sword when he got a hard-on, none of his dreams and hard work had paid off. Some of the women he'd counted on over the years had eventually moved on.

I didn't like it when Wade told me that he'd be with me even if I didn't have a rich husband, whose money had financed some of the best times that Wade and I had shared. I knew that that was a bare-faced lie! Things would have been a lot different had I been as broke as Wade. He probably would not have been with me in the first place. It bothered me, and made me sad, when I thought about Wade's economic status. But I had to think about it, whether I wanted to or not. I was one of the few friends he had left that he could count on. And he was one of the few friends I had that I could count on. Therefore, we needed each other. For different reasons, of course. No matter how people interpreted life, when you looked at it closely enough, two of the most important things in life were good sex and big money.

With a grunt, Wade kicked off his shoes, stumbling so hard, he fell to the floor. But he was as agile as a panther, so he was back up on his feet in no time, his eyes on my moist and hairless crotch. He shaved me himself on a regular basis, telling me that it was the only way for a man to get "pure pussy." I had had some concerns about how I was going to explain that to my husband the first time Wade shaved me. But the next time Jesse Ray slowed down from his busy schedule to

make love to me after my first shaving, he hadn't even noticed anything different. All he'd said was the same thing he always said after
we made love, "Mmmm, baby, that was good."

Wade exhaled and gave me a guarded look. "You ain't got to worry
about my mama. You need to stay focused on this . . . uh . . . thing we
started," he replied, stretching his naked body out on the mattress,
lying on his back. "Come on over here," he ordered, with a grin. "And
get that worried look off your face. I got everything under control."

"We don't know that for sure, Wade," I insisted, flopping down
next to him on the mattress. "What if J.R. calls the cops? What if he
doesn't pay the ransom? I won't be able to go back home," I wailed. It
was hard for me to talk because Wade was covering my face and
mouth with hot, hungry little kisses. His tongue slid across my lips like
a paintbrush. At the same time, he was pulling off the rest of my
clothes. He didn't speak again until I was just as naked as he was.

"You ain't going back to him one way or the other, anyway. When
we get our hands on that money, you take yours and split. Get you a
place in Hawaii like you've been dreaming about. Me, I go on back to
L.A. and resume my career. If we *don't* get the money, I go on back to
L.A., anyway, and you come with me. We've talked about this umpteen
times. It's way too late for you to be getting cold feet." Wade was
squeezing my breasts so hard, it hurt. He frowned when I pushed his
hands away. "What's your problem, woman? We've done this a million
times."

"Wade, what if J.R. calls the cops and has them trace the call you
just made? Shit! This thing is falling apart before it even gets started,"
I exclaimed, sitting up.

"Woman, it ain't that easy to trace a call. And, even if they did, I
could say I'd called his number to check on some videos I wanted to
rent. You told me yourself that the phone in the store rings off the
hook all day long. Remember how long the line was busy before we finally got through?"

I nodded, lying back down, one hand reaching for Wade's dick. He
parted his thighs, with a smile and a wink, looking sexier than ever.

"From what you done told me about the brother, he ain't a stupid
man," Wade added. "Even though he looks like one. He wore them
boxy, horn-rimmed glasses when we were in school, and he looked
like the geek from hell. All the other kids used to call him Clark Kent
behind his back."

Clark Kent. I laughed to myself. Clark Kent was a clumsy, timid geek, but he was also Superman in disguise. I had been lucky to end up with a black Clark Kent. Wade was a sexy beast by every standard, and women, especially lovesick women like me, let him know that. However, some would have argued that my husband had Wade beat by a country mile. Any woman with a practical mind would never have chosen Wade over Jesse Ray. Wade represented a good time, and that was all. Jesse Ray had so much more to offer, especially security. And, to a lot of women, that would have been enough. And, it had been for me for a while.

Wade went on. "Didn't you hear how scared he sounded? I'd be willing to bet my share of the money that he ain't going to call no cops. Shit. You didn't marry no fool, after all."

"Well, from now on, we call him from a pay phone," I insisted.

Wade nodded and smiled as he climbed on top of me. "You are the one paying the cost to be the boss, so whatever you say is fine with me. As long as I get paid, I ain't complaining."

Wade's body was magnificent. Even though he drank everything but shoe polish and lived on junk food, he was all muscle. Just the thought of making love with him was enough to get me off. And thinking about Wade was the only way I could get off when my husband made love to me lately. It had not always been that way.

Sex with my husband was good during the first few years of our relationship. But that was because Jesse Ray had done his best to impress me. Once we got comfortable, he made love to me on the run, often glancing at the clock on our bedside stand and slurping on my titties at the same time. He flipped and flopped around on top of me, sweating and squealing like a banshee, his long, thin body propped up on his bony arms like a brown grasshopper.

Compared to Wade, my husband seemed like a mute in bed. Wade was the noisiest lover I'd ever been with. The way he carried on when he was having sex, you would have thought that somebody was killing him, or at least beating the dog shit out of him. Even though we were the only ones in the big, shabby house in South Berkeley that his mama rented, I covered his big mouth with my hand to keep his mama's neighbors from hearing things they didn't need to hear. It was bad enough that every time Wade brought me to the house, the neighbors on both sides peeped out of their windows.

He was rough, too. He flopped up and down on me like he was riding a bull. The reason the mattress was on the floor now was because we'd finally broken the slats on the cheap bed frame that he'd been sleeping on since he was in junior high.

I removed my hand as soon as he came and rolled off of me, panting, wheezing, and moaning like some creature caught in a trap. He was breathing so hard that the hot air streaming out of his mouth irritated my eyes. The sweat that had dripped from his body had saturated the thin sheet, which had almost slid off the mattress.

"Oh, baby, that was the best yet. Seems like the older you get, the better you get. Ain't a young girl in this state that can snap, crackle, and pop her pussy the way you can! Shit. Even you couldn't do all this when you were a young girl yourself," he told me, slapping my backside. This was one of the few things that I didn't like about having sex with Wade. He slapped me on my rump the way I'd seen the jockeys at Bay Meadows slap their horses' asses.

Wade sat up and looked down at me, wiping his face with the tail of the sheet. I was still on my back, looking up at the cracked ceiling. I had so many thoughts swimming around in my head, I couldn't tell where one ended and another began. One was, I didn't like it when Wade, or any other man for that matter, reminded me that I was no longer a young girl. I had a house full of mirrors, so I knew that. I was vain, so how I looked to other people concerned me. Despite Wade's choice of words, I still enjoyed his company. He did the one thing that my husband now did only every once in a while: he made me feel desirable. I could look and smell like a pile of shit and Wade would still cover me with kisses. The last time I approached my husband, smelling like a rose and wearing my sexiest negligee, he rolled his eyes at me and told me to go put on some clothes before I caught a cold.

"Was it good for you?" Wade asked, once again squeezing my breasts so hard that I pushed him away.

"It was good for me," I told him. Though my mouth said one thing, my mind said another. Like if it bothers me now when people mention my age and I'm only thirty-one, what is it going to be like when I'm fifty-one? Would I still have enough of the ransom money left over to get a face-lift then?

I needed to keep my mind on the current situation. I couldn't afford to let myself get too distracted.

"Why do you still have that worried look on your face, girl? Didn't I tell you that I got everything covered?" Wade asked, looking worried himself.

"Have you ever done something like this before?" I replied, trying to at least look like my mind was focused on the right things.

Wade gave me a puzzled look before he responded. "Kidnapped somebody?" For a moment he looked like he wanted to laugh. "Hell, no, I ain't never kidnapped nobody."

"Then how do you know you've got everything under control?"

"Look, this was your idea," he snapped, with one hand up in the air like he wanted to slap my face. He screwed his face into a frown and patted his stomach. Then he let out a stream of belches, which rolled out of his mouth like thunder. "I shouldn't have ate them day-old sardines and oysters this morning." He belched again, shaking his head and patting his stomach some more. "I wasn't that crazy about doing this shit with you in the first place. Kidnapping is a serious crime! Now, if you was going to back out, you should have done that before I called up your old man and got this ball rolling. But, it still ain't too late. You can go on back home and pick up where you left off, but you better come up with one hell of a story to tell your old man about how you got loose. And, no matter what you tell him, it better not include my name," he warned, shaking a fist in my face.

"I am not going to back out now, Wade. I know it's too late. And I need that money. I need to get up out of this city," I whimpered in a voice that was cracking with each word. "I love Berkeley, and I thought I'd spend the rest of my life here. But I know I can't do that now. Jesse Ray's crazy if he thinks I am going to spend the rest of my life cooking and cleaning and taking care of his family and putting up with their bullshit by myself. And in my own house at that! I am tired of trying to talk some sense into that man's hard head. Now all I want is to get as far away from him and my crazy in-laws as possible." I snarled. I was surprised at how strong and determined my voice sounded when I got angry.

"Then quit worrying. You making me nervous," Wade insisted, giving me an exasperated look. "I know what I'm doing. My mama didn't raise no fool. Shit."

"I'm not worried," I said, with a pout. "I've just got a lot on my mind these days. I just hope that everything works out all right." I sat up again and gave Wade a concerned look. "Maybe you should call

Jesse Ray again tonight. Just so he knows you mean business. He can be pretty stubborn and exasperating. You saw that by the way he dragged you around on the telephone." The insides of my thighs and my crotch were still throbbing. I started massaging myself with both hands, but that didn't help. If anything, it made me ache even more.

"I told him I'd call him again tomorrow. Now if you want this thing to work, we got to follow our own rules, too."

Wade pushed my hands away and started massaging me. That didn't stop the aching in my private area, but his hands felt a lot better to me than mine did.

"I don't trust J.R. I know he said he wouldn't call the cops or tell anybody, but what if he does?"

"Look, if he calls the cops and we find out about it in time, we split," Wade answered, pulling his hands away from my crotch. "I got a Mexican buddy down in Mexico City that owes me some favors. We could hole up with him from now on if it comes to that. The law ain't too fond of him, so we wouldn't never have to worry about him blabbing. Mexico is full of folks running away from something, so we'll feel right at home. And if it comes to that, Jesse Ray will get to keep his money, but he won't have you no more. As long as you don't slip up, he won't never find you or find out what happened to you. For all he'll ever know, you laying dead somewhere in the mountains. Now do you think that the man you married would want to spend the rest of his life with that on his mind? Do you think he'd let something happen to you that he could have prevented?"

"My husband loves me," I insisted. But I had to wonder just how much Jesse Ray loved me after the way he'd hemmed and hawed when Wade called him up. I wasn't so sure anymore.

Wade rotated his neck and brought his lips together with such a quick move, they snapped shut like a coin purse. With his eyes on my face—and with a look on his face so lifeless, you'd have thought that he was watching this year's most boring movie—he slid his tongue out and moistened his lips before he spoke again. "Your husband loves you? Uh-huh," he muttered, nodding. "And is that why you are trying to cheat him out of half a million dollars?" Wade laughed.

CHAPTER 5

"I don't like it when people laugh at me, Wade." I pushed his hands away and gave him the dirtiest look I could manage, but that didn't even seem to faze him. He kept laughing. "I wish you'd stop that!" I snarled, pinching the side of his arm. The two pillows that had been on the mattress were now on the floor, too flat and flimsy to be of any use, anyhow, so it didn't matter where they were. I propped my head up on my arm, with my cheek pressed against my elbow, breathing out of the side of my mouth. Wade had eaten the day-old sardines and oysters, but there was such a foul taste in my mouth, it seemed like I'd eaten some, too.

"Then stop humoring me," he said, looking serious now.

"I signed a prenup," I said in a low, hollow voice, holding back a belch of my own.

"You did what?"

One of the few things that I didn't like about this man was that I often had to tell him the same thing more than once. I couldn't remember how many times I had already told Wade that I'd signed a prenuptial agreement. But I told him again, anyway.

"I signed a prenuptial agreement. If I divorce Jesse Ray, I get next to nothing. I've already told you that." For some mysterious reason, I had a feeling that this would be the last time I'd have to tell him this. I gave Wade a pleading look. "I can't stay on with him the way things are." I cleared my throat, but it was still hard for me to continue speaking. "Jesse Ray has changed. His work, his family, they all come before me now. It wasn't always like that," I said hoarsely.

"Christine, will you get mad if I say something I probably shouldn't say?"

"You are too late for that, so you can say whatever you want to say now," I said firmly, giving him a guarded look. "I'm listening."

Wade took a deep breath and then let it out. He held his hands out toward me, palms up, like he was about to do something I'd like. He was one of the few men I knew who was good with his hands. But he didn't use them to do anything erotic this time. He covered my hand with his. "Baby, I know that what I'm about to say is going to sound crazy coming from me, especially at this point in time. But if you couldn't stand living with your husband no more, couldn't you have just moved in with a girlfriend or back home with your mama or something? Faking something as risky as a kidnapping is pretty extreme."

I didn't like the tone of Wade's voice. He sounded too serious and more than a little frightened.

I gave Wade an exasperated look and snatched my hand out of his. "If you don't want to go through with this, you need to decide now," I said sharply, panic rising in me like a kite on a windy day. "The more time we let pass, the harder it's going to be for me to talk my way out of this if we back out."

"If this is what you really want, I'm still in, baby," Wade told me. "As long as I'm getting paid, I'm going to stay in."

I shook my head. "I just want to get this over with as soon as possible, that's all."

Wade's cell phone rang. But with the room being such a mess, it was hard to tell where the phone was. After six rings, he located it on the floor, tangled up in a jockstrap under a mountain of dirty clothes. "Yeah," he replied, holding up his hand in my face. "Cool. We are on our way." He tossed the phone on top of the same mess and sucked in so much air, he had to cough.

There was a familiar look on his face. Satisfaction was too mild a description. It was more like the look of rapture, because it was a haunting look. His face darkened, his eyes and lips trembled, and his nostrils flared. It was the same look that I always saw on his face right after his dick erupted in me like a volcano. "That was Jason," Wade announced. The way his lips quivered I was surprised that he could even talk. But the words came tumbling out of his mouth like rocks down the side of a mountain. "My homeboy, he got us a motel room in his name down on San Pablo Avenue!"

To reach the dresser, where he'd left his watch, Wade had to hop across the floor to avoid stepping on dirty plates. He was still naked, and it was a sight to watch his long, thick dick swing back and forth like a pendulum. "Go in my closet and pick out some of my shit to wear," he ordered, waving me to the closet in the corner, by the door. He paused and looked around the room. "And don't forget to put on that cap. Make sure to hide all your hair," he told me, sliding his watch onto his wrist, muttering under his breath about how cheap the watch was and how he was going to get himself a Rolex with part of his ransom money.

"Put on my sunglasses and one of my jackets," he added. "A loose one so your titties won't show. If we run into anybody I know, don't you open your mouth unless you have to. If somebody tries to make you talk, act like you from Brazil or Nigeria or some other fucking foreign country and you don't speak English. With the cap and them sunglasses, they might just think you just another dude. Or just some dowdy bitch that they don't want to know, no way, no how."

Even though Wade was obviously impatient, I took my time getting dressed. He stuffed the two-hundred-dollar skirt and the ninety-dollar blouse that I'd worn to his house into a plastic grocery bag and took them out to the trash. By the time he returned, I had slid into a pair of his baggy, tacky jeans and a plaid flannel shirt with sleeves so long, I had to roll them up to my elbows. Both items still had the Goodwill price tags attached. It broke my heart to know that this was the best he could do. And, it also broke my heart to know that he was going to splurge on a Rolex when there were so many other things he needed. Like a decent wardrobe and a car. When I didn't feel like driving us around in my Lexus and when his mama's old jalopy wasn't available, we traveled from one hotel to another in cabs and buses.

I had the sunglasses in my hand, just staring at them. As the wife of a millionaire, it had been a long time since I'd worn something so cheap looking.

"Woman, you better get a move on. Stop standing there looking at them shades like they're something good to eat. We gotta get up out of here before my mama comes home!" Wade barked.

My hands were shaking as I fumbled with the glasses. I dropped them twice before I got them to stay on my face. Wade slapped one of his baseball caps onto my head and pulled it down over my ears, hiding all of my hair. Just a few hours earlier, I'd spent over a hundred dollars on a press and curl at Thelma's House of Beauty. If I had really thought everything through the way I should have, I would have brought a wig with me to hide my hair.

But if I had thought everything through the way I should have, I wouldn't have concocted such a clumsy and desperate plan in the first place. And that was what a little voice had been trying to tell me. But my head was too hard for me to let that little voice penetrate my brain.

"You all right?" Wade asked, with a forced smile.

"I'm fine," I said, adjusting the cap and the glasses. I was still nervous and apprehensive about my role in this crime. But since I was the mastermind and the one who was going to profit the most, I had no intentions of turning back now.

"Aw shit!" Wade hollered, clapping his hands together like a seal. There was a wild-eyed look on his face.

Everything on my body froze except my eyes and mouth. I looked at him, with my eyes stretched open as wide as they could go. "What's wrong?" I asked, with a gasp, looking toward the door, then each window.

"Them shoes!" Wade yelled, pointing at my three-hundred-dollar Italian sandals. Before I could respond, he shot out of the room like a ball of fire. A few minutes later he returned with a pair of limp, brown moccasins. "Put these on. Mama don't wear these no more," he said, tossing the tacky shoes onto the mattress.

Without hesitation, I eased down on the mattress and kicked off my sandals. "Next time you go to Goodwill, take those shoes," I said, with a sigh, nodding toward my sandals. "I spent three hundred dollars on these puppies, and I've only worn them twice." Wade's eyes got as big as teacups.

"Goodwill my ass. I can get a pretty penny for these bad boys at one of them consignment shops. I just wish you had told me how much you spend on your shit before I threw that skirt and blouse you had on in the trash. Now I got to dig that shit out and get—"

Then something hit me like a thunderbolt. "Wade, I just thought of something! You can't donate any of my stuff to Goodwill, and you can't sell it," I gasped. "That's a chance we can't take."

"Who is going to find out and how?"

"I don't know, but I don't want to take that chance," I said, shaking my head. "Detectives are way too smart these days. My DNA is all over my shit." I frowned as I eased my feet into the moccasins.

Wade gave me a thoughtful look; then he looked nervous again. It was ironic that two people who got as nervous as Wade and I did would even be involved in any type of crime together, especially a scheme as elaborate as kidnapping. "So you do think that your old man might go to the cops?"

"I didn't say that," I wailed, rising from the mattress. The moccasins were so flimsy and thin, my feet felt like they were bare.

"Then what the hell are you talking about detectives for? If you don't think that your old man's going to the cops, why would you be worried about detectives going to Goodwill and finding your shit?"

"I just don't want to take that chance. I know enough to know that a lot of people have been destroyed because of DNA. Not only is my DNA on my clothes and shoes, but yours is, too. If, and I do mean if, something happens and the cops do get involved, how would we explain both our DNA on my clothes? It could be that one slipup that ruins everything. The ransom money will be more than enough," I said.

Wade sighed and shrugged. Then he snatched another plastic grocery bag up off the floor and slid the sandals in it. I followed him outside to the backyard to make sure he put the shoes in the trash, where he'd already buried the rest of my things under a pile of filth in a can with two lids.

"Happy?" he asked, marching me back into the house, goosing my ass all the way.

"I just don't want you to get greedy, Wade," I said, turning to face him once we made it back to his bedroom.

"Greedy? Girl, I ain't half as greedy as some of the folks I know," he told me, with a strange look on his face. That gave me something else to worry about because I didn't know what it meant.

CHAPTER 6

Like most of the houses in this neighborhood in the southern part of Berkeley, the house that Wade shared with his mama was on a corner, across the street from a liquor store. Winos and stray dogs patrolled the area more than the cops. The outside of the old house was pretty grim. It hadn't been painted in so long, it was hard to tell the original color. The wraparound porch in the front of the house looked like it was slowly sinking into the ground. With another strong earthquake, it would. Cheap plastic curtains covered the windows downstairs.

But the motel that Wade took me to in his mama's old car was even more depressing than the house we'd left behind. Fast-food containers, empty beer cans, whiskey bottles, used condoms, and women's underwear practically covered the ground that surrounded the cheap motel.

Jason Mack one of Wade's many shady friends who would do anything for money, was in the room, sitting on the squeaky bed, with a large pizza box on his lap. There was a battered shopping bag on the bed, next to him. His run-down shoes sat on the floor, next to his long, sour-smelling bare feet. "So did you make the call?" he asked, looking at Wade.

Wade had added Jason to the mix without my knowledge or consent. I couldn't do anything about that now. But just knowing that somebody other than Wade and me were in on this bogus kidnapping scam made me very nervous. Especially somebody like Jason Mack.

I didn't like Jason, and he knew it. For one thing, I didn't trust him. Who could trust, or like, a thirty-three-year-old unemployed man who bragged about the five children he had with five different women? He supported them all, which was a major surprise to me. But it was with money that he made as a burglar, and any other shady way he could come up with. He'd even done time for robbing the Bank of America where my husband stored his money. But that was just one of the many crimes that he'd done time for. With a prison record as long as a mop handle, it was no wonder I didn't trust him.

Jason and I had associated with some of the same rough crowds back in the day, but we'd never been friends. We had both come a long way. At one time he'd been one of the best-looking black boys on the block, with his golden brown skin and thick, straight hair. His features were so delicate, a lot of people thought he was gay until he started getting women pregnant left and right. But his skin now looked like sandpaper, covered with scabs, scars, sores, and a mysterious walnut-size knot on his lower jaw. He had fewer than a dozen teeth left. All were at the bottom of his mouth, except for one.

"I made the call," Wade said, looking around the room, with one hand on his hip. His other hand was rubbing his nose. "Man, this place is a dump!" he exclaimed, gazing at me with a tortured look on his face. I didn't comment on the motel room, because it didn't look any worse than Wade's bedroom. As a matter of fact, it was cleaner and more organized than Wade's room had ever been during my visits.

"What did you expect for what you wanted to pay?" Jason sneered, still ignoring me. "And, for a man about to come into a half million bucks, you don't need to be so tight. Shit! After this Friday, we'll be living like kings." The thick, beautiful black hair that used to cover Jason's head was a lot thinner now and had more strands of gray than black.

Wade gave me a quick glance. I didn't know what all Wade had told Jason. I just assumed that we were all on the same page. Apparently, Jason didn't know all of the facts, but he did know that half a million dollars were on the table, and that disturbed me. The fact that Wade had been stupid enough to reveal that information to an ex-con like Jason was just one more reason why I had to break off my relationship with him once and for all as soon as I could. Wade and I had gone over our plan at least half a dozen times. Wade was to get fifty thousand for his role. And out of that, he was supposed to break Jason off with ten thousand. The rest was mine.

Once Jesse Ray paid the ransom, I'd be "returned" to him unharmed. After a week or two, I'd still be "traumatized, frightened, and depressed," so I would "leave" Jesse Ray and eventually divorce him. With my share of the ransom money, I could move away from Berkeley. Hawaii seemed like a good place for me to reinvent myself, and that's what I had told Wade. But I had other plans. Plans that I didn't plan on sharing with Wade or anybody else I knew.

I was not going to go anywhere near Hawaii, or any other place where I thought Wade would eventually come looking for me. I had never lived anywhere but California, and I didn't want to give it up. I liked Sacramento, and nobody would think of looking for me there. But I still didn't plan to take any chances. Once I made the move to Sacramento, I planned to change my hair and make a few other alterations to my appearance. By the time I got done with my makeover, my own mother wouldn't recognize me. As far as Mama and Daddy were concerned, I planned to tell them the same story that I planned to tell Jesse Ray and everybody else: I was moving to Hawaii. I even had a story ready for the people who'd ask me how I could afford to move to Hawaii. And that story was that I'd borrowed the money from a friend. It would be a friend that didn't exist, of course, so that was one more lie I didn't have to worry about being exposed.

It saddened me to know that my life had come to this. I had not been happy for years, and my marriage had become a joke. But Jesse Ray wasn't the only man I needed to remove from my life. My relationship with Wade was, and had been, a dead-end situation for years. As much as I hated to admit it, the sex was the main reason I was still involved with Wade. Yes, it was just that good. He could make me come just by rubbing the side of my arm.

Wade interrupted my thoughts by snapping his fingers in my face. "Take off that jacket," he told me, removing the baseball cap from my head and tossing it to the floor. I took off the sunglasses myself. "Jason, get busy," Wade hollered over his shoulder. "Do your thing, brother."

I looked past Wade. Jason removed a grocery-store brown paper bag from the shopping bag on the bed and started walking toward me. I was surprised to see that he now walked with a limp. He ignored me and handed the bag to Wade.

"What's all that?" I wanted to know. I was no angel and never had been. But I did not make a good criminal. Not only was I too nervous for my own good, but I felt that my role as the "mastermind" had been compromised. It seemed like Wade was calling all the shots now. I was still pissed off with him for involving Jason in our plan. And, now it looked like he and Jason had cooked up another part to my scheme without my knowledge or consent.

"We have to make this look real good," Wade said, talking out the side of his mouth. He removed several pieces of rope and a piece of black cloth from the bag. "Where is the camera?" he asked, turning to Jason. Without a word, Jason plucked a Polaroid camera from the shopping bag.

"What's all this for?" I asked, looking from one item to another. "You've already called J.R., and he knows the deal. We don't need to overdo anything," I protested, holding up my hand.

"You got any black make-up or a black eyebrow pencil?" Wade asked me. "A black eye would add a nice touch."

"No. Black eye, my ass. I don't want to upset my husband that much. Taking his money will be bad enough. And you didn't answer my question," I snapped. "I want to know what all of this shit is for?" I asked, pointing at the items that Jason had just produced. "This wasn't part of our plan. And if we, or you and your boy, start making up things as we go along, we are going to slip up and fuck up."

"We just want to sweeten the pot," Wade told me, wrapping one of the pieces of rope around my wrists. "We've come this far. We might as well go all the way," he said, looking from me to Jason. Wade stripped me down to my underwear. And, for the first time, Jason smiled at me, his eyes stretched open wide as he stared from my crotch to my chest.

Jason snorted and gave me a thoughtful look. Like he didn't know what to say next. But then he started talking like he didn't want to stop. "Shit, shit, shit! The brother is right," that snaggletoothed sucker said, grinning. "It might take more than a phone call to make this thing work. A few good pictures will sew this thing up tight as a virgin's honeypot." Jason snapped his lips shut as his eyes roamed up and down my body some more.

I sighed and tilted my head back for Jason to tie the blindfold around my eyes. Now at least I wouldn't have to look at his leering face for a few minutes.

CHAPTER 7

All kinds of prostitutes, from elderly women to teenage boys, worked day and night, seven days a week, rain or shine, along San Pablo Avenue, a gritty street that ran from Oakland to Berkeley and way beyond. They did their business between parked cars, stretched out on the ground, with a homeless person as the lookout; in the backseats of their tricks' cars; or backed up against walls in back alleys.

But the ones who really meant business did theirs in some of the cheap motels up and down San Pablo Avenue and some of the nearby streets. With rooms that they rented out by the hour, some of the motel owners had the nerve to offer cable TV. It had been a long time since I had been inside a motel as tacky as the one I was in now. If Jesse Ray hadn't given me a job and fallen in love with me, I would probably be on my back in bed with some stranger in motels like this one on a regular basis by now. I had not been a bad youth, just confused and impulsive. Back then it seemed so cool to be like that. I had wanted people to like me so I'd eagerly become part of the wildest crowds. Not only had I fucked my brains out, I had done just about everything else, including drugs and thefts. It would have been easy for me to slide into prostitution. But by marrying me, J.R. had saved me from a life of despair. Well, almost. The attention and the respect that he had once given to me had made me feel better than I had in a long time. I had worked hard to reinvent myself and for a while it had worked. The housewives in my posh neighborhood had no idea how happy I was to be among them. It saddened me that it had come to this.

I had to rub my nose because there was a foul smell in the air, and it was so potent, I couldn't tell where or what it was coming from. Last week they found a woman who'd been dead for three days under the bed in one of these motels. The bed that I was standing next to sagged in the middle, but I was not about to look up under it. When I sat down on it, with my hands tied and my eyes covered, I sank into what felt like a deep valley. I gritted my teeth as Jason snapped several Polaroids of me, which he was going to deliver to Jesse Ray after the second telephone call.

"That's right. That's right," Wade said in a breathy voice, rubbing my leg as he squatted on the floor by the bed like a director. "Get one more of her face from the side. Baby, poke your lips out," he ordered, pinching my thigh. "That shit looks real dramatic," he said, clapping his hands.

"All right. This is as much as I can stand of this," I snarled. "Take this shit off me." I had already started wiggling the ropes from around my wrists.

I was disappointed when the blindfold came off because Jason was the one who had removed it. He stood there grinning, with that one tooth he had left at the top of his mouth hanging from his gums like an icicle. When he touched me, with hands that looked like paws, my flesh crawled.

Wade was standing over me, looking at the pictures I'd posed for. I refused to look at them as I snatched my clothes up off the floor and got dressed. I didn't even have to look at Jason to know that he was enjoying every inch of my naked skin that he could see with his beady eyes.

It had been a long day, and it was going to be a long night. Around eight, Wade drove Jason back to wherever it was he lived these days. I didn't want to know any more about that man than I needed to know. And I knew more than I wanted to know already. I was glad that he didn't even know about my bogus plan to flee to Hawaii after we'd collected the money from Jesse Ray. I had warned Wade not to tell him. Especially now that the plan had been initiated.

I knew I would have trouble sleeping. For one thing, I had to wonder how Jesse Ray had explained my absence to his mama and the rest of his family. Since they all lived with us, and were so used to me being there to fix dinner for them and clean up behind their sorry asses, they would get nosy and impatient right off the bat.

After I watched television for a while, I glanced at my watch, surprised to see that it was a few minutes past nine o'clock. Adele, my bitch-on-wheels sister-in-law, sat around with rum and Coke and waited for me to braid her hair every night around nine. I knew that by now she was mad as hell. The fact that I had not been there to prepare dinner and bathe my invalid mother-in-law would have already set her off. These were just a few of the rituals that I'd endured every night for almost a year. That's how long my sister-in-law and her family had been living with us. To them, that's what "a little while, until we get back up on our feet" meant.

I pretended to be asleep when Wade returned to the motel room a couple of hours later, cursing as he tripped over the empty pizza box that Jason had left behind on the floor. He took a quick shower, then crawled into the weak bed with me, naked and rubbing on my butt with both hands and his throbbing dick.

Despite the fact that I had arranged my own kidnapping to get money from my husband so that I could start life over as a single woman, I still had feelings for Jesse Ray. My history with him had not been all bad, and no matter what happened and where I ended up, even if it meant jail, I'd always be grateful to Jesse Ray for all the good he had done for me.

I didn't love Wade the way I had always wanted to. He was not the kind of man that I would marry and have babies with. He was more like a real-life fantasy. And, in the real world, no woman in her right mind married a fantasy. But he'd been my first love and my steady lover for the past several months. I cared enough about him for that. How could I not? The fact that he had been a "maintenance man" in a lot of other women's lives (and probably still was) over the years didn't bother me. He still made me feel special.

Especially when he agreed to help me commit a crime that could ruin us both for life if we got caught.

CHAPTER 8

As much as Wade turned me on, I still ignored him rubbing and patting my crotch. I had had enough sex for one day. He wouldn't let me off that easily, though. He slid my panties off and fucked me, anyway, all the while thinking I was asleep. For the next hour, he rode me like a mule before he slumped over to his side of the bed like a boneless corpse.

I had had some very long nights in my turbulent life, but this was the longest night that I'd ever had to get through. But the ruckus that the hookers made running in and out the rooms on both sides of us, and fussing, fighting, and fucking their tricks, would have been enough to keep me from getting to sleep, anyway. And, even though this was not a family-friendly motel, somebody outside had a baby and a dog that were crying and howling so much, I could barely tell one from the other. I couldn't have slept if I had wanted to. I knew that I wouldn't really sleep well again until after Jesse Ray had paid the ransom money for my return.

If he did.

I was still wide awake when Jason returned to the motel around ten the next morning. Grinning as usual, of course. I was annoyed and angry to see that Wade had given that punk a key to the room. I didn't have a key. Not that I was going to be out taking a morning stroll or anything, but to me, it would have made more sense for me to have a key than Jason.

"I figured y'all would be hungry," Jason said, stumbling into the room, holding a brown paper bag. "These bear claws is a day old and the coffee is kind of weak, but I went to the cheapest and closest place I could find." He took out one of the bear claws and bit into it with that one tooth, his whole face twisting from left to right as he chewed. Then he set the bag down on the dresser, looking me up and down. I was still naked, thanks to Wade. But I had the covers pulled up to my chin, so it didn't do Jason any good to roll his eyes up and down my body, hoping to see my crack through a crack in the covers.

"Thanks, man," Wade said as he fished the two cups of coffee out of the bag. He took a quick sip, making gurgling sounds in his throat. "Baby, you need to eat something," he said, handing me one of the bear claws, which looked like somebody had been playing with it. I shook my head. "Uh, listen, me and Jason, we decided to go call my man from a pay phone today, like you suggested."

"I'm glad to hear that," I said, sitting up. I made sure that the covers were still up around my chin. "I wish you had done that yesterday when you called him." I dragged my fingers through my matted hair and slid my tongue around inside and outside of my mouth. The taste of my gums, teeth, and lips was enough to make me sick. But I didn't want any coffee, any of the beaten-up bear claws, or anything else in my mouth except some mouthwash or toothpaste, which I didn't have. But more than anything, I wanted this episode to be over and done with. "What about those pictures we took yesterday?" I said, looking from Wade to Jason.

"What about them pictures?" Wade asked, talking with his mouth full.

"What are you going to do with them?" I wanted to know.

"We are going to use them. What did you think I took 'em for, woman?" Jason snapped.

"Jason, I wasn't talking to you," I said, shaking a finger at him. "I was talking to Wade."

"Well, I'm talking to you. And while I'm doing it, I want to tell you that you got one hell of a mouth on you, girl. No wonder you couldn't keep your husband happy," Jason sneered, talking and chewing at the same time. A hard look crossed his face, and he stared at me with so much contempt, I felt a sharp pain shoot up my back.

"I didn't want you involved in this in the first place. And if it was up to me, you wouldn't be here now," I reminded. "This is my"—I paused and tapped my chest with my finger—"my game. If you don't want to play it by my rules, you can take your fucking bear claws and get the hell up out of here. And, with your lovely record, I know I don't have to worry about you blabbing about any of this."

Jason was still chewing, but the look on his face had softened. He blinked and swallowed hard. "We ain't going to use them pictures unless we have to," he muttered, looking at Wade.

"Jason, I'm in the room, and I'm the one talking now. I asked the question about the pictures, not Wade. You can address me," I said, with a smirk. "After we get the money, you won't ever have to see me again."

"Woman, I don't know why you be tripping. We are all on the same side," Jason said speaking to me but *still* looking at Wade. Then he slurped from his coffee cup like a hog at a trough.

"Both of y'all need to chill out. We got business to take care of," Wade said, shaking his fist in Jason's face but looking at me. "Baby, you better stay in the room while we're gone. I seen a pay phone about two blocks down the way."

"What are you going to say to my husband this time?" I asked, still glaring at the side of Jason's face. I flinched when he let out a loud belch.

"First, we need to find out where my man's head is right about now. If things are going our way, I'll tell him when and where to drop off the money." Wade paused and gave me a thoughtful look. "Once we get our money, well, it's over. You do what you got to do. I do what I got to do. Any questions?" He looked from me to Jason.

"Hell, yeah! I got a question! When do I get paid?" Jason asked in an anxious voice, moving toward the bed. Crumbs decorated his chin and lips. It was only then that I noticed that Jason looked cleaner and neater than he'd looked the day before. He wore a nice crisp plaid shirt and a pair of jeans that somebody had taken the time to iron. The creases in the legs were razor sharp. Whatever he was doing to the women in his life was working. Or, if he was as lucky as Wade, one of the women taking such good care of him was his mama.

"Calm down, brother. You'll get your money when old J.R. gives me my money," Wade said firmly, giving Jason a hot look.

"I think you mean *my* money," I said, ignoring the ominous feeling that suddenly came over me. The feeling that I had was one thing, and that was bad enough. But the way that Wade looked at me gave me a chill that went all the way down to my bones.

CHAPTER 9

I didn't know how long Wade and Jason would be gone this time. And even though I was nervous and on edge, I was glad to be alone so that I could have some time to myself.

I had no appetite. The way my stomach was feeling, I didn't think I'd eat again until I knew for sure what Jesse Ray was going to do. My throat was dry, but by now the coffee that Jason had brought was too cold to drink. I emptied one of the cups and used it to get some water from the faucet in the bathroom. I was only able to swallow a few sips, and I almost threw it back up. The water was cloudy and tasted like metal.

I tried to get some sleep as I crawled back into the bed and curled up under the covers, still naked. Maury Povich was on the TV screen, with some trashy-looking, big-footed woman screaming at the married man she'd been having an affair with.

But no matter how tired I was or how hard I tried to doze off, all I could do was lie there and think. There were a lot of things on my mind that I needed to sort through. My future was the most important. But I couldn't ignore my past and the things that had happened to me then that had driven me to my present point of desperation.

I had spent most of my childhood looking for love, but in all the wrong places. And I had tried just about every trick in the book to get it. I didn't have any family other than Daddy and Mama. At least none to speak of. But from the vague stories that both my parents had told me, usually in whispered voices, I had a few family members left somewhere in some little rural village in Guatemala occupied mostly by blacks and Indians.

After enduring forty-eight hours of the worst labor any woman had ever experienced, according to Mama, she had given birth to me. "And you was such a homely little beast. You had eyes like a dead fish, hair like barbed wire, and a snout like a pig," she often told me, adding, with a mysterious smirk, "Praise the Lord, your face eventually settled in the right direction." That was as close as my mother ever came to telling me I was good-looking. And coming from her that was quite a compliment.

My untimely, unplanned, and unwanted birth had occurred at home, in the two-bedroom apartment that my parents had lived in at the time, on a dead-end street in North Berkeley, California. We moved from that place when I was eight, but I will remember it until the day I die. Eight other people, from the same oppressed Central American country as my parents, had lived with us. They slept on the living-room floor, on cardboard pallets lined up like corpses. And that was literally the case with one man. One night, as I stumbled through the living room to get to the bathroom, I stepped on the man's head. He was an ugly old creature that we called Abuelo Pato, Spanish for Grandpa Duck. He looked more like a frog than a duck to me, and the one time that I mentioned that to my mother, she slapped me halfway across the living room. When he didn't move or say anything, I knew something was wrong. But I didn't say or do anything. After I did my business in the bathroom, I stumbled back to bed.

The next morning, when I found out that the man I'd stepped on was dead, I thought I'd killed him. I was the only child in the house, so I didn't have a high position. I stayed in a child's place. I spoke when I was spoken to, and nobody bothered to ask me anything about the dead man. I walked around in a daze for the next few days, convinced that I'd caused a man's death. Each time somebody knocked on our front door, I almost jumped out of my skin, terrified that it might be the cops coming to haul me off to jail. I was just about ready to pass out at the funeral when the preacher saved me by muttering something about the old man dying from a heart attack in his sleep. My life returned to normal, which was not saying much.

There was not much in my life for me to be happy about. I had no friends or real toys to play with. The television that we had only got two stations: One was a home shopping channel, which was useless because nobody in our house was interested in costume jewelry or Ginsu knives. The other channel was in Korean.

It was no wonder I was always doing or saying something to upset Mama. Like the time I walked into the bedroom I shared with her and Daddy and saw another man with her on the bed. They didn't see me, but as soon as Daddy got back home from his janitor's job at a nearby office building, I met him at the front door, yelling at the top of my lungs, "Daddy, Mama was sitting on a man's face!" Daddy didn't respond, so I assumed he didn't hear me. But Mama heard me all the way from the kitchen. She flew into the living room and batted my head with a spatula. For the next two days, she reminded me about the long labor she'd survived on account of me and how ugly she thought I was when I was born.

Just before I turned nine, Daddy got a job driving for some shady-looking white man who owned a restaurant with a bar that a lot of rich people went to. I thought that he was shady because every time I saw him, he had on dark glasses, even at night, and a black hat and dark clothes, which made him look more like a bandit than a businessman. Mr. Bloom lived in a big beige mansion in the Berkeley Hills. Up until then, the only work that Daddy and Mama had ever done in the States was farm or janitorial work.

Right after Daddy started driving for the shady businessman, he talked him into hiring Mama as a nanny for his three children. Like gypsies, we moved from one miserable old building after another. Moving around so much was the only way we could eventually get rid of all our "roommates." Each time we relocated to another apartment, it was always one that was smaller than the one before, so Daddy had a good excuse not to drag all of his rootless countrymen along with us. By the time we found a one-room studio apartment that was so small, it looked and felt like a dollhouse, it was just Mama, Daddy, and me.

With the long hours that my parents worked, I pretty much had to raise myself. During that time, I felt that I didn't belong anywhere. The days that my parents would leave the house before I got up and would come home after I'd gone to bed, I felt like an orphan. I roamed the streets like a stray dog. I started smoking when I was ten and drinking a year later. When I couldn't steal any of Daddy's cigars and when there was no alcohol in the house, I stole what I wanted from convenience stores. Sometimes I stole from the parents of some of the unsupervised kids I ran amok with. Nobody ever told me not to do it or that it was wrong. So I kept doing it.

About a year later, the restaurant owner bought up a bunch of old apartment buildings throughout the Bay Area. He made Daddy the manager and maintenance man of one in Berkeley. The neighborhood was fairly rough, but Daddy didn't have to pay rent as long as he managed the building. My folks didn't like to spend money, so I knew that as long as we could live rent free, we would be in this place. And I was glad.

It didn't take long for me to make some new friends. Across the street from us lived a Mexican family with nine kids. The only girl, Maria Cortez, was my age. We hit it off right away and before I knew it I was hanging out with Maria and some of her friends. Like me, they were not really bad kids. But I was glad to see that they were not as confused and impulsive as I was. Our conversations almost always included sex. I was the only virgin in the crowd so I tried to absorb as much information as I could. I couldn't wait to have my first sexual experience so that I could see what all the fuss was about.

Maria had to look after her younger siblings so she didn't have too much free time on her hands. "Christine, be glad you are an only child. You can do whatever you want and not have to worry about changing diapers, cleaning toilets, helping cook dinner, doing laundry and all the rest of the bullshit I have to do," Maria told me. "You can have all your time to yourself. You a lucky girl." Compared to Maria I guess I was. I had time to spare.

After school I would go home and watch television and eat whatever I wanted to eat. It was a good thing I enjoyed healthy things, like fruits and vegetables, as much as I did candy and soda pop. I was as healthy as I was supposed to be. But there were other things around me that were not healthy. The lack of guidance was one. Because there was nobody around too much to tell me what to do and what not to do, I did whatever I wanted, and I didn't have to worry about any consequences.

I was so hungry for attention that I put myself in a situation that cost me my virginity on my thirteenth birthday. Nobody raped me or took advantage of me like with so many of the other girls in my neighborhood. I initiated my first sexual encounter myself.

He was one of the many boys in our neighborhood that a lot of the parents had warned their daughters to stay away from. But that only made him more appealing. My parents had not warned me to avoid this boy or any other boy, so their interference was one thing I didn't have to worry about. Almost every time I saw him, some girl was up in his face, trying to get his attention.

Not only was this boy cute, but he was popular. By the time he caught my roving eyes, he'd already been with just about every black, Asian, Latino, and white girl I knew. He was already in high school, and even though I'd seen him looking at me long and hard, he had not approached me yet. But in the Bay Area, life was too short for some people. I didn't know how much time I had left, so it made sense for me to speed things up. I trotted over to his house the Friday after Thanksgiving to return a roasting pan that Mama had borrowed to cook our turkey in and to bring the twenty dollars that his mama, Miss Louise, was borrowing from Daddy. But my real purpose for going to his house was to claim what I thought should have been mine a long time ago.

As soon as I realized that the boy was home alone, I backed him from behind into a corner in his mama's kitchen, wrapped my arms around his waist, and kissed him on the back of his neck. I still had the twenty-dollar bill clutched in my hand. Even though the house that he and his mama lived alone in was large, the kitchen was small. There was barely enough room in it to accommodate the appliances and the large table in the middle of the floor. But it was neat, and the floor looked like it had just been waxed.

Not only did Miss Louise have a handsome son, but she was a clean woman. She kept such a clean house, you could eat off the floors. But she was also a materialistic woman with extravagant tastes. A lot of people didn't like her, because she borrowed money from everybody she knew to support her expensive habits. She even borrowed from me the pocket change that I made running errands for old people.

"Girl, what's gotten in you?" he laughed, pushing me away. He grabbed my wrists and turned around to face me. He had eyes like a cat. They were gray and shiny and so mysterious that when I looked into them, it seemed like I was looking into his soul. I felt something that I had never in my life felt before, and it was something I would never forget or stop searching for: passion. I would have settled for some kind of affection from just about anybody, but I only wanted to experience passion for the first time with this particular boy. I was getting signals from places on my body that I had never paid any attention to before. My crotch alone felt like it was on fire, so I wanted to get this over with as soon possible so I could cool off and move on to something else. In addition to having sex, there were a lot of other things that I wanted to do while I was still young enough to do them.

I started rubbing his dick with both of my hands as hard as I could.

CHAPTER 10

"Talk to me, Christine. I asked you what done got in you, girl."

"It could be you, *in me*, if you want it to be," I said, trying to imitate a look I'd just seen on HBO the night before, on Kathleen Turner's face in *Body Heat*.

"What are you up to? Could be me what?" he asked, with a dumb look on his face. My hands were still on his dick, and it was as hard as a rock.

It disappointed me to see that this boy was not as smart as I thought he was. Couldn't he tell what I was up to? Did I have to come straight out and tell him I wanted him to fuck me? Or just go ahead and get naked and start the job myself! I didn't think that I could make myself more obvious. "It could be you *in* me," I offered, pushing myself up against him and grinding. He was several inches taller than me, so I was grinding against his thigh. "I've been asking around about you, and I hear that you are going to be an actor," I added. I wanted him to know that he was already on my agenda. "Going to be in the movies and on television and stuff. Just like John Travolta." I spoke in a firm and serious tone of voice. I wanted him to know off the bat that I was not just trying to be funny. "But you are way cuter than John Travolta, so you'll be more rich and famous than he is."

That got his attention real fast. His eyes got big, and his lips curled up at both ends into the biggest smile I'd ever seen on a boy. "Uh, I sure hope so. It's all I ever wanted to do," he said hopefully, turning his head so I could see his profile. "I'm going down to Hollywood as soon as I get out of school," he announced, with a sniff and a glazed look on his face. He was no longer looking at me; he was looking over my shoulder at the wall. When I cleared my throat and pressed against him a little harder, he returned his attention to me. He shook his head and looked at me, blinking a few times before he spoke again. "I figured I'd do a little television first. You know, so I can get my feet wet. I cut my teeth on *Cheers,* but I think I'll concentrate on the serious shows when I get down there. There are too many black clowns out there already. They should have stopped with Eddie Murphy." He paused and gave me a sideways look. "You really think I can do it?"

I nodded. "Uh-huh. I was kind of thinking about doing that same thing myself," I lied. "You seen *Body Heat?* It's my all-time favorite movie. I am going to do movies like that."

His smile faded, and he gave me a harsh look. "Yeah, right." The sarcasm in his voice was so thick, you could stir it with a spoon. Then a sad look crossed his face, and he attempted to move away from me. But I still had my arms around his waist and his back was against the counter. "I really am going down to Hollywood. I will show you. I will show everybody. And, I don't appreciate you coming up in my mama's house, making fun of me! Gimme that money!" he snarled, snatching out of my hand the money that I had come to deliver to his mama.

I stumbled back a few steps, bumping into the wobbly kitchen table. "I would never make fun of you," I whimpered.

That comment didn't seem to impress him. He shot me a dirty look and started to walk away, stuffing the twenty-dollar bill he'd just taken from me into his pocket. "Look, I gotta empty the trash so Mama won't be on my ass again," he said, nodding toward a large trash can in the corner, by the door. "What did you really come up in here for?" he asked, with an impatient wave of his hand. "And don't tell me it was to discuss my show business future."

"I came to return your mama's roasting pan and to bring that money she wanted to borrow to buy her lottery tickets. Honest to God," I said, nodding at the pan I'd placed on the kitchen counter. "And—"

"And what?"

"And to see if you wanted to have some fun." I moved back up against him again, parting his legs with my knee. I didn't care how uninterested he tried to be. That hard bulge between his thighs told me a different story.

"Girl, how old are you?" the boy asked, looking at me out of the corner of his eye. I knew he wasn't too concerned about how young I was, because both of his hands were on my butt, squeezing and sliding up and down in such a way I could barely stand still.

"I'm old enough for you," I insisted. "I know you like older women, but there ain't nothing they can do that I can't do." The "older" women that this boy had already fooled around with were in college. And one already had a baby by some other boy. I hadn't even had my first period yet, so I wasn't worried about getting pregnant. As a matter of fact, I was wearing my first training bra, even though my titties were about the size of two marbles. Which was why I had stuffed both cups with toilet paper.

He leaned back and looked at my face for a long time. "You are kind of cute," he admitted, squeezing my butt even harder. When he looked at my titties and started reaching for them, I got as stiff as a board. "What's wrong?" he asked, both hands inside my bra. Then he froze and looked at me out of the corner of his eye.

"My titties just started growing," I admitted.

He laughed under his breath as he pulled out the tissue, looking at it like it was a snake. I turned to leave, with my head bowed and my eyes already filled with tears. Some sexpot I had turned out to me.

"Where you going, girl?" he asked, grabbing my arm.

"Home to watch *Cheers* reruns. I guess you don't want me now, huh?" I sniffed.

"All I want to know is if you are clean."

"Huh?" I rotated my neck and gave him a puzzled look. "Yeah, I'm clean. I took a shower this morning. I take a shower every morning."

The boy rolled his eyes and grinned. "That ain't what I meant."

I shrugged.

"Some old, funky, Jamaican girl gave me the crabs last year," he confessed, looking embarrassed.

"The what?"

"Never mind," he said, waving his hand and rolling his eyes. "You can stay, and we can have a good time. But, uh, I am telling you now, if you burn me, I am going to kick your butt!"

I had no idea what he was talking about, so I shrugged again.

"Did you know that today is my birthday?" I mentioned.

His eyes were on my breasts as he spoke. "No shit? Damn we gots to celebrate now! Happy birthday. You look clean enough to me, so I'll take a chance on you. Um . . . my room's upstairs. The first one you get to when you get to the top of the stairs. You go on up there and wait on me," he ordered. "I need to go feed my dog first, and then I need to go lock all the doors."

I ran up the stairs leading to the second floor, taking the steps two at a time. I had to force the door to his bedroom open with my foot. There was just that much junk on the floor. It wouldn't be the last time that I entered this same messy bedroom to get fucked like so many other girls before me. But I didn't want to be like the other girls this boy had been with. I wanted to be special in somebody's life, and he was a good start.

He shuffled into the room a few minutes later, nibbling on a candy bar and unzipping his pants at the same time. I sat up as soon as he sat down on the bed.

"Yeah, you are kind of cute. What's your name again?" he asked.

My heart felt like it had dropped down to the soles of my feet. "Christine," I mumbled.

"Oh, that's right. Listen, I got a feeling you and me just might get into something real big one day. And, by the way, my name is Wade."

CHAPTER 11

"Christine, this is Wade. Why are you sounding so strange? What's the matter with you?"

"Huh?" I had been so deep in thought recalling my first time with Wade that I hadn't heard the telephone when it rang on the stand next to the bed. I don't even remember picking it up. But when I heard Wade's loud voice on the other end of the line, I realized where I was and what time it was. "Where are you? What's going on?" I looked around the dreary motel room, frowning.

"Listen, baby, and listen good. This is the thing, see. I know this shit is getting crazy, but I might need for you to talk to our boy again," Wade said, sounding tired and disappointed. "I'm getting real aggravated with your old man." He sounded angry and even more impatient now.

"What did he say? What's the problem?"

"He ain't saying what I want him to say. That's the problem." Wade let out a groan and started cussing under his breath. "That's why I can't stand niggers with money! They ride on such high horses, they done rode clean out of reality. Them *stingy* motherfuckers!"

"Is he not going to pay the ransom?" I gasped.

"He'd better! I didn't go out on this goddamn limb for my motherfucking health!"

"Well, did he say he would, or did he say he would not?" I demanded, my heart beating. Now I was angry and impatient. Not just at Jesse Ray, but at Wade, too. I wanted him to get to the point. "Talk to me, Wade. Is Jesse Ray going to pay you the money or not?"

Wade took his time responding. "Well, I think so, but not without a little more encouragement."

"Wade, please tell me what my husband said. I've talked with him. So . . . so doesn't he believe I've been kidnapped?"

"He said he didn't know if he could pull together half a mil by Friday." There was a lot of uncertainty in Wade's voice.

"Pull it together? Is he trying to tell you that he doesn't have the money? He's got the money in the bank!"

"I believe you, baby. And I'm just as frustrated as you are with that . . . that scalawagging cocksucker myself! Now I wish I had snatched up Mick Jagger's half-black daughter. You know where she live?" Wade snorted and cussed some more under his breath. "Never mind. Knowing that uptown heifer, she won't be that easy to grab, no how. We'll just have to make this here thing with you work. You just might have to chat with your old man again. Sound real bad; cry; beg; do whatever."

"If I have to, I will. I just hoped that we'd be able to get this over with as soon as possible with just a couple of phone calls," I said, with a heavy sigh.

It was a good thing that this was not a real kidnapping. A real kidnapper would not have put up with the shit from Jesse Ray that Wade was putting up with. I would have been dead by now.

"Baby, I don't know what he's up to. That's why I think you might have to put another bug in his ear," Wade told me in a gruff voice.

"I just spoke to him yesterday. You told him he had until Friday to get the money to you." I sniffed. If this plan failed, my life was over. I had run out of options. "I'm . . . uh, in a world of trouble. What is it going to take to get him to realize that?" I didn't even try to hide the desperation in my voice.

"Calm down, baby," Wade hollered. "You just hold on there and calm yourself down. We can't afford to have you falling apart when we so close to the prize."

"Look, I just want this to be over with so I can get up out of this dump," I said, with a heavy sigh, looking around the gloomy room. "I'm nervous and . . . and I'm scared."

"I can understand you being nervous, but you ain't got nothing to be scared about. I got your back."

"Then what do we do now?" I asked, rubbing my nose. "I . . . shit! Somebody's at the door!" I whispered, gripping the telephone with both hands.

"Don't you open that door!" Wade ordered, shouting so loud, it sounded like he was in the same room with me.

I held my breath and stood stock-still, covering my naked body with the thin bedspread.

"Housekeeping," the person on the other side of the door yelled, jiggling the door handle.

"It's just the maid," I said, breathing a sigh of relief. "Let me get rid of her." I didn't wait for Wade to respond. I laid the phone on the bed and put on the sunglasses and the cap. Then I cracked open the door and peered into the tired moon face of a woman who reminded me of my beloved late godmother. I had to blink back a tear that was threatening to slide out. My godmother had not been dead that long, but I got emotional every time I thought about her or saw somebody who resembled her. I smiled as I looked over the maid's shoulder.

"Housekeeping," the woman said again, nodding toward the room, trying to look over my shoulder. She could glimpse just enough of me to see that I was wrapped up in the bedspread. From the smirk on her face, something told me that she assumed I was one of the hookers.

"Um, I don't need any service today," I said quickly. She seemed relieved to hear that. "As a matter of fact, I won't be needing any housekeeping services any other day, either. I'll be checking out on Friday," I said hopefully.

"No towels, toilet paper?" the maid asked, still trying to look over my shoulder.

"No," I said, shaking my head and trying to shut the door. "I have enough toilet paper, towels, and everything else. I brought my own soap, so you don't even have to worry about that, either." The maid had a puzzled look on her face as I shut and locked the door, securing it with the dead bolt and the chain. I stood with my back against the door until I heard her knock on the door of the room next to mine.

"I'm back," I said, picking up the phone. "I got rid of her."

"Don't you open that door no more," Wade hollered.

"It was just the maid," I hollered back. "If I hadn't opened the door, she would have entered the room. What was I supposed to do? I got rid of her for the rest of the week."

"Just don't open that door no more. Do you hear me? I ain't going to jail for you or nobody else."

CHAPTER 12

Jail was the last place I wanted to be. I tried not to even think along those lines. And, it made me angry when Wade brought it up.

"Can we get down to business? I'm naked and smelling like hell, and I want to take a shower. Now what is the deal with Jesse Ray?" I barked. I wanted to make sure that Wade knew I was angry and impatient.

"I told him I'd call him again so I could prove that you are still alive. In the meantime, Jason's going to make sure he sees them pictures we took first."

I didn't like to think about the pictures I'd posed for. I had been hoping that we would not have to show them to my husband. As strange as it seemed, even to me, I wanted to make this monkey business as painless as possible for Jesse Ray. But I knew it was going to hurt him like hell to part with half a million dollars. That part couldn't be helped. Besides, I was in a lot of pain myself and had been for a long time. And, the money from Jesse Ray was the only thing I knew of that could ease my pain.

And, speaking of pictures, yesterday was not the only time that I'd posed for pictures for Wade. One night a few months ago, in a room at the Marriott—paid for with one of my credit cards at that—I'd allowed Wade to take some Polaroids of me. Not a few head shots of me grinning into the camera like a drunken fool, but shots that were so sexually explicit that I could only stand to look at them that one time. Even though I looked much younger in each picture, and in a couple, I didn't even look like myself.

That same night Wade made a video of us making love. I had protested and tried to get out of doing that, too, but after he'd plied me with about a gallon of wine, I became putty in his hands. He'd whined and pouted so much about needing something to help him "get through the days and nights" that I couldn't be with him that I'd agreed to do it just to shut him up. Since he had *promised* me that it would be a one-time thing, and that the video would not end up on the Internet, I'd put on the performance of a lifetime.

I didn't like what I'd done, and the next time I saw Wade, I made him give me the pictures and the tape. As soon as I got home that day, I fed the pictures into my shredder, and I ripped the video apart, disposing of the pieces in four different Dumpsters in Oakland.

When, and *if,* we got the money from Jesse Ray and I made it to Sacramento to start my new life, one thing that I was sure I'd never do again was let somebody photograph me, naked or any other way. The world had become too small, so I didn't want any new pictures of me floating around that might end up in the hands of somebody who knew me. My break from Jesse Ray had to be complete in every way.

"How?" I asked Wade.

"How what?"

"How is Jason going to show my husband those pictures? He can't go up to him in person! And, if he mails them, it could take a day or two before Jesse Ray receives them. Who knows who else might see them first." I rose from the bed, rubbing my stomach with one hand and clutching the telephone in my other hand so hard, my fingers tingled. "And what if they find Jason's and your fingerprints on those pictures? With all this DNA shit going on these days, a serious criminal doesn't have a chance anymore. All they need is a drop of sweat, a strand of hair so tiny that a naked eye can't see it, or a piece of lint off—"

"Listen up! DNA, BNA, triple A, or any other kind of A. Fuck it all. Look, baby." Wade paused and let out a deep breath. "In the first place, I got enough sense to wipe them pictures off real good before we do anything with them. In the second place, I doubt very seriously that our boy is going to call the cops. Fingerprints is the last thing we need to worry about. We need to focus on getting that money and getting the hell up out of Berkeley."

"Then how will you get the pictures to Jesse Ray? He's got cameras all over that video store. Even if you or Jason go there in a disguise to deliver those pictures, these investigators these days have come up with all kinds of ways to identity folks in disguise." I stopped to catch my breath. "Even if he doesn't call the cops now, he probably will once he delivers the money and I'm safely returned. Jesse Ray worked too hard to get the money he's got. He is not going to let it go that easily."

"We'll worry about crossing that bridge when we get to it," Wade snapped. "Me and Jason will be back at the motel in a couple of hours. What do you want me to bring you to eat? You must be hungry as hell by now. You want some tacos? Some ribs? How about a bucket of KFC?"

"A sandwich will do," I mumbled. "And while you are at it, pick me up some deodorant and some clean clothes. And don't forget some underwear."

It was the middle of May. Even though Berkeley was breezy throughout the day and near a lot of water, including the San Francisco Bay, the weather was fairly hot. The sun was already beating down on the cheap motel. The thin plastic curtains on the motel windows didn't keep the sun's blinding rays out. I was sweating everywhere on my body.

I had not cleaned myself since I'd left home the morning before, and I had not showered after my bedroom romps with Wade in his mama's house and in the motel. I was beginning to feel and smell pretty ripe and musty. I was a clean woman. I was used to taking a shower every morning and a long, hot bubble bath every night. There was nothing more disgusting to me than the smell of day-old sex and dried cum caked up on my thighs and face.

I took a quick shower, and I do mean quick. The shower area had water bugs crawling up and down the moldy walls, and roaches sliding across the plastic shower curtain, and the hot water was almost as cold as the cold water. I almost fell when I noticed a used condom in a cracked soap dish on the windowsill.

After I dried myself off with one of the stiff towels in the bathroom,

I slid back into the same clothes that I'd worn the day before and stretched out on the bed.

I could not relax or get too comfortable, because I had so many disturbing thoughts swimming around in my head. As hard as I tried to focus on the present situation and my future, my past came back to haunt me again.

CHAPTER 13

I didn't enjoy having sex with Wade on my thirteenth birthday, even though I had acted like it was the best thing that had ever happened to me. Because I'd already experience a few orgasms—the first one by mistake, by clutching a pillow between my thighs while lying in bed—I thought I knew what to expect.

But the first real sex was painful, just like Maria had warned me. "Listen, girl, it's going to hurt like hell when you lose your cherry. Me, I could barely walk when it happened to me." I was not surprised when Maria told me she'd had sex for the first time when she was eleven. With her long wavy black hair, a cute round face that was almost as brown as mine, and the body of a woman twice her age, I could see why the boys couldn't keep their hands off her.

"I've done it a dozen times and it still hurts," added Denise Conners, one of Maria's friends.

We were in the bedroom that Maria shared with four of her siblings. I looked toward the door to make sure none of them were eavesdropping before I responded. "Well, if it hurts, why is everybody doing it?" I wanted to know. Despite the tone of the conversation, there was a tingling in my crotch that had become quite familiar since I'd started having these conversations with my friends.

Maria and Denise looked at each other, then at me. They shrugged their shoulders at the same time. "We do it because everybody else is doing it," Denise said with a heavy sigh. That was one of the reasons I did it when I did.

Not only was sex with Wade the first time painful, but it looked downright ridiculous. That was bad enough. But the way that he behaved during the few minutes that it took to get it over with—yelling, making faces, and humping like a mechanical bull—you would have thought that it was painful for him, too.

After Wade had what I thought was some kind of spasm, the way he started jerking and hollering even louder and slamming into me, he gave me a few sloppy kisses and told me what a good piece of pussy I was.

My jaw dropped open, and it took me a few moments to compose myself enough to speak again. "What happened?" I asked.

"What do you mean by that? Don't you know?"

"Uh, I thought you was, like, dying or having a heart attack or a stroke or something."

Wade chuckled and tapped the side of my head. "I came. I got my nut."

"Oh," I mumbled.

"Didn't you get yours?" He sounded disappointed.

"Uh-huh. I got mine, too. You really know how to do it. . . ."

He belched and then let out a loud breath. "I know. That's why these damn girls won't leave me the hell alone. They get some good sex, and they just about go crazy. Following me around and shit. . . ."

"I know what you mean," I managed. I didn't have the nerve to tell this boy that I'd had better sex with a pillow than I'd had with him.

After he let out a few more belches and a couple of farts, he just lay there on top of me, breathing loud through his mouth. His body jerked a few more times. Once Wade returned to his senses, he leapt off the mattress and turned on me like a snake. Not only was he mad because I'd made him forget about some ball game, but he cussed me out for getting blood on his mama's sheets, too.

"Oh shit! Damn you, girl! I done missed my basketball game! And, you are going to get me in all kinds of trouble with my mama! Look at all that goddamn blood on them sheets!" he screamed, struggling to zip his pants. "Go home and take a douche!" He gave me a sharp look, and then he laughed. He laughed like I was the biggest joke he'd ever seen.

To this day I can still feel the sting of those words. Knowing that he'd been amusing himself at my expense didn't make it feel any better. That day, I knew that I'd have to figure out a way to put men in a place in my life where they did me the most good. It was the first goal that I'd set for myself. But I had still managed to smile at Wade after his outburst.

"All girls bleed the first time. Didn't you know that?" I said, sliding back into my panties.

"Huh? Yeah, I knew that. But not the girls I been with!" he clucked.

"Do you mean to tell me that I'm your first virgin?" I asked, feeling more special than I thought I would.

Wade shifted his eyes, then gave me a thoughtful look. "Uh, yeah." His voice had softened. He even smiled as he sat down next to me on the messy mattress. "You ain't never done it before? You let me be the first?" he asked, with a proud look on his face.

I nodded, giving him a shy look.

"It was kind of good, huh? I think we should do it again. Spread open them legs," he ordered, glancing at a clock with a Mickey Mouse face on the wall facing his bed. "Hurry up!"

"Do we have time? What about your mama? What about your basketball game?"

"My mama is at the nail shop. And that game is over with," he said, tugging at my panties.

"It still hurts," I confessed, making a face and rubbing my crotch. I slapped his hand away.

"Oh, that's right. Okay, then," he muttered, clearly disappointed. He perked up almost immediately. "Suck my dick then," he suggested, with a shrug, licking his lips.

I shuddered and made another face. "I never done that before," I whimpered. Despite what my girls had told me, and what I'd seen in some of the nasty magazines they'd shared with me, sucking dick didn't appeal to me. I didn't want anything to go into my mouth that I couldn't swallow, and I told him so.

Wade talked me into doing it, anyway. He talked the whole time I was down there between his thighs, my head bobbing up and down like a cork. He told me which way to do it, and which way not to do it. Except for sore cheeks, I wasn't getting a damn thing out of this dog and pony show. But I did everything I could to keep Wade from realizing that. I grinned like a joker when he squirted everything he had into my mouth. It was the most disgusting thing that had ever happened to me.

While Wade was on his back, hanging off the mattress, breathing through his mouth hard enough to blow out a burning bush, I was quietly spitting his juices onto the floor. Then I swiped my lips with the corner of the sheet, wondering what I had got myself into.

CHAPTER 14

"**M**ama, I'm home," I yelled tentatively, letting myself in the front door of the second-floor apartment we lived in on Prince Street, in a big, brooding beige building facing another building that looked just like it. There was nothing but plain-looking apartment buildings on our block. From the outside, most of the buildings looked presentable. Some even had an orange, a lemon, or a palm tree or two. But in some, where the stairwells had no lights and the halls that separated the units were so eerie, you could hear the wind howling through cracks you couldn't see. There was also a sense of despair that seemed to cover our building like a shroud. Some days I got depressed as soon as I opened the front door.

But not today.

My neighborhood was located near Shattuck, Telegraph, and Alcatraz, three of the most well-known streets in Berkeley. Shattuck contained a lot of business offices, our main library, and several restaurants and movie theaters.

Berkeley was still one of the most prestigious college towns in the country, despite that ruckus that the hippies and the demonstrators had caused during the sixties. And, a lot of those activities had occurred on Telegraph and Alcatraz years before my mother brought me into the world, after enduring forty-eight hours of labor.

Things were fairly quiet in Berkeley now. But the city still had a dark side that could not be ignored. There were a lot of crimes committed on our street, often in broad daylight. Just last week a man down the street had been attacked and robbed in his own garage in broad daylight by two men in ski masks. The thieves had made off with the man's wallet, his watch, his briefcase, and his new shoes.

I'd been lucky, so far. I had managed to avoid the pedophiles and other garden-variety thugs that had given our part of Prince Street such a bad name.

Before I'd left Wade's house, I'd rinsed out my mouth with warm, salty water, but I could still taste him. Wade had cooled me off, but my crotch still felt like it was on fire. That didn't bother me half as much as the turmoil that was going on in my mouth. I wondered what kind of nasty-ass motherfucker had dreamed up oral sex!

Even though where I lived sometimes depressed me, I was glad to be home. This was the only place in the world where I knew I could hide not only myself, but my feelings, too. My parents didn't bother me, and I didn't bother them.

I didn't know what it looked like inside the other three units in our building, but ours was pretty dull. We had dreary plaid furniture that didn't match, a gooosenecked lamp with a 40-watt lightbulb in a corner in the living room, roach paste on the walls in every room, and carpets so thin, you could see the hardwood floor beneath.

I peeked into the living room, where my mother and my father were watching reruns of old television shows from the fifties on a nineteen-inch black-and-white TV.

"Mama, Miss Louise wasn't home, but I left her roasting pan and the money she wanted to borrow with her son. You remember Wade? He's a nice boy," I said, grinning. I had gargled so hard with the salt water and rubbed my lips so hard, they were numb. And, my throat was so dry, it ached when I swallowed.

"Did you shut that front door?" my father asked, not even turning around to face me. From the back, Daddy's head looked like a large peanut, and the front of his head didn't look too much better. Daddy had never been a handsome man. At least not that I could remember. His looks had slid even further down the drain. He looked like a hound dog, and I didn't know when that had happened, because the last time I took a long look at him, he'd looked all right to me. Unfortunately, Mama was the female version of Daddy. They had been together so long, they now looked alike. As a matter of fact, they'd always looked alike as far back as I could remember. They both had nut brown skin and large, sad, droopy black eyes that looked like they'd just been carelessly dug into their long, narrow faces. Mama and Daddy even had the same kinky gray hair, which they covered in stocking caps every night, when they went to bed.

"Yes, sir. I did shut the door. And, I would have been back home sooner, but I ran into some girls from my gym class," I volunteered.

It had only taken a few more minutes of my time for me to suck Wade's dick long and hard enough for him to come. But he'd enjoyed it so much, he invited me to stay with him and cuddle on the bed for a little while so he could share his thoughts with me. He made some popcorn and split the last Pepsi in his mama's refrigerator with me.

"I don't tell too many people, because they make fun of me when I do, but I *am* going to be a big movie and television star some day," he told me, with his arm around my shoulder, as we lay on the bed. "I play a lot of sports to get in shape so I can do my own stunts when the time comes." The smile on his face was contagious.

It pleased me to know that he was ambitious. I smiled, even though there was popcorn stuck to the roof of my mouth. Of all the junk food at my disposal, popcorn was one thing that I didn't care much about. But in this case, I ate it, anyway, even though half of it was still unpopped, because it seemed to please Wade.

"Let me get you some more popcorn," he offered, rising.

"That's all right," I said fast and loud, holding up my hand. "I'm not that hungry."

He lay back down, tilted his head to the side, and gave me a guarded look.

"Uh, why would somebody laugh about you wanting to be a star?" I asked.

"You know how these kids around here be tripping. They think acting is sissified," Wade said, with an angry tone in his voice. "Same as hairdressing and ballet dancing. They think any dude that do shit like that *gots* to be a fag."

"Do these same kids go to the movies?" I asked, sipping from the can of Pepsi, which I didn't care that much for, either. This one had an odd taste. I glanced at the side of the can, not surprised to see that the soda was diet. I drank some more, anyway, because it helped rinse the taste of Wade's juices and that half-cooked popcorn out of my mouth.

"You know they do," Wade said, rising up enough so that he could look at my face. The expression on his face told me that he was wondering where I was going with my end of this conversation. "What's your point?"

"Well, Al Pacino and all the rest of those big stars had to start somewhere. I bet the kids in their neighborhoods didn't make fun of them when they first started talking about going to Hollywood. And, what about those real mucho macho stars, like Sylvester Stallone and Clint Eastwood? Nobody in their right mind would call them sissies."

Wade gave me a thoughtful look. "Shit," he said in a low voice. He smiled and blinked twice, looking at me like I had just revealed the secrets of the universe. "Girl, I never even thought about things like that. Them big stars did have to start somewhere. They had to tell their relatives and friends what they wanted to do. You don't think I'm talking crazy?"

"No, I don't think you are talking crazy. I think it's cute that you want to be a big star," I said, caressing Wade's face. That was not what he wanted to hear.

"Fuck you, bitch!" he screamed through clenched teeth.

"What?" I managed. My mouth dropped open and stayed that way as I watched Wade's face turn into one of the most frightening things I ever saw. His gray eyes looked black and evil. Both of his cheeks twitched, and for a minute, his nose looked like it was going to wiggle right off his face.

"What's wrong with you, girl?" he roared, pushing my hand away.

"What did I say?" I gasped, surprised and frightened.

"Cute? You think what I want to do with my life is *cute?* Winnie the Pooh is cute. A poodle in a dress is what you call cute! I ain't going down to Hollywood to do no Disney movies or *Sesame Street* or nothing like that. I want to be taken serious. You understand?"

"I understand," I muttered. I was glad when Wade laid his head back down. "Uh, do you want me to go now?"

He rubbed his chin, sighed, and shook his head. "Naw," he said, waving his hand. "You can stay, but just watch what you say to me from now on. Do you hear me?"

"I hear you," I muttered, my head bowed like a puppy.

Wade cleared his throat. "You know what? I do kinda like you, Christine. You are cute—uh, not *cute*—you are a real fly girl. Turn over here so I can lick your pussy."

"Huh?"

"This old, funky college girl that I hang with, she told me that most women like getting licked better than they like getting fucked. She showed me how to do it real good."

"What about the blood down there on me?"

Wade let out a sharp laugh and made a face like he was in pain again.

"Damn! I forgot about that," he hollered, slapping the side of his face with the palm of his hand. "Well, I'll do it some other time when you ain't bleeding. But guess what? I wouldn't mind having my dick sucked again before you go home."

"What you got to be smiling about?" Mama asked, bringing me back to the present.

"Nothing," I mumbled, my eyes on the floor.

I could not imagine what my parents, especially my mother, would say if they knew what I'd done with Wade. As a family, we rarely talked among ourselves, anyway, about anything. I never knew what they were thinking and vice versa. Sometimes it seemed like I lived with mute strangers. Sex was a subject that was *never* discussed in our house. As a matter of fact, the closest that my mother ever came to discussing sex in my presence was to tell me about all of the difficulties she'd endured to bring me into the world, always including the fact that she'd had such a hard life that she'd never wanted a child in the first place. She always made the forty-eight hours of labor, loss of blood, and extreme pain sound like it was something that I had caused on purpose. And, each time I ended up apologizing to her for being born. It was one thing to know that I'd been a "mistake." But that didn't stop me from making enough mistakes of my own along the way. I had no way of knowing it at the time, but Wade would turn out to be the biggest mistake I'd ever make in my life.

CHAPTER 15

I dreamed about Wade that night, lying naked on his back in a field of roses, beckoning me with his dick. I woke up with my face glazed with sweat, a pillow clamped between my thighs, and a wicked smile on my lips. I couldn't wait to see him again.

I didn't care if we had sex again or not. The more I thought about that, it wasn't such a big deal, anyway. I had more fun with a pillow between my legs. But pillows couldn't talk or do other things to a girl that a boy could do. I liked lying in Wade's arms and talking to him. He was one of the few people who actually listened to what I had to say. I knew boys who liked to feel me up and down for hours on end, and a minute later they couldn't remember a single thing I'd said.

I went to Wade's house three times after school the following week. But the only person I'd been able to see was his mother. Each time she told me that Wade was out with his friends. On the third day, I got bold enough to ask her exactly where he was with his friends. Miss Louise was a mean old woman, at least to most of the kids in the neighborhood. When she caught kids stealing oranges off the tree in her front yard, she chased them with a broom.

She had gray eyes like Wade, and she had a pretty face for a woman her age. But she wore a wig that was so fake looking, it looked like it belonged on a rag doll. She wore clothes that looked like they belonged on a female my age, so not too many people took her seriously. I sure didn't, but I treated her with respect because she had something I wanted: her son. And, I had something she wanted: money. Not much. Sometimes less than a dollar. But Miss Louise was the kind of moocher who would take candy from a baby. My parents always broke her off a twenty or a fifty loan at least four or five times a month, so she was fairly nice to me.

"Christine, you are going to worry me to death over that boy of mine. Now if he wanted to see you, don't you think he'd let you know that?" Miss Louise told me, giving her wig a strong tug. "What do you want with him, anyway?"

"Uh, I just wanted to talk to him. He told me about his plans to go to Hollywood," I said in a cheerful voice.

"Oh?" Miss Louise said, fanning her hand out like she wanted to make sure I saw she'd just gotten her nails done. She stepped out onto the lopsided wraparound porch hugging the front of her house like an ill-fitted bra.

"He's going to be a real big star one day. I told him so to his face," I added, pleased to see that she was feeling more cordial. A smile from her, even to me, went a long way.

"He sure enough is, baby. And I know my boy. He won't forget the folks who was there for him on his way up. I am sure he appreciates your encouragement and support." Miss Louise sniffed, patting her chest.

Miss Louise was a strange woman. She had a lot of relatives in the area, but the way she talked about Wade, you would have thought that he was the only one she had left. I didn't know much about Wade's father other than Miss Louise's claim that he was a "low-down, funky black dog." Miss Louise was a waitress, and she had a few men friends here and there, but she still couldn't make ends meet without borrowing money. But even though she struggled to make ends meet, she had some expensive habits. She liked designer clothes and fancy restaurants, not to mention the extravagant things that filled her shabby house. Like a big-screen television set, state-of-the-art computer equipment, and leather furniture, which she liked to replace ever other year.

"Baby, can you break me off a few dollars? I had some unexpected expenses this week, and I'm a little short," she cooed.

"Yes, ma'am," I said eagerly, removing the five-dollar bill and three ones that I had in my Windbreaker pocket. The woman who lived in the apartment below ours had paid me ten dollars to do her laundry and bathe her dog two days ago. "How much do you need?"

"How much you got?"

"I can let you have five," I told her in a sheepish voice.

"Is five all you can spare?" she asked, looking at the three remaining dollars I was clutching in my hand.

"Uh, I was going to buy me some magazines and some gum," I replied.

"All right then," she said, then sniffed. "The boy's over on Shattuck, at the Eye-talian restaurant all you kids like to go to. Gobbling up one of them spicy-ass pizzas they sell over there. Damn them dagos," Miss Louise said, with a smirk, snatching the five out of my hand so fast, she almost pulled my arm out of the socket. The money disappeared into her apron pocket as she mumbled a thank-you under her breath. Then she folded her arms and gave me a pensive look. "When my boy makes it big in Hollywood, he's going to buy me a house, a new car, some new frocks . . . everything but a mockingbird. And guess what I . . ."

I didn't even hear the rest of Miss Louise's sentence, even though she followed me off her front porch out onto the sidewalk, still talking. As soon as I got to the corner, I took off running toward Shattuck Street, almost dashing in front of a bus.

When I got to nearby Giovanni's, where Wade was supposed to be, I was glad to see him sitting with some white boy that I'd never seen before in a booth in the back. Wade had on a black leather jacket and a baseball cap turned sideways, looking straight-up awesome. I had to close my eyes, hold my breath, and blink. The space between my thighs started itching and sweating, and for a minute, I thought I was going to cream all over myself right there in the middle of the restaurant floor.

I waved and ran over to Wade's table, almost knocking a waiter to the ground. The boy with him had on a sweater that had a snowman on the front with crossed eyes and a joint sticking out of his mouth.

"Hi, Wade! Your mama told me you was here," I squealed, waiting for him to invite me to join the party.

First, he looked from me to the white boy and back. "Do I know you?" he asked me, with a shrug and an annoyed look on his face.

I swallowed hard and blinked at him. "It's me," I said sharply, pointing to my face.

"Me who?" Wade demanded. The white boy covered his mouth with his hand and snickered so hard, the snowman on his sweater moved in a way that made it look like he was puffing on the joint hanging off his lip.

"I . . . I was at your house day after Thanksgiving," I stammered, hoping I would not have to explain any more than that. "My mama had borrowed a roasting pan from your mama to cook our turkey in, and I brought some money that your mama wanted to borrow." At this point, I leaned over the table and lowered my voice. "You, uh, *showed* me your room . . . ," I said, with a nod.

"Oh. That was *you?*" he gasped, looking embarrassed, then amused.

"That was me," I mumbled, my face burning with anger. Who the hell did this nigger think he was? I had heard that some boys treated girls like shit after they'd fucked them. But I never thought that it would happen to me.

"Well, what do you want me to *show* you now?" he sneered. That motherfucker! I didn't know if he was being for real or if he was just trying to entertain and amuse the boy across from him at the table.

"I just wanted to say hi," I said. I didn't give him the chance to make me feel any worse. I slunk out of the restaurant and ran all the way back home, with tears streaming down the sides of my face, wondering if anybody would ever really care about me.

I had no cigarettes or alcohol to ease my pain. And, because Miss Louise had talked me out of most of my money, I didn't even have enough to buy any from some of the older kids I knew.

Mama and Daddy still occupied the same spots that I'd left them in. They didn't even look up when I stumbled across the living room floor to my room. I could not have felt more insignificant if I'd tried.

CHAPTER 16

Christmas was the one thing that made my family seem normal. Well, almost normal. But that wasn't saying much.

What was different about Christmas was the fact that Mama cooked a big meal, Daddy put up a tree, and we even exchanged gifts. Each year I gave Daddy either a pair of socks or some Old Spice aftershave, which he used as a breath freshener. I always gave Mama something practical, like a new frying pan. Me, I never knew what I was going to get from them. One year all I got was a pair of boots with a note that had both Mama's and Daddy's names scribbled on it.

When I was twelve, I received two dolls, some clothes with the tags from Kmart still attached, and a Monopoly game. I hadn't played with dolls since I was five, the clothes were three sizes too large, and I knew as much about Monopoly as I did about rocket science. But I played with the dolls, anyway, sold the clothes to a fat girl and used the money to buy some similar outfits in my size, and traded the Monopoly game for a carton of Newports and two cans of Coors Light.

I had to kick Denise's butt when she came to my house and tried to sneak out with half of my Newports and a pair of my new jeans in her backpack. There was quite a ruckus in my room as we rolled around on the floor, pulling each other's hair and cussing. When Daddy knocked on the door and told us to, "turn off that damn rap music," Denise and I laughed so hard we couldn't fight anymore. Even though we laughed, I could tell from the look on Denise's face that she was not happy I'd won the fight, but I assumed we'd make up and still be friends. I had fought with other girls before and still stayed friends with them but Denise never came around me again after our fight.

Denise had scratched my face and I still had some of the scars by the time New Year's Day rolled around. I coated my face with a lot of makeup to hide the fact that I'd been fighting. But I got drunk at a New Year's Eve party at Maria's house and told everybody about the fight anyway. I had a good time dancing with Maria's brothers and some of their friends, but the only boy I really wanted to be with was Wade.

I was in love for the first time. Ever since I'd fucked Wade in his mama's house, I'd been on cloud nine, and I assumed that he was, too. I had gotten over that little stunt he'd pulled on me at Giovanni's. Somehow I managed to convince myself that that white boy I'd seen him with had something on him. Something that kept him from admitting that he was my man. I refused to believe that a boy who had fucked the daylights out of me had lost interest in me that fast.

I began to think otherwise because I hadn't seen or heard from Wade since I'd cornered him at Giovanni's. "I ought to go to his house and smash his windows!" I told Maria. "I ought to steal that mangy dog of his and drop him off in East Oakland somehere."

"Then you won't hear from him again for sure and you might get arrested," she replied.

"He could at least call me up and tell me he don't like me no more." I pouted. "What am I supposed to think or do? I don't like this shit! He can't fuck with me like this and just forget about me!"

"I think he already did," Maria said with a nod. "Give the boy another chance. There might even be a good reason why he hasn't called you up."

I gave Maria a thoughtful look and then I rushed home.

We didn't have an answering machine, so I didn't know if he'd tried to call me during the day, when nobody was home at my house. But he didn't call in the evening or at night when I was home, either. And the evenings and nights that I was out lollygagging, there were never any messages left for me with my parents when I got home. But I always asked, anyway.

"Did a boy call for me?" I asked Mama. I had just come home from a party at a skating rink a few blocks from my house. I had had a few beers and a little tequila, and had taken a few hits off a joint, so I was a little tipsy. I didn't know if my parents knew about me drinking and getting high, because I never did it in front of them. I never looked or acted drunk or high, so they never knew when I was. I was the kind of girl who could get drunk as a skunk and as high as a flying monkey and still not stagger or slur my words. I had that much control over myself. That was one of the reasons I had such a hard time believing that I'd been played by Wade.

Even though I missed him, and would have jumped at the chance to marry him and have his babies, his absence was beginning to get on my nerves. But I still wanted to see him again. If he didn't like me anymore and wanted nothing more to do with me, I wanted him to tell me so, to my face. "This boy that I'm expecting a call from, he's a good friend," I said, more to myself than to Mama. I wasn't convinced that that was true.

"A lot of boys call you," Mama told me, not even looking up from the television. Daddy was stretched out on the sofa, snoozing like a cat. He was on his back, with his arms folded across his chest. He was already a dull and lackluster man. When he slept, he looked like a dead man. The only reason I knew he was still alive was because he snored like a freight train.

"Did any of them leave any messages?" I had to talk loud so that Mama could hear me over Daddy's racket.

"Naw," Mama said, with a grunt.

There was a rolled-up *Enquirer* in Mama's hand that she had been reading off and on for over a month. She glanced in my direction as she swatted a fly the size of a nickel on the arm of her chair with the old *Enquirer*. Then she unrolled it and started reading stuff that was so old by now, it no longer mattered. Like the two stars on the cover celebrating their lavish wedding. They'd already gotten divorced. But that didn't matter to Mama. She had magazines that were older than me that she was still reading and using to swat flies.

I dragged my feet to my room, hoping that I would never have to introduce Wade to my parents. It was bad enough that he had a strange mama to deal with, too. Just thinking about Miss Louise, with her greedy self, made me smile as I flung myself across my unmade bed. I always stuffed a few spare dollars into my sock every time I left the house because I never knew when I was going to run into Wade's mama. She had paid back the hundred dollars that she'd borrowed from Mama three days after I'd delivered it to her house, leaving it with Wade. But she'd come to borrow it back two days later.

I was so confused about my relationship with Wade that I could hardly think about anything else. Even though almost every girl I knew had told me at least one story about some boy fucking her, then disappearing. I never thought that one day it would be my story, too. But that's just what it turned out to be. Wade had disappeared so completely from my life that it was like he had never existed. There were even a few times that I found myself wondering if I'd imagined the whole thing. I even went so far as to kick off my panties, straddle a mirror on the floor in my room, and stick my finger inside myself, checking to see if my cherry was still in place. But my innocence was gone. Just like Wade.

CHAPTER 17

As dull and out of touch with reality as my parents were, I was sur-prised that Mama bought me a blue suede jacket that was too stylish and cute for words for Christmas this year. It was a nice change from the mammy-made, dull-colored things she usually bought for me off the discount-store racks. That was the main reason I got so caught up in shoplifting.

My parents rarely came into my bedroom, and when they did they had no interest in what was in my closet, but I kept it locked anyway. When I wanted to wear one of my stolen outfits, I waited until my parents were in bed. When they stayed up later than they usually did on a night I had a party to go to, I left the house dressed in one of the frumpy outfits Mama had bought for me. But my party clothes were in my backpack. Half of my closet was full of hot "hot" outfits.

It was a cold and dreary Saturday evening, with puffy black clouds sliding slowly across a sky that looked like a gray blanket. I had just gotten over a cold that had been so serious, I hadn't even been able to crawl out of bed for the last two days. But on the third day, I was well enough to hit the streets again.

"Mama, can I go over to the skating rink and hang out? I want to show my friends the new jacket you got me for Christmas."

My mother was in the kitchen, washing dishes. She turned and looked at me with a blank expression on her face, which had become so familiar over the years. "Ummm," she muttered. "You can do whatever it is you want to do."

I already knew that. But out of respect and because I knew that it was the right thing to do, I asked, anyway. Neither one of my parents really cared about what I did. No matter what it was. I could skip school, ignore my household chores, eat junk food for days, stay out all night if I wanted to, and not have to worry about any consequences. Even though some of my friends lived in neighborhoods rougher than mine and had parents that drank, fought, and abused them, they had curfews and rules that they had to follow. To them, I was living a kid's dream. And, it was fun, but only up to a point.

I was still in middle school, and I didn't know what to do with myself most of the time. It was an awkward time for me. I was so confused, I didn't know if I was coming or going.

As much as I hated school, I liked going sometimes because my teachers made sure I followed their rules. Even though I bitched and moaned about it, it made me warm all over when one of my teachers scolded me for not turning in my homework or for acting up in class.

Two weeks after Christmas, I came home after hanging out with a few of my friends a few hours later than I normally did. All of the lights were out. The old Chevy that my daddy drove was not parked in front of our building like it usually was this time of night, and my parents were not home. They had no friends that were close enough to visit, so there was nobody for me to call except the man that they worked for.

"Mr. Bloom, this is Christine Martinez. You seen my mama and my daddy?"

Mr. Bloom coughed for a full minute before he spoke. "Reuben's girl?" he asked, clearing his throat.

"Yes, sir," I muttered impatiently. "Are my mama and daddy still at your house?"

"Why, no, sunshine. They are supposed to be in Gilroy for some kind of festival. They bugged me about it for a week before I finally told them they could take the weekend off to go. Did you not know that?" Mr. Bloom asked, sounding surprised. I didn't really care that much for Mr. Bloom, with his big red face and wiry gray hair. It didn't matter to me that we lived rent free in one of his buildings. I thought that he took advantage of my parents, making them work long hours and paying them low wages. I usually hid, ignored him, or rolled my eyes at him when he came to the house. He knew I didn't like him.

It was no wonder that he was surprised to be hearing from me, and just as surprised to hear that I didn't know where my parents were. But he was not as surprised as I was that they had not mentioned the festival to me, invited me to go along with them, or even left me a note telling me their plans.

"Oh yeah! I remember now. Ha ha ha! Dummy me! They did tell me they were going to that festival in Gilroy. It's some kind of celebration that the black people from Guatemala get off into every year." I sniffed. "Mostly old folks. I didn't really want to go. I told them that I wanted to spend some time with my friends."

"I see," Mr. Bloom said. A stony silence followed. "Is there anything else I can do for you?"

"Uh-uh." I hung up and sat on the hard sofa in our living room for several minutes, wondering what I should do next. And that's where I ended up sleeping that night.

As many friends as I had, and as much as I got myself into, I was a very lonely child. That's why when I woke up the next morning, I wandered over to People's Park, where there was always something exciting happening.

Even though the park was not that far from downtown, people put up crude tents, which they slept in until somebody killed them or until they got thrown in jail. People got drunk or stoned, fucked people they didn't even know, and even walked around naked. One drunken woman had even given birth during the middle of an orgy one night. It seemed like every time I looked up, People's Park was in the news. Most of my friends were not allowed to go anywhere near that place, because in addition to the occasional murders and rapes in or near the park, there were a lot of fun activities going on there that involved drugs.

There were a lot of white kids in the notorious park, some even younger than me. Most of them had run away from home. A lot of them were the kids and grandkids of the same hippies that had slept, fucked, and got high in People's Park back in the day. These were the kids who always had the best weed.

I saw Wade before he saw me, but I had no intentions of acknowledging that sucker. He was with some big-butt white girl, anyway. I was stunned when he galloped over to me, with a cocky grin on his face.

"Hey, Christine," he greeted, squatting down on the ground where I was sitting. I hid the joint that had just been passed to me behind my back.

"Do I know you?" I asked, with a profound smirk. It pleased me to see the hurt look on his face. Now he knew how I'd felt that day at Giovanni's when he'd disrespected me in front of his friend.

Wade stuck out his bottom lip, and for a moment, I thought he was going to cry. "So it's like that, huh? You treat your brother like a piece of shit when you with your *Caucasian* friends." He said the word "Caucasian" like it was a cuss word.

"I don't have no brother," I snapped firmly, giving him a hot look. All the other kids laughed, and that seemed to make him madder than everything I'd said.

"I'll see you around," he said in a weak voice, grabbing the white girl who had come to the park with him by the hand and leading her away.

"That a friend of yours?" one of the kids asked me.

"He used to be," I said sadly. I watched him until he had disappeared from my sight.

CHAPTER 18

One of the white boys who had been with me when I'd clowned Wade in the park that day invited me to have dinner with him at a Greek restaurant a few blocks away. He planned to pay for it with a credit card that he'd stolen from his uncle's wallet the day before.

"Order whatever you want. You can even order something to take home, too," he told me, waving the gold American Express card in the air. We plopped down in a booth close to the door in case there was a problem with the credit card and we had to leave in a hurry. Like if we had to jump up and run out the door before the manager showed up.

"Can I get me a steak and a lobster, uh, dude?" I didn't even know this boy's name. But "dude" was so universal that people who didn't know my name called me that, too. "And I'll take another steak to go." Anyway, my mysterious friend had long, silky hair that was as white as snow and a nose so long and narrow, it looked like a clothespin. Whatever his name was, he was a lot of fun.

After dinner I sat on the ground in front of a liquor store near my street, smoking Newports with the same boy. He was as gay as an Easter basket, so I didn't have to worry about having to fuck him or suck his dick like I had to with so many of the other boys I'd recently met. Unlike me, this boy had a nice home in Silicon Valley to go to. But he didn't want to, and I could understand why. His daddy was a big shot in the marines and wasn't about to tolerate a sissy for a son sashaying around his macho friends, making him look like a punk, too.

I gave the steak that I had ordered to go to a homeless man who wandered by. When the white boy left, I felt so alone and unloved. I wanted somebody to hold me, and I didn't care who that somebody was. If Wade had come back around at that moment, I would have mowed him down like a steamroller and clung to him like paint. I regretted what I'd said to him in the park and decided that I would apologize as soon as I saw him again.

I didn't go home that night. One reason was, I didn't like being in the apartment alone. I felt safer on the street with a bunch of strange runaway kids than I did in our apartment.

One night last year, I woke up in the middle of the night, and there was a man standing over my bed. He was dressed in dark clothing, and there was a ski mask covering his face. Before I could scream, he clamped a gloved hand over my mouth. He smelled like a combination of kerosene and underarm funk. I threw up, but since his hand was over my mouth, I almost choked on my own vomit. Somehow I managed to whimper loud enough for Mama to hear me when she got up to go the bathroom, which was across the hall from my bedroom.

As soon as she entered my room and clicked on the light, the intruder fled. He sprinted across the floor and jumped out of the open window.

"Girl, don't you get tired of entertaining your friends? Do you know what time it is?" Mama hollered. She rubbed her eyes and yawned. "Some of us have to get up and go to work in the morning."

I was so afraid, it took several attempts for me to get my words out. "He wasn't my company, Mama."

"Then why was he in this room? Why did he run off like he did?"

"A crazy man broke into my room!" I blurted. I jumped out of the bed and ran to the window and closed it so hard and fast, it cracked. "Mama, we have to call the police!" I yelled, whipping my head around so abruptly, I almost fell to the floor.

"Did he hurt you?" Mama asked, sounding concerned, looking around the room.

"No, he didn't hurt me, but he broke into my room, so I know he wanted to!" I wailed.

Mama stood there looking at me for a long time, like she didn't know what to say or do. Her hands were shaking, and I couldn't describe the look on her face. She seemed to be just as frightened as I was. "Are you all right?" she asked in a low, shaky voice. I could barely hear her, and I was in the same room with her, so I was surprised when Daddy stumbled into my room.

"What's all this ruckus?" he asked, blinking his owlish eyes.

"If I've told this girl once, I've told her a thousand times to keep that window locked," Mama said, with a heavy sigh. She turned to me, with a look of pain on her face. Like a woman in labor. For a minute, I expected her to remind me about the forty-eight hours of labor she had endured to give birth to me. But she surprised me this time. "We worry about you all the time," she said in a surprisingly gentle voice. "We don't know what to do with you anymore."

I bit my bottom lip and looked upside the wall. That wasn't what I'd expected her to say, but it was close enough.

"Well, maybe now she'll do just that," Daddy said. He strolled up to me and felt my forehead. "If he comes back, you holler," he said to me, rubbing my back. Then he turned to Mama. "Juanita, remind me to put some bars on this window. All we need is to get our names in the paper."

I stayed up the rest of that night, with the light on. The man didn't return, but the next morning I found a ladder outside my window, which the man had used to climb up to the second floor. I knew that it belonged to Mr. Royster, the old man who owned the shabby house next to us, so I removed it and dragged it back to his property.

I didn't even bother to tell my parents about the ladder, but when I told old Mr. Royster about it, he had one of his sons come over and chop the old ladder to pieces. When he realized how scared I was about what I'd experienced the night before, he told me that from now on, he'd leave his back-porch light on and his pit bull in the backyard. I wanted to cry when he gave me a big hug. The only reason I didn't cry was because by now I had learned to hide my true feelings. Mr. Royster didn't like my parents, so he didn't bother to tell them what he'd done with his ladder or anything else that he had discussed with me about my traumatic experience. And neither did I.

But that same day Daddy replaced the window that I'd cracked, and he installed some bars. The day after that, he gave me a baseball bat to defend myself with in case some intruder got into my room again, anyway.

A couple of nights later, something happened in my room that shocked me almost as much as the man who'd broken in. As I lay there in the dark, with my eyes closed, I heard my door creak open. A few moments later, I felt a warm hand touch my cheek. I was still playing possum when a pair of rubbery lips kissed the side of my face.

CHAPTER 19

I forgot all about the intruder, and before long things were back to normal. I had fun bringing some of my friends to the apartment to show them the bars on my bedroom window. The bars made me feel safer, but I still had some concerns about sleeping alone in the same room where I might have been raped or murdered if Mama hadn't come in when she did. When I asked Daddy if I could start sleeping on the sofa in the living room with him, he didn't even answer me. He just looked at me like I was crazy. I didn't even bother to ask Mama. One rejection was enough.

I still didn't know which one of my parents had come into my room that night and kissed my cheek, and I didn't care. It made me feel good just to know that one of them had taken at least one step forward. I couldn't even begin to imagine what my life would have been like if my parents had shown me more affection—and out in the open. But I was glad to get any affection at all.

When nobody paid any attention to me I felt alone and unwanted. And the only times those feelings didn't bother me was when I was drunk or in somebody's arm. If somebody gave me some attention I felt better about who I was. And I didn't care how I got that attention or who gave it to me.

I spent so much time helping Maria take care of her baby brothers they had started to call me Aunt Christine.

By the end of that year, I had slept with more than a dozen boys, and I'd contracted gonorrhea three different times, twice in the same month. Even with several free clinics throughout the Bay Area, each offering free birth control, I only went when I needed a shot of penicillin.

When I slept with a boy who told me *after* he'd fucked me that he thought he had some type of disease, I sucker punched him so hard a crown fell off his front tooth. The only reason he didn't hit me back was because I threatened to say he'd raped me. I noticed a smelly discharge in my panties the very next day so I made another trip to the clinic. Then I almost hit one of those smart-mouthed bitches at the clinic who had seen me in there one time too many. "If you insist on sleeping around you should be a little more careful," that heifer had told me with a smirk on her face. And that was while I was on my back, propped up with my feet in stirrups and with every hole on my body below my waist exposed so I was already in a funky mood.

"You need to mind your own fucking business and just do your job. I didn't come out here to get lectured," I hissed. "Give me my shot, or whatever it is I need this time so I can get the hell up and out of here." When I needed to be treated again two months later, I went to the clinic in Oakland. Somehow I had managed to avoid getting pregnant, but almost every girl I knew had had at least one abortion. Maria had had two. The free clinic offered free and confidential abortions, anyway, so the possibility of getting pregnant didn't even faze me.

I don't know how I managed to graduate from middle school, but I did. And with a B average! The kids I knew were excited at the thought of the upcoming summer, but I was not. To them, it meant having a lot more freedom, but I already had more freedom than I knew what to do with. There was very little left for me to get into. I was already doing drugs, smoking two packs of Newports a day, and fucking every boy who asked. There were times when I got so lonely that I did the asking.

I drank when I could get my hands on some alcohol. And, when I got really bored, I shoplifted things, which I usually sold or gave to cool kids so that they would want to hang out with me.

I got caught stealing a bag of potato chips in a liquor store one afternoon. I was relieved that somebody was finally going to chastise me and recite that story to me about how they were going to punish me for my own good. But even that backfired. Instead of calling the police, like I'd wanted him to so that I would know what it felt like for somebody to try and steer me in the right direction, the store clerk just gave me a stern warning and sent me on my way. I stopped at another liquor store on the way home and stole some cigarettes and some Doritos.

I went on a shoplifting rampage that summer. I even stole things right in front of some store clerks' noses. The one time that a store manager caught me and called the cops I cried so long, loud, and hard they didn't arrest me. But even though they read me the riot act and told me that the next time I wouldn't be so lucky, they escorted me home.

When the cops told my parents that I'd been caught stealing makeup and a Rick James tape, all my mother said was, "Well, at least she didn't kill nobody or rob no bank."

The two young officers gave me a puzzled look, shrugged, and told my folks I shouldn't be out so late, and then they left. Ten minutes later, I waltzed right through the living room, past my parents, toward the door.

"*Hey!*" my daddy yelled. I wanted to stop, but I didn't. And, neither he nor my mother attempted to keep me in that night. I made a beeline to the park, where I knew a lot of people would show me some love.

I still saw Wade around the neighborhood, but he ignored me just as much as I ignored him. He had a steady girlfriend now, and he seemed happy with her. A relationship with one boy was what I wanted, but that didn't seem like something that was going to happen for me anytime soon. None of the boys I slept with wanted to see me after three or four times. And none of them ever took me to a movie or home to meet their parents. I expected that kind of treatment from the white boys that I'd fucked, but not from the brothers. As a matter of fact, a couple of the white boys that I had fooled around with eventually invited me to parties and other gatherings. But by the time they did, I'd already lost interest in them.

High school was an exciting time in my shaky life. Kids were more focused, even me. Most of us knew what we wanted to do with our lives. Some of my classmates wanted to attend UC Berkeley. A lot of the others wanted to join the military, or get married. I just wanted to experience a normal life, which to me meant, I wanted someone in my life that really cared about me and showed it.

Even though my parents rarely showed me any affection, I was convinced that they loved me in their own strange way. They just didn't know how to show it. When I won a citywide spelling bee, a reporter from a local newspaper came to our apartment to interview me and take my picture. Everybody in our building and on our block got excited. I was at a nearby grocery store, helping Mama shop for groceries one day, and several adults came up to Mama and told her she should be proud of me.

"Oh, we are very proud of this girl," Mama said, patting the top of my head. She looked at me in a way that she had never looked at me before—at least not while I was awake. There were tears in her eyes, but she did as much blinking as she had to to hold them back.

We walked home in silence, like we usually did. But later that evening, Mama stuck her head into my room and said, "I meant what I said back at the store a little while ago."

"About what?" I asked, not even looking up from the *Playgirl* magazine one of my friends had passed on to me. I was so used to her and Daddy not showing any interest in me that I honestly didn't know what she was talking about.

"I am proud of you. Your daddy is, too," she muttered in a meek voice. "Me and Reuben, we didn't get too far in school. Nobody in our family did."

I looked up. "They have school programs for people like you and Daddy," I offered. "Do you want me to go to the library and get some brochures? Maybe some day we can all visit Guatemala, look up some of our family, bring them to the States, and get them into school, too."

My mother looked at me like I had just spewed out some pea soup. *"We can never ever go back to that place,"* she said in a voice just above a whisper. Then she clicked off my light and left the room. Her going back to school was never mentioned again. Nor was the fact that she was proud of me.

CHAPTER 20

"Woman, don't you flip out on us now. We got work for you to do."

"Huh?" I felt a hand on my shoulder and somebody's hot breath on my face. I shook my head and struggled to bring the rest of my body back to 2007. "Wade, when did you get back?" I asked. I was still on the bed in the tacky motel room. Wade hovered over me, with his arms held open, like a bear about to crush me to death.

I couldn't remember the last time I'd spent so much time reminiscing about my past. But now it was something that took over my thoughts whether I wanted it to or not.

"Me and Jason have been standing here talking to you for five minutes. For that whole time, you've been just sitting here looking like a zombie. I know all you can think about right now is that half a million fucking dollars we got coming, because that's all I can think about myself," Wade told me in an excited voice, talking so fast he had to stop to catch his breath. He leaned back on his heels and folded his arms, giving me a critical look, and I didn't like that. It made me nervous. "But you need to stay focused, baby. There's too much money at stake for you to be spacing out on us."

Another thing that made me nervous was the fact that Wade had shifted most of his affection from me to the money ever since he had made that first telephone call to my husband.

"And, you look like hell with them red, swollen eyes," Jason, whose eyes looked like shooting stars, had the nerve to add. "I say, we take a few more pictures of you looking like that."

"I was just sitting here thinking, that's all," I mumbled, rubbing my arm.

"You sure was," Wade clucked, tossing a plastic bag at me. You didn't even hear us come in this door. Anyway, I got you some Right Guard, some toothpaste, and some gum from Walgreen's."

"Did you bring me some clean underwear?" I asked, patting the plastic bag.

"I said Walgreen's, not Victoria's Secret. The closest thing Walgreen's got to women's panties is them adult diapers," Wade said, then guffawed.

"I need some clean underwear, Wade," I insisted.

Wade stopped laughing and gave me an impatient and exasperated look. Something he'd been doing a lot of lately. "We'll swing by Target after we make that call," Wade told me. "Look, I think we are making some real progress. My man seen them pictures, and that shook his ass up like a milk shake."

"Jesse Ray saw the pictures of me tied up and blindfolded? How did you get the pictures to him?" I gasped, rising from the bed.

"Jason got one of his boys, a homeless dude, to deliver. When homeboy came back to the coffee shop where we was waiting at, he said old Jesse Ray looked like he seen a ghost when he opened that envelope. He got so upset, he broke down and cried like a bitch. I had to see that with my own eyes. I ducked into his store, and sure enough, he looked like a lost man."

"He saw you? You let him see your face? How stupid can you get, Wade? What if this thing falls apart?"

"Well, as long as he don't know me from Moses, we ain't got nothing to worry about."

"He's seen you before."

"A lot of people have seen me before. That don't mean shit. As far as he knew, I was just another customer in his video store." Wade gave me a dry look and shook his head. "Baby, you need to get a grip and let me and my boy handle this thing. You've done your part. Now all you gots to do is just sit back and let things fall into place."

I looked at Wade's face. I saw eyes that now looked like they belonged on a madman. And, the more we talked about the tax-free fortune he had coming to him, the more desperate he looked. "Did you call him yet?"

Wade fired up a joint and took a long drag before he answered. "Woman, how many times do I have to tell you that *you* need to talk to him again? Put on them sunglasses, and let's take a little trip down to a pay phone. And one far away from here. We can't take no chance on none of them busy hoes overhearing nothing, or seeing you and me together and getting nosy."

Jason had borrowed one of his lady friend's battered old Honda Civic. He did the driving as we rode around for about twenty minutes, looking for a pay phone where there was not that much traffic. I was hunched down in the backseat with Wade. He had his arm around my neck, holding on to me like he was afraid I might leap out of the car.

That thought *had* entered my mind.

"Now, when you talk to this rich-ass nigger, don't forget—you need to sound *real* desperate. We need to get this thing situated here so we can make some real plans. Shit," Wade said as soon as the car stopped.

He led me by the hand like I was a blind woman to a pay phone at the corner, near a deserted building on Telegraph. There was a funeral home across the street. "Shit," Wade grunted when he saw the mortuary's sign and a big black hearse parked on the street. "I need for you to make this conversation short and sweet. This is some bad Karma around here. This place gives me the creeps," he said, releasing my hand.

He fished a few coins out of his pants pocket, counted, and cursed under his breath. "Baby, give me a quarter," he ordered. I didn't say a word as I rooted around in my purse and found some loose coins and handed them all to him. He dropped what he needed to into the payphone slot and then slid the rest into his pants pocket. With the tip of his tongue sticking out of the corner of his mouth, Wade dialed my husband's number. He screwed up his face and held his breath like he was about to deliver the performance of a lifetime. And I guess he was.

He cupped the receiver in his hand as he spoke in a low voice, which he didn't do too good of a job disguising. "Listen carefully. Don't try to trace this call, and don't say nothing stupid. Are you alone? Good! Did you see them pictures of your wife we took? Good! Uh-huh. Yeah, man, she is still alive and kicking. Now how long she's going to remain alive and kicking is up to you, my man."

Wade made a face at the telephone like he wanted to break into it. But, instead, he handed it to me. Then he did a strange thing. He pressed his finger against my forehead, like it was the barrel of a gun, and made a clicking noise with his tongue. I didn't know whose benefit that ominous little gesture was for. It meant nothing to me, and Jesse Ray couldn't see it. But I still didn't like it. I snatched the telephone and turned my back to Wade.

"Honey . . . honey, it's me." I threw in a few sniffles before I started crying. "Hon . . . honey . . . I want to come home," I sobbed, a real lump rising in my throat. I was amazed that I was able to squeeze out some real tears.

"Oh my God, Christine! Oh my God!" In all the years that I'd known Jesse Ray, this was the first time I'd heard him cry.

I stopped crying, and I let a few moments of silence pass before I responded. "J.R., they . . . they are going to kill me if you don't pay them the money."

"Aarrrggghhhh!"

"J.R., please stop crying. I love you, and I want to be back with you. Please pay them the money so I can come home," I pleaded. Wade gestured for me to do some more boo-hooing myself. "Honey, they said they were going to rape me first," I sobbed, but I was not as hysterical as Jesse Ray was. "And please don't call the police! They've got a gun! I don't want to *die*!" I wailed.

"Baby, listen to me! You be strong." Jesse Ray sounded like he was choking on his own words. "We are going to get through this thing, and everything is going to be all right. I swear to God it is!" he vowed.

"You . . . you are going to pay them the money then?" I asked. "They . . . they are getting real mad."

"Put whoever's in charge back on the phone! Put him back on the telephone right now!" Jesse Ray commanded. "I want to end this shit right now!"

I handed the telephone back to Wade.

"Yeah," Wade said, with a grunt. "Uh-huh. Uh-huh. Huh?" he gave me a stunned look and held the telephone away from his face. A look that included a mysterious smile crossed his face as he cleared his throat and prepared to speak into the receiver again. I glanced at Jason, who was standing next to the car, with a look on his face that was so smug, it looked like it had been painted on. It didn't take long for his expression to change. He gave me a cold look and pointed to his watch. I held my arm up to Wade and tapped my watch. He responded by holding up his hand in my face. "Now listen, my man. I want you to repeat what you just told me to your little wife here," Wade said, then put the telephone up to my ear.

"J.R., it's me, baby," I mumbled, my voice sounding as weak as a newborn kitten's.

"Christine, honey. I can't stand this. I love you; I love you; I love you. I told him if he turns you loose *unharmed,* I'd give him *double* what he's asking for. And, that means he can't rape you or even touch you in the wrong place. Has he already—"

"No, I haven't been raped or touched or anything . . . yet," I croaked.

"And . . . and I told him I'd give it to him today if I could, but I need time to work this out with my banker. Please be strong, baby. We are going to get through this all right!"

"J.R., did I hear you right? You told him you'd give him a million dollars?" I mouthed, sounding stronger than I should have. I realized that immediately. "A . . . *million* . . . dollars?" I asked, speaking in a weak voice again. I got so light-headed, I stumbled. Wade threw his arms around my waist just in time to keep me from falling to the ground.

"They can have every dime I got if they want it. I just want this thing to be over with. I swear to God, I will make this up to you. We'll go off somewhere so you can relax and put this behind you!"

"I . . . I want to come home, honey. I don't care what you have to do for them to let me go." I handed the phone back to Wade. He had such a satisfied look on his face, you would have thought that he'd won the lottery. And, in a way, that was exactly the case.

But I had one immediate concern: now that Jesse Ray was going to pay double what I'd expected, how much of an increase was Wade going to expect?

"Ten o'clock," Wade said, looking at the cheap watch on his wrist. "I will call you at ten o'clock sharp on Friday morning at the same number. If you got my money, I'll tell you where to drop it off. Once I get it, I'll call you exactly one hour from the pickup time and tell you where you can pick up your woman. Don't try nothing cute! Don't try to punk me with no money that can be traced or nothing like that. I want used bills, all hundreds, fifties, and twenties. Don't even think about involving the cops . . . I know where everybody in your family lives. Any questions?"

"No," Jesse Ray muttered.

"Now you have a nice day, brother. And look on the bright side. I don't care what you pay out. You'll still have enough bling to keep living like a king. You ain't never going to be as broke as some of us."

I gave Wade a sharp look and gestured for him to hang up.

He finally hung up and looked at me long and hard. "Girl, you sure you want to leave this goose? I didn't know it was going to be this easy to get him to pay us. If I was you, I'd stick to this nigger like white on rice. He got insurance?"

"Yes, he's got all kinds of insurance," I stated. "That precious main store is insured up the wazoo. Fire, earthquake, theft, vandalism."

"I am not talking about that kind of insurance," Wade said, waving his hand. "I'm talking about *life* insurance."

He looked away when I looked at him, with my mouth hanging open. "We take what he's offering. Nothing more," I said in an angry voice.

"All I asked is whether or not he got insurance," Wade said, with a pout. "I'm just curious."

"Jesse Ray's well insured," I said. "But if you're thinking about doing something to him so you can get your hands on that insurance money, too, you can get that out of your thick head right now. I would never hurt Jesse Ray for money."

Wade and Jason looked at each other and snickered.

"You don't want to hurt the brother? Well, baby, I got news for you. I think it's a little bit too late to start worrying about hurting old J. R. Thurman," said Wade. He laughed again and winked at me. "Girl, if punking a black man out of a million dollars ain't going to hurt him, I don't know what will."

"Fuck me! A whole one million fucking dollars? Shit, I ain't never even seen more than a few hundred at a time in my whole life! I . . . I wonder what the fuck a million goddamn dollars look like stacked up all nice and neat? Shit!" Jason could barely contain himself in the car on the way back to the motel. No matter how I looked at it, the fact that this man was part of my plan made me extremely uncomfortable. "And tax free at that!"

"One million dollars. Uh-huh. That's what the man said," Wade shrieked, slapping his knee. "Ooh wee!" His involvement was beginning to disturb me, too. "Looks like Christmas is coming early this year. Thank God I've been a gooood boy."

I was in the backseat, alone this time, huddled in a corner, with the baseball cap still hiding my hair and the sunglasses hiding my eyes. I was glad that I was in disguise. I was glad that nobody could see the concern on my face or know what was going through my head. This new development gave me even more to worry about.

Traffic was heavy, and there were a lot of people on the street. Even though I was disguised, I was afraid that someone I knew would see me hunched down in the backseat of the car and would recognize me, anyway. I knew that that was unlikely, but I didn't want to take any chances. I had taken enough already. I hunched down some more, so low that I was practically lying on the seat.

When we stopped at a red light on Alcatraz, not far from my husband's video store, I slid down even farther in my seat. I almost shit my pants when somebody ran up to the car and tapped on the window. I closed my eyes and held my breath.

"Get your spic ass away from this car!" Wade yelled, slapping the window.

I opened my eyes and looked up. A young Latino man stood next to the car, waving a cheap watch in one hand and a used DVD in the other. He frowned at Wade, then looked at me with a leer on his face.

"And don't be eyeballing my woman, amigo!" Wade hollered, slapping the window again. "How come you so quiet back there, baby?" Wade asked as we drove off, turning his head around just far enough so he could see me. There was a glazed look on his face. His jaw twitched. He narrowed his eyes and licked his lips, moaning under his breath the same way he did when he went down on me. It was no wonder that the only other time I'd seen such a look of ecstasy on Wade's face was during sex. "You ought to be shouting for joy! I can't believe my woman is going to be a fucking millionaire!"

I didn't like hearing Wade refer to me as his woman. In all the years that I'd been hopping in and out of bed with him, he had never referred to me that way. And, it was all because of the money. Money that I truly felt I deserved and couldn't get from my husband any other way.

It amazed me how money could have such a profound effect on people. I never thought that I would see the day that it would mean so much to me that I would be a part of something this extreme.

"A million dollars is not that much money in this day and age, Wade," I said in a strained voice.

"Oh, no! You are hella funny, baby! To you, it might not be. You been living so close to it for quite a while now. A big, fancy house in the hills, a husband with his own business, credit cards up the asshole . . . Everything I ever wanted!" Jason said, adjusting the rearview mirror so he could see me better. I didn't like the hungry look on his face, not that I liked any other look on his face, either.

"Tell me about it, my man!" Wade yelled, waving his hands like a country preacher. It seemed like everything Wade did or said now annoyed me.

"Uh, I'll have to decide exactly how much I want to keep now," I said, sitting up and moving close to the edge of the seat. Jason and Wade looked at each other at the same time.

Jason reacted in a way that made him turn two shades darker. "So? And what the fuck are you trying to tell us?" he asked, talking so loud, my ears rang.

"I mean, I could sure use the additional money, and I know both of you could, too," I said meekly. "The pie is a lot sweeter and bigger now. Uh, but y'all don't have to worry, because you'll get paid."

Wade and Jason looked at each other at the same time again, each one frowning like he was in pain. "Get paid? Get paid? What the hell! Woman, what's wrong with you? You goddamn right we are going to get paid! And we better get paid right! Tell us what the hell you mean by that," Jason demanded through clenched teeth, his eyes back on the road now. "Man, I knew this bitch was cuckoo when you told me what she was cooking up, but I didn't know she was this damn crazy."

"Well, to be honest with you, baby, me and Jason are the ones that's been taking the most risks," Wade told me. He looked out the window as he spoke, like he was afraid to look in my eyes now.

"What risks?" I asked, gripping the back of the front seat.

Wade twisted around to face me, making it look like his head was on backwards. He blinked and then glared at me. "Woman, don't play dumb. You know damn well that if this thing falls apart, me and my boy here are the ones who will likely end up in the joint," Wade insisted, talking with his lips barely moving.

"If things fall apart, I'm in trouble, too. I could lose everything, including my freedom," I insisted.

"Just as long as you treat me fair, I ain't going to complain," Jason said, with a groan.

"What do you call fair?" I wanted to know, my anger rising.

"What the hell do you think I mean? I am in this thing just as deep as you, and I expect to get paid for my troubles. That's the deal!" Jason yelled, swerving to avoid hitting a man on a bike.

"Keep your eyes on the road, brother. You ain't Batman, and this ain't the Batmobile," Wade barked, grabbing the steering wheel. Riding in a car with Jason behind the wheel was like riding on a roller coaster. A few seconds later, he turned a corner on two wheels. I looked at him in the rearview mirror. That single serpent's tooth at the top of his mouth looked like a stiletto now.

"Like I said, I made a deal here!" Jason hollered, still driving like a madman.

"A deal between you and Wade," I reminded.

"But you the one getting the money! Wade ain't the one controlling this project, girl. That's you! We can't get nothing without you!"

"You got that right. But like I said, your deal is between you and Wade. I didn't make any arrangements with you, Jason." I was so angry, I was about to explode. "I want to make sure you understand that *whatever* you get is up to Wade. You are not getting a damn dime from me!" I boomed.

Wade glanced around at me, then back at Jason. "Brother, you ain't got nothing to worry about. I told you I was going to break you off real nice. Now I will just break you off a little bigger piece of the pie." Wade exhaled and turned to look at me again. "Happy?"

I stared at him and blinked before I nodded.

But I was a long way from being happy. I was glad that Jason got us stuck in a traffic jam and that the car had come to a complete stop. I reared back in my seat and closed my eyes, but I knew I was not about to go to sleep.

I had too much to think about—past, present, and future.

CHAPTER 21

One of the happiest periods in my life began about six months after my fifteenth birthday. I finally got to know what real love felt like. Not with another lover, but with someone who was probably as starved for affection as I was: an old woman who had already buried three husbands and had one foot in the grave herself.

Odessa Wheeler moved into the apartment across the hall from me and my parents. The same week she moved in, I began doing all kinds of errands for her to earn a little extra spending money. Even though I had no trouble stealing the things I wanted (including the portable color television in my bedroom), I actually felt good about myself when I paid for something with money I'd earned.

Every time I ran to the corner store to pick up this or that for Miss Odessa or when I helped her move a piece of furniture, she paid me a few dollars and often gave me a big hug, too. "Christine, I don't know what I'd do without you. You are precious," she told me one Saturday afternoon. I left in a hurry after she told me that because I didn't want her to see the tears in my eyes. I couldn't remember the last time somebody said something so nice to me.

It didn't take long for me to reach a point where I looked forward to the hugs more than I did the money. This was so new to me that I didn't know how to handle it at first. It made me want to avoid a lot of the people who had had a negative effect on me. Sadly, this included my parents.

"Now, Christine. Today is Mother's Day, and you should be spending it with your own mother," Miss Odessa told me. I had just steamrolled into her living room that Sunday evening, with a Mother's Day card for her.

"My mother doesn't celebrate Mother's Day," I said glumly, handing Miss Odessa the card, which I'd bought at Walgreen's and which had set me back three dollars.

"That's not the point. She is still your mother," Miss Odessa told me, fanning her face with the card.

Miss Odessa was so old, her hair was completely white and lines crisscrossed her face like a road map. But I figured that she must have been a good-looking woman once upon a time to have had three husbands. She had small, dainty features on a heart-shaped face, and her skin was the same color as honey. She was not a big woman, but what was left of her body had begun to sag so severely that bras and girdles did her no good. Decked out in a pale blue cotton dress and the matching hat that she'd worn to church that morning, she stood in front of me, with one hand on her lumpy hip and the other hand waving the Mother's Day card at me.

"This is a real special day for mothers and their children, Christine. Even to the mothers that don't deserve to be mothers," she added, giving me a stern look. It didn't bother me when I got scolded by Miss Odessa. As a matter of fact, I was glad when she did.

I gave her a sheepish grin, shuffled my feet like an idiot, and shrugged. I don't know why, but one thing I couldn't do was sass old people. Even when they were mean to me. I figured it had something to do with that incident when I was a little girl and stepped on that old man's head in our old house and thought I'd killed him. Even though I had found out that that man had died of natural causes, to this day I still felt a twinge of guilt about stepping on him and not telling anybody about it.

"Are your kids coming to spend Mother's Day with you?" I asked.

A sad look immediately appeared on Miss Odessa's face. It was the same look that slid across my face when people asked me something I didn't want to answer. But she answered me, anyway. "I doubt it," she replied in a hollow voice, shuffling across the floor to one of two shabby easy chairs in her congested living room. She had one of the smallest units in our building, but she had more possessions than anybody I'd ever seen. As petite as I was, I often had to walk sideways to get around in her apartment, and I still sometimes managed to knock over something along the way. "They hardly do anymore. Not since they all grew up and moved into their own places. I had me three husbands, a bunch of kids, and I still ended up alone," she said, with a dry laugh.

It amazed me how much I actually had in common with this old woman. Miss Odessa was even older than my parents, and from what I'd learned from her in bits and pieces that day, all five of her kids lived in or around Berkeley, but they practically ignored her. Her youngest son had a new wife and a year-old daughter, whom Miss Odessa had never met, and they lived just six blocks away.

I could see the sadness in the old woman's eyes when she talked about her children. I decided to change the subject for now and avoid it in the future. In the next breath, I started rambling about something I'd seen on television, and before long we were laughing.

As footloose and fancy-free as I was, I was fairly sensitive. It didn't happen that often, but I got emotional from time to time. I had cried off and on for two days when, a few months before, old Mr. Royster next door died.

I spent the rest of the evening stretched out like a python on one of Miss Odessa's two living room sofas, watching one rerun after another. She liked beer, and she usually kept a couple of six-packs in her refrigerator. She kept dozing off, so I could have drunk as many of her beers as I wanted to, but I didn't. I didn't need a buzz to feel good when I was with her.

It was a school night, and if Miss Odessa had not chased me home around eight o'clock, I would have stayed even longer, watching more television and poring over the magazines that she had stacked up in boxes throughout her apartment. She also had an incomplete set of encyclopedias, which I found fascinating. Through them, I entered a whole new world, and I started to see a lot of things in my old world in a better light, including myself.

CHAPTER 22

Even though Miss Odessa had become a positive influence in my life, I was still running with a wild crowd.

I had not seen Wade Fisher around the neighborhood in over a year. And whenever his name came up, I changed the subject. I'd almost forgotten about him completely until Miss Odessa and I ran into his mother at a fruit stand at the Ashby Street weekend flea market one Saturday afternoon two weeks before the Fourth of July.

"Oh, Wade is already doing so well in Hollywood! He's got him an agent and an apartment near the big studios. And, he got him a Jewish agent, so I *know* my baby is in good hands," Miss Louise squealed, spit dribbling from both sides of her mouth. Somehow she had managed to slide her stout, bell-shaped body into a denim jumpsuit that was two sizes too small and thirty years too young for her.

She opened her matching denim shoulder bag and whipped out a sealskin wallet. My first thought was that she was going to show me how empty it was and then put the bite on me for "a few dollars," like she usually did when I ran into her. But she surprised me this time. With her eyes bugged out and her tongue licking her bottom lip, she flipped open her wallet to a picture of Wayne in the spot where her driver's license should have been. It was a good head shot of Wade. He looked every inch a big Hollywood star. But I had a feeling that was not the case.

"What has he done so far?" I asked in a casual voice. My question made Miss Louise uncomfortable, because her mouth dropped open, and she gave me a look that made me uncomfortable, too. "Uh, I go to the movies a lot and I watch a lot of television, but I haven't seen Wade in anything yet," I said, with a forced smile.

"My boy's done a lot of stuff," Miss Louise snapped, like she was saying it more for her benefit than for mine. She patted her wig and sucked in a loud breath. "But you know how them Hollywood bigwigs do black folks. Black actors can't get too far in them movies, because the producers and directors usually edit them out of whatever they put 'em in when they run over budget or some other stupid reason." Miss Louise let out a sigh that made her screw up her face in such a pained way that I thought she was going to cry.

Miss Odessa fished a pair of horn-rimmed glasses out of her big straw purse and held them up to her eyes. Then she looked at the picture with so much awe on her face, you would have thought she was admiring something holy. "Well, the boy is certainly handsome enough to be in the movies," she said, swooning.

"Oh yes. The boy goes to parties where all the biggest stars go. And, you ought to see all of them pretty girls chasing him all over that Hollywood. Them white girls especially. He all but has to beat them off with a stick. I don't know what it is about my boy that drives the girls so crazy, but his daddy had the same problem. Irresistible is what he is," Miss Louise said, with a proud sigh, looking directly at me.

"He's my son and I love him to death, but the boy is a ladies' man. The girl he's with now is white, but she's a nice girl, and I think I can deal with her in the family if I have to. She rich. You want to see her picture?" Miss Louise asked, already flipping open her wallet to another compartment. This time she plucked a picture out of the change compartment. Miss Odessa leaned so far forward to look at this picture, it looked like she'd suddenly developed a hump on her back.

"Oh, my God, what a beautiful girl," Miss Odessa said, looking at the picture like it was something good to eat.

I glanced at the picture so fast, all I saw was a blond blur and two rows of sparkling white teeth. "Tell Wade I said hi and best of luck," I mumbled, backing away. I didn't want to hear any more about Wade's glamorous new life, and I certainly did not want to look too long at a picture of his pretty new girlfriend. I wasn't looking where I was going. I stumbled and accidentally backed into a stand across from the fruit vendor, where a boy was selling old comic books and lemonade.

"What can I get for you today, baby sister?" the boy asked. This boy was also from the neighborhood, but he and I ran in completely different circles. I didn't even know his name, but I knew that he was always involved in some kind of moneymaking venture. One week I saw him running up and down the street selling newspapers, even going up to cars waiting on red lights to change. The next month, he was on the street selling something different each week: newspapers, bean pies, roses, and fish sandwiches. When he got tired of doing that, he sold lemonade on the sidewalk in front of his mama's house. I even used to see him rummaging through Dumpsters, fishing out aluminum cans and empty pop bottles.

"Is that lemonade fresh?" I asked. I glanced over my shoulder and saw that Miss Odessa was still talking to Wade's mama. Given the way Miss Louise was waving her arms and wiping sweat off her face with the back of her hand, I assumed she was still bragging about Wade. Then I saw Miss Odessa pull a wad of bills out of her purse. Miss Louise's hand looked like a lobster's claw as she reached out and snatched the money. She did it so fast that I would not have witnessed it if I had blinked. That's when I looked away and focused my attention on the boy and his lemonade in front of me.

"I made it myself out of lemons from my own tree," he said proudly. Before I could even tell him that I didn't have any money, he filled a large Styrofoam cup and handed it to me, tossing in a wedge of lemon.

"Uh, I spent all my money getting my fortune told," I explained, pointing to a booth down the same aisle, occupied by a gypsy psychic. She had told me that I'd meet a tall man who would one day be very important to me. I didn't pay too much attention to her prediction, because every psychic I'd ever been to had told me, and most of the other girls I knew, the same thing. "I'll have to pay you later," I said. I drank until the cup was empty.

"You're Christine Martinez, right?"

"You know my name?" I gasped.

He nodded. "Martinez is Spanish or something, right?"

I nodded. "My folks are from Guatemala. How do you know my name?"

"I asked around."

I gave him a surprised look. "I don't know you, do I?" I had had sex with so many boys, I couldn't remember a lot of the names or faces. There was a possibility that I'd already been with this boy! If that was the case, I had to change my ways because I didn't like the way I felt about myself at that moment.

"No, we've never met," he said, shaking his head. "I know some of the kids you hang with, so I didn't think I was your type," he said, with a chuckle. "Hey, maybe I'll see you around somewhere. Movies maybe?"

He was not bad looking. He had a round, cinnamon-colored face with shiny black eyes. His lips were rather generous, and he was a little too thin for my taste. He was tall, at least six two. His lanky arms looked like they could wrap around me twice. "What's your name, anyway?" I asked, turning to leave. "I know your mama is Miss Rosetta Thurman because she goes to the same laundromat that we go to."

"Jesse Ray." He paused and stuck out his chest. "My family and my friends call me J.R.," he said proudly.

"J.R.," I repeated. "I like that. It's easy to remember," I told him. "Well, I hope I see you again."

"You will," he replied, with a wink and a mysterious smile.

Something told me that I would see Jesse Ray again. Because he looked at me like no man had looked at me before, like he was already sizing me up and planning our future.

CHAPTER 23

I had enjoyed meeting and chatting with Jesse Ray Thurman, but I didn't give him another thought after I left the flea market that day. I spent the rest of that Saturday afternoon with Miss Odessa. I had to laugh when I thought about how I'd gone from hanging out with some of the coolest kids in town to hanging out with a woman old enough to be my grandmother.

Unlike a lot of old people I knew, Miss Odessa wasn't nosy and meddlesome. She'd asked me only a few questions about my folks, like where they worked and what they did in their spare time. The basic information was all she seemed interested in. And, each time I attempted to tell her what my folks were really like, she changed the subject. I guess in her own way, she already knew by the way I'd latched onto her.

I spent so much time at Miss Odessa's apartment that when some of my street friends came looking for me, they came straight to her door. Jesse Ray Thurman was the last boy on the planet that I expected to pay me an uninvited visit.

I felt so comfortable and at home at Miss Odessa's that I answered her door when he knocked a few days after I'd seen him at the flea market.

"Hi, Christine. Your mama told me you were at your godmother's apartment," he said, grinning from ear to ear.

"How did you know where I lived?" I asked, my mouth hanging open after I stopped talking.

"I asked around," he admitted, cocking his head to one side. He was so much taller than me that I had to look up at him. When he looked down on me, his eyelids slid halfway down his eyes, like shades, giving him that "hooded eye" look that made some men seem so mysterious.

"Uh . . . that's right. My, uh, godmother," I said, with pride I didn't know I had. I was surprised that somebody as out of touch as my mother would refer to Miss Odessa as my godmother. From that day on, that was what I considered Miss Odessa to be. It had a better ring to it than "friend" did when I told my friends who Miss Odessa was.

The sight of Jesse Ray standing there in that dimly lit apartment hallway had really taken me by surprise. I stood there, reared back on my heels, with my head tilted back, squinting my eyes so that I could see him better. He was better looking than I'd thought. I didn't know how to deal with a boy that I didn't know who was going around asking questions about me.

"I guess you came for the money I owe you for the lemonade." I grinned, patting the pockets on my jeans, my head still tilted back. My neck had already started to ache, but I didn't care.

"Oh, you can forget about that. I already did. I, uh, thought you might want to go see a movie." I didn't know any shy boys, but the way that Jesse Ray was blinking his eyes and shifting his weight from one foot to the other, he was acting like one.

"With who?" I asked.

He shrugged. "With me. Your mama let you go out on dates yet?"

"Not really," I admitted. Neither of my parents had ever discussed my social life with me. "I'm just fifteen."

"Oops!" Jesse Ray looked like he was going to faint. "I'm sorry. I just thought . . . I thought you were at least sixteen!"

I shook my head.

"Listen, I'll catch up with you some other time." He laughed, backing away, with his hands up in the air, like I'd just pulled a gun on him. "I just thought . . . Well, I've seen you out with some of the kids from the university, so I thought you were older. And, you do look at least sixteen. I don't want your daddy cracking me upside my head." He laughed some more, wiping sweat off his face. He didn't seem shy now, just nervous.

"You still want me to forget about paying for the lemonade?" I asked, following him down the hall, toward the exit.

"Don't worry about that," he said, walking away even faster.

"Who was that at the door? Was it one of my kids?" Miss Odessa asked as soon as I returned to her living room. The biggest problem with having such an old person for a best friend was the fact that she had health problems on top of health problems. Today her arthritis was bothering her so bad, it was a struggle for her to get up once she'd sat down. She was wobbling like a spinning top now, trying to get up from her sofa. I padded across the floor and grabbed her by the arm to keep her from falling. "I asked who that was at my door," she said, flopping back down on her seat so hard, she took me with her.

"Nobody," I replied, with a shrug. "Just some boy knocking on the wrong door."

CHAPTER 24

I didn't go home after I left Miss Odessa's house that day. Instead, I ended up at the house of a tall, lanky girl, with a cute round face, named Tina. I had recently met Tina through Maria. A month after I met Tina, Maria's family moved to San Jose so now I spent most of my time with Tina. Unlike some of the other girls I knew, who would steal your clothes and your man, I trusted Tina because she was always honest and up front with me. She was probably the only real friend I had now that Maria was gone. I had promised that I'd help her braid her hair that night. Like with most of the kids that I roamed the streets with, I didn't even know Tina's last name. And, it didn't really matter, because most of my so-called friends never stayed around too long, anyway. Either they moved away like Maria, got themselves caught up in some criminal situation that cost them their lives, ended up missing under suspicious circumstances, or got locked up. Three of my late friends, two girls and a boy in the same family, had all died in the same year. The girls had been murdered, and the boy had committed suicide when he found out he had AIDS. The fact that I was still alive and walking around free was as much a mystery to me as it was to other people.

Tina said she liked hanging out with me because I was smart. But she'd only started saying that after I started sharing information with her that I'd sopped up from the magazines and encyclopedias in Miss

Odessa's apartment. Other kids started to look at me with admiration when I used some of the big words I'd learned.

I was doing something constructive and positive for another person, besides fucking or getting high, and that made me feel good about myself. It saddened me to know that some kids, some even older than me, didn't know that there were black folks from Guatemala. Tina was one of those kids. She didn't even believe me when I told her that that was where my parents had come from until I dragged her to our apartment one night and had Mama say something in Spanish. I didn't know much Spanish, but I knew enough to know that Mama had used a few cuss words when she chased me and Tina out of her kitchen while she was trying to fry a fish.

Tina and I didn't speak again until we were a block away from my building, and even then, we were still running. "Girl, your daddy didn't speak when I spoke to him, and your mama spewed some gibberish and looked like she wanted to bust my brains out with that frying pan. No wonder you like to hang out so much," Tina told me, looking behind her. "I hope you don't take none of your other homies to your home," Tina said in a serious tone of voice. "With your folks being so strange, you won't keep no friends too long."

After I finished braiding Tina's hair in her tiny bedroom, we shared a joint and a can of beer. And, before I left the run-down house on Martin Luther King Jr. Drive that she shared with her alcoholic mother, she told me something that shocked me.

"You remember that boy Wade?" she asked, sniffing and rubbing her runny nose. Tina used to be pretty, but the drugs and fast life had taken a heavy toll on her. She already had dark circles around her eyes and a face that looked as hard as concrete. She didn't bathe on a regular basis or do much with her hair. I felt so sorry for her and the way she looked. That was why I always volunteered to braid her hair for free, when I charged other girls twenty to thirty dollars to hook them up with the same hairdo.

Tina's mother was always fussing about the water bill being so high, so Tina didn't take baths but a couple of times a week. I really liked Tina and I tried to look out for her. Every time she came to my house I encouraged her to take a long shower and to use my deodorant. But I could only do so much for her. She still looked and smelled downright foul most of the time. That's why she couldn't keep a boyfriend. Some of the boys that she used to fool around with ran when they saw her now. And, some of the boys that I used to fool around with did the same thing to me, but for different reasons. I didn't stink, and I did my best to make myself look good when I went out. I honestly didn't know why I couldn't keep a boyfriend. Just hearing the name of the one boy that I would have walked on water to be with made my heart skip a beat.

"You do remember Wade, don't you?" Tina asked, grinning.

I blinked and bit my bottom lip, trying my best to keep from smiling. But Tina saw me smile, anyway. She rolled her eyes and shook her head, patting the neat braided designs I'd just completed.

"Wade Eddie Fisher? What about him? His mama came to my house yesterday to borrow some more money from my daddy," I complained. "As usual, she was going on and on about him doing so good down there in Hollywood. I haven't seen him in anything yet, and you know how much television I watch."

"I seen him on a commercial for Pepsi," Tina informed me.

"Humph! Well, a Pepsi commercial is a long way from him being in a movie," I muttered bitterly. "The way he went around bragging about how he was going to take Hollywood by storm, I expected him to be costarring with Eddie Murphy by now."

"But a commercial is better than nothing. I read in one of those magazines you gave me that people can make a lot of money doing commercials. Somebody with Wade's looks and body can make a living just doing commercials."

"I guess so," I offered, the bitterness still in my mouth, coating my tongue like venom. On one hand, I was happy that Wade was doing so well and living his dream—if that was the case. But I still had a lot of resentment toward him for the way he had treated me at the restaurant that day, especially after all the sex we'd had in his messy bedroom. "Why did you bring his name up?"

"I seen his mama at Safeway last night. Poor Miss Louise. She was ahead of me in the checkout line. When the clerk ran her credit card through and it got declined, I had to loan her twenty dollars to pay for her groceries."

"Well, if her son is doing so good down there in Hollywood, how come she can't pay her credit card bills?" I asked, giving Tina an amused look.

"Hell if I know," Tina said, with a shrug. "Anyway, she waited until I paid for my shit, and we walked out together. Wade was sitting in that old car of hers."

"So what?" I asked, rising from Tina's lumpy bed.

"They gave me a ride home, but along the way, Miss Louise stopped off at Mr. Bailey's house, you know, that old barbershop man she's been fucking around with all month. She wanted to borrow some money from him so she could pay me back. While I'm sitting in the car with Wade, he starts talking a bunch of shit about the old days. Who's still in Berkeley, who's dead, and who's in jail. When I tell him that you are the only friend I got left, he tells me that if he ever settled down with a black girl, it would be you."

"I don't know why he told you that," I responded, with a gasp. "But I know for a fact, he likes white girls."

"That's probably true. Most of the brothers I know do. But Wade likes at least one black girl, and that's you," Tina told me in a serious tone of voice. "Why else would he say some shit like that if he didn't mean it?"

I didn't know what to say next. For one thing, I was not impressed. As far as I was concerned, I was too good for Wade Eddie Fisher. But I was willing to give him another chance if he wanted it. "I wonder why he would say something like that about me." From the look on Tina's face, she was wondering the same thing herself. I had told her about the incident in the restaurant.

"Because you are the only one around here that didn't laugh and make fun of him when he said he was going to Hollywood," Tina explained. "He said he would never forget that."

I gave Tina a thoughtful look. "But he forgot my name that day at Giovanni's," I said, with a pout, anxious to leave now.

"Oh, girl. You know how dudes trip when they are around their friends. Or maybe he had a thing going with that boy or something. Fags are coming out of the closets left and right these days."

I had no reason to believe that Wade was gay, so I didn't even bother to comment on that.

"Well, what Wade said might have meant something to me if he had told me himself." I smirked, heading toward the living room, where Tina's mother, Miss Honey, was passed out drunk in the middle of the floor. I hopped over her on my way to the door. It took me a while to undo the three locks on it.

"He's having a party next Saturday night. You want to go?" Tina asked, squatting down on the floor to put a pillow under her mother's head. This is what Tina did when her mother passed out. It did no good to haul Miss Honey to the sofa or her bed because somewhere along the line, she'd end up back on the floor, anyway.

"I'll think about it," I said, with a sniff. "If I don't have anything better to do, I just might go."

CHAPTER 25

I didn't even mention Wade or his party to my parents. From the indifferent looks I received from each one over the next few days, I had a feeling that they didn't want to hear about that boy and his party, or anybody else's party.

My parents would go for hours at a time without speaking to me while we were in the same room. As a matter of fact, they would also go hours at a time not even speaking to each other. As far back as I could remember, they hadn't even shared the same bedroom. My mother slept in the largest of the two bedrooms in our apartment; I slept in the smaller one. Daddy slept on the sofa bed in our living room. I knew enough about adults at the time to know that some couples had similar sleeping arrangements. It usually meant that one was having an affair but was staying in the marriage for other reasons. Usually "for the sake of the kids." But that was not the case with me. I knew that my parents were not staying together because of me. Why they stayed together at all was as much a mystery to me as everything else with them.

I didn't leave home at eight to go to Wade's party that Saturday night like I had told Tina and a few other kids I would. I had stolen some jeans and a new pink T-shirt the day before from the Gap, some fresh new make-up and some condoms from Walgreen's, and some perfume from Macy's to wear to the party. I'd cancelled my plans to go to Wade's party at the last minute. But I did go out that night at eight: to be with Miss Odessa.

It was the old lady's seventy-fifth birthday, and she had been going on and on about it all week. She'd wept and wailed about how happy she was the Lord had allowed her to live so long. She praised God for keeping her safe in such a violent environment and for sending me to her.

One of Miss Odessa's sons had sent her a cheap bouquet of flowers. Another one had dropped off a cake that was so lopsided, it looked like somebody had dropped it and then stepped on it. None of her daughters had even called or sent anything. Even though she tried to act like it didn't bother her, I had a feeling that it did. If anybody knew what it was like to be ignored by family, it was me. As soon as I found out that Miss Odessa was going to be alone on her birthday, I decided that she was more important to me than Wade's party.

While Miss Odessa was taking her nightly bath, I slipped out and ran down to the corner convenience store. The cashier behind the counter was new, so he refused to sell me some beer like the cashier he'd replaced. And, I didn't feel like hanging around outside, waiting for an older person to come by who might purchase for me the beer that I wanted to give to Miss Odessa as a birthday gift. I ended up buying her a bag of rock candy and a birthday card with a black woman on it.

"Christine, shouldn't you be out with some of your friends at the movies or the roller-skating rink or something? It don't seem right for a popular young girl like you to be sitting here with me and my old self," Miss Odessa commented, clutching the card like it was gold.

"Oh, I can see them anytime," I said, with a wave of my hand, wondering what she would say or think if she knew just how and why I was so "popular." I had a feeling she already knew. With us being right across the hall, it had to be hard for her not to notice how many boys I let in and out of the apartment when Mama and Daddy were at work. But like I said, she was not as nosy as the rest of the old people I knew.

"And, besides, today is a special day. Your special day. You'll only be seventy-five this one time," I chirped.

"I didn't expect to see seventy-five this one time," she said, almost choking on a sob. She sniffed and dabbed at her eyes off and on while we sat in front of her television, eating that lopsided cake. When she said she wished she had some beer, I told her that I'd pay for it if she'd escort me back to the store and buy some.

I left Miss Odessa's apartment when she fell asleep in the middle of *America's Most Wanted,* with her fifth can of beer still in her hand.

As soon as I entered my own living room, I immediately wished that I had someplace else to go. Since Daddy slept on the sofa bed in our living room, I couldn't watch television once he turned in for the night. I couldn't see him under all the blankets on the sofa, but I had heard him snoring before I got inside the door. The television in my room was on the blink, so there was not much else for me to do on a Saturday night. I went to my room and flipped through a few magazines I hadn't read. But I couldn't concentrate on anything other than the fact that there was a party going on at Wade's house and I wasn't there.

Now that I felt better about Miss Odessa, I returned my thoughts to Wade. I was still mad at him for the way he had treated me. That made it so hard for me to understand what he'd said to Tina about me. If what he'd told Tina was true, I owed it to him to let him know I knew. Since I already had on my party clothes, I decided to go out and party, after all. Besides, my pussy had been itching for days, and if anybody knew how to scratch me right, it was Wade Fisher.

CHAPTER 26

There wasn't much light in the living room as I strutted past Daddy, curled up in a fetal position on the edge of the sofa. Before I left, I walked back across the floor and leaned over my daddy and kissed the top of his head. If my parents could show me some affection only when they thought I was asleep, I decided that I could do the same for them. I turned and looked toward the room where Mama slept, and I started to walk in that direction. But I stopped when I heard her cough and mumble under her breath. When her bedroom light came on, I made a U-turn and was out the door within seconds, galloping down the street like a pony.

It was late, and I should have taken a cab the four blocks to Wade's house. But after buying the beer for Miss Odessa, I didn't want to spend any more of my money, in case I needed a few dollars to lend to Miss Louise. I knew that if I wanted to resume my relationship with Wade, one of the things I had to do was keep his mama happy.

I had to dodge a few nasty men on the street. They thought that because I was dressed like I was looking for a good time that I wanted to have it with them.

It must have been that I wasn't meant to attend a party at Wade's house. At least not that particular night. The music was so loud, it did me no good to knock on the front door for five whole minutes. And, right after I stumbled off the porch to go back home, the cops showed up, almost knocking me to the ground as they ran up the steps leading to the front door.

From the sidewalk, I stood and watched as Miss Louise came outside and talked to the cops. I couldn't hear what she was saying, but whatever it was, it must have been what the cops wanted to hear, because they left right away and Miss Louise rushed back inside.

Just as I was about to go knock again, two girls, one black and one white, spilled out onto the porch. I took a few steps back and stood under a streetlight, in the shadow of a tree with a trunk wide enough to hide my whole body. Then about five other girls stumbled out the door, and all hell broke loose. One girl slapped another girl, and all of a sudden every single one of them was screaming and throwing punches. I had never witnessed a smackdown like this one. I let out my breath and trotted back down the street and went home.

I would have slept until noon if somebody had not come banging on the door like they were coming through it. My parents rarely had guests, and none of my friends were crazy enough to be knocking on our door before noon on a Sunday. I snatched open the door, all prepared to cuss out a bunch of Jehovah's Witnesses.

To my surprise, the visitor was about as far away from a Jehovah's Witness as you could get. It was Wade.

"Hey, girl," he said, leaning in the doorway.

He was taller and more handsome than ever. "Uh, hi," I muttered, clutching the front of my thin nightgown. "What in the world are you doing here?" I asked, a grin brewing on my lips.

"My mama sent me over here to pay your mama back the ten dollars she borrowed last week," he explained, reaching into his pocket. His jeans were so tight, it was a struggle for him to get his hand all the way in his pocket. And, I could see the outline of everything he had to offer between his legs. "One of your girls told me you was coming to my party last night. I didn't see you," he said, waving a crumpled ten-dollar bill in my face like it was a carrot.

"Oh, me. Uh, I had to do some stuff around the house," I lied, gently removing the money from his hand. "I hope I can make it to the next party you throw," I offered. His eyes were dangerous, and I realized that when I tried to stare him down. I even got dizzy.

"I hope you can make it the next time, too. But you know something, baby? We don't have to wait on no party to hook up." He paused and looked me up and down. "You sure have grown up since that . . .

uh . . . day you came to my mama's house on your birthday that time. I think about that day all the time. . . ."

"Yeah." I glanced behind him to make sure Miss Odessa wasn't lurking about. "Well, do you want to come in or what? I would like to hear all about Hollywood and all the show business you've been in."

He scratched his head and started talking, with his eyes looking at the floor. "I'm just getting started. I haven't made my mark down there yet."

"You can still come in if you want to," I said, opening the door wider. He looked behind him and over my shoulder. "My mama and daddy are at church. They won't be back home for at least a couple of hours."

"Do I want to come in and be up in here with you by myself?" he teased.

"That's up to you."

Wade brushed past me and strolled in like he owned the place. "You sure your folks won't be home for a couple of hours?" he asked, smoothing his hair back with one hand.

I nodded. "And, I won't forget to give my mama the money Miss Louise sent back," I insisted, folding my hand with the money in it into a fist. Wade looked at my face, then over my shoulder again.

"Uh, I ain't got nothing else to do today," he said, shuffling his feet.

"So?" I shrugged and turned my head to the side.

"Well, you already seen my bedroom. Now can I see yours?" he asked.

CHAPTER 27

It was the first time I ever spent the whole night in bed with a dude. I knew that it was going to happen sooner or later, but I never expected it to happen in my own house, with my parents just a few feet away. And, I never thought that it would be with Wade.

Wade and I had been holed up in my room ever since he had come to our apartment that morning. Other than to run to the bathroom or to the kitchen to get some snacks, we stayed in my bedroom.

One of the few things that I was proud of was my room. It was clean, and everything was where it was supposed to be. Even though the bed was older than I was, and the curtains were so stiff, they could stand up by themselves, I was proud of what I had. I was happy to entertain Wade in my room. And, it was not just about sex, even though it was mind-boggling. I enjoyed talking to Wade.

"I just hope you don't forget me when you hit it really big down there in Hollywood," I told him, gently jabbing him in the side with my elbow.

"I ain't forgot about you yet, girl. Like I told Tina, you about the only sister I'd ever think about settling down with," he admitted.

A muffled sound distracted me. I lifted my head and looked toward the door. "Shhhhh," I said, my finger pressed against my lips. "My folks just came home from church!"

"Oh, shit!" Wade tumbled out of my bed and started hopping

around the room like a man with one leg. "I thought you said they wouldn't be home for hours!" he hissed, scrambling around for his clothes.

"That's right. I did say that. But, baby, we've been in here for *hours*," I reminded, trying not to laugh. "But you don't have to worry about my folks coming in here. They don't care what I do," I told him, looking away because I didn't want him to see the sadness in my eyes.

"Don't take this the wrong way, but your mama and your daddy is kind of strange. I noticed that a long time ago," Wade said, returning to the bed.

"Well, I noticed it a long time ago myself," I replied. He propped himself up with two pillows and looked at me with curiosity. "What's up? Don't y'all get along?"

"Oh, we get along all right. I go my way; they go theirs." I sighed. "In some ways, I am used to my parents' indifference. In some ways, I'm not. I feel like a puppy that nobody wants."

"If it'll make you feel any better, I'm the kid that always got stuck with the puppies that nobody else wanted," Wade said, with a dry laugh.

I shrugged. "Anyway, every now and then, and I do mean every now and then, one of my parents looks at me like they care. But it's always during one of their rare weak moments. Like a few months ago, when Daddy was laid up with some kind of intestinal infection so severe, it almost killed him. I hugged him, and for the first and only time, he hugged me back. And, now that I look back on that moment, I think he only did it because he thought he was dying. The only other times they show me some love is when . . . is when they think I'm asleep. One of them will creep into my room in the dark, pull the covers up to my neck, and either rub my cheek or kiss me on it."

Wade gave me a thoughtful look and caressed his chin. "Well, that's better than them showing you no love at all. Look at it this way, they kept you. Some folks throw their babies in the trash as soon as they are born or kill them before they are born. You got a place to sleep, food, clothes. A lot of kids would love to trade places with you," Wade said, making a sweeping gesture with his hand as he looked around my neatly arranged room.

"I wish my mama was more like yours," I said, getting misty-eyed.

"No, you don't," Wade said in a low voice. He looked away when I glanced at him, talking, with his eyes on the floor. "My mama thinks

I'm some kind of prince that can't do no wrong. You don't know what I have to do for her to keep on thinking that way." Then the strangest look appeared on his face. It was a look that I rarely saw on a man. For about five seconds, he looked unbearably sad. "Do you mind if I take a nap now?"

Wade didn't wait for me to reply. He curled up and turned his back to me. And, he stayed that way for the rest of the night.

I got slightly depressed when Wade tiptoed out of the apartment the next morning, a few minutes before my folks got up to get ready for work. I didn't even bother to go to school that morning, but later in the day, I wished I had. At least I would have been distracted. At home by myself, all I could think about was Wade and how I couldn't wait to see him again.

After two days had gone by and he had not called or come back to the apartment, I took it upon myself to go to his house. I armed myself with a crisp ten-dollar bill in case I encountered Miss Louise. I got there just in time to see Wade crawling into a cab with his two battered suitcases and his backpack. His mama was hanging on to his arm like he was going to the moon. He was halfway into the cab when she pulled him back out.

I stumbled over a dog stretched out on the sidewalk as I ran up to Wade and started tugging on the sleeve of his jacket. "Wade, are you leaving?" I asked, feeling stupid because it was so obvious that that was exactly what he was doing.

Just thinking about how he had made love to me in my bed made me tingle all over. He had learned a lot over the years about how to please a woman, so it had been a totally different experience from our first encounter. And, after all the boys I had been involved with since Wade had helped himself to my virginity, my body had adjusted to all that poking and pumping, so sex wasn't so painful anymore. I wanted to throw myself to the ground and take Wade down with me and fuck his brains out. And if Miss Louise and that cabdriver hadn't been in the way, that's probably just what I would have done.

"Oh, Christine," he muttered. I didn't know how to interpret the look on his face. He was either annoyed or surprised. "I been meaning to call you," he said, his arm around his weeping mama. "My agent called me last night. I need to get back down to L.A. to read for two very important parts," he said, glowing like a firefly.

"They are just commercials, but that's better than nothing," Wade's mama said through her tears. From the look on Wade's face, I knew that this was a piece of information that he was not that excited about sharing.

"Can I call you sometime?" I said as fast as I could, his mama and I playing tug-of-war with his body. She had a hand clamped around one of his arms, I had my hand clamped around the other, and we were both pulling him in the opposite direction.

"Yeah, yeah, sure you can. That's cool," Wade said, looking embarrassed and talking fast. He gently pulled away from me and his mama. "Uh, I am going to miss you, and I really wish that you could come with me." He gave me a brief hug and a cold, quick peck on the cheek. Then he slid into the backseat of the cab and slammed the door shut. He didn't even look back, but I stood there until the cab was out of sight.

I didn't realize Miss Louise was still standing there, too, until I heard her voice.

"How come you ain't in school today?" she asked in a gruff voice. She blew her nose into a piece of tissue and looked at me with red, swollen eyes.

"I wasn't feeling too good," I lied, adding a fake cough. But now that I knew Wade was leaving, I did feel sick. A knot had formed in my stomach, and I was more confused than ever. Not just about Wade and the way he seemed to slide in and out of my life. I was also confused about what I wanted to do with my life from this point on. "Miss Louise, can you give me Wade's address so I can write him a letter sometime?"

"Just a fan letter, I hope," Miss Louise said, with a smirk.

"Huh? Oh yeah. I just want to write him a fan letter."

"Good. The boy just getting started, and he don't need a lot of distractions in his life right now."

"I know. I won't distract him," I insisted, nodding my head for emphasis. "I'd appreciate it if you'd give me his, uh, phone number, too."

"I guess I could," Miss Louise said, looking puzzled. "But you are the only girl I'm giving it to. My baby already got too many girls on his back, riding him like he some kind of mule."

I followed Miss Louise into her house, where she scribbled the information I'd requested on the back of a *TV Guide*. Then I left her house, running.

That night, as soon as I heard Daddy snoring, I eased out of my room and tiptoed out the front door. I hung out at Tina's house until the next Greyhound bus was ready to leave for L.A. I climbed aboard that bus, with Wade's address on the back of a matchbook in my backpack.

CHAPTER 28

I hated buses. Other than the local buses, which were bad enough, I had never been on any other kind. The Greyhound bus was a nightmare on wheels. For almost ten hours, I had to look at and smell some of the most desperate-looking people I'd ever seen before in my life. The big, bull-faced man in the seat next to me smelled like an unwashed ass, but that didn't bother me as much as his hand landing right on my thigh every time he dozed off. The woman in the seat in front of me had a stout baby in her arms that squealed like a pig for most of the ten hours. A large, shabbily dressed group of people speaking a language I didn't recognize occupied almost half of the side of the bus opposite me. One of the males had a large, bloody knot on the side of his face, and one of the kids had only one eye. Three of the females were pregnant; one looked to be about twelve. Behind this miserable family sat a snaggletoothed redneck with a limp ponytail. Every few minutes he would mumble under his breath about how America was being taken over by "all them nasty gypsies."

I was afraid to go in the bathroom. But when I had to go, I had to go. The stench was unholy, and there was no toilet paper or toilet seat protectors. Not only did I have to hover over the seat to keep from sitting in somebody else's waste, once I finished doing what I had to do, I had to shake my bottom parts dry like a dog.

I couldn't believe that I was still sane by the time the bus finally pulled into Los Angeles. My feelings were a combination of relief, excitement, and impatience.

The inside of the bus station looked more like the lobby of a flophouse. Wild-eyed, foul-smelling people wandered around, with dazed expressions on their faces. I could not believe that I was in the same city that the media called "one of the most glamorous locations in the world."

Nobody paid much attention to me, and after I caught my reflection in a window near the ticket counter, I understood why. I looked just as dazed and confused as some of the other people.

I scurried around like a drunken squirrel for twenty minutes, until I found a pay phone that worked. Before I could dial Wade's telephone number, a homeless man with old newspapers wrapped around his feet popped up out of nowhere. He started mumbling and waving an empty tin can in my face. I was not too far from being homeless myself, so I was in no position to part with any of my money. Between what I had and what I had borrowed from Tina, I didn't have much. I slapped the man's hand, and for a minute, I thought he was going to slap me back. After he gave me a dirty look and mumbled obscenities under his breath, he shuffled on to the next person. I held my breath, dialed Wade's phone number, and prayed that the boy was at home.

"Yo," he muttered, answering on the fourth ring.

"Hello? Wade, is that you?" I asked, breathing a sigh of relief. I smiled for the first time since I'd boarded the bus. My face was so dry, it felt like it was going to crack. I rubbed my cheek and sucked in some stale air. But the air around me was so stale, it made me cough. "Thank the Lord you're home," I wailed, patting my matted hair. I had not slept much on the bus, and my eyes were so heavy, I could barely keep them open. I blinked and sucked in some more air, coughing again. "It's so good to hear your voice, Wade."

"Christine? Girl, what's wrong with you? It's after midnight. What's going on? Who gave you this number?" He didn't sound that happy to be hearing from me, and for the life of me, I could not understand why.

"I just got here," I said, wondering why he was so concerned about me calling him after midnight when I could hear what sounded like a party going on in the background on his end. I hated using pay phones. Especially in areas like where the L.A. Greyhound bus station was located. Another homeless man staggered up to me, with his empty hand held out, babbling some shit I couldn't understand. As soon as I shooed that sucker away, another one replaced him and was standing a few feet away, sizing me up.

There was a pause before Wade responded. "You . . . you just got *where?* What the fuck is this all about?"

"I'm in L.A. I'm at the bus terminal, and let me tell you, this is not a place where I want to be too long. Three bums have already tried to get money from me," I complained.

"What the hell are you doing at the bus station in L.A.?" Wade asked. His question surprised and depressed me at the same time.

I didn't know how to respond at first. I sniffed and cleared my throat so that I could speak clearly. I wanted to make sure he heard everything I had to say. "Wade, didn't you tell me you wished I could be down here with you?" I didn't even give him the chance to answer. "Well, here I am."

"Fuck!" His response stunned me. And, he'd said it in such a loud, angry voice, it hurt my ear. It was not what I wanted to hear. But I would hear a lot of things from Wade during the next few days that I didn't want to hear.

"Does that mean you're not glad I came down here to be with you?" I whined. "Are you not going to come pick me up?" I held my breath and waited for him to speak. He took so long, I thought he'd left the phone. "Wade, are you still there?"

"Shit! You just stay right where you are at, girl. I'll be there as soon as I can get there! Shit!" he yelled.

I was twice as dazed and confused now. Wade had just put me in a position where I didn't know where I stood with him, again. I got dizzy, and it felt like the floor was moving beneath my feet. I had already done a lot of stupid things in my life. But running away to L.A. to be with a man took the cake.

Two hours after I'd called Wade, he showed up. He saw me before I saw him. When he came up behind me and touched my shoulder, I whirled around with my fist raised, expecting to see another aggressive homeless person.

"Thank God it's only you," I blurted, wrapping my arms around his waist. He turned away when I attempted to kiss him. "Where did you park?" I asked. Wade rolled his eyes and looked at me like I was speaking Greek. He grabbed my backpack and started to lead me toward the exit. "You don't have a car to get around with?"

"A car? Girl, I ain't even got a skateboard to get around with," he told me in an impatient and tired voice. I looked down and saw that he had on a pair of thin house shoes with holes on every side. "Come on. The next bus is coming in five minutes. There ain't no more express buses to my place, so it's going to take us a while to get there," he said, almost spitting out the words. He talked without looking at me, and I had to run to keep up with him as we rushed to a nearby bus stop.

Two city buses and an hour and a half later, we arrived at Wade's place. I was horrified when I saw the building he lived in. It was a three-story gray stucco decorated with obscene graffiti and gang signs. Some of the windows were covered with old newspapers; some were not covered at all. At least not with curtains. One window, propped open with a beer bottle, had a dingy sheet for a curtain. An old car with no wheels was parked in front of the building. Next to two overflowing trash cans on the sidewalk was a pee-stained mattress. There was a hole where a lock should have been in the door at the entrance to the building.

It looked like some of the same derelicts from the bus station area had followed me. A man squatted on the floor right inside the door, holding out his hand as we passed him, mumbling through brown teeth.

Wade lived in this dump with two other aspiring actors, in a studio apartment that was slightly larger than a closet. The fact that this was the best that the three of them could do together said a lot. There were three sleeping bags on the floor, with rolled-up blankets for pillows. The only seats were a red beanbag and an empty crate with a flat pillow strapped on top. Other than a tiny gas stove next to a sink with one faucet, a mini-refrigerator, and a shit box of a radio, there was not much else in the apartment.

"I thought you were doing so well," I whispered to Wade.

"Huh? Oh . . . um . . . I am doing well . . . when I work," Wade replied. "But L.A. is like San Francisco, real expensive." He acted like he didn't even want to look at me. His roommates, two white boys named Bob and Nick, looked even younger than me. "You can sleep over there by the stove with me," he said, pointing to one of the sleeping bags. "You hungry? We got some buffalo wings left over from last night."

"I had some Doritos on the bus," I said, looking around the bleak room. The hairs on the back of my neck stood up when I saw an albino roach crawl up the wall a few feet in front of me. Wade saw it, too. He lunged across the floor and smashed it with his fist. Then he swiped his hand on the leg of his pants. I didn't get too upset, because I had seen worse things than albino roaches. Back in Berkeley, Tina had flying roaches in the house that she shared with her mama.

The boy named Bob crawled into his sleeping bag, with a copy of *Rolling Stone.* When Wade reluctantly introduced me as "a friend from his old 'hood," Bob glanced up and gave me a weak wave. The other boy, Nick, was already in his sleeping bag in the middle of the floor, with a bottle of beer in one hand and a tape player in the other, which explained the music I'd heard in the background when I'd called Wade from the bus station. All Nick did was look at me and blink. He didn't even speak. But from the look on his face, and on the other boy's, too, they were just as annoyed to see me as Wade was.

The room had an overwhelming stench, which made me think that the bathroom was not too far away. But I didn't see it. As a matter of fact, other than the door leading out of the apartment, I didn't see any other doors. And, the biggest window in the room was about the size of a porthole. "Where is the bathroom?" I asked, rubbing my nose.

"It's next door, but you need a key to get in it. We keep the key on top of the refrigerator. When you use the john, don't forget to flush, and make sure you lock the door back up. We have problems with the homeless people coming up in here to do their business and sleeping on the bathroom floor," Wade told me. He opened the refrigerator and removed a bottle of beer, which he popped open with a bent fork.

I set my backpack down and took the bathroom door key. The closer I got to the bathroom, the more potent the stench got. Once I got inside, I could see why. There was just a toilet. No sink, no shower, no bathtub. It looked like the bathroom had not been cleaned in days. The last person had not even flushed the toilet. To make matters worse, I discovered that my period had started. I had "packed" in such a hurry, I'd forgotten to bring something to sleep in. Wade gave me one of his big T-shirts to sleep in as soon as I returned from the bathroom.

As soon as he turned out the light and pulled me into his sleeping bag with him, his hands started roaming all over my body, tugging on my panties and patting my crotch. His hand froze when he felt my tampon string hanging out of my pussy. I knew that most boys didn't like to have sex with a girl when she was on her period. Wade was no different.

"Shit! You better keep yourself plugged up real good so you won't drip no blood on my shit, like you did that time on my mama's sheets, or on Nick's floor. He just mopped this morning," Wade said, with a groan. I was glad it was dark, so I couldn't see his face. "Uh, look you can stay here tonight. But in the morning you gots to find yourself someplace else to stay."

"Uh-huh," I mumbled. "I was planning on doing just that." Like I said, traveling to L.A. the way I did was the worst thing I'd ever done. I had no money for an apartment, and I didn't even have enough money to go back home.

CHAPTER 29

By the time I woke up the next morning, so groggy I thought I was dreaming, Wade's roommates were gone. Wade told me that Bob worked as a security guard at some big office building downtown. And, with an embarrassed look on his face, he told me that Nick worked the streets, sucking the dicks of older men on their way to their fancy offices in the morning. "A lot of kids do shit like that to survive down here," he explained. "It ain't no big deal. Bob and Nick got part-time jobs, too."

"And what do you do for money?" I asked. I was surprised that he'd told me about Nick being a male prostitute. It would have been just as easy for him to lie about it. I would have. I couldn't help but wonder if Wade was going to be honest with me about what he did for money. He took his time responding, walking around the gloomy room, dragging a mop that looked like a cheap wig across the floor.

"Who me? Uh, I do different things from time to time. Right now I wash dishes at this Mexican restaurant around the corner," he said, giving me a quick glance. He must have been embarrassed or lying, because now he was mopping a dry spot.

"Dishwasher?" I howled. I couldn't have been more surprised and stunned if he had told me he had a job selling balloons on the beach. "Dude, your mama said you go to parties with big Hollywood stars! You got a job washing dishes? Do the other stars know that?"

Wade stopped mopping and gave me a hostile look. "Look, it ain't easy to make it big down here," he said. He got even more defensive. He dropped the mop to the floor and folded his arms, lifting his chin and looking at me down his nose. "What's wrong with washing dishes? It's a job, ain't it? Some folks can't even get a job washing dishes."

"So your mama was lying about you going to parties with the stars?"

"You know how parents like to exaggerate about their kids. But my mama goes by what I tell her, so she didn't lie," he said, shaking his head. "I didn't lie when I told her I went to the same parties a lot of the stars go to. I do. But . . . as a waiter."

My heart felt like it wanted to drop to the floor. I felt so sorry for Wade. But I shrugged it off like a pro. With a big, fake smile, I said, "There is nothing wrong with being a waiter . . . I guess. I think I read somewhere that Dustin Hoffman was a waiter when he was just start- ing out. I'm sure a lot of the other big stars were, too. Whoopi Gold- berg used to work in a funeral parlor, doing dead folks' make-up."

"I heard that same thing myself," Wade told me in a dry voice.

"I won't tell anybody. Not even your mama," I promised.

"Look, baby. I don't really care if folks back home find out or not. A lot of big stars worked worse jobs than waiting tables before they made it. A baby gots to crawl before he can walk. I'm just paying my dues. And, while we're on the subject, I usher at a movie theater over in Westwood when I can. I do whatever I have to do to eat and have a place to stay," Wade confessed. He was walking around the apartment in just his shorts. He stopped and slapped his hands on his hips. "At least I don't turn no tricks on the street like Nick, if that's what you thinking. Shit." He scratched his chin and gave me a serious look.

"I know you wouldn't stoop that low," I said, giving him a serious look.

He seemed pleased to hear me say that. So pleased that he offered me a big smile. "Um, uh-uh, I wouldn't. Uh, I'll get off early so I can help you find a place."

An awkward moment of silence passed before I spoke again. "Did you mean what you said about wishing I was down here with you?"

"Look, Christine. I like you a whole lot, and I think you know that by now. But your timing is way off. I did mean I wished you was down here with me when I said it. But I didn't expect you to jump on a bus and come down here without me asking you to, or without me even knowing! That's some crazy-ass shit, girl! What's wrong with you? You can see I ain't in no shape to be the host with the most," Wade said, making a sweeping gesture with his hand. "If my mama wasn't sending me money every month, I'd be eating in a soup kitchen."

He trotted across the floor and flung open the refrigerator so hard, it shook and the dim light inside blinked off and on. There was nothing inside but a few more bottles of beer and a block of green cheese. "Now if you plan on staying in L.A., that's fine with me," he added. "We can have some good fun together when I have the time. But you can't stay up in here with me and Nick and Bob. This place ain't big enough, no way."

"I don't take up much room," I whined, holding my hands out, palms up. "I'll even sleep in that nasty bathroom, on the floor, if I have to. And, you won't even have to worry about feeding me. I know how to go into any store I want, go down every aisle and nibble on something, and then sneak out the door without paying. Me and my friends have been doing that all over Berkeley since I can remember."

"There's more to it than that. See, this is Nick's place. His name is the only one on the lease. Me and Bob have to sneak in and out of this motherfucker like burglars so the landlord won't see us. Now, like I said, you can't stay here."

"Where will I go?" I asked in a meek voice, with my eyes on the floor.

"If you're as smart as I think you are, you'll go on back home," Wade told me.

That was not what I wanted to hear. But I knew that he was right.

CHAPTER 30

Wade washed up in the kitchen sink, with a blue washcloth that was so stiff, it looked like it could stand up by itself. As soon as he got dressed and left the apartment, after kissing me on the cheek like I was an elderly relative, I had myself a good cry. I had never felt so unwanted in my life. I cried so much, my eyes puffed up. Snot oozed out of my nose and dribbled down my face. Spit and other slime that I didn't even know my mouth could produce glazed my lips and chin like gravy.

I didn't want to use the same washcloth to wash my face that Wade had used to wash his ass. But since I couldn't find anything else to clean myself with, I ripped a page out of Nick's *Rolling Stone* magazine, and I used that. I closed my eyes and rubbed them until I couldn't feel them anymore.

I was hungry, but with roaches marching up and down the walls like soldiers, and swarms of gnats descending on the floor like locusts, it didn't take long for me to lose my appetite.

"Girl, what have you got yourself into this time?" I asked myself out loud, wiping my neck with the wet paper that I'd used to clean my face.

I didn't think that things could get any worse. I couldn't talk to my parents, and other than Tina and old Miss Odessa, I didn't have any real friends that I could fall back on. Since I'd already hit Tina up for a few dollars, I didn't have the nerve to call her. I had no choice but to call Miss Odessa. I snatched the cordless telephone up off the floor and dialed her number so fast, my fingers cramped.

It was a weekday, and I expected her to be home like she usually was on a weekday. I was wrong. I called every hour on the hour, and she didn't answer. And, she was one of the few people I knew who didn't like answering machines, so I couldn't even leave a message.

I was leaning out the window, trying to get some fresh air, with the telephone still in my hand when Wade came home around four that afternoon. I had heard thunder earlier, but it hadn't rained yet. The sky outside looked like a gray ceiling. That made everything seem even more gloomy. "You find a place yet?" Wade asked in a gruff voice, not offering any other greeting. He had that look on his face that people got when they saw somebody they didn't want to see. And, I could tell that he was agitated. He kept letting out loud breaths and looking at me out of the corner of his eye.

"Um, yes and no," I said. I left the window and set the phone back on the floor where I'd found it, squeezed between a box of Fruit Loops and an empty peanut butter jar.

"Yes, you found a place? No, you didn't find a place?" Wade's hair was flat on both sides of his head and sticking up on top like a fan. His lips were dry and cracked. The bottom one had a scab that had not been there that morning. I couldn't imagine what he'd been doing for his hair and lips to end up looking like that. He looked like he had been mauled. He looked like anything but a movie actor.

"Huh?" As fast as I was living and as much as I thought I knew, I was still a child, and I sounded like one. One stupid thing after another slid out of my mouth like bubbles. "Who me?"

"Yes, *you*! What the hell is yes and no supposed to mean?" Wade strutted across the floor and stood in front of me. I was already backed up against the wall. And, the way he was looking at me, I wished that I could just disappear into the wall and get it over it with. He had made it clear that he wanted me out of his sight. And, because of the way he had been treating me since I'd arrived, I decided I never wanted to see his punk ass again after I got my crazy self out of this mess.

"Um, two landlords told me to call them back," I lied.

"Uh-huh." Wade folded his arms. He stood so close to me, our faces almost touched. I had never noticed how big his Adam's apple was until now. It looked like a rock stuck in the middle of his long neck.

"Well, there ain't no newspapers up in here, and I know you didn't leave out that door today. How did you find these two landlords?"

I dropped my head. "I'm going home. I don't have enough money for any apartment, and even if I did, who is going to rent to a girl my age with no job?" I muttered. I looked back up at Wade's face, and he looked even more annoyed. "I will leave as soon as I get the money from my folks," I snapped.

I was glad when Wade left to go to his evening job, or wherever he went, a few hours later. As miserable as the apartment was, I felt better in it when I was alone. I called Miss Odessa three more times in less than an hour, and she still didn't answer her telephone. I knew then that I had to come up with another plan, and there was no other option for me except my parents.

One of my fears was that I would not be able to get help from some other source before Wade ran out of patience with me. But my biggest fear was not Wade kicking me out on the street. I was more concerned about whether or not I could depend on my parents to help me get back home.

CHAPTER 31

Around eleven that night, Wade and his two roommates came home together, paying more attention to the roaches than they did me. As soon as they got inside the apartment, Nick grabbed a magazine and started smashing roaches. Bob strolled over to the stove and removed a cigar box from the oven. He rolled some joints, and I was surprised when he handed one to me. But other than that, the way Bob, Wade, and Nick behaved, you would have thought that I was invisible.

My period was heavier than usual this month, and I had some cramps that made my stomach feel like it was upside down. I knew that the stress that I was under had a lot to do with the way my body was breaking down. I flopped down on the beanbag and enjoyed my high while my thoughts swam around in my head.

I spent as much time as I could in that tacky, smelly bathroom next door to the apartment. By now I was bleeding like a stuck pig, and my cramps were even worse. I'd never been in labor before, but the way my mama had often described it to me, I was pretty sure that my cramps were on that level. That was enough to make me feel like shit. But Wade's reaction to my presence made me feel even worse. Instead of sharing the sleeping bag with me again, he made a pallet on the floor with some cardboard and a blanket and slept there.

The next morning all three of the boys were gone when I woke up.

Wade had left the key to the apartment, a five-dollar bill, and a note telling me to use the money to get something to eat. I had not eaten since the day before. It was still early, and I knew that if I moved fast enough, I could reach my parents before they left for work. I stumbled across the floor to the telephone on the wall. My hands shook as I dialed the number. For the first time in my life, I was glad to hear my daddy's voice.

"Mmm . . . hallo!" he said in his usual gruff voice, grunting under his breath. This was the first time I'd heard my own father speak from the other end of a telephone line. He didn't have any kind of accent or anything, but the way he greeted me made it sound like he did. "Mmm . . . hallo!" he said again, sounding impatient and annoyed.

"Daddy?" I managed, my hand covering my heart because it was thumping so hard. "Daddy, it's me."

"*Me who?*" my father asked.

I almost dropped the telephone. I was his only child—as far as I knew. I was the only person I knew who addressed him as "Daddy." The fact that he had to ask who I was made me wish that I had tried to call Miss Odessa again instead.

"It's Christine, Daddy," I said firmly. "Your daughter."

"Oh. Where are you calling from? Wherever you at? Shouldn't you be getting ready for school?"

"Daddy, I'm in L.A.," I said in a flat voice.

"L.A.? Los Angeles?"

"Yeah," I mumbled, my heart beating like a bongo drum.

"Well, what . . . what you doing down there, girl? And when did you go down there?"

"I came down here on Sunday."

"Is that right? No wonder them dirty dishes is still in the sink."

"You didn't even know I was gone?" I wailed, my voice cracking.

"You know I don't get in your business," he admitted.

"No. No, Daddy, you don't," I said, and I wanted to say, *"But I am your business."*

"Aye yi yi! All this time I thought you was shet up in that room of yours. Either there or across the hall with that busybody Odessa. So what are you going to do now? You done finally quit school or what? And who you down there with? You ain't going to stop till you ruin yourself."

"I want to come home, Daddy. I'm down here with a friend, but he said I can't stay with him. He's got two roommates, and their place is really too small. I need for you to wire me the money for a bus ticket to come back to Berkeley. I need thirty-five more dollars."

"Hold on. Let me get your mama in on this. You know she handles everything in this house when it comes to money."

There was dead silence for the next five minutes. I kept looking at my watch, wondering how much the long-distance call was going to cost and how mad Wade was going to be when he got the bill.

"Christine," my mother finally said in a loud voice. Then, to my surprise, her voice sounded extremely soft and gentle. She didn't even sound like the woman I'd known all my life. "Are you all right?" There was so much concern in her voice, it almost broke my heart.

The last thing I ever wanted to do was hurt my parents. But I didn't know what they wanted me to do and what they didn't want me to do. As far as I was concerned, the only person I needed to try and please was myself. "I'm all right, Mama," I said, almost choking on my words.

"I hope so. Thank the Lord, you sound as strong as a *burro*." My mother and father rarely spoke Spanish in my presence. For all I knew, they had forgotten most of it. Whenever one of them used a Spanish word, it threw me for a loop. Yes, I sounded strong, but I didn't like being compared to a donkey. "What the devil are you up to now? You left that kitchen looking like a train wreck. Dishes all over the place."

"I'll do the dishes as soon as I get home, Mama." I sighed. "Mama, I'm in L.A., and I want to come home. But I don't have enough money to buy a ticket. Can you and Daddy wire me some money?" Mama was taking too long to answer, and I didn't know what her silence meant, but it frightened me. I said the next thing that came to my mind. "I will get a job and pay you back."

"How much does this ticket cost?" she asked, with a weak sigh.

"I just need thirty-five more dollars," I said sharply.

"Thirty-five dollars is a lot of money for piss-poor folks like us. And, how do I know that you ain't planning on spending this money on something other than a bus ticket? I never know what you are up to."

"I'll even pay you back with interest," I offered. I stopped talking because I was close to tears. My parents had not seen or heard me cry since I was a baby. I was too proud to let my guard down around them.

"I'll go to the Western Union place as soon as they open up."

"Thank you, Mama. And, Mama . . . I do love you, and tell Daddy I love him, too."

"Of course, you do," she said in a distant voice. "And you should," she added.

I didn't wait for Wade or his roommates to come home. Right after I took a birdbath in the kitchen sink, using another page from the *Rolling Stone* for a bath cloth, I fished some clean underwear out of my backpack and slid into it. Then I gathered up all of my shit and left that miserable place. I was thankful that the nearest Western Union station was only six blocks away. The additional money that I needed to help pay for my bus ticket was there when I got there. And, that was all that Mama had sent, nothing extra for food or anything else.

The few dollars that I had left home with and the crumpled five-dollar bill that Wade had left for me that morning was all the money I had to my name. Since I had to use part of it to cover the cost of my ticket home, there was not enough left over for me to take a cab home from the bus station, which was in Oakland a few miles away, from our apartment. Even though I'd fucked strangers, I was too afraid to hitchhike. Three girls that I used to run with had all been killed after accepting rides from strangers. If I had not found enough loose change in my pockets and in the belly of my backpack to take the local bus from Oakland to Berkeley, I would have walked the four miles home.

I got back to Berkeley around one a.m. that morning. The apartment was dark, but when I let myself in the front door and clicked on the light, Daddy lifted his head off his pillow on the sofa bed, looking at me with his eyes still half closed. He offered a rare smile. And then he lay back down.

About an hour later, after I'd gone to bed, I heard my bedroom door open. The lights were out, and I didn't budge, so I didn't know which one of my parents had entered my room, tiptoeing across the floor, bumping into things like a clumsy thief. But whoever it was, they lifted the covers off my face and kissed me on the cheek.

CHAPTER 32

The next day was just like every other day in our house. My parents got up and got themselves ready for work, not once mentioning my unauthorized trip to L.A. However, my mother did get close to me and peer into my eyes in the kitchen. "You look all right to me," she said, with relief, slapping a tortilla onto a cracked plate and setting it in front of me.

When I got to school that morning, I told everybody I'd had the flu. I kept to myself, and every quiet moment I got, like in study period and during lunch, I did some serious thinking. I was tired of the life that I'd been living. There was no doubt about that. I knew that if I wanted things to change for me, it was up to me to make that happen.

Right after school, I rushed home and put on the most conservative outfit I could find: a mammy-made plaid skirt with a matching blouse, which one of my dowdy friends had left in my room, and a pair of low-heeled shoes. That evening I visited every shop and restaurant that I could get to on foot in Berkeley, looking for work.

It was getting dark, and a lot of the businesses that I wanted to approach had already closed. But I didn't let that stop me. I'd already been turned down or told to come back in a couple of years by more than ten managers when I wandered into a video store on Alcatraz, between a sandwich shop and an ice cream parlor. Two young Asian women were behind the counter. They stopped talking and gave me a puzzled look.

"Is the manager in?" I asked, looking from one to the other. Before they could answer, a tall, slender man entered the main area from a back room, walking backwards. When he turned around, I gasped. It was that nerd-ass Jesse Ray Thurman. I hadn't seen him in over a year. But I'd heard that he'd graduated and attended some type of business classes at UC Berkeley. In addition to that, he had made money running a refreshment stand on a busy street downtown, where he'd sold hot dogs, cold drinks, and other snacks to construction workers and other people who worked in the area.

From the look on Jesse Ray's face, he was surprised to see me. But I was even more surprised to see him. I never expected to see him working in a video store. He seemed too independent for a job like that.

"Christine," he said, giving me the biggest smile I'd seen on a man's face in months. He seemed genuinely pleased to see me, and that made me feel better than I'd felt in a long time. "Girl, I thought you'd left town or something. I haven't seen you since that day at your apartment building, when you were a *little* girl." His eyes roamed up and down my body, and he seemed pleased that I was no longer "little." And he was right. I had filled out a lot since the last time he saw me. I didn't need much make-up to look good, and my shoulder-length black hair was so manageable, it seemed like it had a life of its own. I tossed my head to the side and raked my fingers through thick black curls and waves, which a lot of jealous people swore was a weave.

"Jesse Ray, do you work here, too? I'm looking for a job, and I was just asking for the manager," I chirped.

Jesse Ray dismissed the two young Asians before responding. "What kind of work are you looking for?" he asked.

"Anything," I said, with a pleading look. "But I can only work nights and weekends."

"Oh, that's right. You still go to Berkeley High?" he asked. He sniffed and caressed his chin.

I nodded. "I hope to graduate next year." I let out my breath and looked around, hoping to see the manager. "Is the manager here? I'd like to apply for a job."

"I assume you're eighteen now, hmmm?" he said, with his chin tilted up and his eyebrows raised.

"Me? Uh-uh, not yet."

"*I assume you are eighteen*," he said again, glancing around. He got closer and lowered his voice.

"I assume I can be eighteen," I said, talking in an even lower voice than he was. "If that's the only way I can work here."

"When can you start?" Jesse Ray asked, his head tilted to the side. The fact that he glanced at my breasts a few too many times made me uncomfortable, but it was nothing I couldn't deal with. Shit. I had more fingerprints on my titties than a hooker.

"What?"

"I manage this store, and I can sure use another clerk in the evenings and on weekends."

"You . . . *you* are the manager? You're giving me a job?" I asked, with an incredulous look on my face. I was so overwhelmed, I could barely speak. It was one of the few times that a man had offered me something other than dope or sex. I didn't count the five dollars that Wade had donated for me to get something to eat before I left L.A. But I did count that time at the flea market when Jesse Ray gave me a free cup of lemonade.

"You know, I always wondered if I'd ever see you again. Every weekend for the next six months, I set up a stand in that same spot where I met you at the flea market, hoping I'd see you again," Jesse Ray confessed. "To be totally honest, I was glad you didn't come back. I don't like trouble, and so I knew better than to mess with a young girl like you. Even though I wasn't that much older than you."

I had never felt so shy before in my life. And so sad. I was not used to men treating me with such respect. I didn't know what to say next, so I just stood there, with a weak smile on my face.

"So. When can I start?" I finally managed.

"Come back around next month and fill out an application."

"Oh, I can't wait that long. I need a job real bad now. I owe my, uh, somebody some money." I had promised Mama and Daddy that I would pay them back the thirty-five dollars they had wired to me in L.A. as soon as possible. "If it's all right with you, I'd like to start right away. Tomorrow. Or even today. Right now would be all right with me," I said, looking around. It was a busy place. More than a dozen people had entered and started browsing since I'd walked in.

Jesse Ray pursed his lips and nodded his head. His hair was so thick and curly, it looked like the backside of a black sheep. He had nice full lips and a neatly trimmed goatee. He was more handsome than Wade, but that was something that I didn't realize until now. "Do you have any references?"

"References?" I asked, my voice drifting toward the floor, dragging my heart along with it.

"Somebody who could vouch for you, uh, like a former employer."

"I've never worked before," I said, my hopes floating out the door. I dropped my head and started to leave. "Thanks, anyway."

Jesse Ray clamped his hand down on my shoulder and spun me back around. "Come into my office, and let's talk," he said, leading me toward the back. My first thought was that I was going to have to suck his dick for him to hire me. But I was in for the surprise of my life. Even though I was not the required age of eighteen, Jesse Ray offered to hire me and pay me minimum wage under the table. It was a secret that he made me promise not to share with any of my friends. And, I knew that I didn't have to worry about my parents getting in my way. For one thing, I had a feeling that my parents worked for Mr. Bloom and got paid under the table, because they never filed taxes. For another thing, they wanted back the money I owed them, and they probably wanted me to be able to support myself so that they wouldn't have do to it anymore.

"When you turn eighteen, if you want to stay, I'll do the paperwork," Jesse Ray told me.

I could barely stay still, sitting across from him at a desk in an office crammed with boxes and bags of videos. Nobody had ever done something so nice for me in my life. I didn't know a lot about the employment rules and regulations, but I did know that Jesse Ray was taking a big chance with the IRS and the people who made the child labor laws. He did all of that for me.

"You won't regret this. I promise I will be the best clerk in the world. I won't disappoint you, Mr. Thurman," I assured him.

"You just did," he said, with a frown. I froze. Then he smiled again. "Don't you ever refer to me again as Mr. Thurman. You call me Jesse Ray, or J.R., like everybody else. Is that clear? Now you be here Saturday morning at ten sharp."

I ran almost all the way home. Once I got inside my apartment building, I didn't stop running until I made it to Miss Odessa's door. I had not seen or talked to her since I'd returned from L.A. She must have sensed I was coming, because she snatched open the door before I even knocked. The sweet smell of a freshly baked cake almost knocked me out.

"Praise God, you are all right," she said, crying and hugging and kissing me as soon as I got inside her door. She had on a housecoat. A hairnet covered her head like a spider's web.

"I tried to call you from L.A. a bunch of times," I told her. "I, uh, went down there to visit a friend." I felt bad enough about what I'd done. I didn't see any reason to drag Miss Odessa into my foolishness. "But I . . ." I stopped and stood there in the middle of her living room floor, with my mouth hanging open. There was a bandage on the side of Miss Odessa's nose. "What's the matter with your nose?" I asked in a shaky voice.

"Oh, it's nothing serious. Just a little skin cancer," she said, laughing and waving her hand. I didn't know how to respond. I had never heard somebody laugh when they talked about cancer. Especially if they had it. As far as I was concerned, cancer was way up there on the shit list, just below the devil.

"Cancer?" I mouthed. The word itself was enough to make my head swim. "You've got cancer?"

"Oh, it ain't nothing to worry about." Miss Odessa laughed again. "I got warts on my feet that are more serious than this little bugger," she said, pointing to the bandage on her nose. "See, Dr. Stine scraped it all off, and he guaranteed me, it won't come back. Now, what are you so excited about?"

I didn't like what Miss Odessa had just told me. I didn't care how "little" her cancer was. Cancer was cancer. "You were in the hospital when I tried to call you from L.A.," I told her, unable to take my eyes off the bandage on her nose. I blinked a few times and looked around the room, sniffing that cake and hoping she'd offer me a big slice.

"Yeah, I guess I was. But I told you, it wasn't nothing serious. They did the surgery and sent me home the same day. I had my telephone turned off so I could rest." Miss Odessa folded her arms and dipped her head. These were the two things she often did when she was serious. "Now tell me why you so excited," she ordered.

"I got a job!" I yelled. "I got a job and I'm back in school and everything is going to be all right now." I had finally done something constructive for myself, and it felt good.

Miss Odessa still didn't get all up in my business, but I knew she was dying to hear about my journey to L.A. So I volunteered the information on my own. I left no stone unturned. By the time I finished talking, she knew as much about Wade as I did.

"And how do you feel about yourself now? Did all them drugs and fornicating and running away to Los Angeles make you feel any better?" she wanted to know, handing me a glass of cold milk and a large slice of homemade lemon cake.

"Uh, it did when I was doing it," I admitted.

"But it don't now," Miss Odessa said in a stern voice. "I've heard all I want to hear about that Wade boy. From what you say, he sounds a lot like my second husband. All dick and no brain. You don't need that. If that's all that boy got going for him, you can get that from one of them adult shops on Telegraph. All you need is some batteries." She laughed. I bowed my head and laughed, too. "Now tell me all about this job and this Jesse Ray Thurman."

"He is so nice to me. I think we're going to get real close," I said hopefully, meaning every word.

CHAPTER 33

In some ways, Jesse Ray Thurman saved my life. I don't know what I would have become of me if he had not offered me a job in the video store that he managed and would eventually own.

It was hard to believe that so many years had passed. I couldn't believe that I was now sitting in an old wreck of a car with Wade Eddie Fisher, depending on him to get me—and a million dollars—away from Jesse Ray.

"You awful quiet back there," Wade said, with a snort. "You want some pancakes or a Egg McMuffin or something? There's a McDonald's at the corner."

"I'm not hungry," I said. "I just want to get this over and done with." I covered my mouth with my hand and yawned. I knew that sooner or later I would really have to catch up on my sleep. I was beginning to feel weaker and weaker. And not just that. I also felt disoriented and paranoid.

"It's almost over, baby. The next call to my man will be to make sure he's got that damn money ready for us. Then, once we get situated, I call him and tell him where he can pick you up at," Wade explained, looking at the side of Jason's knotty head.

As if on cue, Jason glanced at Wade, then over his shoulder at me. I didn't like the look on his face. It was the same smug look he'd had on that ugly mug of his since he'd heard that my husband was going to pay a million dollars for my release. I didn't like the look that was on Wade's face, either. He looked twice as smug as Jason.

"We need to talk about who gets what," I suggested, hoping that I sounded firm enough for Wade to realize that I was still the one in charge.

"Now hold on, baby. Keep your thongs on. I told you we'd get to that later," Wade snarled. "We'll talk about that later."

"No, we need to talk about it now. I don't want to wait until we get the money. And, anyway, you agreed to take fifty grand. That should be all I give to you," I said in a hot tone of voice. Wade and Jason looked at each other again, then at me.

"Look, I agreed to fifty grand because half a million was all I thought you was getting at the time. But this new thing here, what your old man offered up on his own, it changes everything. You need to be fair. I went way out on a long-ass limb for you. I ain't going to be short-changed after all I went through," Wade snapped.

"Look, I am the victim here. I am the one who is giving up the most," I reminded, stabbing my chest with my finger.

"Victim? You think you are a victim?" said Wade. He rose up on his seat and turned all the way around, looking at me so hard, my face stung. He laughed so hard that a large tear rolled down his cheek like a pebble.

"You know what I mean," I said sheepishly.

"Oh, I know what you mean all right," Wade said, still laughing. "You are the victim, but me and Jason are just as much victims as you if we get caught, girl. Shit." He sucked in a deep breath and turned back around to face the road. "Any way you look at this thing, you are still going to come out smelling like a rose. You'll still have enough money to live on for the rest of your life if you spend it like you got some sense. By the way, where exactly in Hawaii do you plan on doing your thing?"

"What? What are you talking about?" I asked. Wade turned around again, his mouth stretched open like a hole in the wall. With my mind being in such a shambles, I had temporarily forgotten that I'd told him that I was going to relocate to Hawaii with my share of the ransom. "Oh! Uh, Maui. That's where I'm going to rent me a little apartment and live a quiet life."

"What the fuck! Whatever!" Wade threw up his hands in exasperation. "Look, you better eat something. With them dark circles around your eyes, you look like hell. I don't want you to look like you been mistreated when you go back to your old man," Wade said, motioning with his hand for Jason to turn into the McDonald's parking lot at the corner. "After you eat something, we'll drop you off back at the motel and let you have some time to yourself. You might want to go over in your head what you want to say, and how you want to act, when . . . uh . . . your old man picks you up. Rehearse your speech and shit so you can play your part right. This is a one-time deal, baby. You got to do it right the first time."

"I don't need to rehearse anything," I replied in a cool, level voice.

"Look, lady. This ain't no game. We can't take no chance on you saying nothing stupid once we turn you loose. I ain't going back to jail no matter what happens! If we get busted, they ain't taking me alive! Like Wade just said, you need to figure out everything you are going to say and do once we turn you loose," Jason hollered, turning into the McDonald's parking lot. "And we want to know just what it is you plan on saying!"

"No, you look, you snaggletoothed motherfucker!" My words shot out of my mouth so loud and violently, my throat ached. I had to lower my voice for my own sake. "I've said it once and I will say it again, this is between Wade and me. I didn't bring you into this, Jason, and I will be damned if I am going to sit here and let you give me orders," I hissed, leaning toward the front seat, gripping the back of the seat so hard, my knuckles ached.

As soon as the car stopped, another car pulled up and parked next to us. I immediately slumped back into the corner of my seat and held my breath. My poor heart had been thumping and pumping so hard and fast the last couple of days, I was surprised that it had not stopped beating altogether by now. Even with the cap on my head, hiding my hair, I didn't want anybody to see me. Even people I didn't know. Like the strange Hispanic man who had just parked his car next to us.

"Baby, we are all in this together. I know we are beginning to get on one another's nerves, but it'll all be over soon. Now give me some sugar," Wade said, pursing his lips. He growled when I turned my head away. "That's how you want to be now?" he asked, sounding hurt. I ignored him and remained huddled in the backseat as he and Jason left the car, mumbling profanities.

CHAPTER 34

I felt weaker and even more disoriented. It seemed like everything was spiraling out of control. I was afraid that one of the things that I was going to lose control of was my mind. And, even though I didn't have much of an appetite, my mouth started to water for that Egg McMuffin that Wade had bought. I thought that if I put some food in my stomach, it might help settle my nerves. The last time I stood up, I felt so light-headed, my legs buckled and I almost fell.

I was glad to be back in the motel alone. After I ate, I took a shower. I scrubbed myself until my flesh ached, but I still didn't feel clean. Especially since I had slid back into the same underwear and clothes, which were all pretty ripe by now.

I couldn't sit still; I couldn't concentrate on anything on the television screen. I couldn't call anyone I knew, and I couldn't go anywhere on my own. I had truly begun to feel like the victim that I was pretending to be.

The room was small, but as much pacing as I did, I had probably walked enough to cover a football field. Other than one of those dollar-store Bibles in the nightstand drawer, there was nothing in the room for me to read.

I had some make-up in my purse, but I didn't want to hide the dark circles around my eyes. I wanted them to stay there and get even darker if possible. For the first time in my life, I wanted to look like a frump. I had to look like a woman who had been through a kidnapping ordeal when Jesse Ray picked me up.

Wade had to go home to check on his mama. She'd called him up on his cell phone three times in the last hour. He'd cussed and fussed about it nonstop for twenty minutes. I knew he loved his mama, but Miss Louise had become a major thorn in his side over the years. To calm her down, he took with him twenty bucks that he had "borrowed" from me to give to her.

I didn't know where that Jason went, and I didn't care. All I cared about was the fact that the next time I saw Wade, he would have made the call to Jesse Ray from another pay phone to make sure he had the money.

I managed to eat half of the food from McDonald's; then I decided I'd try to take a nap. I was so worn-out and anxious, I knew that if I did manage to fall asleep, I'd sleep like a log. I don't know when I finally dozed off or how long I slept. But I woke up in a hurry when I realized there was a rough, hairy hand over my mouth. I was so groggy, I thought it was a monkey's paw. I tried to bite it, but the skin was as thick and tough as rawhide.

"What the hell? Jason, what the hell are you doing?" I shouted, pushing him and his hand away. I sat up, coughing and glaring at him as he leaned over me. "Motherfucker, what the fuck are you doing?" I hollered, wiping his filthy DNA off my lips. Jason's touch was enough to make my stomach turn. I wished that it had been just a monkey's paw. For one horrific moment, I thought that he was trying to rape me!

"Be quiet!" Jason snarled. "Shet the fuck up!" His breath was as foul as cow dung.

I swung at him, aiming for that one upper tooth that he had left, hoping to knock it out. He turned his head just in time for my fist to land on his cheek. "Fuck you! What the hell do you mean by coming up in here, putting your funky hands on me?"

"I didn't want to surprise you and have you jump up swinging at me," Jason said, pouting.

"Surprise me? Well, you did just that! Don't you ever touch me again, Jason. You don't know me well enough to be putting your nasty hands on me like that! My own husband doesn't put his hand over my mouth, motherfucker."

"Fuck you and that punk-ass husband of yours. You ain't got to worry about nothing no more, so you can calm your ass down," Jason boomed. There was a strange look on his face. "We got the money," he continued in a hollow voice. "All neat and pretty in a little black suitcase."

My breath felt like it was stuck in my windpipe. I coughed and cleared my throat. "What?" I asked, looking around the room and behind Jason, surprised that Wade was not present. "Where's Wade?" I demanded. I had to slap the side of my head and then shake it to keep my thoughts from rolling around in so many different directions. A headache came on so fast, it felt like somebody had just batted my skull with a baseball bat.

"He's around, close by," Jason replied, snapping a finger. "He's getting everything situated so we can get you back to your old man."

"Well, what's that got to do with you putting your hand over my mouth? Where is Wade?" I asked again. I leaped up from the bed, so fast, I almost knocked Jason to the floor. "Where is the money?" I asked, my hands on my hips, looking around the room some more.

"Wade and the money is at my pad over on Telegraph."

"Why is he there? Why didn't he come with you?"

"Lady, a million bucks is a heap of money. He couldn't leave it laying around his nosy-ass mama's house, with her broke ass roaming from room to room. That woman spends money like it's going out of style. Can you imagine what she would do if she stumbled upon a million bucks? And, that's bad enough, but Wade didn't want to be riding around town with it, with all these crazy motherfuckers around here."

"Shit!" I hollered, stumbling to the bathroom, where I splashed cold water on my face. "I intend to let Wade know I don't appreciate you coming back here, pulling a stunt like you just did, Jason!" I yelled, moving back toward the bed, drying my face with a wad of toilet paper.

"Christine, I want you to know right here and now, this ain't my idea," Jason said, with a leer. "I was beginning to like you. Even though you've been treating me like an ugly stepbrother. If you wasn't already hooked up with Wade, I would make you my woman. I like women with big legs." He paused and cleared his throat, his eyes locked with mine. "But I wouldn't put up with that smart-ass mouth you got. I'd straighten you out in no time if you was my woman. With your hardheaded, bigmouthed self—just like a black woman! That's why I'm going to get me an Asian woman next! A *pure* one straight off the boat so I can train her real good! You black women done got so out of control, it's a damn shame," he declared, shaking his head. "I don't know what this world is coming to. Shit."

I fought, with a gasp that was so brutal, it almost choked me. My legs buckled again, and I plopped down on the bed. I had to close my eyes for a moment, and when I opened them again, I choked some more. Jason was standing over me again. But this time there was a gun in his hand.

CHAPTER 35

"Jason, now you tell me what the hell this is about," I demanded, folding my arms, my eyes on the gun. "Look, I'm already a nervous wreck, but you are really beginning to scare me. Now if Wade's got the money, and he's at your place, I want you to take me over there. We need to wrap this thing up so I can go on back home." I didn't even recognize the squeaky voice coming out of my own mouth. I couldn't take my eyes off the gun in Jason's hand. The fact that his hand was shaking made me even more concerned and scared. But scared was too mild a word to describe the way I felt. I was terrified, to say the least.

Jason sniffed and wiped his nose with the sleeve of his shirt. "You ain't got nothing to be scared of," he assured me, growling under his breath. "I ain't going to hurt you."

"You've got a gun in my face, and I don't know why. Why shouldn't I be scared?" I wailed, sounding stronger now.

Jason tilted his head to the side and gave me a pitiful look, confusing me even more.

When I attempted to get up from the bed, he pushed me back down, pinning me in place with his knee on my chest. Now that really made me mad. My breasts felt like somebody had set a cement block on them, and I could hardly breathe. But Jason's gun was too close to my face for me to overreact. I responded with as much caution as I could manage. "Be careful, Jason. And get that gun away from me, *please*," I pleaded, shaking a shaky finger in his face. "Now I want you to get the hell away from me and tell me what is going on. I'm tired, and I want to get the fuck away from you and your boy Wade."

Jason gave me another pitiful look, and this time he looked truly sincere. "My oldest daughter is named Christine," he muttered, looking at the floor. I was glad that he had pointed the gun away from me.

"So what the fuck do I care?" I yelled, attempting to rise again. He pushed me back down on the bed, still pinning me down with his knees on my chest.

"Christine, I . . . see, I just want to say something first. I don't know what you seen in Wade, in the first place. He ain't nothing but a dumb-ass punk. He couldn't even make it in Hollywood," Jason declared. I didn't know what to say to that, so I just kept my lips pressed together. His eyes looked like two black holes that somebody had cracked open in his face as a cruel joke.

"Well, this is the deal," Jason continued, pausing again. "Me and Wade, uh, we decided to cut you out of the deal." His nose was running. He wiped it with the back of the hand that held his gun. "Shit, I don't even want to be doing this. But, see, Wade said if you try anything, I'm supposed to shoot you. And, he told me to make sure I shoot you in the head." Jason looked at me and blinked. One moment he looked sorry, and the next moment there was so much contempt on his face, you could have peeled it off with a knife.

"I just wish your name wasn't Christine," he whispered, rising. I didn't bother to try to get up again. I was too stunned to move. "If some asshole was to play my daughter Christine like you about to get played, I'd teach him a lesson he'd never forget!" Jason turned his back to me, but he continued talking. "And, I don't know if it'll make you feel any better, but if you *was* my woman, this wouldn't be happening." He whirled around to face me again, holding his gun up in the air.

I rubbed my eyes and blinked, jerking my head back and forth. I looked from Jason's face to the gun in his hand. But I still didn't move off the bed. I slapped the side of my head and shook it, like I didn't believe what I was hearing. And I didn't. "I don't believe this is happening," I whimpered.

"Well, it's happening, baby. Now you get your shit, and let's get the hell up out of here." Jason waved the gun and glanced at his watch.

I leaped off the bed, landing on my feet, with my hands on my hips.

I was so angry by now that the gun no longer scared me. "You crazy son of a bitch!" I hissed. It was a struggle to keep my voice low. I could hear voices in the rooms on both sides of me. I didn't want them to hear mine.

Jason folded his arms and looked me up and down. "If anybody in this room is crazy, it's you. Did you really think that me and Wade was going to let a million bucks slip through our fingers, woman? I mean, *get real,* bitch! This is a chance of a lifetime. How many black men get something handed to them on a platter like this? I been praying for this kind of opportunity all my life," he said. His tongue flicked in and out of his mouth. Beads of sweat dotted his forehead like pebbles.

I stumbled toward Jason, with my fist raised. Even with the gun still in his hand, he looked frightened. With every step I took in his direction, he backed up in the opposite direction. I stopped when I realized I had backed him up against the wall. "Jason, you listen to me and you listen good. You are not a stupid man," I said in a hoarse, desperate voice. "You don't need to do something this stupid. You are going to get paid, brother."

"Correction! I done already got paid," he said, with a hollow laugh. "Half a million dollars!" He lifted the gun, touching my nose with the barrel.

"That money belongs to me," I hissed, moving back toward the bed. "I'm not leaving this room until I speak to Wade," I said, holding up my hands. I dropped back down on the bed, crossing my legs.

Without a word, but not taking his eyes or the gun off me, Jason fumbled around in his jacket pocket and removed his cell phone. He punched in a number and handed it to me. When Wade answered on the first ring, I didn't know where to begin.

CHAPTER 36

"Wade, your boy just pulled one hell of a stunt on me, and he just told me some shit I refuse to believe," I began.

"Christine, don't talk. Just shut up and listen," Wade told me, talking in a voice that sounded like he was a million miles away. And, in a way, I guess he was. "I don't like what you dragged me into. I mean, jail ain't one of my favorite places to be. I know I ain't got half of what you got to lose, but I don't want to lose what I do have. And right now, that's a million dollars. I think I deserve every penny of it."

My heart skipped a beat, and then it almost stopped completely. The pain that shot through my entire body was excruciating. I was surprised that I was still conscious. "Wade, you can't be serious. I know you and Jason both expect more money now since Jesse Ray paid double what we asked for. But I was planning on doubling your take, anyway, baby. I will overlook this little stunt Jason just pulled. We can all sit down and talk this thing over. And, I promise you I will be fair. And, the sooner I see you, the better."

"I can't see you no more," Wade told me, with a deep sigh. "This thing we've had off and on all these years, it's over. It's over with for good. It's time for us both to move on."

"That's fine if you want to end our relationship. I can live with that. And, to tell you the truth, I had planned to break it off myself, anyway," I said in a bold voice.

"I can't *see* you no more, period. Now if you know what's good for you, you will do everything my boy Jason tells you to do."

"Wade, don't do this to me! Don't be a fool! How far do you think you'd get with my money?" I wailed, glaring at the telephone in my hand like it was a time bomb. I didn't know my small body could produce so much sweat. My hair and clothes were soaking wet.

"No, baby, this is my money as long as it's in my hands. And, you and I both know that there is plenty more where this came from."

I was so stunned, I could barely think of what to say next. It was like my mouth and tongue were on hold. It took me a few more moments to get more words out. And they gushed out like lava. "Wade, what are you saying? Was my money all you cared about?" I whimpered. I was glad to see that Jason had sat down on the bed and laid the gun across his lap. But the glare from his evil eyes had almost as much of an effect on me as the gun.

"Christine, I know you might find this hard to believe, but I still care about you, and I always did. I know I acted like a piece of shit when we were kids, but I outgrew all of that. I still want you to be happy, and I think you can . . . but I can't be the one to help you get to that point. You got a rich old man, a big-ass house, and you still a fine-looking woman."

"Wade, I'm having a hard time here. Please listen and let me talk," I sobbed. "I know . . . I mean, we had a lot of fun together. You came back into my life just in time, and I appreciate that. But you are not making much sense right now. I just don't believe what I'm hearing. Are you telling me that you are going to keep all of the money that my husband paid to get me back? Or are you just trying to be funny? And, if this is a joke, and I sure as hell hope it is, it is not funny." I had to stop because what I'd just heard out of Wade's mouth was too god-damn incredible to believe. I laughed. I actually reared my head back and laughed until my throat and eyes hurt. "There is no way in hell I'd let you get away with this. You will spend the rest of your life in jail, motherfucker!"

"Uh-uh. I don't think so. I know that, and you know that, too," Wade assured me in a voice so calm, you would have thought that he was reciting the Lord's Prayer. "Jason is going to drop you off where I told your old man to pick you up. You are going to go on home and love your man, bake some cookies, give yourself an egg facial, and do whatever else the hell you rich housewives do."

"The hell I will!" I shouted, shaking my fist in the air,

"The hell you won't. Remember that little photo session and that little moviemaking deal we done at the Marriott a while back? Remember them pictures, that video? Well, baby, I didn't give everything to you like you thought I did."

"You wouldn't—"

"Oh yes, I would."

"And what does that prove? I could say that I was forced. And drugged."

"Uh-huh. And, if you believe anybody else would believe that, you better think again. What about all them phone calls you made to my mama's house to me?"

"What about them?"

"You want to know how many of them sweet messages you left on my answering machine I still got? How would you prove I forced you to do that?"

"Wade, I need to talk to you face-to-face. Either you have your boy bring me to wherever you are, or you'd better get back over here right now," I hollered. My voice was so weak, it couldn't even intimidate me.

"In exactly one hour, your husband is going to come pick you up. And, I'm going to tell you the same thing I told him: Don't you never, I mean never, involve the cops or nobody else. If you do, you will regret it for the rest of your life. You can run, and you can hide. I know where your two kissy-poo girlfriends live. I got friends, too, and if something happens to me, they got the same information I got. You remember that. This ain't just about you. Do you hear me?"

There was a lump in my throat so large, I had a hard time finding my voice.

"Do you hear me?" Wade asked again.

"I do," I croaked.

"Now you go with my boy and do what he tells you to do. And, one more thing, I did care about you. If I was ever going to settle down with a black woman, it would have been you." Wade hung up.

Without another word, I followed Jason to his car and crawled into the backseat. There were no words in the English language that could describe my feelings.

"This could have turned out a whole lot worser," Jason said as soon as he started the car. "At least nobody got hurt. And, to tell you the truth, you lucky to have latched onto you a man like old Jesse Ray Thurman in the first place. I don't understand why you didn't realize that! Maybe y'all can work things out, after all. I heard you and him go way back, to when you was still in school. . . ."

I didn't bother to remind Jason that Wade and I also went way back, to when I was still in school. My history with Jesse Ray suddenly didn't mean much to me now. But my history with Wade still did.

And, it was those memories that got me through the next few hours.

CHAPTER 37

None of my friends graduated from Berkeley High when I did. Some of the ones who had been smart enough to stay in school had fallen back a year or two and had to do some repeats. But there were more who had strayed as far away from an education as they could get.

That fiasco with Wade in L.A. had hurt me more than I thought it would. For days after I'd returned home I had felt like a piece of shit because that was how Wade had treated me. And because I was now making an effort to improve my situation I deserved something better than Wade had offered, or not offered I should say. Now I wanted to be with somebody who wanted to be with me, and not just to fuck me. I wanted to see what the other side was like. But I knew most decent men avoided girls like me so I knew I had to make some changes in my life.

I had not done any drugs, not even a joint, since the day I started working for Jesse Ray at the video store. I still drank, and I still liked to smoke a few Newports throughout the day, but I had dropped some of my bad habits. I had not had sex for five months by the time Jesse Ray got around to asking me for a date.

"I don't know much about your personal life, and if you don't want to tell me, you don't have to. But I like you, Christine. I did the first time I saw you at the flea market that day. If you are interested, I'd like to take you out sometime," Jesse Ray said. "But . . . ," he said, then paused and looked away. He looked at the floor a moment before he returned his attention to me. "If you are already involved with somebody else, I respect that. And, if that is the case, all I can say is, he's one lucky man."

It was a Saturday night, just before closing time. He and I were in the store alone, restocking videos that had been returned that day. His confession brought tears to my eyes. It was the first time that a man had shown an interest in me in such a noble way.

"How do you know it's not a woman?" I teased.

"Excuse me?"

I laughed and touched the side of his arm. Then he laughed.

"I don't have a boyfriend—or a girlfriend—if that's what you want to know," I said and smiled. I had not given much thought to Jesse Ray as a possible lover or anything other than an employer. But he was so nice to me, letting me take off when I wanted, and listening to me ramble on about things that meant nothing to anybody but me.

Things were still pretty dismal at home, but I still had Miss Odessa next door to fall back on. I had not seen or heard from Wade since he'd chased me out of L.A., not in person or on television or anywhere else. And, neither had any of my friends. But Miss Louise was still running all over town, bragging about how good her "baby boy" was doing in Hollywood. She was also still borrowing money left and right, even more than ever before. The last time she'd hit on me, I was down to my last quarter. She took that. But, true to her word, she came to the apartment the following weekend and paid me back.

"Well, I know you like movies," Jesse Ray laughed, holding up a copy of *The Color Purple*. He let me take as many movies home to watch for free as I wanted. "You've borrowed this one more than half a dozen times. But movies are so much more enjoyable on a big screen. If we leave now, I'm sure we can catch the last screening of something else you might like."

In addition to movies, he took me to dinner a couple of times a week. Being the enterprising brother that he was, Jesse Ray was always looking for more ways to make more money. He borrowed money from the bank and took over the video store. He opened his second store on Cedar Street in North Berkeley a month later, leaving me to manage the first one.

I had just restocked some returned videos one evening, just before we closed for the night, when I decided to check out the adult section for the first time. Not that I was interested in watching any X-rated movies, but the fact that so many people rented the damn things made me curious.

The adult section was located in a small back room behind the manager's office. Jesse Ray had decided that this was the only way to keep minors from looking at some of the lurid titles. I was standing in front of the shelves, shaking my head at some of the titles. With each one I picked up, I frowned. Then one title jumped out at me: *Ball in the Family*. This particular title caught my attention because it reminded me of the old television show *All in the Family*. On the video cover were several white women and one handsome, well-hung black man. I blinked and rubbed my eyes because at first, I couldn't believe what I was seeing, or who I was seeing. I recognized the actor even with a mustache. Splayed on a king-size bed, naked to the world in a bedroom too tacky for words, was Wade. He was the very first and the last man (I hoped) who had had me acting like a fool. His stage name was King Dong. I looked through several more tapes and came across four more that featured Wade in the lead role. I held up the two most disgusting ones and shook my head. The titles alone were enough to make me sick: *Tricky Dick* and *Tittie City*.

As strange as it was even to me, I was still interested in Wade. I felt good about the fact that I had encouraged him to pursue his acting career, but I never expected him to end up as a porn star. Knowing what I knew now made me feel unbearably sad and sorry for Wade. Now I understood why my presence in L.A. had irritated him so much.

Just two days earlier, I'd run into his mama at the bus stop where I caught my bus home after work each evening.

"Oh, my boy is doing so well down there in Hollywood," she'd declared, swooning. "It's just a matter of time before he gets the lead in one of his movies."

I sighed to keep from rolling my eyes. I watched a lot of television, and I rented a lot of movies. So far I had not seen Wade Eddie Fisher in anything legitimate. Surfing the Web had not even turned up anything, and that was really strange because I'd been able to find movies featuring some of the most obscure entertainers in the business and other related information.

Well, Wade had finally landed the lead role in not one but several movies. With a heavy hand and sad heart, I returned the videos to the shelf, wondering what I'd say to Wade about his career if and when I ever saw him again.

CHAPTER 38

I never mentioned the videos of Wade to Jesse Ray. As a matter of fact, I never mentioned Wade to him at all. One of the many things that I admired about Jesse Ray was the fact that he had no interest in my past. At least that was what he had led me to believe. Even though I'd told him that I'd been "pretty wild" during my younger years. Whenever I did bring up my past, he promptly changed the subject.

"Baby, what you did before you met me was your business. And vice versa. I don't know what you did or who you did it with. All I care about now is our future," he told me. "Let's go get some Chinese food."

Jesse Ray spent a lot of time talking to me about his family, which included his widowed mother and his two siblings and their families. From what he'd told me, his was a close-knit family. They got together on a regular basis. But the first few weeks into our relationship, I declined all of his invitations to attend this or that family gathering. One of the reasons was, I didn't want to get too close to somebody else's family, because of the relationship I had with mine.

I didn't like to talk about my parents with outsiders. Mainly because there was not too much I could say about them that would make them look good.

Things had changed in our house, but not for the better. Daddy was even more withdrawn and sullen. And, Mama was as cantankerous as ever, still reminding me about all the hours and pain she had to endure to give birth to me. Which made the fact that they had attended my high school graduation even my mysterious. They had shown very little interest in my education, attending PTA meetings only when they had to, glancing at my report cards, with no comments. But I blamed myself, too. I never shared much with them and did very little to encourage them to be more active in my life.

Three weeks before graduation, Daddy glanced at me sitting on the sofa next to him and cleared his throat to speak. "So, you'll be finishing up school soon, eh?" he asked. He and I had been sitting on the same sofa alone for three hours, watching television in silence. It took me a few moments to realize he was talking to me. I gave him the same kind of blank look that he and Mama usually gave me.

"Me?" I asked dumbly, pointing at myself. "Uh, that's right."

"Uh-huh," was all he said. He nodded and returned his attention to the television screen. And the subject never came up again.

Mama and Daddy were at work when I got ready to leave for the graduation ceremonies. Even though it was an exciting day for me, it was also a sad one. I had no plans for my future. I enjoyed working for Jesse Ray, and I enjoyed his company, but I didn't know where the relationship was going. I didn't even mention my graduation to Jesse Ray. In some ways, it was just another day for me. I didn't notice Mama and Daddy sitting in a back row until I actually walked across the stage to receive my diploma. I don't know how I managed not to stumble. I saw them leave before I even got back to my seat.

"I never expected to see them sitting there. I didn't think they cared," I told Miss Odessa after everything was over. I had come home with her in a cab.

"They are still your folks, baby. They are proud of you. If they wasn't, you wouldn't be with them," Miss Odessa assured me, stroking the side of my head.

"It wouldn't hurt if they told me or showed me that once in a while," I said, my lips pursing into a pout. "They have never told me they loved me or that they were proud of me or anything. I know I was not planned or even wanted. Mama is never going to let me forget what a burden it was to carry me for nine months and how my birth almost killed her. Why they feel the way they do about me is a mystery."

It had been a while since one of my parents had snuck up on me in my bedroom and kissed my cheek when they thought I was asleep.

But I had to admit that there was the possibility that they had done it while I had actually been asleep. I had mixed feelings about them doing something so odd, and it was one of the few things that I didn't even want to discuss with Miss Odessa.

"Baby, have you ever sat down with your folks and tried to talk to them?"

"Why should I?"

"Because there is a reason for everything. I bet there is a lot of things they want to say to you."

"Then why don't they? They see me every day."

"Honey, some folks don't know how to say what's on their mind. Some folks don't know how to show their feelings. Now your folks had a very hard life in Guatemala. A life me and you can't even begin to understand."

"They talked to you about Guatemala?" I asked, with a surprised look on my face. "They *rarely* talk to me about where they came from and what it was like. Why would they tell you?"

"Because I asked them."

"Why?"

"Well, because I wanted to know. If you really want to understand your folks better, I suggest you go up to them and ask them whatever it is you want to know."

I gave Miss Odessa's words a lot of thought over the next few months. But I didn't take any action, and I didn't know if I ever would.

When I finally did accept an invitation to have dinner with Jesse Ray and his family, I was glad I did so that I could see firsthand that having a close family was not all that it was cracked up to be. His sister, Adele, walked around with her nose in the air like she was a supermodel. She was tall and thin, but she was as plain as she could be. Her eyes were too big for her long face, her nose was all over her face, and she had one of the worst cases of acne I'd ever seen on a woman her age. The brother, Harvey, was lucky. He looked like an older version of Jesse Ray, but he was loud and obnoxious, and so were his clothes. The first time I met him, he wore a red polyester suit. He told stale jokes and did horrible impressions of famous people. I didn't know which sibling was the most irritating. But I was nice and friendly with them at all times, no matter how difficult it was.

"So look here, Crystal—"

"It's Christine," I corrected, cutting Adele off. "And it's spelled with a *C*." From the scowl on Adele's face, she let me know right away that she didn't like the move I'd just made. But I'd done it for more reasons than one. First, I wanted her to get my name right. Second, I wanted her to know off the bat that I was no wuss. I defended myself whenever I had to.

"Whatever," she said, continuing, with the scowl still on her face. "I don't know what you are doing to my brother, but whatever it is, it must be good. I ain't never seen his nose open for no women this wide," Adele said, gnawing on a pork-chop bone.

We had gathered for dinner, which I'd cooked in Jesse Ray's spacious condo, in one of the nicest areas in the northern part of Berkeley.

"Well, as long as you don't open it too wide, I ain't going to complain," Harvey muttered, a fork in one hand and a large glass of wine in the other. "My baby brother is a businessman, and he needs to keep his wits about him."

It was a struggle for me to smile, because all eyes were on me, giving me critical looks. But Adele's husband, Mel, had the only set of eyes that made me nervous. He'd winked at me several times already. And, with the last wink, he had licked his lips in a very suggestive manner.

"I think J.R. and I are going to be fine," I said, with confidence. "We get along all right," I added.

"Well, if you are going to be cooking up meals this good, I don't care what you do to old J.R.," Mel said, chewing so hard, I was afraid he'd snap his tongue in two. "These chops is screaming."

"Next time don't be so heavy-handed with that pepper, though," Adele said, with a fake smile, twirling a knife and a fork in the same hand.

"Baby, don't let anything these heathens say bother you. They're this way with everybody," Jesse Ray said. He rose from his seat at the head of the table and came around where I sat next to Harvey and hauled off and kissed me so passionately, it made me squirm. It made Adele squirm, too, because when I looked at her, she looked at me like she wanted to use that knife and fork on me.

I hadn't even slept with Jesse Ray yet. However, he often spent more money on me in one month than the rest of the men I'd been with had spent on me put together. And, speaking of money, from what

Jesse Ray had told me, and from what I'd seen the same evening I'd met them, his family was one set of people that I would have to keep both my eyes on.

Other than Wade's mama, Jesse Ray's family had more financial "emergencies" than anybody I knew. Three days after that dinner in Jesse Ray's condo, Adele returned while I was there to borrow money for an emergency she was too embarrassed to identity. A week later I called up Adele to invite her to lunch at my expense. I did it because I had been feeling guilty about scolding Jesse Ray for being so generous to his family. I was horrified when Mel told me she was "still on her Mexican cruise."

Two months later Adele borrowed money from Jesse Ray to get American Express off her back. She owed them over two thousand dollars. I found out later that most of the charges had been made at Disneyland.

It was hard for me to ignore all this foolishness, and I tried to as much as I could. But there was no way I was going to sit back and let people continue to take advantage of my man. I was not bold enough to confront his family, but I did let him know how I felt. "Baby, it's only money," he told me. "I got a few dollars, and everybody I know is wondering how much I'm going to leave behind when I die. I'll tell you the same thing I tell them: I'll be leaving it all behind. I can't take it with me, so I plan to enjoy it while I can. And, part of my enjoyment is being there for my family."

Jesse Ray's older brother, Harvey, reminded me of Wade. Not that they looked alike or anything like that, but Harvey had shyly confessed that he'd once considered pursuing a career in show business. But the closest he'd been able to get to show business was an appearance on *The People's Court* when he sued a former friend for not repaying a loan. And, that was a story in and of itself, because Jesse Ray told me that Harvey rarely repaid any of the money he "borrowed" from him. Harvey had stayed at the dinner just long enough to tell a few lame jokes, fix a plate to go, and borrow a "few more dollars" from Jesse Ray. I had already learned that to Jesse Ray's family, a few dollars could mean anything from a few dollars to a couple of thousand.

"My brother and sister have more financial problems than anybody I know," Jesse Ray told me, like I couldn't already see that for myself. I gave him a thoughtful look, thinking about Wade's mama and all the times she'd borrowed my last dollar. "I usually don't see or hear from them until they are in a bind. Now Mama, she never asks for anything unless she really needs it. And, then she goes out of her way to pay me back, not that I ever take it. But you know, family is family. If you can't depend on family, you can't depend on anybody else," Jesse Ray told me, with a wistful sniff.

I liked it when he showed his emotions. In addition to being smart, generous, and thoughtful, he was sensitive. I knew that it would be a good move on my part to take my relationship with him to another level. And I planned on doing just that. This was one man I wasn't about to let get away. I knew I could not depend on my family, but I knew that I could depend on Jesse Ray.

We finally made love six months into our relationship, on a king-size bed at the Hyatt Hotel in downtown San Francisco. I had come a long way from fucking anonymous guys on the ground in People's Park and Wade on that saggy mattress in his bedroom.

Jesse Ray was not as good in bed as Wade, but he was adequate. And, he seemed to get better each time, because I was not shy about telling him what I wanted in bed. Before long I couldn't keep my hands off that man. But it was not just about sex and his generosity. Jesse Ray did something for me that no other man had ever done. He made me feel special. Being special was one of the few things that I'd ever wanted in my life. And, for that reason, he would always be special to me.

CHAPTER 39

"This Jesse Ray sure enough sounds like a good man. And probably the best a girl like you can do." Mama paused and looked me up and down, frowning, squinting her eyes, and shaking her head. "You ain't no Janet Jackson, but you look better than some of these girls around here." She turned her head but not fast enough. I caught a slight grin on her face. Neither of my parents had a sense of humor. I couldn't remember the last time I'd seen either one of them laugh at anything. Mama looked at me again with that stern look back on her face. "Me, I say you better snatch him up before he gets away."

This was one of the few times in my life that my mother had shown an interest in my social life. I was still in a state of shock over her and Daddy showing up at my graduation. But just like the smile she had not been able to hide from me, her true feelings were beginning to come through, anyway. That's why I was able to ignore Mama's "put-down" about my looks.

We stood side by side in the kitchen, where Mama spent most of her time when she wasn't working for Mr. Bloom. She was chopping onions with a dull knife, ignoring the tears streaming down the sides of her face. The fumes from the onions were so potent, they made me cry, too.

"Too bad I can't be as lucky as you," I teased, not knowing how

Mama was going to react to my statement. Every now and then, I tried to forget how bizarre my relationship with my parents was.

Mama gasped and wobbled against the counter. When she composed herself, she gave me a look that was so sharp, I felt it. My face actually stung. "What's that supposed to mean?" she asked in a hoarse voice. Her breath, drifting into my face, was hot and sour from the onions and other exotic tidbits that she'd been nibbling on. With that and the sting of her sharp words, I almost wobbled against the counter myself.

"I don't think I'll find a man like Daddy," I replied, looking away because I didn't want to see what kind of expression she offered this time.

"You sure won't," she muttered. "Not on this planet. If this Jesse Ray boy is kind to you, be kind to him and you'll be fine. Treat him the same way you would treat a dog you love, and he won't complain. Happy dogs don't complain or stray." My mind flashed on that time I'd seen Mama in bed with another man. If my daddy had been a happy man back then, I could not imagine what he could have done for her to end up in the arms of another man. She must have read my mind. "Too bad it doesn't go both ways. The only woman a man truly respects is his mama." Mama lifted her chin and nodded at me, looking at me out of the corner of her eye. "Always remember that."

Mama gave me a quick nod, which usually meant the conversation was over. But I had more to say, and now was as good a time as any to say it. For the first time in my life, I felt important to somebody other than myself. I'd never felt important to my parents or the many fly-by-night boys I'd gotten high with and fucked for no other reason than them asking. Besides returning to school and getting my diploma, hooking up with Jesse Ray had been the best move I'd ever made in my life.

I didn't like the direction that Mama had taken the conversation, so I took a slight detour. "Jesse Ray asked me to marry him last night," I announced abruptly. "But there are a couple of problems," I mumbled, wiping my eyes and face with the back of my hand. "He wants me to sign a prenuptial agreement."

Mama's mouth dropped open, and the knife almost slipped out of her hand. "How bad is it?" she asked, with a cough. She finally brushed off some of the tears on her face as she chomped on a wedge of onion.

I shrugged and blinked at Mama. "If I divorce him, I get a little money for a year. Not much."

"You call that a problem? If I was a self-made man like he is, I'd want to protect my interests, too. Next?"

"Ma'am?"

"What's the next problem?" Mama asked, turning her attention back to the onions on the counter.

"I might have a few problems with his family," I said, frowning. "They have their own jobs and homes and stuff, but they depend on him for a lot. I don't know if I can deal with that."

Mama let out a heavy sigh and gave me a pitiful look. "Girl, that's what some families do. Don't worry about them until you have to."

"There's something else . . . I don't even know if I love him," I admitted.

"Love?" Mama threw her head back and laughed. No, she howled. She had to wipe tears and snot off her face with the tail of her apron. I gave her an amused look because I didn't know how else to react. It was funny to see her laugh. The skin around her mouth and eyes looked like it was going to crack. But then she got serious again. "Look, girl, love is nothing but a four-letter word. Just like *hell*. Love can't pay your bills."

"But Jesse Ray *loves* me," I said. "That's why he wants to marry me."

"Phttttt!" Mama snapped, giving me a look that was a cross between pity and anger. "Security is what's important in this life," she insisted. A frightened look slid across her face and covered it like a mask.

"What about family?" I asked.

"What about it?" Mama looked away and started talking to me over her shoulder.

"Family is very important to me," I said, hoping that I was opening a door for her to enter.

She turned to me, with more tears in her eyes. "Like I said, security is the most important thing in this life." As if on cue, Daddy shuffled into the kitchen, already in his sleeping attire.

"This girl says that boy wants to marry up with her," Mama told Daddy.

"What boy?" Daddy asked, looking at me like I was a stranger. He wore a drab floor-length housecoat over a pair of plaid pajamas with legs so long, they dragged on the floor. The years had not been kind to my parents. Deep lines ran the length of their faces, and large liver-colored spots covered their hands.

"Jesse Ray, Daddy," I said. "Jesse Ray Thurman."

Daddy looked from Mama to me and shrugged. Then he rolled his eyes and scratched the side of his head. It was obvious that he had no idea who we were talking about.

"Rosetta's boy," Mama said in a stiff voice. "He wants to marry this girl."

Daddy shot me a hot look. Then he squinted and shaded his eyes with his hand and stared at me so hard, I squirmed. "Oh, do you have a boyfriend?" he asked, looking surprised. I was surprised, too. Jesse Ray had been to the house several times and had had conversations with both my parents. "Well, I hope you treat him good so he'll stay with you." As hard as my daddy tried to hide his feelings from me, he got careless every now and then. Like now. Just like Mama a few moments earlier. His eyes blinked a few times, and he tried to keep his lips together, but it didn't work this time. Even though the weak smile didn't stay on his face but a few seconds, that was long enough for me.

"I will, Daddy," I said, glad to see a smile on my daddy's face for a change instead of the usual blank expression. It was an awkward moment for all of us. Mama and Daddy stood in front of me like statues. When I lunged at Daddy and hugged him, he almost fell to the floor. Mama's eyes got wide, and she moved back a step when I turned to hug her, but she opened her arms and hugged me back. As soon as that emotional moment was over, Mama went back to what she was doing, and Daddy snatched open the refrigerator and fished out a beer, then went back into the living room. And I got ready for my date with Jesse Ray.

Compared to Wade, Jesse Ray was a knight in shining armor. But on a warm afternoon in June, as I stood in front of a white-haired, red-faced preacher in a cute little chapel in Reno, about to become Jesse Ray's wife, Wade was the one on my mind.

CHAPTER 40

As a married woman, I felt like a totally different person. I still visited and called Miss Odessa when I could, and I kept in touch with my parents. And that was not easy. I'd been married for two months before I was able to catch up with them and invite them to see the condo I'd moved into with Jesse Ray. Miss Odessa had already let me bring her over for a few visits, and she'd been more excited than I was about me moving into such a nice building in a neighborhood with nothing but professional people.

"And you say you got a doctor and a lawyer in this building?" she'd exclaimed on her last visit, stumbling from one room to another in awe. Even though she'd seen everything more than once already, each time she visited, she acted like she was seeing it all for the first time. "Well, if I fall out up in here and bust up my hip, you run get the doctor downstairs and the lawyer upstairs," she laughed, giving me another one of her bear hugs. "I am so happy for you, baby," she added, with a sniff, looking around my spacious living room. She gasped when she saw my extensive library. One of the six shelves contained a set of encyclopedias. "And I am happy you keeping up with your reading. It's one of the most enriching hobbies a girl like you can have," she told me.

"I have you to thank for that," I admitted. And it was true. Had she not been there across the hall from me when I was younger, with all those magazines and that incomplete set of encyclopedias for me to bury my head in, I might not have ended up where I was now. All that reading had a lot to do with me developing more constructive interests.

I was feeling so good after I drove Miss Odessa home that I slipped a note under my parents' door and invited them to come for a visit. To my surprise, they showed up the following evening, coming by straight after Mama left work at Mr. Bloom's house.

"We can't stay long," Mama told me as she and Daddy entered the living room, looking as grim as ever. It was warm outside, but they both had on long dark coats, and it looked like they had on several layers of clothes under the coats. Mama wore a flowered scarf wrapped around her head like a turban. Daddy had on a wide-brimmed black hat, with a stocking cap on under that. They both wore the same dark, severe-looking shoes with toes so pointed, they looked like missiles. With a few adjustments, they could have passed for Muslims.

They looked out of place in the living room, which I'd recently redecorated with new furniture, all in various shades of gold. Mama couldn't seem to keep her eyes off of my thick brocade drapes and the thick carpets. As soon as I'd hinted to Jesse Ray that his place needed a woman's touch, he'd slapped a credit card in my hand and told me to do whatever I wanted to do as long as it made me happy. "This place don't even look lived in," Mama remarked. I could never tell when she was making a rude statement, lodging a complaint, or paying a compliment.

"Oh, but there is a lot of life between these walls," Jesse Ray said, breaking the uncomfortable silence that had followed Mama's comment. "Now . . . I hope you two can stay long enough to have a few drinks," Jesse Ray said, rising from the La-Z-Boy facing the sofa, where Mama and Daddy had dropped down, still bundled up in their coats. Despite the fact that Mama and Daddy seemed so indifferent toward Jesse Ray, he always greeted them with a smile.

"I was just about to fix myself and Christine some very large drinks, rum and Coke," Jesse Ray said, dancing a jig. "What can I fix for you two fine folks?" he asked, rubbing his hands together. "Let's get this party started," he sang. He motioned toward the new entertainment center I had purchased, across the room, next to a television with a

sixty-inch screen. "What kind of music do you folks want to hear? I got
something for everybody, gospel, reggae, jazz. I've even got a few
blues tapes around here."

Mama looked at Daddy, and then they both looked at Jesse Ray.
The expression on Daddy's face remained the same. He looked as
stiff as a tree. But Mama's mouth dropped open, and she was clearly
horrified. "I don't know what kind of mess this girl's been feeding you
about us, but we don't *party*," she insisted. "But we'll take them drinks.
A beer for Reuben. Onion soup for me," Mama said, with a sniff. I
looked away when she shot me a look of contempt. "Girl, I hope you
don't spend your time partying. I think you done enough of that
when you were younger."

"My party days are over," I muttered. "All I care about now is making my husband happy. Uh, we don't have any beer in the house, and
we certainly don't have any onion soup, but we can sure get some for
you," I said, looking at Jesse Ray, with a pleading look on my face.

He didn't hesitate to respond the way I wanted him to. "Well, it'll
take me just a few minutes to run over to Andronico's to get some
beer and the soup," he said, already moving across the floor to get his
car keys.

I waited until he left before I initiated a conversation. "I'm glad you
both finally came over here," I said, easing down on the wing chair
facing the sofa. "Would you like to see the rest of the place?" I asked,
looking around the room, beaming like a lighthouse.

Mama and Daddy looked at each other again. "Just lead me to the
toilet," Daddy said, with a cough.

"Me, I'd like to see where you cook and sleep," Mama said, rising.
She didn't like the large bed in the master bedroom, whispering to
me that it was proof that Jesse Ray was the dog she thought he was.
"Men like a big playground to do their business," she added. "But you
can nip that in the bud by making him sleep on the sofa from time to
time. After a while that's the only place he'll want to sleep. Your
daddy, he won't leave his sofa now to go to heaven." I laughed, and as
much as Mama tried not to, she did, too.

She thought the kitchen was too big, too, but she didn't say why.

"Mama, I hope you and Daddy will come visit on a regular basis.
You are the only family I have," I said, getting misty-eyed.

"Pfft!" Mama replied, giving me a dismissive wave. "Your man is your family now. We are just part of your background. Point me back to that living room so I can sit down before I fall down."

The beer loosened Daddy up a little. He smiled a few times, even laughed at some joke Jesse Ray repeated that he'd heard from his brother, Harvey. Mama sucked up her onion soup so fast and enjoyed it so much, Jesse Ray had to run out and get her some more. It turned out to be a pleasant evening. Even though Mama and Daddy never removed their coats.

The next few times I took it upon myself to visit my parents, they were as remote and distant as ever. Mama even suggested that I not come to the apartment unless I called first. I called a few weeks later just to see how she was doing, and the first thing that came out of her mouth was, "This is not a good time. Call back later." After hearing that or something like that the last four times I called, I decided to stop calling for a while. When I visited Miss Odessa across the hall, I didn't even bother to knock on my parents' door.

CHAPTER 41

Being married to Jesse Ray was more than I expected. Much more. I was so happy, there were times that I had to pinch myself to make sure I wasn't dreaming. I didn't have to work, and one of the things he put his foot down about during the first year of my marriage was for me to give up my job at the video store. "Baby, you know I can't keep my hands off of you in public, so you'd be doing me a favor by terminating your employment," he'd said, with a grin. I quit my job without hesitation. I was sick of being there, anyway, stocking movie videos and dealing with rude customers. I had much more fun spending my days at the mall, shopping up a storm with platinum credit cards with limits so high, I never had to worry about going over. Jesse Ray was the most generous man I'd ever met. Unfortunately, he was the same way with everybody. And, that turned out to be the first thorn in the side of my new life.

It seemed like people sat around waiting their turn to approach Jesse Ray with one tale of financial woe after another. I lost count of the number of his so-called friends who seemed to drop in out of the sky, but only when they needed some "financial assistance." Given that I was one of the people in that line, needing this or that from Jesse Ray myself, I didn't feel it was my place to interfere. But Miss Odessa thought it was.

"Girl, if anybody got a right to grab Jesse Ray and shake some sense into his head, it's you. At the rate he's doling out his hard-earned money, he's going to end up in the poorhouse and take you with him," she told me in a stern voice.

"I can't tell him what to do with his money," I wailed, sorry now that I'd shared this information with Miss Odessa.

"The hell you can't. He's your husband, and I don't care about no prenup or nothing else. What's his is yours as long as you stay with him!"

I'd been poor most of my life, and it was a condition I never wanted to experience again. Even though I didn't like all the money Jesse Ray was handing out like candy to other folks, I decided to keep my mouth shut for as long as I could. I didn't want to start up something that might backfire. If I talked him out of being so generous to everybody else, there was a possibility that he'd eventually include me in that sweep. I was not ready for a smackdown like that. It had taken me too long to get to where I was.

I was on a long-ass gravy train, and I was enjoying the ride. And, the best part of the ride on that train was that I was in the first car, in a seat next to the conductor. I had more credit cards than I knew what to do with. Within a year I had everything I'd ever wanted: a beautiful four-bedroom house in the affluent Berkeley Hills, a wardrobe fit for a film star, and my own vehicle. Jesse Ray had a lot of friends, both male and female. And, it was not long before I had a whole new set of girlfriends to hang around with. And, these were respectable women with good jobs and strong values.

One day I went to finish my Christmas shopping downtown with one of my closest new female friends. Jeanette Harrison was the ex-wife of Jesse Ray's financial adviser. Walking toward us, moving like she was in pain, was Tina from the old neighborhood. Girlfriend had on some wrinkled, soiled, ill-fitting clothes and a coat that I wouldn't put on a scarecrow. Not only was Tina pregnant, she had two children, both in diapers and howling like wolves, clinging to her. She looked so dowdy, I almost didn't recognize her. And, with my expensive clothes and chic hairdo, she didn't even recognize me at all.

"Now that's a damn shame," Jeanette said to me in a low voice, moving to the edge of the sidewalk as we strolled down Shattuck Avenue. "With all these programs available to women like that these days, there is no excuse for a sister to be out in public looking like a refugee. She reminds me of my trifling folks back in Philly—four generations of women in the same house and every single one on welfare! Whew!"

"It is a shame," I mumbled, turning my head toward the street. I didn't want to see Tina, and I didn't want her to see me. We passed one another like strangers, which was pretty much what we had become.

I didn't like to spend too much time thinking about the people I used to know, but I continued to think about Wade whether I wanted to or not. Other than his mama, the only connection I still had to him was his porn movies. One night when I was home alone, I shoved one of the X-rated movies that Wade had starred in into the VCR. Not only did I find it disgusting to watch, I ended up feeling so sorry for Wade. Even though it was a porn movie with not much of a story line, Wade did display some talent. I sincerely believed that with his determination and ambition, he could have made it as a legitimate entertainer if he'd tried hard enough.

I destroyed the video after I watched it. And, the only good thing that came out of it was the fact that seeing Wade fucking five different women inside out on film had turned me on. Jesse Ray saw a side of me that night that he had never seen before.

"Girl, if I'm not careful, you are going to wear me out. I've never seen you like this before," he managed, almost out of breath. He was so tired and worn-out, he could barely get up out of the bed. "What brought all this on?"

My sex life with Jesse Ray was still just average compared to Wade. However, it was better than it used to be. Jesse Ray didn't do that much in bed, even though he had the kind of equipment that most men would envy. But I never complained. I was so thankful for what I did have. I kept reminding myself of that. Besides, I'd already had my share of good sex before I met Jesse Ray.

As time went on, I continued to visit Miss Odessa on a regular basis. And, as uncomfortable as it was, I also visited Mama and Daddy as often as I could. But the communication lines between me and my parents were still weak. Months would go by without us speaking. They rarely called me up. And, after so many unsuccessful attempts to reach them, I bought them an answering machine. They never acknowledged or returned any of the messages I left. One night, four months after my last visit with my parents, I knocked on their door.

Daddy, wrapped up in all kinds of dark clothes, like a Muslim again, cracked open the door.

"Can you come back some other time? We are not receiving company just now," he told me, talking in a low voice.

"I just wanted to say hi and see how you and Mama were doing," I said quickly. I stuck my foot in the door. "I want you and Mama to know you are always welcome in my house. And, you don't have to call before you come to visit."

Daddy looked at my foot, then back up at me. "Okay," he said. "Go home now. You don't belong here no more. You got that good man in your house, and that ought to be more than enough. Now git!"

Anybody who didn't know any better might have thought that I was a bill collector or a peddler. I didn't even speak again. Instead, I just nodded and slunk out the apartment building's front door.

I had so much going for me now that it took a lot to get me down. But I could always count on somebody in Jesse Ray's family to give me a run for my money. Or Jesse Ray's money, I should say.

It didn't take me long to realize that his family regarded him as a cash cow, which they milked like it was going out of style. Two months after Jesse Ray and I had moved into the new house, Jesse Ray's brother, Harvey, started making regular trips to the house. Harvey had never married, but he'd been living with the same woman for fifteen years, and he'd been working as a baggage handler at Oakland International Airport for twelve years. That told me he was stable in some areas, despite his financial problems. But knowing that he had a job and a woman who had a job made it that much harder for me to sit back and keep my mouth shut. I got so used to gritting my teeth that I started doing it in my sleep. When Jesse Ray told me about it, claiming it woke him up, I just laughed.

"J.R., I need a little favor," Harvey would say, almost every time, five minutes after he'd entered our house. Then he and Jesse Ray would disappear into an unoccupied room. A few minutes later, Harvey would make a hasty getaway. It was not that I didn't like my brother-in-law, but I did not like the way he treated Jesse Ray. Jesse Ray had told me how jealous his siblings were of his success. His being the baby of the family made his position even worse.

"When we were kids, I was always the one that Mama and Daddy used to brag about. I was born with an enterprising spoon in my mouth, they would say. And, if there is one thing parents should not do, it is to brag about one child in front of the others," Jesse Ray said. "And, anyway, what good is money if it can't be enjoyed."

"I agree with you on that. But why should other people benefit from all your hard work? It's bad enough you don't get paid back most of the time." No matter how hard I tried, I couldn't keep my thoughts to myself any longer.

Harvey was enough of a pain in my ass, but Jesse Ray's sister, Adele, was a real piece of work. Not only did she and her husband, Mel, and their two kids stop by the house at least once a week around dinnertime, now they "borrowed" money on a weekly basis, too. It had been bad enough when it happened once in a while, but this was too much. Adele and Mel both had jobs, but when it came to money, they were the most irresponsible people I knew. These people had nothing on Wade's mama. Miss Louise borrowed money like it was going out of style, but she always managed to pay back her loans. Even if it meant borrowing from one person to pay back another. Jesse Ray's relatives rarely paid back any of the money they borrowed from him. I had a major problem with that now, and I told my husband so.

"This is getting way out of hand," I insisted. "They are not going to stop until they bleed you dry, honey."

"Baby, as long as you got everything you want and need, don't get too excited about what I do for my folks. I was doing this way before I met you, and I plan to keep on doing," he told me. "You've just got to remember that there's enough for all of us and you. You are the one getting the biggest piece of the pie."

I didn't like to complain, and I tried to control my tongue when my in-laws got on my nerves. It took a lot of willpower for me to do that.

Harvey was always cordial to me during his brief visits, but Adele eventually made it clear that she had *no* use for me. I hated answering the telephone when she called.

"Put my brother on the phone," was how she usually started, as soon as she realized it was me on the other end of the line. And, when she came to the house, she'd strut right past me without saying a word. The only time that bitch spoke to me was if I spoke to her first. One of the reasons I tolerated her behavior was because I adored my mother-in-law. Miss Rosetta was one of the sweetest people I'd ever met. She had a warm, round face, with a smile that could lighten even the darkest mood. She still lived alone in a little cottage not far from us that Jesse Ray had purchased for her. And she limited her visits and phone calls. She led a very active social life and preferred spending most of her free time with her friends from church and bingo.

When I didn't feel like shopping or spending time with any of the people I'd met through Jesse Ray, or anybody else, I visited Miss Rosetta.

"I appreciate your spending so much of your free time with me, but don't you think you should pay a visit to your own mama from time to time?" Miss Rosetta asked me during my last visit. She knew from conversations with Jesse Ray that I had practically no relationship with my parents. "I'm sure they would enjoy seeing you more often . . . before it's too late."

I didn't answer Miss Rosetta's question. As far as I was concerned, it was already too late.

CHAPTER 42

I was so happy that I didn't even notice how fast time was passing. Jesse Ray and I had been married for eight years when things began to really unravel. For one thing, I had begun to wonder if we'd ever have a family of our own. I loved children, but I had mixed feelings about becoming a mother. And, the reason for that was the fact that my childhood had been so bleak. But for some reason, I felt that I still had to prove to myself that I was incapable of being as cold and remote to my children as my mother was with me.

Jesse Ray had told me on several occasions that it didn't matter one way or the other to him if we ever had children. But it mattered to my mother-in-law. "Maybe if I'm lucky, I will have some grandbabies that I can be proud of," Miss Rosetta told me, half serious. "I have very little use for those two heathens of Adele's," she added. As much as my mother-in-law complained about the only two grandchildren she had so far, she treated them like gold. I got sick of hauling her back and forth to the mall to buy gifts for those two, which they never even acknowledged or thanked her for.

Last year, when she didn't send them a personal check for five hundred dollars each, like she did every year on their birthday, Adele jumped on the telephone the next day and called up Miss Rosetta. Adele told her that the twins had been counting on that money and that it was a damn shame that their own grandmother was "clowning"

them in such a mean way. Like Jesse Ray, Miss Rosetta was too generous and kind for her own good. I drove her to Adele's house to drop
off the checks because neither Adele, the twins, nor their daddy had
time to come get them. The only way she knew the kids got the money
was when she received the cancelled checks in the mail the following
month.

The more I observed people in general, the more I wondered if I
really did want to reproduce. I was afraid that I would repeat history
in more ways than one. There was the situation with me and my parents, which was the oddest relationship between relatives that I'd ever
known. Then there was Miss Odessa and her no-good, grown-ass kids,
who didn't have time for her. Now I had to deal with the in-laws from
hell. Had it not been for Miss Rosetta, it would have been a lot easier
for me to make up my mind. But she made me happy because she was
so kind to me, and I thought that if my having children would make
her happy, it was the least I could do.

The next two years, I fucked Jesse Ray inside out, and nothing happened. I was examined by three different doctors, and each one assured me that everything was in working order. I was fertile and healthy.
The problem was not with me. Jesse Ray was always too busy with his
work to go get checked out himself, assuring me that his equipment
was in tip-top shape, too.

"Well, *somebody's* love juice is too weak," Jeanette told me over coffee in one of the mall coffee shops one Saturday afternoon. "I get
pregnant if a man looks at me hard enough," she said, rolling her big
brown eyes. Jeanette, the real estate agent who'd sold us our house,
had two daughters and three sons by her current live-in boyfriend,
and she'd had two miscarriages with her ex-husband.

"And you don't have to rub it in," I told her, turning to Nita Talbot,
who had six rusty-butt boys, all under the age of twelve. "Do you think
I should take some of those fertility drugs like you did?" Nita's husband was an officer in the military, stationed in Guam. She was a stay-
at-home mom and loved every minute of it.

Jeanette and Nita were cousins who were about as different as night
and day. Nita had never worked a day in her life. Her days revolved
around car pools, bake sales, and PTA meetings. Jeanette was a career
woman. She was almost thirty-five but looked more like twenty-five.
Nita had just celebrated her thirtieth birthday. Jeanette dressed like a
fashion model, even for a casual trip to the mall. Nita lived in sweats,

jeans, and T-shirts. I fell somewhere in the middle. Today I had on jeans and a plain white silk blouse.

It was a big change for me to finally have some females in my life that I could be proud to know. Neither Jeanette nor Nita could ever come between me and Miss Odessa, but it was nice to have friends close to my age, too. And, as it turned out, they liked Miss Odessa almost as much as I did once they met her. They didn't know what to make of my parents. They had only been in their presence a few times, and that had been enough for them.

"Honey, you can take all the fertility drugs, and every other kind of drug in the world if you want to, and it won't help your problem. Your problem is Jesse Ray," Nita informed me.

When my period didn't show up when it was supposed to that weekend, I got hopeful. So hopeful that I went to the bookstore and bought a book with baby names. I was in Wal-Mart later that same day, picking out baby clothes, when I felt a familiar cramp in my side. A reluctant trip to the ladies' room confirmed what I didn't want to know: I was not pregnant.

I got so depressed, I could hardly eat. And, it was only because Jesse Ray got sick of seeing me moping around the house that he came clean.

"Baby, I know you want kids mostly to please mama, but I don't think that's a good enough reason to have kids," he started.

"So? Are you telling me that you don't want any?"

"I didn't say that. If we have some, that's fine. If we don't, that's fine, too. But what if you have kids and regret it? Mama would be happy, but Mama is not going to live forever. Any children you have will be our responsibility long after my mama's gone."

"I know all of that, but it means so much to Miss Rosetta. And, I can't think of any other way to do something to make her happy. She's been so nice to me," I said, a sob in my throat.

Jesse Ray sucked in a deep breath before he continued. There was a look on his face that I didn't know how to interpret. He actually looked scared. I knew that what he had to say next was serious by the way he took my hand in his and started squeezing it. "Baby, I lived with another girl before I got with you. She got pregnant and made me the happiest man in the world. I really wanted kids back then. But when she gave birth to a blue-eyed blond baby, I knew that she wasn't the woman I wanted to spend the rest of my life with."

"The baby wasn't yours?"

"I didn't think it was. Not with blue eyes, blond hair, and skin almost as white as an albino. But she kept going on and on about there being a lot of white folks way up at the top of her family tree." Jesse Ray shrugged and shook his head. "DNA testing was not around back then, so I got myself tested in other ways. My sperm count was, and is, so low, I could fuck every woman in this country from now on and probably not get a single one pregnant."

A wave of depression covered me like a blanket. But that didn't last long. Because the next thing I felt was a wave of relief. I was so emotionally confused, I didn't know how to respond. I couldn't even stand to look at Jesse Ray as I spoke. "So . . . so I'm never going to have a baby?" All of the things that went along with being a parent that I had feared seemed to float right out of my head. But a sharp pain shot through my side when it dawned on me that I'd never fulfill Miss Rosetta's dream.

"I didn't say that. Anything is possible. Think about it, baby. Do you really want to bring a child into this fucked-up world?"

"I don't know what I want to do anymore," I wailed, shaking my head so hard, my teeth rattled. Like doing something like that was going to help me make up my mind about what I wanted. "But why didn't you tell me before now? How could you keep something like this from me for all these years?"

"Because I love you so much that I couldn't stand the thought of losing you," Jesse Ray mouthed, looking at me with tears in his eyes. "Baby, I have so many other things to offer you. And we can still be parents. There are thousands of babies out there that we could choose from. Will you at least think about that?"

"I could divorce you for this," I said. I didn't have the nerve to tell him that in the last few seconds, I had been more relieved than anything. It had been a while since my mother had told me her well-worn story about the forty-eight hours of labor she'd endured to have me, and that horror story was one of the things that had me leaning away from the idea of having children. I hated physical pain.

"Divorce?" Jesse Ray gasped so hard and sucked in so much air, I had to slap him on the back to keep him from choking. "Christine, don't ever say that word in my presence. I love you more than I've ever loved any other woman in my life. Please don't ever even think about divorcing me. Look, I will do anything and everything in the world to make you happy."

I had never seen Jesse Ray look so desperate. However, he had no idea how desperate I was. I was angry and hurt by what he had just told me. But I didn't want to cut off my nose to spite my face. I could still have a full and happy life without a child of my own. And, I wanted to keep the lifestyle that I had grown accustomed to. One thing I didn't want to do was to look back, because I didn't want to see if my past was trying to catch up with me.

I had no way of knowing it at the time, but my past was going to catch up with me, anyway.

CHAPTER 43

I never let on to Jesse Ray that I was more relieved than I was disappointed about us never having children together. The one thing that we did agree to was to not share this information with Miss Rosetta. And certainly not with the rest of my in-laws, because telling any one of them would have been like broadcasting it to the world. I decided that if I told anybody else, it would be Miss Odessa.

Thinking that I was depressed about the whole situation, because I walked around the next few days with a long face, Jesse Ray whisked me off to Hawaii a week after his confession. We had planned to spend two weeks frolicking on the beach in Waikiki and eating in all the best restaurants on the island.

The weather was so nice, I was tempted to walk naked up and down the secluded beach outside our window, like I'd seen a few other women do. But Jesse Ray didn't like that idea, so I wore a wide sarong over my thong bikini.

"I wanted to have a child as much as you did, baby. But I couldn't risk losing you by telling you I couldn't," Jesse Ray told me over a tall pitcher of mai tais on the balcony of our luxury beachfront hotel room. He wore a flowered, short-sleeved shirt and a pair of baggy shorts. Earlier that morning, before I woke up, he'd gone out and picked flowers, which he had pinned to my hair. He was doing every little thing he could to help me get over what he'd told me. I was enjoying all the extra attention, so I decided to "milk that cow" dry.

"But I found out, anyway," I said, feeling light-headed. I had already had three drinks and was working my way through the fourth. Jesse Ray nodded and looked away. "If we want this marriage to work, we have to be open and honest," I said. "About everything. I don't care how small a situation seems to you, if it involves me, I want to know about it. And I want you to be one hundred percent honest. You can expect the same from me," I stated, looking my husband in the eye so hard, he had to blink and look away again.

I was learning more and more about Jesse Ray each day. One thing that was clear to me now was that he was the kind of man who always said what he thought somebody wanted to hear. That had a lot to do with his success. However, I didn't think that that was a good characteristic to apply to marriage.

It didn't take me long to realize that I was going to do the same thing to Miss Rosetta. I knew she would continue to badger me about having a baby. And, I was all prepared to tell her one lie after another about why I didn't get pregnant. The best one I could come up with was the one about me having a tilted womb. I had read about a woman with that same problem in one of Miss Odessa's magazines years ago. It was the kind of lie that I could get a lot of mileage out of. And, since Miss Rosetta was already in her golden years, I didn't think that I'd have to use it for too many more years. It saddened me to know that I could deliberately deceive someone I loved. But that's exactly what Jesse Ray had done to me! I told myself that if Miss Rosetta made too much of a fuss about having more grandchildren, Jesse Ray and I could take in a few foster children. That way if they started acting a fool, like so many kids I knew, we weren't obligated to keep them.

Jesse Ray coughed and cleared his throat, interrupting my thoughts. I was glad he did, because my mind was off on a tangent. "That's the way it'll be from now on. In that case . . . ," he said, then paused, scratched his neck, and gave me a mysterious look. His eyes roamed up and down the entire length of my body. "Please dispose of that sarong as soon as you can. It makes you look like a piñata." I bolted from my seat and ran into one of the two spacious bathrooms in our suite. Behind the door was a full-length mirror. I didn't agree with Jesse Ray's assessment of my appearance, but I changed into some white shorts and a plain halter top, anyway.

The best thing about the sudden vacation was the fact that nobody knew where to reach us. Well, I had told Miss Odessa and Jeanette and Nita, but I'd made them promise not to call me unless it was a matter of life and death. At the last minute, before we left the house, I called and left the same information on the answering machine that I had bought for Mama and Daddy. But I wasn't even sure that they'd use it, even if one of them died.

When Jeanette called me eight days into my vacation, the first thing I said to her was, "Woman, somebody better be dead."

There was a long pause before she told me. "Your mother-in-law had a massive stroke last night."

CHAPTER 44

One of the advantages of not having a lot of family or other loved ones is that you don't have too many people to worry about losing to death, unlike people with large, close-knit families. I loved Miss Odessa. I loved my parents dearly despite their peculiarities. And, as ghoulish as it was, I often wondered how I was going to react to their passing. I had added Jesse Ray and Jeanette and Nita to that list because I loved them all dearly, too. I wasn't particularly crazy about Adele and her clan, or Harvey and the Chinese woman he lived with, Flossie Ming Lee, but I had come to adore Miss Rosetta. She was as much a loving mother to me as she was to Jesse Ray and his two siblings. One of the first thoughts that had shot through my head after Jeanette's call was the fact that I had cooked up that lie to feed to Miss Rosetta about me not having babies for her to fuss over. I felt worse than shit, and I wasn't too far from it. Because right after I got off the telephone with Jeanette, I ran into the bathroom and I threw up from both ends.

Jesse Ray and I immediately cancelled the rest of our vacation and booked a reservation on the first available plane back to California. Neither one of us ate or drank anything during the five-hour flight. We must have looked like pallbearers, sitting there, with our long faces and tear-stained eyes. It seemed like I was taking it harder than

Jesse Ray. I couldn't stop crying. By the time the plane landed, I looked like a Panda bear, the dark circles around my eyes were so profound.

"She don't know nobody. She can't even speak or move," Harvey told us in the car on the way from the airport. There was so much traffic that the freeway looked like a parking lot. I had so many knots in my stomach, and the inside of my nose was so dry, I had to breathe through my mouth. Even though I knew that Miss Rosetta would not know if I was there or not, I didn't want to be in the same room with her until I could get a grip on myself.

"What does the doctor say?" Jesse Ray asked in a weak and tired voice, looking straight ahead. He was in the front passenger seat of the new Altima that he'd cosigned for Harvey to get last year.

I was huddled in a corner in the backseat, directly behind Jesse Ray. I knew that it was not the time and place, but I couldn't stop myself from thinking about the fact that Harvey had defaulted on his loan after the first two payments. When the bank didn't receive the third payment three weeks after its due date, they promptly called Jesse Ray. When Jesse Ray confronted Harvey about the past-due payment, Harvey offered up some sob story about losing his wallet and trying to borrow the money. He eventually did find somebody fool enough to lend him enough money to make the delinquent car payment, plus pay the late charges: Jesse Ray. Six months and six payments into the loan, Jesse Ray was still the one making the payments.

"Mama ain't never going to be the same," Harvey said in a shaky voice. For a brief moment, I thought he was going to burst into tears. And, from the way he looked, I guessed that he'd already shed quite a few tears. His eyes were red and swollen. But that was nothing new. His heavy drinking and the late hours that he and Flossie Ming Lee kept hanging out in the casinos in Reno were usually responsible for his haggard appearance. "The doctor done already told us that she'll probably need round-the-clock attention from now on. She won't be able to live on her own no more," Harvey reported, his voice cracking.

I loved my mother-in-law, and I knew that I was going to jump in and do whatever I had to do to make the rest of her days comfortable. And, when Harvey announced that she would no longer be able to live on her own, my first thought was that he would jump at the chance to move himself and Flossie in with her so they could live rent free.

They had attempted to move in with Miss Rosetta before, but she had vigorously opposed it. Harvey didn't waste any time removing that idea from my mind.

"Me, I can't see myself moving up in there with Mama to take care of her. Not with my bad back and high blood pressure. Flossie Ming's mama is over there in San Francisco, driving everybody in Chinatown up and down the wall. She's been flat on her back for six years. I hope I don't live long enough to be that kind of a burden to nobody," Harvey said, with a heavy sigh.

"Well, we've got to come up with some kind of a plan," I offered, wringing my hands. "Baby, what about a live-in nurse?" I suggested, gently tapping Jesse Ray on the shoulder.

"I'll look into that right away. But in the meantime, we all got to do what we have to do," Jesse Ray said. He turned around and gave me a pleading look.

"Christine, you are the only one home all day, doing nothing. All the rest of us got jobs," Harvey stated. I didn't know where this conversation was going, and at the time I didn't care. My main concern was my beloved mother-in-law. "I hope you don't mind keeping an eye on Mama until we come up with a better plan. She's crazy about you, and I know she'd appreciate you doing that for her. And, God'll bless you for it, too. I tell my brother all the time what a good woman he married." Harvey paused and glanced at me through the rearview mirror. There was a pleading look on his face, which would have been more than enough to back me into a corner of submission. But it wasn't even necessary.

"I'll do whatever I can to help out," I stated. I didn't know what else to say. The last thing I wanted to do was make Jesse Ray feel even worse by saying something stupid or something that sounded selfish and uncaring. But in the back of my mind, I had to ask myself, *Girl, what are you getting yourself into now?*

CHAPTER 45

There were also some disadvantages to not having much of a family. I knew that if I outlived my parents, one day I would probably have to provide some level of caretaking services to them. The entire responsibility would land smack-dab on my shoulders.

The fact that Mama and Daddy rarely showed me any affection didn't matter. I cared about them. I was proud of myself for being able to say this and mean it. I used to know people who despised their parents. And, one of the boys I used to sleep around with used to beat up his own mother.

Since Mama and Daddy were the only blood relatives I had, this issue was especially important to me. Especially now that I knew I'd never have a child of my own—at least not with Jesse Ray. They were still my parents, and I was still going to be there for them. They had both been in their forties when they conceived me, so the chances of them falling apart not that far into the future were pretty high. The last time I visited the apartment on Prince Street, Daddy looked like he was about to keel over at any minute. He'd lost most of his hair and was losing the vision in one eye. Mama complained about dizzy spells and an assortment of other ailments. Despite all of these obstacles, they both continued to work for Mr. Bloom.

Miss Odessa had one foot in the grave, and had for years, for that matter. Her days of independence were numbered. She was losing her memory and was using a walker to get around with now. But she had children and other relatives who I was sure would step up to the plate should she have some serious physical setback. As much as I loved this sweet old sister, I was thankful that I didn't have to worry about her well-being, too. But never in my wildest imagination did I think I'd end up taking care of an elderly invalid, anyway. And that's exactly what happened!

I could not believe how Jesse Ray and the in-laws ganged up on me. Instead of hiring a full-time live-in nurse to take care of Miss Rosetta in the house that Jesse Ray had bought for her, they insisted on moving her in with Jesse Ray and me so that it would be easier for me to attend to her needs. The only thing that kept me from screaming was the fact that this was supposed to be a temporary solution. Every single one of my in-laws (some in other states, whom I'd never met) constantly justified this decision by reminding me that I was the only one who had nothing to do, anyway, but lie around the house all day, watching Jerry Springer and Oprah, and getting fat.

It didn't take long for Jesse Ray to use that same "excuse" to lock me into a responsibility that I did not deserve. Miss Rosetta had to be fed, bathed, and clothed like a baby. It was so ironic, and it seemed so unfair, that I even had to diaper her like a baby, too. Just like I would have done for the baby I would never have with Jesse Ray. As much as I loved Miss Rosetta, by the end of the first week, I was ready to jump off the Golden Gate Bridge.

I thanked God for the well-timed visit from Jeanette and Nita that following Monday morning. It derailed my plan to commit suicide. Jesse Ray had already left to go to work. I loved my man dearly, and he was a good man by anybody's standards, but he often did things that made no sense to me. He didn't open for business until ten each morning. And he kept all three of the video stores open every night until eleven, seven nights a week, 365 days a year. Several times a week, he spent a couple of hours at the main store *after* closing time, tying up loose ends that he never explained. When I tried to pry more information about these "loose ends," they became "this and that."

Anyway, since the man didn't open until ten and he took care of the loose ends at night, I could not understand why he went to work every morning before dawn. This was something that I discussed with Jeanette and Nita on a regular basis. This Monday morning was no different.

"Maybe he's got him a chick on the side," Jeanette said, with a laugh.

"That's the least of my worries," I told her, leading her and Nita into the kitchen, where I'd already put on a pot of fresh coffee. "And speaking of work, why aren't you at yours?" I asked Jeanette. "And what is your story?" I asked Nita. "Shouldn't you be at home, baking cookies, little mama?"

"This is about you," Nita told me, touching my hand. I sat down hard at the table. Jeanette and Nita helped themselves to a cup of coffee, then joined me at the table.

"So do you two hens want to tell me what this surprise visit is all about?" I asked, looking from one to the other. Jeanette, with her smooth dark skin and almond-shaped eyes, looked like Naomi Campbell and was dressed like her, too. She wore a white silk blouse, a brown suede skirt, and boots that matched her skirt. Nita, shorter, heavier, and much lighter skinned than Jeanette and me, had on a muumuu under a yellow Windbreaker. A yellow scarf hid some of the pink sponge rollers covering her head. She had on a pair of men's house shoes that had seen better days. Both she and Jeanette carried Gucci purses.

"Christine, I want to take you to lunch. I want to do something good for you because I know you need a break," Jeanette informed me.

"I can't go today," I said, holding up my hand. "You know my situation. I can't just up and leave the house like I used to," I said, nodding toward the living room, where Miss Rosetta was propped up in the wheelchair that Jesse Ray had purchased for her. "I have to find somebody to stay with Miss Rosetta every time I leave the house."

"And that's a damn shame," Nita shouted.

"It's just during the day. At night, when Jesse Ray comes home, he takes care of her," I explained in a weak voice, still looking toward the room where Miss Rosetta was withering away like a dying plant. I didn't bother to tell my friends that my husband's idea of "taking care" of his own mother meant him inspecting her from head to toe to make sure I'd cleaned her properly. All he had to do was help me haul her to bed.

"And what's there for you to do that time of day, or night? Everything is closed except the strip clubs by the time Jesse Ray unhooks himself from his precious video store," Jeanette wailed. "Girlfriend, we know what you are going through, and there is not a whole lot we can do about it. But you don't have to be in this situation if you don't want to be."

"I know I don't, and I won't be as soon as . . . as soon as . . ." I couldn't even finish that sentence, because I didn't have a backup plan. "Jesse Ray keeps putting off hiring someone to come to the house to take care of his mother, and Adele and Harvey scream like hyenas every time I mention putting her in a nursing home. I can't go to lunch with you heifers today," I said, blinking hard and shaking my head. "I can't leave Miss Rosetta alone, and I can't take her with me."

"That's why I'm here," Nita told me. "Miss Thing is going to take you to lunch and a movie if you feel up to it. I'm going to stay here and keep Miss Rosetta company."

Tears immediately formed in my eyes. "I can't do that to you," I hollered, blinking hard to hold back my tears. "Miss Rosetta has to be watched like a baby. I have to move her around, from her bed to her wheelchair, and then turn her over so she won't get sores. I have to change her . . . underwear, too. I couldn't do that to you."

"But you're letting your husband and the rest of those motherfuckers do it to you!" Nita shouted. "Look, Christine, I grew up in a house with both sets of my grandparents and my great-grandmother living with us—all at the same time. There was never a time when there wasn't some old crow interfering with my plans. Especially during my teen years. You are not doing anything now that I didn't do then. And this time, I'm offering to do it. Back then I didn't have a choice. Mama made us all help out."

"I haven't been to lunch during the day in . . . since Miss Rosetta got sick," I said, staring at the wall.

"Well, you are going to lunch during the day today with me. Even if I have to carry you on my back. Case closed," Jeanette said, waving a threatening finger in my face.

Nita, with her short but stout arms, removed Miss Rosetta from her wheelchair and transferred her to her bed in one of the downstairs bedrooms like it was the most natural thing in the world. I took a shower, pulled my hair into a ponytail, and put on a pair of slacks that were still on the hanger, with the price tag still pinned to the waistband. I had dozens of new outfits that I had not worn.

Jeanette let me pick the restaurant. There were a lot of places for me to choose from, but Giovanni's was closer, and it was one of my favorite spots. I had spent a lot of evenings at Giovanni's, nibbling on pizzas and garlic bread with some of the wild crowd I used to hang out with. It was a favorite spot for a lot of people. I had forgotten that it was one of the places where Wade used to hang out back in the day before he moved to L.A.

Our friendly waiter, an Asian woman with a waist-length ponytail, escorted us to a booth in the back, facing the fireplace. If we had come a minute later, it would have made all the difference in the world. Wade was on his way out, leaving a table just a few feet away from us.

"Christine? Girl, look at you. I'm scared of you! I heard you got married," he said, rushing over to me. I didn't recognize the tall, lanky, sad-faced man with him, and Wade suddenly seemed like he'd forgotten him. I almost collapsed when Wade leaned over and wrapped me in his arms, covering my face with lip-smacking, loud, hungry little kisses. For a moment I almost forgot where I was. I had to squeeze my thighs together to keep my crotch from itching. Wayne's touch was still enough to arouse me!

I blinked hard, and I wanted to fan my face, because it felt like it was on fire. Instead, I lowered my eyes and grinned, hugging Wade back. I think that for a moment he forgot where he was, too. His embrace was so strong and extended, I had to pull away. But only after Jeanette cleared her throat and kicked my foot under the table.

"Uh, this is my friend Jeanette," I said, introducing them. From the look on Jeanette's face, she was enjoying every minute of this scenario. Her back was to the fireplace. The flames from the fire illuminated her face, making her look ghoulish. And, the amused and curious look on her face only enhanced her ghoulishness.

"I'm Wade," he said, shaking Jeanette's hand. "Me and Christine go way back," he said and grinned, giving me a wink. "We used to be real close."

"I figured that," Jeanette remarked just loud enough for me to hear. I kicked her foot and shot her a threatening look because she had a stupid look on her face.

"How long are you in town?" I asked Wade. Before he could answer, I turned to Jeanette. "Wade's in show business and lives in L.A.," I told her. She had raised her eyebrows so high that it looked like they'd relocated to the top of her forehead.

"Uh, I'm not sure," Wade said, glancing around and scratching the side of his neck. "Hey! This is Dave Sauer. He's an old friend, too."

Wade slapped his friend on the back. It was obvious that Wade didn't want to talk about his career. I suspected that things were not going the way he wanted them to. For one thing, I still had not seen him in anything on television or in the movies. Not even a commercial. At least nothing legitimate. However, I had come across two more porno- graphic videos that he had starred in, both just last year! I couldn't re- member the titles, and I had not even viewed them.

"How are you ladies doing?" Wade's friend asked, shaking my hand, then Jeanette's. "One thing I can say about Wade is, him and beautiful women go together. And, both of you ladies are at the top of the line."

I glanced at Jeanette. She was blushing just as hard as I was.

"How's married life treating you?" Wade asked.

"It's . . . it's nice," I said quietly and slowly. I looked in Wade's eyes and blinked. "Marriage is a blessing."

"I feel you on that one. I couldn't agree with you more."

"Oh. You're married now?" I asked, my heart slowly breaking into a million little pieces. I sniffed and straightened up in my seat.

"I was, but it didn't work out." My question seemed to make Wade uncomfortable. "Well, it was nice seeing you again. You sisters enjoy your lunch." Wade gave me a light slap on my back, smiled, nodded at Jeanette, and turned to leave.

Jeanette opened her big mouth, but before she could speak, Wade returned to our table.

"Christine, if you'd like to have a drink or something, here's my cell number," Wade said, handing me a napkin with his number writ- ten on it in red ink. Then he was gone. I turned to Jeanette. That stu- pid look was still on her face, and now her arms were folded, too.

"What?" I snapped, stuffing the napkin into my purse. "I know what you're thinking, and you are dead wrong. Yes, Wade and I had a real hot thing going at one time. But, I'm a married woman now."

"I've only got one thing to say, Miss Thing," Jeanette said as she sucked in her breath and placed her arms on the table, giving me a look that was so serious, it scared me. "With the way things are going for you these days, you'd better hold on tight to that number. If you don't use it, pass it on to me."

CHAPTER 46

Miss Rosetta rapidly went even further downhill. She didn't eat much and spent most of her time sleeping. In a way, it looked like she had lost her will to live, like she didn't want to be around any longer. At least not the way she was. But the truth of the matter was, she was not going to get any better. Dr. Haywood and two other doctors had assured us that she would never walk or talk again. She would have to be cared for like a baby until the day she died. And that saddened me. What saddened me even more was the fact that I didn't want her to go on, either. Not because I had come to hate her. I still adored my mother-in-law. But because she'd become such a burden to me. I could not count the number of times in a day that the sight of her gave me thoughts so evil, they made my flesh crawl. I had known some despicable people along the way, but I had never wished anybody dead. And I certainly didn't wish that on Miss Rosetta. What I really wanted was for her not to be my burden anymore. Her death was not the only solution. I got angry when I tried to address the situation with Jesse Ray, because it never did much good.

"I don't see why you won't hire a nurse to come to the house . . . at least a couple of times a week," I said. I had just bathed and fed Miss Rosetta while Jesse Ray kicked back in his La-Z-Boy, with a beer in front of the television. It was the first night that week that he had come home from work before ten, and that was only to watch and record an episode of *The Sopranos* that he didn't want to miss.

"You know why I can't hire a nurse," he said, not taking his eyes away from the television screen and speaking out of the side of his mouth. "I can't afford it right now. I just bailed Harvey out of that mess with his taxes. Mama can't be that much trouble. She sleeps most of the time, so I don't know what you got to complain about."

"I have to bathe her. I have to wipe the woman's butt hole, J.R. Do you think I enjoy doing that every day? Do you think I enjoy having to find somebody to come sit with your mother whenever I want to go somewhere?" Since Jesse Ray refused to turn around to face me, I shot across the floor and stood in front of the television. That shook him up real fast.

"Christine, do we really need to discuss this now?" he asked. He motioned with his hand for me to move.

I moved away from the television and sat on the arm of his chair. "I make doctor appointments that I often have to reschedule because I can't find a babysitter. I can't even visit my own parents like I want to. I'm a young woman, but I'm beginning to feel like my life is over, too."

"What do you want me to do? Other than hire a nurse," he said, staring straight ahead. He took a sip from his can of beer and patted the side of my thigh.

I didn't like looking at the side of his head, but I did as I continued talking. "Adele and Harvey have not done a damn thing for Miss Rosetta since she had her stroke. Not once has either one of them offered to sit with her, bathe her, feed her, or anything else. They come over here after I've done it all, and then they sit around talking about how they are not going to let us put Miss Rosetta in a home. And, that bitch Adele, she even told me to my face, no nurse was going to come up in here and abuse her mama."

Jesse Ray whirled around to face me, with his eyes wide open and both his eyebrows arched. "I would appreciate you not calling my only sister a bitch."

I leaped up and gave him the dirtiest look that I could manage. "Fuck her and fuck you, too." With one hand on my hip and my other hand balled into a fist, I stormed out of the living room and stomped all the way to my bedroom. I ignored Jesse Ray when he came to bed, naked and pawing me all over. One of the things I couldn't under-

stand and hated about men was how they always tried to use sex like it
was some kind of an elixir when a woman was mad, sad, lonely, or anything else they considered to be negative. I pinched his dick and
kicked the side of his leg so hard, he almost rolled off the bed. He left
me alone after that.

I don't know when I went to sleep, but around midnight I woke up.
Jesse Ray was sitting on the side of the bed. I was glad to see that he
was no longer naked. He had on his navy blue silk pajamas and the
white terry-cloth housecoat that I'd given to him last Christmas.

"Baby, I just had a long talk with Adele. Uh, we came up with a solution. She's, uh, having some problems with Mel. I told her years ago
not to marry Mel Howard. That man, and most of the men in the
Howard family, are straight-up dogs. Did you know that his granddaddy's brother is in prison for life for killing his girlfriend?"

"Do you think there's a chance that Mel might kill Adele?" I asked,
my voice dripping with sarcasm and hope.

"That's not funny, Christine," Jesse Ray scolded. "I love my sister,
and when she's in pain, I'm in pain."

I sat up so fast, I pulled a muscle in my back. "And what about when
I'm in pain?"

"I feel your pain, too, baby. I've never loved a woman the way I love
you."

"I hope you never will," I said in a tired voice. I lay back down,
keeping my eyes on Jesse Ray's face because I wanted to see his expression when he finished what he had to say. Since it involved Adele,
I already knew that it was going to be something that pissed me off.

"So what is Adele's pain this time?" I hissed.

"Uh, like I said. The men in the Howard family are dogs. Anyway,
Mel's been drinking up a storm, just lost his job, and he's hit her a few
times. Tonight some woman claiming to be Mel's whore called the
house looking for him, and that was more than Adele could stand. I
told her to bring the kids over here for a few weeks. That way she'll be
away from Mel, and she'll be here in the house to help you out with
Mama before and after she goes to work. And, I made it clear to her
that Mama is her responsibility on the weekends and in the evenings,
when she comes in from work. The twins can help out, too. That's the
least they can do for their own grandmother after all she's done for
them. Most kids don't get five hundred dollars from Grandma every

year for their birthday like those kids did." Jesse Ray sniffed hard and touched the side of my face. "That's the best I can do for Mama, you, and Adele and the kids."

I didn't know how to respond. Miss Rosetta was a handful, but the thought of living in the same house with Adele was a nightmare that I refused to think about.

I stared at Jesse Ray, with my mouth hanging open. My lips were moving, but no words were coming out. I had to clear my throat before I could speak again. "You what?" I couldn't believe how hoarse I sounded now. Black bile and hot sour air rose in my throat. "You told Adele, she and her kids could move in with us, without discussing it with me? You know your sister hates my guts, J.R."

"Well, if you can come up with a better solution, please let me know. In the meantime, my sister and her kids will be here tomorrow evening. I know it'll be rough at first, but you'll get used to it. I want to see a smile on your face again."

"You want to see a smile on my face again, and you think that moving Adele and her kids in here will make me smile?"

"Christine, I am just trying to help this situation. Until I can afford to hire a nurse, you'll have some help now in the evenings and on weekends. Now you can go do whatever you need or want to do during those hours." Jesse Ray paused and rubbed his head. I didn't like the tortured look on his face. "But if you really don't want them here, I'll call Adele right now and tell them not to come." He paused again and sniffed, looking around the room. "I guess I could get her a hotel suite somewhere for a little while."

I opened my mouth to speak again, but I couldn't. I didn't want Adele and her kids to move in with us, and I didn't want Jesse Ray to pony up the money for them to move into a hotel. Knowing Adele, she and those kids would be at that hotel from now until eternity. And not some flophouse or dingy hostel! She would insist on something expensive. Just like she did with everything else when it was coming out of my husband's pocket. That bitch!

I didn't sleep the rest of that night. But that morning I did smile again for the first time in days. Right after Jesse Ray gave me a sloppy kiss and ran out the door and climbed into his SUV, I dialed the telephone number that Wade had given to me.

CHAPTER 47

"Um . . . hello, Wade. This is Christine," I stammered.

"I know who it is," he laughed. "You don't have to identify yourself, girl. I'll never forget your voice."

"When we were kids, you used to forget my name." I said it in a light, teasing voice, but I was serious.

"We ain't kids no more, baby," he said in that seductive tone of voice that I'd never forgotten. That was all it took to make me tremble. The fact of the matter was, he had offered his phone number, so he must have really wanted to be with me again. I had not, and would not have, asked him for it. The situation at home had made me so bitter over the last few months, I didn't need to add to it by chasing after a man that didn't want to be caught. At least not by me.

"I think I need that drink you offered," I replied. Jesse Ray was just pulling out of our garage and onto the street. I was at the living-room window, with the drapes parted. I could see out onto the street with one eye, and I could still keep the other eye on Miss Rosetta, who was propped up in her wheelchair in front of the television. She couldn't talk, but she could moan and whimper when she wanted some attention. And I knew that she could hear. But since she couldn't speak or communicate any other way, I didn't bother whispering into the telephone.

As a matter of fact, I was glad she could hear my end of the conversation. Of all my in-laws, Miss Rosetta was the only one who had ever been on my side. I knew she loved her son, but I'd got to know her well enough to know that she would not have approved of what was happening to me. I recalled all the times she used to tell me, "Girl, J.R. is my son, but don't you let him, or no other man, make a fool out of you." Miss Rosetta's words rang in my head as I waited for Wade to respond. He'd already made a fool out of me. He had used me. But it had made me stronger and smarter. Now I would use him.

"I've been expecting to hear from you," he said, then laughed. "And I'm glad to hear from you."

"Can we meet at Giovanni's in a couple of hours?" I said in a bold voice.

Wade took his time responding. "You want me to make love to you, don't you?" he asked, saying the words loud and strong, like he wanted to make sure I heard him right.

"No, I want you to fuck me," I told him. He got silent again. I immediately wished that I could take back my words. All of a sudden, I felt uncomfortable. So uncomfortable that I wanted to hang up the telephone and tear the napkin with his phone number on it to shreds. Despite everything, I was a married woman. And, even though it was a struggle now, I still cared about my husband. However, the relationship that I had with my husband and his family now was the reason I'd called Wade in the first place! My face ached because I suddenly smiled in a way that was literally painful.

I didn't know what to say next. Wade must have felt the same way, because neither one of us spoke again for several moments. I didn't know what was going through his mind. There were things going through mine that I could not ignore. Like the way he'd treated me that other time I saw him at Giovanni's and the way he'd treated me when I had turned up on his doorstep in L.A. But we were a lot older now. And, I didn't know about him, but I was a lot wiser than I'd been in my youth.

"Uh, Giovanni's is cool, but I think we'd be more comfortable at my place. Well, my mama's place. I'm staying with her for a while. When do you want to hook up?"

"What's your mama's schedule for the next few days? I don't want to visit when she's there."

"She's at a friend's house, getting ready to go to Reno with her. She'll be gone for the next four days."

"I'll get there as fast as I can," I assured him.

I was sweating so hard when I got off the telephone, I had to drink two glasses of iced water and place a cold, wet paper towel across my face.

I was so excited, I could already feel myself getting wet between my legs. My hands were shaking so violently, I had a hard time dialing Nita's telephone number. She answered on the first ring.

"Can you come over and sit with Miss Rosetta for a little while?" I said. Even though it was before nine in the morning, I knew Nita was probably still asleep. She usually went back to bed after she got the kids off to school.

"Who is this?" she asked, letting out a loud breath.

"You know who it is. Shit!"

"What's up?" Nita asked, laughing. "Girl, some of us are still in bed. Where are you going this early?"

My silence gave me away.

"You nasty puppy you," she said and laughed. "What took you so long? Jeanette and I were wondering how long it was going to take before you hooked up with your hunk from the past. I'll be there as soon as I can get dressed." She paused and laughed some more before she hung up.

I had already bathed, dressed, and fed Miss Rosetta. She was staring at the television when Nita arrived, in a see-through raincoat over her pajamas and her hair still in rollers, less than twenty minutes after I'd called her up.

"I didn't expect you to get here this fast," I told Nita as she entered my living room, with her keys in one hand and a large cup from Starbucks in the other. I looked at my watch.

"You sounded desperate," she said and grinned. She lowered her voice to a whisper when she realized Miss Rosetta was in the room. "Where is he?"

"At his precious video store by now, I guess," I said, with an annoyed shrug.

"I don't mean J.R. I meant . . . that long-legged piece Jeanette keeps telling me about. Wayne."

"Wade," I corrected. "He's at his mama's house," I whispered back, patting my hair. I had pulled it into a ponytail, which was the most practical hairdo I could think of for what I was about to do.

"All I can say is, you deserve to have a good time." Nita looked at

Miss Rosetta and back to me, shaking her head so hard, one of her rollers fell out. "I'll stay with Miss Rosetta for as long as you want me to," she said, catching the roller in her hand and returning it to its place on her head. Nita was the only sister I knew who didn't perm her hair or bother with wigs, hairpieces, or weaves. But of all the women I knew, she was the one who spent the most time rolling and unrolling her hair. "Or at least until I have to go pick up the kids from school." Nita touched my face. "You look a little more disgusted than usual. Did something else happen?"

"Adele and her crew are moving in this evening," I said in a flat voice, through clenched teeth.

"Fuck me!" Nita gasped. "Girl, I will get a prayer chain going for you because you are going to need that and more." Then she wrapped her arms around me, rubbing my back. "Christine, I don't mean to get up in your business, but you need to sit down with your husband and have a long talk with him. You are nursing *his* mama, and now you are telling me that you are going to have to play hostess to his sister and her family, and I would not want a flirt like Melvin Howard in my house. How Adele can stay married to that pig is a mystery to me."

"Mel's not coming. As a matter of fact, he's the reason Adele and the kids are moving out for a while," I said and sighed. I glanced at my watch again. "I'll be back as soon as I can," I added. I grabbed my sweater off the coatrack by the door and ran out of the house.

Wade was standing on his mama's front porch, with his hands on his hips, when I pulled onto his street. He had on a pair of jeans and a light blue shirt, which was unbuttoned. His well-developed chest, his gray eyes, and full, wet lips were almost enough to hypnotize me. I parked my car in front of the house and jumped out so fast, one of my shoes came off.

CHAPTER 48

When I married Jesse Ray, I'd promised myself that I would honor my vow and be a faithful wife. But since things had changed so drastically since my wedding day, that damned vow was the last thing on my mind when Wade carried me in his arms upstairs to his bedroom. I didn't *plan* on establishing an ongoing affair or even seeing him again after today. So I had to make every minute of this rendezvous count. Shit!

I was so turned on, I couldn't even wait until I got out of all of my clothes. I jumped on Wade like a tiger and sat on his face so hard, he couldn't breathe. The last thing I wanted to do was smother the man, so I rolled off just long enough for him to catch his breath. I don't even remember how the rest of my clothes ended up in a heap on the floor.

"You still got it," he told me, sliding off my quivering body to his side of the bed after our first session. "After all these years, you still got it." He blew out a breath and sat up, looking down at me. My ponytail had come undone, so my hair was all over my head, and a thick lock partially covered my eyes.

"I was surprised to see you back in Berkeley, and even more surprised that you wanted to see me again," I said, brushing my hair back. I was breathing so hard, my chest hurt.

"Why wouldn't I want to see you again? We were always good together," Wade said, giving me a surprised look of his own.

"But it wasn't always good for us. I'd like to forget that little episode in L.A. when I showed up at your door," I said.

"Things have changed. You're not a little girl anymore," he said and laughed, slapping my naked thigh. A door slammed downstairs, and we both froze.

"Shit!" Wade hissed, holding a hand up in my face. "Stay here. Don't make no noise," he told me, struggling to get back into his jeans. He left the room, running his fingers through his hair. "Shit! Mama's back. What the fuck did she forget this time?"

With the door to his bedroom closed, I couldn't hear much of what was going on downstairs. But I could hear Miss Louise's throaty voice. I got up and put my ear to the door long enough to hear her tell Wade that she had come back to get her lucky cigarette lighter. Then she asked him for a hundred dollars so she could go play keno when she lost the rest of the money that she had when she got to Reno. His response was so low and muffled, I couldn't understand what he said. But when I heard him padding back up the stairs in his bare feet, I ran back to the bed.

"Hey, baby. Listen, I'm going to have to make a quick run," he whispered, even though he'd closed the door behind him. "I'm a little short on cash," he said, sliding into his shoes. "One of my homeboys owes me a few bucks."

"You need a ride?" I asked, rising.

"No, baby. You stay right where you at. I don't want Mama to know you are up here."

"But my car is out front," I reminded, scrambling around for my clothes.

"That don't mean nothing. That car could belong to anybody. I should be back in about ten minutes. My boy lives just around the corner."

I didn't want to be left alone. I didn't want Wade out of my sight until I was finished with him. "How much do you need?"

"I don't need nothing. It's for Mama. You know how she is about her keno and shit. A hundred-dollars would do it." I immediately opened my purse and plucked out a crisp hundred dollar bill. As soon as I held it up, Wade held up both hands and shook his head. "Baby, you don't have to do that." I noticed how weak his protest was.

At the same time he was turning the money down with his mouth, he was reaching for it with both hands.

"I'll pay you back as soon as I can," he said, moving toward the door.

I didn't plan on seeing Wade again, so I didn't expect him to pay me back the money. So I planned on fucking the hell out of him as soon as he got rid of his mama. That was worth more than a hundred dollars to me.

Wade didn't promise me anything about seeing me again before I left his mama's house, with a massive grin on my face because I had been fucked the way I should have been fucked. I didn't care that he didn't promise me anything. I didn't promise him anything, either. As odd as it was, I reminded myself that I was still a married woman. But I was human, so I was bound to make mistakes and bad choices. I couldn't think of a better mistake or worse choice than the one I'd just made.

I almost cried as soon as I turned onto my street. I had to blink, close, and rub my eyes because I didn't want to believe what was in front of me. Parked in our driveway like a gigantic stink bomb was Adele's jalopy, with the trunk open. There were boxes on top of boxes stacked up on the sidewalk next to her car and on my front porch. I was disappointed not to see Nita's car. But before I could even park, Nita pulled up behind me. Sitting in the front passenger's seat in Nita's Taurus was Adele's smart-mouthed daughter, Odette, looking at me like I'd stolen her purse. Odette and her twin brother, Odell, were fifteen going on forty. The boy, even though he was strange and sneaky, wasn't that bad. But Odette thought that the world revolved around her. And, for a girl who was just as plain as her mother, she had a lot of nerve thinking so highly of herself.

I didn't move until Nita parked her car and came over to me. She had to motion for me to roll my window down.

"What the hell is going on?" I asked, ignoring Odette as she strutted up on my front porch, with a large suitcase in one hand and a tennis racket in the other. A tennis racket! One thing I had to say about my in-laws was that for people who were always complaining about being broke, they sure lived high on the hog. The kids would only wear designer clothes and had to eat in the most expensive restaurants in town. But only when it was at somebody else's expense. That usually meant that the money for their extravagances usually came out of Jesse Ray's or Miss Rosetta's wallet. Now that Miss Rosetta was incapacitated, Adele and Harvey did all her banking. Her pension and Social Security checks were deposited directly into her checking account, which Adele and Harvey controlled. Every month they took turns spending what they wanted to on themselves and leaving nothing for Miss Rosetta but some change.

Now I loved money just as much as the next person, and I spent my share of it. But I figured that what belonged to Jesse Ray belonged to me, so it was not like I was mooching off of anybody. But it never ceased to amaze me how people like Wade's mama and Jesse Ray's family could be so brazen about spending money they were not entitled to.

"Like I said, I am going to pray for you," Nita said, shaking her head. "Your sister-in-law left work early and snatched the kids out of school, and they've been hauling their shit over here since this morning," Nita told me, looking at her watch. "I didn't think you'd be gone this long."

"I didn't, either," I confessed. "Uh, Wade was glad to see me, and we had a lot to talk about."

"I bet you did. Well, all I can say is, I am glad you got to do something for yourself today. From the looks of things, it's going to be a while before you get your cookies again." It felt like I was having an out-of-body experience as Nita opened my door and pulled me out of my car.

"They are only going to be here for a little while. A week or two," I said in a tentative voice, nodding toward the house. Adele was peeping out of the front window, looking at me with a smirk on her face.

"For your sake, I hope that's the case. But judging from what I've seen so far, a little while means one thing to me and you, and something else to these folks. Odette just had me drive her back to the house—for the third time—to get more of her shit, including her cat, Bruce."

Adele left the window and came out to the porch, hands on her hips, looking at me and Nita. There was a cigarette stuck between her ashy lips. She took it out and shook ashes into one of my best coffee cups, knowing that I had placed ashtrays in every room of my house, including the bathrooms. I was too horrified to comment on Adele's smoking etiquette, but I couldn't overlook the fact that she had invaded my wardrobe.

"That bold hussy is wearing one of my best housecoats," I hissed, rocking from side to side on my weakened legs. My body was still feeling the effects of my marathon fuck fest with Wade. My nipples were still tingling. My crotch was vibrating like I was still riding up and down on Wade's huge dick. The state of my body was probably the only thing that kept me from running down the street, screaming.

"And how was your . . . uh . . . date?" Nita asked, with a wink.

Even though I was preoccupied, I managed a smile and a thumbs-up.

"Uh-huh. I feel you," Nita said, nodding. "When are you going to see him again?"

"I . . . we didn't discuss that," I said, with a shrug, my eyes on Adele, who was still standing on my porch, with her cigarette.

"Well, if I were you, I'd keep his number real close," Nita advised, rolling her eyes and nodding toward Adele. "I have a feeling you are going to need it again."

I let out a disgusted breath and shook my throbbing head. "I have the same feeling myself," I said through clenched teeth.

CHAPTER 49

The day that my in-laws invaded my house marked the beginning of a battle that would have put the infamous movie *Gunfight at the O.K. Corral* to shame. I was glad that I did not have access to any lethal weapons, because I probably would have used them. And, the "support" that I received from my husband was so weak, you couldn't even tell that he was involved in this mess. I knew I had to fend for myself. I went into battle with Adele and her kids with no allies, except for Jeanette, Nita, and Miss Odessa. I couldn't count Miss Rosetta, because she didn't even know where she was, let alone what was going on in the same house. One thing I could say for myself was that, thanks to my experiences with street life, I was a fighter and a survivor. I was going to do whatever I had to do to keep Adele and her kids in line.

By the end of the second day, everything was in an uproar. It felt like I'd been set up, because it seemed like my in-laws' behavior had all been carefully planned, rehearsed, and staged. Even their cat was in on it! I loved animals, but Odette's heavyset, five-year-old calico cat, Bruce, became a major pain in my ass within hours after moving in. Even though the cat had enough sense to use his litter box, which Odette had set in a corner in the kitchen, that damned creature strutted around like royalty on top of my kitchen table whenever he felt like it, which was every hour on the hour. Nobody but me yelled at Bruce and chased him off the table. What was even more irritating was the fact that Adele thought it was "cute" the way Bruce leaped up on my smoked–glass top table to strut his stuff.

"I don't know why you are making such a fuss. My cat is clean," Odette snapped every time I scolded Bruce.

"I don't care how clean Bruce is. I don't want him shedding hair all over my kitchen table," I shot back. I didn't even mention the fact that Bruce had also clawed the bottoms of all my expensive living-room drapes, already. Odette dismissed me with a wave of her hand and ignored me as much as she could. But I could not ignore her presence any more than I could ignore her mother's.

Clothes and boxes had been dumped just about everywhere but where they were supposed to be. A box full of toys for the cat had been set on my kitchen counter. Toiletries, magazines, books, and even wig heads had been piled up on the living-room floor, right by the door.

Adele and Odette were supposed to share one of our two spare bedrooms. Odell was to occupy the other. Yet nobody had bothered to store any of their belongings in the room to which they'd been assigned. I ended up doing it, thinking that I was doing a good deed. But even that "good deed" backfired. Even though they were "homeless," Adele and Odette had the nerve to be the most territorial and touchy females I'd ever met.

"What's wrong with you? Why are you hanging up my good clothes like that?" Adele asked as I finished storing the last of her dresses in the closet in the room she'd occupy.

"Like what?" I wanted to know.

"You don't just slap my shit onto no pole all unorganized and mixed in with my pants and blouses," Adele hissed, brushing off a dress that looked like it belonged to her daughter. "I paid good money for this frock."

"Then you take care of it," I advised, hands on my hips. My attitude and body language stunned Adele, and I didn't know why. She had known me long enough to know I didn't take anybody's mess lying down. "You do whatever the fuck you want to do with your shit then. But whatever you leave lying around in *my* house, I will move it and put it where it should be," I warned.

"This is my brother's house, too," Adele said in a meek voice, which was rare for her. She usually sounded and acted like a frustrated fishwife.

"And your brother is my husband. What's his is mine," I reminded.

"Look, Christine. I don't want to be here any more than you want me here. I got other places I can go. But part of the reason I came here was so I could help take care of my mama. Now either we can get along or we can't. But me and my kids are here, and we will be here until we leave."

"Adele, as long as you treat me with some respect, I will treat you with some," I said, mumbling profanities under my breath as I backed out the door.

"Don't start no mess, there won't be no mess," she said in a low voice, following me, looking toward the stairs. The living room was just off the landing and next to the ground-floor bedroom that Miss Rosetta occupied. The last thing I wanted to do was upset Miss Rosetta. Even though she could not respond to much of anything, she could still hear.

No matter what I said or did, it provoked somebody. That was why I decided to hide out in my bedroom until Jesse Ray got home from work on day two of my nightmare. I couldn't keep my eyes off the clock on my nightstand. The hands seemed to be moving so slowly, I thought they had stopped. I fumbled around until I located my watch in my purse, but the hands on it moved just as slowly as the hands on the clock.

I don't know if Jesse Ray planned it, but it just so happened that he had to stay at the store a little later than usual to do some inventory. He didn't seem the least bit sorry when I called him. "Baby, we had a few emergencies down here that I needed to straighten out. I don't know what time I'll make it home tonight," he told me. He sounded impatient, but my mind told me that that was just to throw me off.

"Jesse Ray, your last emergency was a missing copy of the *Godfather* DVD. It took you two hours to find out it had been misfiled. You want to talk about an emergency. There are a whole lot of emergencies going on in your house right now, and you need to be here to help me deal with this shit!" I hollered.

"Well, I got a real emergency down here tonight—"

"Can't it wait until tomorrow?" I wailed. "I'm going crazy up in this house with all these people downstairs. There's boxes of shit everywhere you look, and I've already had to listen to Odette's smart mouth. I can't deal with this by myself!"

"Baby, have a glass of wine and stay in your room. I'll be home soon. The cops are here and—"

"The cops? Did you get robbed or something?"

"We had a shoplifting incident tonight. I was able to hold this motherfucker until the cops got here. Now let me get off this telephone so I can wrap this thing up. Don't hold dinner for me. I got a pizza on the way."

I hung up. During the few minutes that I'd been on the telephone talking to Jesse Ray, I'd heard glass breaking downstairs, and the television and the stereo were blasting at the same time. I counted to a hundred and asked God for strength before I went back downstairs.

I waltzed into the living room and turned off the television and the stereo. Like a zombie, I stumbled into the dining room, where Adele and the twins were at the dinner table, gnawing on the baked chicken and turnip greens that I'd prepared for dinner. And by the way they were grabbing, gobbling, grunting, and chewing, I knew that there would be nothing left for Jesse Ray when he got home, anyway. "We don't play the television and the stereo at the same time in this house," I told them, looking from one scowling face to another.

"You been tripping ever since we got here," Odette said, talking and chewing at the same time. "Ain't she, Mama?"

"This is her house, sugar. We got to respect her," Adele said, giving me one of the most fake-looking smiles I'd ever seen.

Odell gave me a pitiful look and a real smile, but I was even suspicious of that. Even though he was fairly nice compared to the rest of his immediate family, this boy was too quiet for me. Quiet people made me nervous. That was one of the reasons I never liked being alone with my daddy.

Quiet people even disturbed elderly Miss Odessa. "Still waters run deep," she told me. Her translation was: "Watch your back." But my in-laws were as destructive to my face as they were to my back. I was not only going to watch my back, I was going to watch all the rest of my body parts as well. Speaking of body parts, Wade's were definitely among the many thoughts swimming around in my head. I was glad I still had his cell phone number.

CHAPTER 50

Somehow I made it through the first week without committing a crime against my in-laws or going stark raving crazy.

"Baby, I know this is hard on you, but it won't be but for a minute. You know, if it was your family, they would be just as welcome in our home," Jesse Ray told me, speaking too casually for my tastes. My family? That was a joke, but I wasn't laughing. Other than Mama and Daddy, I had no family. And, they were the last people in the world I expected to come to me for help of any kind. I visited my parents every now and then, but they had never even been to my new neighborhood, let alone my new house. Even though they declined every invitation I extended to them, I continued to invite them. "I can't turn my back on my family," he added, trying to show me some affection by squeezing my breast. All that did was piss me off even more. Sex didn't distract me the way it used to. At least not with him.

This man had lost a lot of credibility with me. His lip service was bad enough, but his position in the bedroom had dropped from a B minus to a very low D. That made me think about Wade even more. I knew that my relationship with Wade, with his penniless self, had nowhere to go beyond a bed. And, with the situation in my house being what it was, I wanted more than sex. I wanted peace of mind even more.

I was glad I still had my relationship with Miss Odessa. But since I couldn't get out of the house that often anymore, I couldn't even visit my elderly friend as much as I wanted to. And, she was so hard of hearing now, trying to communicate with her by telephone was a waste of time.

My in-laws were just as rude to Jeanette and Nita as they were to me, so my girlfriends had practically stopped coming to the house. But every chance I got, I met one or both of them at a bar or a restaurant. This particular Saturday afternoon, I'd met Nita at Otto's, a dark little bar on a side street a few blocks from my house. As soon as the waiter delivered our drinks, I guzzled up half of mine in record time. I needed it, but not to release the hold I'd had on my tongue. I would have said what I had to say with or without a rum and Coke.

"Those damned people are driving me up the motherfucking wall! If I don't do something soon, I'm going to lose what's left of my mind! That bitch Adele sat in the kitchen, filing her claws, while her daughter's fat cat dragged a pork chop off the counter last night! One night I walked in my bathroom just in time to see Odell jacking off and shooting his black sperm into one of my best towels! One of my credit cards is missing! I'm going crazy up in that house!" I paused so I could catch my breath.

Nita sat in silence, sipping her drink and nibbling on some bread sticks and looking at me like I had already lost my mind. "Adele uses my make-up and perfume without asking! Odette used another one of my best towels to clean up a pile of shit her cat left in the middle of my living-room floor! And, they are supposed to be helping me take care of Miss Rosetta! Ha! When they are home and she shits herself, do they change her diaper? Hell, no! They wheel her into whatever room I'm in and tell me, 'Grammy had a little accident,'" I said, imitating Odette's whiny voice.

Nita looked around the bar, then back to me. "Are you finished? Do you feel better now?" she asked, squeezing my hand.

"I'm fine," I muttered. "No," I said, pausing to drink some more. "I am not fine!" I slammed my glass down so hard on the table, it shook. Our waiter was nearby, and I motioned for him to bring me another drink.

"Girl, you need a vacation," Nita said in a calm voice, shaking her head.

"I need a lot more than that," I mumbled, staring at the top of the table. As soon as the waiter set my second drink in front of me, I took a long swallow and let loose again. "Not only do I clean up behind everybody, cook most of the meals, and take care of Miss Rosetta, I get victimized in other ways. Two days ago some money disappeared from my wallet. I didn't even bother to accuse anybody of stealing it, but I mentioned it to Jesse Ray. His theory was that I'd misplaced it. He said the same thing yesterday, when I told him one of my credit cards was missing.

"On another occasion, I caught Odette fucking on the living-room couch some little, narrow-ass boy that she'd sneaked in during the night. Adele gave her a mild scolding, then turned around and accused me of "spying" on them. And, I finally found out why Odell is so quiet: the boy is an alcoholic and is often drunk as a skunk. One day I caught him drinking vodka straight out of the bottle! Because of the showdown with Adele about Odette and her little boyfriend glazing my sofa with their love juices, I didn't even bother to expose Odell's drinking habits." I stopped ranting long enough to finish my drink.

"And, just as you would expect, people like Adele and her kids have the kinds of friends that you wouldn't want to visit your house too often. I do what I can to keep that under control, and to my surprise, Jesse Ray backs me up. There are to be no visitors after nine at night, and no visitors are allowed to roam around the house unescorted. I had to impose a no smoking rule, using Miss Rosetta's failing health as an excuse, which was more than a little valid. I even gathered up all the ashtrays and stored them in the garage. Even though nobody smokes in my presence now, the house still smells like smoke. And not just cigarette smoke. When I washed Odell's clothes—yes, I do their laundry, too—I found half-smoked joints in his pockets and enough condoms for an army! Those things don't disturb me that much. Odell is a typical teenage boy. But this morning I went to do his laundry and found a pair of my panties in one of his shirt pockets! I'm afraid that if I go off on a vacation, I won't come back!" I told Nita, beckoning the waiter to bring me another drink.

"Girl, don't you let those people run you away from your own home," Nita said sternly, waving a finger in my face. "You can't go on like this. Why don't you call up that hunk Wade?"

"For what?" Just the mention of his name brought a smile to my face. "Should I?" I asked, leaning forward.

"What's wrong with you, girl?" Nita snapped, rolling her eyes. "You need a tune-up, and he's got the tool you need," she said, with a chuckle.

"I'm married," I said, snatching my third drink from the waiter, who was as cute and sexy as Wade. I didn't realize I was still staring at his butt as he walked away until Nita cleared her throat and slapped the top of the table.

"So? That one little detail didn't stop you before!"

"Yeah, well, that one time was a mistake. I've got enough problems. Like I said, I'm married." I could feel myself getting wet between my thighs.

"That's part of the problem. You are too married. You are trying so hard to keep your husband happy that you are neglecting your own feelings. If I was in your shoes, I'd either leave or get me some regular outside action."

I gave Nita's words some thought, but I didn't comment. Instead, I went to the ladies' room and grabbed a wad of paper towels. Then I pulled down my sticky panties and mopped up all the juice sliding down my thighs.

Nita and I had come to the bar in separate cars. I was thankful for that because I wasn't ready to go home when Nita was. I drove around aimlessly for an hour, thinking about what Nita had suggested. I still had Wade's phone number, and I knew that as long as that was the case, there was a chance that I would call him.

But by the time I reached my street, I had talked myself out of hooking up with Wade again. I had convinced myself that he probably didn't want to see me again, anyway. A man who had made several X-rated movies probably had women coming out of his ears. Besides all that, I didn't even know if he was still in the Bay Area. It had been a month since our romp in his mama's house. A *month*! It had also been a month that my in-laws had been under my roof. And, it didn't look like they were leaving any time soon. Mel, Adele's husband, had been coming to the house, trying to talk her into moving back home. That gave me a hopeful thought. But that thought went out the window as soon as I reached my house.

To my everlasting horror, Adele's husband, Mel, was climbing out of his battered minivan, toting two of his suitcases. My mind refused to believe what my eyes were seeing: he was moving in, too!

CHAPTER 51

"J.R., I need to talk to you," I yelled into my cellular phone, struggling to control my anger and frustration. But I was losing the struggle. I wanted to scream my head off. I couldn't believe what was happening this time. I was still in my car, sitting in front of my house, watching Mel, Adele, and the twins haul more boxes from Mel's van into my house.

"Baby, we are real busy right now," Jesse Ray said in a nervous and weak voice. I had a feeling that he already knew why I was calling. "Can I call you back in a couple of hours? How about us having dinner at the Hometown Buffet?"

"Fuck the Hometown Buffet!" I shouted.

"Oh Lord, you are in one hell of a bad mood!"

"You're just now noticing that! I've been in a bad mood ever since your *savage* family moved in! I'm beginning to feel like I landed on the Planet of the Apes!"

"I'll call you back in a couple of hours, when you're feeling better."

"Feeling better? Why the fuck do you think I will be feeling better in a couple of hours?"

"We'll talk then, anyway. Now will you let me get off this telephone?"

"Oh, *hell*, no! Fuck that fucking shit! Don't you dare hang up this telephone! If you do, I am coming over there!" I roared, slapping the dashboard so hard with the palm of my hand that the windshield wipers came on. The irritating noise that they made scraping against the dry window made the situation even worse. My head was spinning like I'd just tumbled sideways off a merry-go-round. I thought that I was losing my mind for sure this time. I thought I was turning off the wipers, but I ended up turning on my lights. I fumbled around until I located the wiper switch, but I was still in such a wild state, I left the lights on.

"Christine, you know I don't like to hear women cuss. And, you, you got way too much class to be acting like one of those heifers from the 'hood," Jesse Ray said in a gentle voice. The fact that he could speak so calmly when it was obvious that I was on the verge of a nervous breakdown compounded a situation that was already out of control.

"Fuck this shit! We need to talk, and we need to talk right now. I am sitting here in my car in front of the house, watching Adele and the twins help that punk-ass Mel carry boxes and bags into our house. Either Mel is moving in, too, or they've been on one hell of a shopping spree."

"Mel couldn't make his rent this month. He hit a jealous coworker and got fired," Jesse Ray said, with a hopeless sigh.

"The man delivers pizzas for Domino's. Who'd be jealous of that?" I screeched.

"I don't get up in the brother's business. I just know what he told me." Jesse Ray stopped talking for a moment and cleared his throat. I think he did that because he had to pull his foot out of his mouth. But that pause didn't do him much good, because he kept talking crazy. "Mel's family, my only sister's husband, and he needs my help, too. He just needs a place to stay until he can get himself another gig."

"Well, that's his problem. He's got family everywhere except Mars, so why is he not moving in with them?"

"Now, baby, you know Mel doesn't get along with his folks. And, he wants to be with his wife so they can work things out. It'll only be for a little while, baby. I promise."

"Your promises aren't worth a counterfeit food stamp. You said the same thing about Adele and the twins. Exactly what do you call 'a little while'?" I yelled. "Adele and the twins were supposed to be with us for 'a little while,' and they've been with us for over a month now."

"What do you expect me to do, Christine? I am not going to stand by and let my family end up on the street. You know how I believe in family. If you can't count on family, you can't count on anybody. If you don't do for your family, who will you do for?"

I didn't like it when J.R., or anybody else for that matter, started talking about family this and family that. I couldn't make that claim, so I would never really know what it was like to feel that family loyalty that some of the people I knew experienced. Nita and Jeanette both had relatives all over the place. Once Nita dragged me to a family re-union that involved over three hundred of her relatives. It saddened me to know that even though I still had my parents, the only other family I would have was J.R. and his. I had accepted the fact that I would not have any biological children, and the way things were going, I was glad that I only had to worry about myself. If worse came to worse and I had to run away, it would have been a lot harder to do if I'd had a baby to drag along with me.

"Besides, I believe in giving back," he mumbled.

"What the fuck are you talking about, man? Giving back what and why? What has your sister done to deserve all you've given her? You paid her American Express card last month—over three thousand dollars. Her claim was that she'd only used the card for some emer-gencies. Well, I happened to see her bill from last month, and all of her emergency charges were made at *Disneyland*! The dates of the charges was that same weekend that she and the kids said they were going to L.A. to visit some old friends that she went to school with. They all went to Disneyland, and we ended up paying for it! Not just for Adele and the twins, but her friends, too. That makes no god-damn sense to me. What is it going to take, and how long is it going to take, for you to see that these people are milking us dry?"

"*Us*? Look, lady, you need to stop right now before you go too far. We need to get one thing straight right now. Nobody's taking any-thing away from *you*."

"It's our money that's paying for your sister and half of the Bay Area to live so large. We are the ones paying for it all."

"That's not what I meant," he said in a steely voice. This conversa-tion was already on dangerous ground, and it seemed to be sinking fast.

"And just what do you mean?" I wanted to know. My head was still spinning, and now I was gritting my teeth and twisting around in my seat. I didn't want to know what this mess was doing to my blood pressure.

"Correction. *I* am the one paying. You keep forgetting who is bringing home the money in this deal. You don't have a damn thing to be complaining about, woman. You got it better than every other woman I know. You don't even have to work. You don't have to get up out of the bed until you feel good and ready. What more do you want?"

My mouth was hanging open so wide and I was sucking in so much air, I could barely breathe. "I don't believe my ears. I spend my days and some of my nights feeding and bathing *your* mama. I can't leave the house during the day unless I find somebody to come stay with *your* mama. I haven't been able to sleep as late as I wanted since *your* mama had her stroke. And, if you think I don't do any work, what do you call all the cleaning and cooking I do for *your* family?"

"Baby, please—"

"Please my ass! Do you think it's easy for me to drag myself up and down the aisles at Safeway, buying groceries to feed a house full of people who are all too lazy to help me go get groceries and too stingy to contribute a nickel for all the junk they put on the grocery list? I never had to buy sunflower seeds, licorice, and chicken gizzards until they moved in and started demanding them."

"Christine, please calm down—"

"Calm down my ass! Your family complains about my cooking, yet they all but lick the plates clean after one of my meals. And, did you know that your nephew stole a pair of my panties one time? Did you know that I caught him peeping through the keyhole in our bathroom while I was taking a shower one night? And, don't get me started on that sister of his—"

"Christine, like I said, I am really busy right now. You go in the house and have a big glass of wine. Go in the den or our bedroom, and watch one of your videos. Don't let Adele and the kids and Mel bother you. We are going through this together."

"Together? And that's another thing. How can you say we are going through this together when ninety percent of the time you are not even in the house? I can't take too much more of this," I wailed. I felt like I was coming undone. No, I had already come undone. My head had stopped spinning, but now it felt like it was about to crack open.

The back of my neck was itching, and my stomach felt like somebody with big-ass feet was inside it, stomping on my insides.

It took Jesse Ray a while to respond to my last comment. "Are you making plans that don't include me?"

"What do you think?" I choked.

CHAPTER 52

"I love you to death, Christine. One day I will make all this up to you if you let me, baby."

"Make me know it!" I snapped. "Try a little harder, and maybe we'll get somewhere. Because, brother, I got news for you. What you are doing—or not doing, I should say—is not working."

"Adele looked at an apartment in Oakland two days ago. She's just waiting for the landlady to get back to her. If everything checks out, her job and credit, the place is hers."

"I'll believe it when I see it happen. But that's just part of the problem, Jesse Ray. I love your mama just as much as I love my own mama. And, to be honest with you, I think I love Miss Rosetta even more, because she's treated me more like a daughter than my own mama. But taking care of her . . ."

"Oh, hell, no! You are not going there, lady! Leave my mama out of this! I'm working on that, too!"

"Exactly what does that mean, J.R.?"

"Don't worry about it. All you need to know is that I'm working on it."

"Well, you are not working hard enough for me, Jesse Ray. I've got to make some plans on my own, I guess," I said, so tired of talking, my cheeks ached. Jesse Ray didn't respond right away, and I didn't know what else to add to my threat.

"I see," he said finally in a gruff voice that I rarely heard. "You do what you have to do, and I'll do what I have to do. But you just remember one thing, if you do decide to divorce me, you will leave this marriage with what you brought to it. Go on back over to the 'hood to your chicken wings and cheap liquor and carjacking homeboys. Let's see how well you do without my money."

Apparently, Jesse Ray was way ahead of me. Leaving him was one thing, and it had suddenly crossed my mind. Divorcing him was an entirely different story. It saddened me to know that one of the first things he associated with a divorce was money. And, he never let me forget that the money in question was *his* money.

"I didn't marry you for your money, J.R.," I said, disappointed that he'd chosen to go in this direction. "This is not about what's yours and what's mine."

"The hell it's not! This is all about money, and you know it. You bitch and moan about me paying my only sister's credit card bills. You bitch and moan every time I help my brother out. You complain about all the food my folks eat. I have always been good to my family, and marrying you is not going to change that. You should know that by now."

"I see," I said flatly, feeling totally defeated. "I am your wife, but your family comes first?"

"I didn't say that," Jesse Ray said in a cautious voice, but it was too late. "And, I don't appreciate your putting words into my mouth."

"Why did you marry me, Jesse Ray?"

"Christine, I married you because I love you. I will always love you. I didn't mean to go on off you a minute ago, making fun of the 'hood. Hell, you know that's where I started out myself. And . . . and no matter what you decide to do, I will always love you. Don't you forget that. Let's end this conversation right here and resume it where we left off when I get home. I'll even leave work early tonight. We'll go somewhere nice and quiet where we won't be disturbed. Now let me get off this phone so I can get back to work."

I hung up before Jesse Ray, or I, could say anything else. I had heard enough from him, and I had said all I wanted to say for the time being. At least to him.

My in-laws were still moving Mel's shit into the house, everything from fishing poles to a limp gray blanket, which Mel had flung over his shoulder like a dead body. They all saw me sitting in my car in front of the house, but nobody acknowledged my presence. I turned away when Odette looked in my direction and gave me one of her smug looks. Her stiff braids looked like horns growing out of her bowl-shaped head.

My cellular phone was still in my hand. A warm feeling suddenly came over me. My body seemed drained. I felt empty. Like somebody had pulled a plug out of me. And, it seemed like my fingers took on a life of their own. I dialed Nita's number, but I hung up as soon as she answered. When I dialed the next number, I honestly thought that it was Jeanette's line I was calling. The voice that answered startled me so much, I had a spasm.

"Yo," he grunted.

"Huh?" I gasped. "Wade, is that you? I didn't realize I had dialed your number!" I was amazed that I had subconsciously remembered Wade's cell-phone number. "Uh, I didn't mean to call you. I thought I was calling a friend," I stammered.

"Well, I thought I was a friend of yours," he said, then laughed.

I laughed, too. And, the warm feeling that I had experienced a few moments earlier suddenly got so hot that I had to fan my face.

"Uh, when did you go back home to L.A.?" I asked.

"Who said I was in L.A.? Berkeley is my home."

"You don't live in L.A. anymore?" I asked hopefully. I looked toward my house. Odette and Adele were standing on the porch steps, looking at me. Their lips were moving. I didn't even want to know what they were yakking about, but I was fairly certain that I was the subject.

"Yes and no. Things are kind of slow down there right now, so I thought it'd be a good time to stay up here and spend some time with Mama. She's getting old, you know. By the way, how are your folks? Are they still in Berkeley?"

"As far as I know, they are still in Berkeley. They were fine the last time I saw them," I said. "We've never been close," I admitted, though I had told Wade this detail before. "Well, it is good to hear your voice again, Wade." It was amazing how much better I was feeling now. I was actually smiling. "I didn't mean to call you, but I am glad I did. I was having a bad moment."

"I am glad you called, Christine. I was having a little bit of a bad moment myself." Wade lowered his voice to a whisper. "Lookie here . . . uh . . . I'd like to see you again. I really enjoyed myself that last time I saw you, and I have a feeling you did, too."

"I did," I confessed, my lips curling into a wicked smile. "Wade, I'm still married. "My husband and I . . . we have our share of problems, so things aren't the way they should be between us right now. I've been a little depressed."

"And is there anything I can do about that?"

"Maybe. But I don't know if I can get too involved with you right now. After all the years I've known you, I really don't know you that well. I don't know where I stand with you. I don't know where our relationship is going."

"I know where I want it to go. You know that Marriott Hotel off the freeway going toward Oakland?"

"I do." I sighed. "What about it?" I asked dumbly. I prayed that we were on the same page. If I ever needed to throw myself into the arms of another man, it was now. I needed some serious attention. Oh, what the hell! I needed a serious dick!

"Can you meet me there, baby?"

Before I answered, I looked toward my front porch again. Adele and Odette had gone inside, but Mel was standing at the top of the porch steps, leering like a gargoyle in my direction. That smug look on his homely face was all I needed to see to help me make up my mind.

"Just tell me when, baby," I said, my body heat so hot and thick, my voice came out in a hoarse whisper.

"What are you doing right now?"

"Me?" I kept my eyes on Mel's miserable face. I knew what I should have been doing. And that was to go into my house. But other than hide out in my bedroom and drink myself into oblivion, I didn't know what I'd do after I got there. What could I say to Adele? What could I say or do about Mel moving in? Jesse Ray had made it clear that this was his call. That thought made a sharp pain shoot through my chest. And, I was already mad as hell, so I couldn't even go further in that direction.

"Yes, you. We are wasting precious time with all this small talk? How soon can I see you, baby?"

"I can be there in fifteen minutes," I told him.

CHAPTER 53

I had gotten used to locking horns with Adele and the twins, so having Mel in the house now, too, didn't really faze me that much more. I did give him credit for going out and finding another job right away. Even though it was driving a snow-cone truck, and it didn't pay enough for him to get another place. Adele told me that she was saving half of her paycheck, every payday, from her job at the post office, and that as soon as they found a suitable place that she could afford, they'd be gone. I didn't have much hope in that. She and Mel had looked at over a dozen places, and so far nothing had panned out. For people with such bad credit and such limited incomes, Adele and Mel had the nerve to be choosey. They didn't want to live in just any old place. They didn't want to live around too many blacks or Hispanics. They didn't want this; they didn't want that. I almost didn't care anymore. And, Jesse Ray must have thought that that was the case, because he didn't even mention it unless I did.

As far as I was concerned, I had lost the battle, but I had learned to adapt, so to speak.

I had Wade to thank for that. It had been two months since I'd called him up by mistake and ended up on a rendezvous at the Marriott. I had spent the entire two hours with Wade in bed, fucking him like I was auditioning to star with him in his next porn movie. I'd been with him either at the Marriott or his mama's house several more times since. Because of him, I was still able to walk around my house, with a smile on my face. And, I was unusually polite to my in-laws even when they didn't deserve it. One night at the dinner table last week, Adele tried to get my goat.

"Christine, you might want to borrow one of my wig hats. People are getting tired of looking at that same do on your head every day. The way your hair is standing up on your skull, you look like you been flying," she said, triggering nods and snickers from her kids and husband, who flirted with me every chance he got.

"Thank you, Adele. I like that brown one with the bangs," I responded, with a broad smile. Somebody gasped. Everybody gave me a sharp look. "And, one more thing, Adele, I'll be a little late braiding your hair tonight. I promised Nita I'd go to the movies with her this evening after dinner."

"Again?" Mel said, gnawing on the bone from the T-bone steak on his plate.

As usual, Jesse Ray was missing in action. I knew that my husband loved his work. But ever since the rest of his family had moved in, he seemed to enjoy his work even more. Some days he left the house before I even got up and didn't come home until I was in bed.

"You sure J.R.'s not dropping his bucket into another woman's well?" Mel asked one evening, when he'd cornered me alone in the kitchen. I was in the middle of washing dishes and didn't care enough to turn around to look in his mincemeat pie of a face.

"My husband doesn't fool around like some men, so I have nothing to worry about," I said, my eyes on the dishes in the sink in front of me. I had reached a point where I didn't even complain about cleaning up the mess my in-laws made.

"What about you?" Mel asked, leaning so close behind me, I felt his sour breath on the back of my neck.

"What about me?" I asked, my heart pounding. I whirled around and faced Mel, searching his dark, fishlike eyes, wondering if he'd seen or heard something about me and Wade. Adele was no Halle Berry, so there had been no gallery of men for her to choose from. But even I thought that she deserved someone better than Mel Howard. He had a body like a board, thin and flat. One night I walked into the bathroom just as he was stepping out of the shower. With his oversized head, his bony arms and legs, and a pencil-thin dick, he looked like a brown praying mantis.

"Do you fool around? When a juicy woman like you gets left alone as much as you do, you're bound to start itching for something extra," he said, with a hopeful grin.

I didn't have to answer Mel's question. Adele pranced into the kitchen in one of her negligees, waving her hands. After seeing Mel naked and now Adele in her see-through gown, I could see why she lusted after him the way she did. Her body was even more worn down than his. Her breasts long and flat, hung down the front of her chest like sleeves.

"Christine, I just wanted to let you know I'm taking off work tomorrow so I can look after Mama. I know you must be tired of being cooped up in the house all day, almost every day," she said, tickling Mel's chin. He cleared his throat and replaced his grin with a much more serious look.

It was not often that Adele gave me much consideration. But I appreciated it when she did.

As soon as I finished cleaning up the kitchen, I made a beeline to my bedroom. I slammed the door shut so fast, I almost fell. Then I called Wade, praying that he had his cellular phone turned on and would answer.

"Yeah," he said in a tired voice.

"Wade, it's me. I have the whole day free tomorrow," I told him in one breath. It took him a while to respond, and that made me nervous. "Wade, are you still there?"

"I'm still here, baby. So what are we going to do for a whole day tomorrow?"

"We'll think of something," I teased.

CHAPTER 54

I still cared about my husband, but I wasn't sure what it was I felt for Wade. I enjoyed his company and his magnificent body, but I knew in my heart that there was not much chance of a future with him for me.

A whole year had slid by, and things were pretty much the same. Even though I had my thing with Wade and it was stronger than ever, my in-laws' presence had begun to wear on me in a way that I could barely tolerate anymore.

And, Jesse Ray's indifference made it even worse. Not to mention the fact that I was still the one doing most of the work where Miss Rosetta was concerned. Her condition was worse than ever before. I'd spoon-feed her, and then she'd spit up everything she'd swallowed, plus a few ounces of slimy bile. I'd bathe her, and then she'd relax her bowels before I could get her dressed again. Sometimes it almost seemed deliberate. More than ever before, I found myself wishing that my mother-in-law would go to sleep and not wake up. I felt guilty for having such evil thoughts, but I was only human and couldn't always control what I felt or thought.

One Friday evening in March, when Wade didn't answer his cell phone, I decided to pay Miss Odessa a visit. It had been two weeks since I'd seen her. I couldn't remember the last time I'd seen or talked to my parents. It was one of the rare days that Jesse Ray came home in time to have dinner with the rest of the family. He had encouraged me to "go out and get some fresh air," telling me I looked a little peaked. When Wade didn't answer, I called Miss Odessa's number from my cell phone. I had already climbed into my car and was halfway to her apartment when I called to let her know I was on my way to see her. Normally, I would have called way ahead of time.

"Hello." The husky voice that answered Miss Odessa's phone didn't belong to Miss Odessa or anybody else I knew.

"Is Miss Odessa home?" I asked, really anxious to talk to my elderly friend.

"Who is this?"

"I'm a friend of hers. I used to live across the hall from her, but we still keep in touch," I explained. "Is she all right?"

"Are you Christine?"

"Yes."

"This is her daughter, Corrine. Didn't you get my message?"

"Excuse me? What message?"

"I called and left a message at your house last Monday. I called everybody in Mama's address book."

"I didn't get the message. Is Miss Odessa all right?" I asked again. Just from the tone of this woman's voice, I knew before she told me that she had some bad news to report. An ominous chill swept over me like a tidal wave. I braced myself for the worst.

"My mama died last Monday. It was some rare skin cancer that she's been battling off and on for years. We buried her yesterday. I'm over here cleaning out her place and trying to get rid of all this junk she had up in here." I was so stunned, I didn't know what to say next. There was an uncomfortable moment of silence before Miss Odessa's daughter spoke again. "Every time I called Mama, she bragged about you. I was a little disappointed when you didn't come to the funeral, send flowers, or even call."

"I didn't get your message," I said again, with emphasis.

"Well, I left it with some young girl."

"That was my husband's niece," I managed, so angry with Odette that if she had walked up to me at that moment, I probably would have ripped her head off. "Is there anything I can do?"

"Not now," Corrine said dryly. "Do you want any of this junk out of

Mama's apartment? That woman never threw *nothing* away. You can have anything out of here that you want as long as you pay somebody to haul it."

"Just those encyclopedias and any magazines she left."

"Oh, you can forget about that shit. That was in the first load I had my husband haul to the dump. Anything else you want?"

I couldn't believe that this woman could speak about her mother's possessions in such a cold manner. "I don't think so. Where is she buried? I'd like to take some flowers to her grave," I said, my voice cracking.

"And that was another thing. Mama lived in the dark ages, which is one of the biggest problems with us black folks. Do you know she never used an ATM? And, I know you won't believe this, but she was scared of cell phones! She read somewhere in one of them books of hers about cell phones causing some kind of cancer of the ear. But it was a cancer that took her out of this world, anyway! That woman. She was my mama, and I loved her to death, but she was a fool most of her life. We had her cremated. It was cheaper. Would you believe that she still had clothes she wore six sizes ago? A pair of broken eyeglasses, a black pump with no mate, and old jars full of shit I can't even identify. And . . ." Corrine paused. I could tell that she was crying, but I didn't let on that I knew that.

"I'm going to miss her so much," I offered.

"Christine, I never met you, but I appreciate all you did for my mama. She had so many good things to say about you. I just wish . . . I just wish I had spent more time with her when I had a chance. Life is so short. I don't know what you got going on now, but try to get as much enjoyment out of life as you can. You don't live but once. Mama wouldn't want you to mourn her. She'd want you to celebrate her passing, because it was her time to go, and you can't keep God waiting! Get out and enjoy life if you can. Life is too short."

I hung up and turned my motor off, with Corrine's words still ringing in my ears. Especially the last part. I had tried all of my life to enjoy my life. But every time I thought that things were going well for me, I was wrong. I cried for twenty minutes before I went back home.

I found Odette in the kitchen, burning up some popcorn. Her CD player on the windowsill over the sink was blasting 50 Cent so loud, the windows were rattling. I marched right over and turned it off.

Odette whirled around and faced me, with contempt. I slapped her hand when she attempted to turn her music back on.

"What's your problem?" she demanded, hands on her narrow hips.

"Odette, did you take a message for me from a lady named Corrine last Monday?"

"I take a lot of messages. I don't know no Corrine," she snarled.

"She called to tell me her mama died. You remember Miss Odessa, that old lady I used to live across the hall from. Corrine said she left a message with you."

"I don't remember taking no message from no Corrine," Odette snapped. "You want some popcorn?" she asked, reaching for a bowl next to the CD player. There was popcorn, some burned and some still unpopped, all over the counter, waiting for me to clean it up.

I was seething with so much anger, I knew that if I didn't get away from this girl in time, I would not be responsible for my actions. I just looked at Odette and shook my head. Then I left the room.

It was around eight o'clock when I finally got in touch with Wade. His mama was in the hospital, having her breasts lifted with money she'd borrowed from a dozen people, so we didn't have to check into a hotel this time. He had left the back door open for me to get in, and I had to stumble over a dozen beer cans to get to him in the living room. For the first time since we'd resumed our relationship, we didn't rip one another's clothes off. He was in a pretty rotten mood himself.

"My unemployment checks ran out this week, and I can't get an extension," he complained, his arm around my shoulder as we lay on the lopsided sofa, facing a huge window in the front of the house. "I need new clothes to go looking for a job. I need money for transportation. Mama helps me when she can, but she's struggling, too. And, I'd hate to have to borrow money from you."

"And I'd hate for you to ask me for money," I gasped, sitting up so I could see his face better. He looked stunned and disappointed. "Wade, I don't have any money," I told him, shaking my head.

"What's that supposed to mean? You are living large, if I don't say so myself. Fine clothes, fine car. Credit cards with sky-high limits." Wade chuckled. He gave me a critical look, his eyes looking me up and down like I was up for inspection. "Me, I'm eating neck bones and rice almost every day."

"Jesse Ray controls all the money in my house. He gives me money for household necessities and credit cards, but other than that, I'm almost as broke as you are." I looked at the wall. "Being married to a millionaire is not all that it's cracked up to be," I complained, letting out a sour breath. I was still sad about Miss Odessa's passing and still angry with Odette for not telling me in time so I could attend the funeral.

"Millionaire? Big-lipped Jesse Ray is doing that good? The video rental business is that hot?"

"It is for Jesse Ray. But he's got other things on the side going on, too. He cleans up in the stock market. If he's nothing else, he's a shrewd businessman."

"You can't get out of that prenup you signed?" Wade asked, scratching his chin. There was a sparkle in his eyes that I'd never seen before.

"No. It's rock solid. If I leave Jesse Ray—and if things don't change soon, I will—I'll leave with nothing."

"Nothing?"

"Well, next to nothing. I'd get a few dollars for a year, not much. Then I'd be on my own. Unless . . ."

"Unless what?"

"Unless I can come up with a plan." The voice drifting out of my mouth like smoke sounded nothing like me. It was hollow and low and husky. It was the voice of a desperate woman. And, that's exactly what I had become.

"What kind of plan are you talking about? You going to set him up to get robbed?" Wade laughed, slapping his knee.

"No, nothing like that," I said, shaking my head. "He never has more than a couple of hundred on him at a time, and there's too much security at the stores. He's got teeny-weeny cameras hidden in places where even I can't find them." I sucked in a deep breath and looked in Wade's eyes. Our eyes locked until I looked away. "Wade, I think I know a way. I think I know a way I can leave Jesse Ray with enough money for me to start all over. But I need your help." I pressed my lips together and looked at Wade again. His gray eyes had darkened in the glow of light above his head.

"Look, baby, I don't know what you got on your mind, but jail is not on my agenda. I found that out the hard way when I let some Mexican chick talk me into helping her pull an insurance scam down in L.A. And, all I got for my troubles was two years in the joint and two years probation. Uh-uh. Count me out. With all these smart-ass cops these days, you can't kill your old man and get away with it."

"What are you talking about?" I spoke so fast, I almost choked. "I didn't say anything about *killing* anybody. I would never think about hurting Jesse Ray, or anybody else for that matter," I insisted. Even though I was a desperate woman, and I was willing to do just about anything to change my situation, I drew the line when it came to causing Jesse Ray physical pain.

"Then what do you have in mind?"

"You don't have to worry about jail if we do this right," I said in a subdued voice. "What if you kidnapped me and asked for a ransom? Half a million dollars is what we'd get. I'd give you, uh, fifty grand, and then I'd take the rest and stash it away somewhere until things cooled off. Once you released me back to my husband, and once things settled down I'd divorce him. Then, eventually, I would just up and leave town with my share of the ransom. It would be more than enough for me to relocate and start a new life. And I think we can make it work."

Wade looked at me like the voice coming out of my mouth belonged to a demon. It was the first time I'd ever seen fear on his face.

CHAPTER 55

"What's wrong with you, woman? Have you completely lost your mind?" Wade asked, pushing me away like he'd just heard that I had a fatal disease and was contagious. Then he reared back and stared at me in slack-jawed amazement. "I can't believe my ears! Kidnapping is one of the most serious crimes you can commit in this country. That ain't too far from being a terrorist!" He wobbled up from his seat and stood in the middle of the floor, with his hands on his hips, staring at me now, with his mouth hanging open in a yawn so wide, I could see the base of his tongue.

"Not if you don't get caught. And, if we do everything right, there is no chance of that happening," I assured him.

As far-fetched as my scheme sounded, even to me, I had given it a lot of thought. It had been on my mind for several days now, but this was the first time I'd felt brave enough to put it on the table.

"But it won't be a real kidnapping," I added. "I'll hide out with you somewhere, and you make the call."

"What call?"

"The threatening voice that calls my husband to tell him that I've been kidnapped and am being held for ransom," I answered, not even trying to hide my exasperation. Wade was supposed to be so streetwise, but he was as dense as he could be.

Wade opened his mouth to speak, but nothing came out at first. He shook his head as if that was the only way he could get the words to move. "You think I could pull it off? Do you honestly and truly think that I could pull something like that off?"

"You're an actor, brother," I snapped. "If you can't, I don't know who can."

Wade shook his head and then looked at me out of the corner of his eye. "How do I know you ain't trying to set me up?"

"Why would I be trying to set you up?" I asked, rolling my eyes. "What the fuck would I have to gain by sending you back to jail, Wade?"

He massaged the side of his head and let out a loud sigh. "All right. Talk to me," he ordered. "Tell me everything I need to know."

"Then you'll help me?" I asked, my eyes as wide as a child's on Christmas morning. "You'll do it?"

Wade nodded, but with noticeable hesitation. "If we don't do this thing right, it might be the last thing we ever do," he warned.

"It's a simple plan, baby. Now listen . . ."

It was a simple plan, my plan. It took me only ten minutes to lay it out. If Wade followed my instructions, we'd both be very happy with the outcome.

When I stood up to leave, Wade grabbed my hand. "I just want you to change one detail."

"What?" I asked, annoyed and alarmed. "I thought we had everything worked out."

"We did. I mean, we do. It's just that I need a little more time."

"More time for what? You want to give this some more thought?"

"Not really. I am going to do it, but I just don't want to do it tomorrow like you said. I think we should wait at least a couple of days more."

"What is there to wait for? You're going to rent a motel room for me to stay in. You're going to call up my husband and tell him you're holding me for ransom."

"What if he won't pay? Then what? Do you go on back home and pick up where you left off with him and his crazy-ass family, or what?"

"He'll pay," I said firmly. "He's all about money. He's never turned anybody down that asked him for money."

"Christine, this is not the same thing as that snow-cone truck–

driving brother-in-law of yours asking your husband for a few dollars. Or that Harvey or Adele asking for money to go on cruises and shopping sprees with. Those are not crimes, but they should be," Wade said, with a dry laugh.

I gave Wade a pensive look. "If he doesn't pay, I leave, anyway. I might even go to L.A. with you."

"And if he does pay? What is your next move? Whatever it is, it better be good."

By the time I left Wade's mama's house, we had ironed out our plan some more. If Jesse Ray paid the ransom, Wade would take his share and go back to L.A. and resume his Mickey Mouse "acting" career. If he was smart, he'd use some of his money to hire a good manager or a publicist who could help open a few doors for him. And, from what I knew about his career, he was going to need all the help he could get if he wanted to do something that he could be proud of.

Besides Wade, I didn't know any other people in the movie business. But I knew enough about the business from reading the tabloids and watching shows about entertainers on the E! channel to know that Wade had had his fifteen minutes of fame. In his case, he'd even been cheated out of that. His fifteen minutes had been more like two. But the saddest part was the fact that it had been two minutes of shame. I didn't know about other people who had been reduced to starring in porn movies, but I knew enough about Wade to know that he had too much pride to let his mama and the rest of us know the truth.

I told Wade that my plan was to go to Hawaii and start over. Other than that, I was as vague and evasive as possible. I avoided telling him where in Hawaii I planned to go. When he asked me for the fourth or fifth time, I said the first thing that came to my mind. "Uh, Maui."

"I'll wait a few months; then I'll come visit you," he told me. "But"—he paused and let out a tired sigh—"if dude don't pay and you still want to get away from him, you can come on down to L.A. and stay with me, if you don't mind sleeping on the pallet in a studio with two other folks. . . ." Wade paused again and let out another tired sigh. I was not counting, but I was convinced that he had let out enough sighs to blow out a streetlight. "Until you find a job. It's the least I could do."

I knew in my heart that my relationship with Wade had finally run its course. What he had to offer as far as a future was concerned didn't appeal to me at all.

"Sure," I mumbled. I said whatever I thought he wanted to hear because I knew that if things went the way I wanted them to go, Wade would not see me in the future.

And neither would Jesse Ray.

CHAPTER 56

I had come to believe that anybody who chose to commit a serious crime had to be stupid in the first place. But I'd only felt this way since I'd married Jesse Ray and become "respectable." However, I knew from experience that a lot of people committed crimes out of necessity. The most honest man in the world would steal food if that was the only way he could feed his starving family. That was all about survival. I felt that I had something in common with that honest man trying to feed his starving family. I needed to survive. I had convinced myself that I wouldn't survive if I stayed with Jesse Ray.

Leaving him was going to be painful because I would be giving up a lot. I loved the house he had bought for us to grow old in. It was kid friendly, with a recreation room and a spacious backyard. But none of that mattered now. Because even if I stayed, the only kids who'd enjoy all that would be Adele's and their obnoxious friends.

The next night I called up Wade a few times on my cell phone from my spacious bathroom, a location I used to enjoy being in. Right after we'd moved into the house, Jesse Ray had installed a plasma television with a flat screen in our master bathroom so that I could watch my favorite shows during my long bubble baths. Those days were gone. With so much going on in the house now, my time was severely limited. I had to use it wisely. An hour-long bubble bath was a luxury that I rarely enjoyed anymore. I didn't even like to use the bathroom at all unless I had to. Especially after I'd caught Odell peeping at me through the bathroom-door keyhole and jacking off while I was doing my business on the commode. Now I always covered the keyhole with a towel. And just to make it even more difficult for that sick puppy to get off with the help of my bathroom activities, I ran the water in the bathtub and in the sink so he couldn't hear what I was doing in there, either.

Even with all the background noises in my bathroom, running water, and Anita Baker on my CD player, I still whispered into the phone. "Wade, I just wanted to go over one more detail. When you release me, you'll have to keep and destroy my purse and everything in it."

"Why?" he asked, breathing hard.

"Wade, if somebody really did kidnap me, one of the first things they'd probably do is dispose of my purse. A real kidnapper would not want me to have access to the cell phone that I always carry in my purse when I'm away from home. And, what if the cops stop us and ask for ID before you get me to wherever you're going to hide me? As a brother, you of all people know that if the cops stop you when you are 'driving while black,' they want to ID everybody in the car."

"And that's another thing," replied Wade. "Speaking of cars, what are we going to use for transportation? I don't know any kidnappers, but I doubt if any of them haul their victims around on a bus or in a cab."

"We can rent a car," I said.

"And now you're talking about leaving a paper trail, too? Christine, why don't you just forge your old man's signature on a piece of paper and take it to the bank and get you some money that way? Or why don't you find somebody that looks like old Jesse Ray and have him go to the bank with you?"

"Wade, now that is a straight-up felony if ever there was one," I hissed.

"And kidnapping is not?"

"How many times do I have to tell you this is not a *real* kidnapping?"

"You don't need to tell me no more. You save all that for the man when they slap them cuffs on you."

"So what are you telling me? Are you backing out? There is fifty thousand dollars in this for you."

Wade took his time responding. "Okay. Be cool, baby. It's all good. I just want to make sure we got every little deal worked out," he told me.

I got sick of going over "every little detail" three and four more times all in the same conversation. Each time that Wade attempted to talk about us getting caught, I steered him in another direction, assuring him that if we stuck to my original plan, that was not going to happen.

When I met up with Wade again a few days later at his mama's house to go over the plan *one more time*, Miss Louise was still in the hospital, but Wade was not alone.

"This is Jason. He's going to be our backup," Wade told me as soon as I got inside. "He's got a car, so now we don't have to worry about taking a risk with a rental." I gave Wade a horrified look. I wanted to make sure he knew how I felt. But he tried to minimize it by shrugging his shoulders and giving me a weak smile. I looked at Jason, giving him the same horrified look that I'd just given to Wade.

"Wassup, sister?" Jason said, walking toward me, with his hand out for me to shake. "Long time no see." Jason Mack was no stranger to me. He'd been in a lot of my classes at Berkeley High, but he'd spent more time in jail than school for burglarizing homes and businesses and robbing old ladies on the street in broad daylight. And, with his shifty snake eyes and snaggletoothed grin, he looked like the type who'd knock an old lady down and run off with her purse. But that had not stopped him from having an extremely vigorous social life. He'd married one of the girls from my old gang, but he'd also carried on affairs with several other women at the same time. Every now and then, I caught a glimpse of him out in public with one of the five women that he'd had five babies with. This was the closest I'd been to him since the tenth grade, and I didn't like it.

I ignored Jason's ashy hand and turned to Wade again. "What the hell is this?" I gasped, rotating my neck. I took a few steps back toward the door. I still had my car keys in my hand, because I didn't plan on staying more than a few minutes. It had not been easy for me to get away from my house. I had not been able to reach Nita so that she could come stay with Miss Rosetta. Out of desperation, I'd wheeled Miss Rosetta out to my Lexus and loaded her into the backseat. The only other times I did that was when Miss Rosetta had a doctor's appointment. I was glad that that happened only a couple of times a month.

"What did you tell him?" I asked, glancing out the window to make sure my vehicle was still parked in front of Wade's house, with my mother-in-law in it. I knew of two other people who had been carjacked in this same neighborhood. One woman's car had been taken with her toddler strapped in his car seat.

A painful memory shot through my mind, which distracted me momentarily. I sucked in a deep breath and closed my eyes. It felt like the floor was moving beneath my feet, and I had to lean against the door for a moment to keep from falling. I recalled a night during my teens when I had participated in a carjacking myself. My friends and I had needed a ride to Oakland and decided it was cheaper to jack somebody's vehicle than it was to waste our money on bus fare. Other than the terrified driver, there had been no one else in the car. But even if there had been, that would not have stopped us. Those crime-filled days were behind me. It saddened me to know that I'd backslid all the way to orchestrating a kidnapping. And, it angered me now to find out that my plan had been compromised without my knowledge or consent. I let out air that I'd just sucked in and opened my eyes. Wade and Jason were standing there, looking at me like I'd just sprouted a mustache.

"Christine, you ain't got nothin' to worry about. Your secret is safe with me," Jason said, his hand still out for me to shake. I glared at him before he finally got the message. He threw his hands up and moved off to the side.

"I thought my secret was safe with Wade," I wailed. I looked at Wade with so much contempt, he flinched. "You can forget about everything," I said, turning to leave.

"It's now or never, baby," Wade yelled after me. "If you want me to help you do this thing, it's now or never."

"What's Jason supposed to do? What is he going to get out of this?" I asked, turning back around.

"Don't you worry about that. That one's on me," replied Wade.

"Wade can't do it all and do it right, baby," Jason said. "He might need somebody to watch his back."

"And why would he?" I snarled. "All he has to do is get a place for me to stay for a few days, make a few phone calls to my husband, then collect the money. Why would he need somebody to watch his back? I can do that myself," I insisted, pointing at my chest. I shook my head and let out a deep breath. "How do I know I can trust you?" I asked Jason. "How do I know you won't drag one of your homeboys into this mix?"

"You don't. But this is the way it's going to be if you want me to help you. Otherwise, you can get yourself another boy," Wade said, his words taking me by surprise.

"All right," I said, slapping the side of my throbbing head. "The sooner we do this, the better. I want it to happen on Monday. My car will be in the shop for maintenance, so he'll have to drop me off at the beauty shop to get my hair done."

"What about that old woman you take care of?" Wade asked.

"I've already taken care of my mother-in-law. One of my friends agreed to stay with her until Jesse Ray picks me up from the beauty parlor and brings me back home." I had felt guilty about asking Nita to come to the house and sit with Miss Rosetta until I returned. Especially since I knew that I'd be gone a lot longer than a couple of hours like I'd told her. The twins got home from school around three in the afternoon, and Adele and Mel got home from work shortly after that. Nita could go home then. She had no idea that she was part of my plan, and I didn't want her to know.

I would have trusted Nita and Jeanette with my life, but I knew that this was one thing that I could never share with them. Even years down the road, when we would all be sitting on a porch, sipping tea and complaining about various ailments. This was one secret that I would carry with me to my grave. And I prayed that Wade and Jason would, too.

CHAPTER 57

The following Sunday night was as typical as all the others. Around nine thirty Harvey rushed into the house and led Jesse Ray into the kitchen. As usual, he'd left his lady friend in the car in our driveway, with the motor running. A few minutes later, Harvey rushed back out of the kitchen, almost knocking me to the floor as I passed him in the hallway on my way into the kitchen.

"Christine, I didn't even see you," he said and grinned. I guess that was his way of apologizing for almost knocking me down, because that was all he said before he fled, brazenly clutching in his hand a wad of bills that he'd just gotten from my husband. I nodded at Harvey and smiled to myself because that greedy motherfucker really wouldn't *see* me after tonight.

In the back of my mind, I was wondering how my departure was going to affect my in-laws. They would never know about the kidnapping plot unless they heard about it from Jesse Ray, and I prayed from the bottom of my heart that he wouldn't tell them. But once they heard from Jesse Ray that I had "moved" to Hawaii, they would probably try to come visit me so they wouldn't have to pay for a hotel. I smiled again when I pictured them and Jesse Ray calling a fake telephone number in Hawaii, and I hoped that they would show up unannounced at the fake address I planned to give them. I wouldn't be there to see the looks on their faces, and I didn't care. Jesse Ray had saved me from a dismal life, and I would always be grateful to him for that. But now it was up to me to save myself, and he was one of the things I had to save myself from.

I seduced Jesse Ray that Sunday night. Not because I was in a sexy mood, but because as far as I was concerned, it would be the last time. I didn't plan on staying with him more than a week or two after I returned from my kidnapping ordeal. And, during that time, I would be so "traumatized," and he probably would be, too, that sex would not be on our agenda.

Ironically, he was more passionate than he'd been in years. Instead of lying there like a corpse, or rising up to make a phone call because he'd forgotten to tell one of his employees something, he was wild and insatiable. And I had his undivided attention. It was almost like he knew he was fucking me for the last time and wanted to get as much out of it as he could. I couldn't remember the last time he'd kissed so many parts of my body that I felt like I'd had a tongue bath.

"Oh, baby, that was so damn good," he crooned after coming for the third time in an hour. He was still lying on top of me, with his face against mine. Then he sat up and clicked on the lamp. "Christine, things are going to change for the better around here real soon," he said in a gentle voice. *They sure are,* I told myself. "I know it's been hard for you, taking care of my mama and all. And, I know Adele, Mel, and the kids are getting on your nerves. And, to tell you the truth, I've been working on a few things. Things that I know will make you real happy."

"Like what?" I asked, not that it mattered now. But I was still curious.

"I still can't bring myself to put my mama in a nursing home. I've heard too many stories about how they abuse and neglect those old people, who can't fend for themselves. How would you feel about me hiring a full-time live-in nurse?"

"Where is a live-in nurse going to live? Every bedroom in this house is occupied now. Are you planning on buying a bigger house?" I asked.

Jesse Ray laughed and playfully thumped the side of my head with his finger. "That's the other thing I've been working on. Mel has been after me for years to give him a management job, but the only way I could have done that was to let one of my other managers go, and I don't work that way. But Kim Loo is getting married and moving to San Jose. And, you know, I can't manage the store on Alcatraz by myself. I've interviewed a few folks to replace her, but I haven't been impressed by any of them."

"And you are thinking about making Mel your assistant manager?" I gasped.

"I could pay him a decent enough salary so he could take my sister and the twins and live anywhere they want to live." Jesse Ray threw his head back and laughed loud and long. "But I plan to tell him I'll hire him only if he agrees to find them a place way across town." Jesse Ray got quiet and looked at me, but I had to turn away. I didn't want him to see my eyes.

"That's nice, honey," I replied, my voice dragging.

"Well, you don't have to jump up and down and shout about it. I promised you a long time ago, I would take care of my business with my family. I thought this was what you wanted."

"It was," I muttered.

"Was?"

"Uh, it is," I said.

Jesse Ray had promised me a lot of things where his family was concerned. But so far he had not kept any of those promises. I had no reason to believe him now.

Even if Adele and her family moved into their own place today, and a nurse moved in to take care of Miss Rosetta tomorrow, it would still be too late. What would I say to Wade? How would he react? He was counting on that fifty grand. And then there was Jason for me to worry about. What if he blabbed to one of his numerous lady friends?

"Why don't we have lunch tomorrow, baby? Is Nita still coming to sit with Mama while you get your hair done?"

"Uh-huh," I replied, still feeling bad about dragging Nita into my mess.

"Well, I'll pick you up from the beauty shop, and we'll drive into Frisco. We haven't been to Fisherman's Wharf in a while. How about dinner at Alioto's? How's that sound?"

"That sounds good, baby," I said. It was so ironic that tonight Jesse Ray was behaving like the man I'd fallen in love with so many years ago. But like I said, it was too late.

CHAPTER 58

That Monday morning, I rose from bed ahead of everybody in the house so that I could bathe Miss Rosetta, comb and brush her hair, and change her soiled underwear. It was something I did almost every morning. Even on weekends.

Miss Rosetta got pretty sticky during the night, so by morning she was pretty ripe. Every now and then, Adele got up on a Saturday or Sunday morning and took over that unpleasant chore, but it was something I never counted on. I didn't mind doing it this particular morning, because I believed that it would be the last time.

I couldn't remember the last time I'd seen or spoken to my parents, but I promised myself that I would spend some time with them before I fled the area. It saddened me to know that Miss Odessa didn't even have a grave where I could go and leave a bouquet of flowers before I left.

I deliberately stayed upstairs until I was certain that Adele and Mel had left for work and that the twins had left for school. Nita showed up a little early so that we could have a cup of coffee before Jesse Ray drove me to the beauty shop.

"Is everything all right?" she asked, leaning across my kitchen table. I loved Nita like the sister I never had but always wanted, but at the same time I was jealous of her. Not in a bad, malicious way. But in a way that made me believe that I'd be happy if my life had turned out like hers.

"Uh-huh," I nodded. "Why do you ask?"

"You seem a little more distracted than you normally do when I come over here. Anything going on that you want to talk about?"

I shook my head.

"Did Jeanette ask you about next weekend?"

"What about next weekend?"

"We're going to drive up to Calistoga for the whole weekend. After a tour of some of the wineries, she thought it would be nice for the three of us to get mud baths and really pamper ourselves. We don't get to do things like that with you since . . . well, you know. You can't get away as easy as we can."

"If Adele doesn't have any plans, I'd love to go," I said in a meek voice. "She said something about going to Fresno with her bowling team."

"Girl, sometimes I want to slap the shit out of you! Now I don't mind one bit coming over here to baby-sit your invalid mother-in-law so you can get out of the house. But to be honest with you, I'm getting a little fed up with you letting these people take advantage of you the way they do. You could stop all this shit if you wanted to!"

"I know, I know," I said in a low voice, looking over my shoulder.

"I don't care if J.R. does hear me! I'll tell him the same thing I'm telling you. You need to put your foot down and tell these mother-fuckers to go to hell. These grown-ass, able-bodied niggers need to get out and get their own place. They had a place of their own before! This has gone on long enough!" Nita shrieked, her big brown eyes shining with fury.

"Nita, I'm working on it," I said. It took a lot of effort for me to re-main calm, because I was burning with anger inside. "I'm not going to put up with too much of this too much longer."

"Well, sister, you better work harder on it. You're losing weight, you're looking older than you should, and it's a damn shame that you let this mess get this far. When are you going to sit your man down and give him an ultimatum? I don't know any sisters from Prince Street that would let this kind of shit go on for as long as you have."

"Prince Street is a million miles away from me now," I told Nita. "I'm not a round-the-way girl anymore. Do you expect me to get a stick and start swinging at my in-laws?"

"Why the hell not? Nothing else seems to be working. And, to be honest with you, if I was them, I wouldn't be trying to leave, either. They got it made up in here," Nita said, making a sweeping gesture with her hand.

"Nita, you are beginning to sound like my mama," I quipped.

"Now don't get me started on that sister. I've seen her several times in the last month, and not once did she ask me about you. Have y'all stop speaking altogether?"

"I'm going to go see her soon. She's getting old. . . ."

"We are all getting old, baby girl. And, that's all the more reason why you should take care of your business in your house. Sit that man of yours down, and talk some sense into his head." Nita slammed her fist down on the top of my table so hard, the salt and pepper shakers fell over.

"We are going to talk about things over lunch today. Jesse Ray wants to take me into San Francisco for lunch after I get my hair done. Can you stay a couple of hours longer?"

"Girl, I don't have to be home till the kids get home from school. And, to tell you the truth, I don't really need to be there then. Those monkeys are old enough to fend for themselves for a little while. You spend as much time with your husband as you want to," Nita said in a much softer, calmer voice. She gave me a warm smile and a big bear hug. I don't know how much of the conversation Jesse Ray heard, but he had a strange look on his face when he came into the kitchen. He barely acknowledged Nita. He didn't mention her until we'd climbed into his SUV.

"Baby, we need to do something nice for Nita soon. I appreciate her coming to sit with Mama when you need a break," Jesse Ray told me.

"I'll tell her you said that," I croaked, blinking hard. There was a construction crew on Shattuck, so we had to take a detour down Prince Street to get to the beauty shop. When we drove past the apartment building where my remote parents still lived, my head started spinning. I knew that no matter where I ended up, I had to see them at least one more time. Especially if the unthinkable happened and I ended up in jail.

The beauty shop where I got my hair done a couple of times a month was just three blocks from Jesse Ray's beloved Video-Drama, where he planned to go after he dropped me off.

"Give me a call when they get through," he told me, giving me a quick peck on my cheek.

"It's only a short walk, and I really need the exercise. I'll walk," I told him.

"All right, baby. I'll see you in a bit."

About an hour and a half later, I left the beauty shop. I didn't even look in the direction of the video store, let alone walk toward it. It took me an hour to walk to Wade's mama's house. It would have taken less time if I had not avoided walking down Prince Street. I didn't think that I could stand to see my old apartment building twice in the same day. Especially on this particular day.

Wade was waiting for me, with the kitchen door open, as I stumbled up onto the back porch of his mama's house, the place that was about to become the scene of the biggest crime I had ever pulled off.

"You ready to get this thing off the ground?" he asked, pulling me inside.

"I guess so. If we don't do it today, I can't go through with it," I said, my hands trembling. "I saw somebody peeping out of the window next door," I said, with a worried look on my face.

"So? Everybody knows you know my mama, and they've seen you over here before. And, besides, if we can convince our boy not to call the cops, nobody but us ever has to know about this."

"You didn't say that when I talked about us renting a car. You were so concerned about us leaving a paper trail."

"Well, I am not worried about any of that now." I watched as Wade pulled a telephone out of a plastic bag on the table.

"What's that?" I asked, watching as he plugged it into an outlet by the door.

"A little something I picked up at Wal-Mart. It's got a speaker on it, and I want you to hear everything your man says when I call him up."

CHAPTER 59

"Wake up back there!"

I wasn't asleep, but my mind was not alert, anyway. I had just relived the last half of my life. It took me a while to realize where I was and who was talking to me.

"Jason? Where are we?" I said as I lifted myself up enough to look out the window. All I could see was a Dumpster. My neck hurt when I turned my head to look out of the window on the other side. All I could see was another Dumpster. The stench coming from both receptacles was unholy. It smelled like everything dead had been stuffed into these two containers.

"I ain't got all day," Jason told me as he snatched open the back passenger's door on his side, snapping his fingers. "Come on. I got places to go, things to do."

"Where is this place? How am I supposed to get home? What is going on with my husband? What am I supposed to say to him?"

"Baby, you don't tell him nothing but what he already believes what happened."

"Did my husband really pay the ransom? A million dollars?"

Jason ignored me, but the satisfied look on his face answered my question.

"When you get out to the street, turn left and keep walking until you get to University Avenue," he said in an impatient voice, nodding toward the left side of the alley we were in. "Keep on walking until you get to that Everett and Jones rib joint on the corner. Your man will be waiting on you there in the parking lot. If he ain't there when you get there, wait on him. That's where he's supposed to pick you up."

"I feel sorry for you. Wade is not your friend," I insisted.

"Apparently, he wasn't no friend of yours, neither!" Jason scoffed.

I wiggled myself out of the car, stumbling against it. "You tell Wade, I said he won't get away with this," I said in a voice so weak, my words didn't even scare me.

"Get away with what?"

"After all I went through, do you think I am going to let you two motherfuckers get away with this shit?"

"Don't be stupid and move into a burning house, baby. What's done is done. This was *your* idea, and that's something you don't need to forget," Jason said, shaking a finger in my face. "I heard them tapes Wade made of the phone conversations he had with you. Ain't no court in this universe going to let you off if they hear them tapes. Things just didn't work out the way you wanted them to, but things usually don't. From what Wade told me, you still got a good thing going with your man, if you still want it. A big-ass house, a video business, credit cards up the ying yang. I should be so lucky!" That was the last thing Jason Mack said to me as he climbed back into his car and sped off, making such a sharp turn at the corner, he knocked over a mailbox.

I looked in both directions before I started walking. I didn't stop until I reached University Avenue, where Jesse Ray was standing by the side of his SUV in the parking lot of a rib joint, looking so bad he could haunt a castle.

As soon as he spotted me, he broke out running in my direction.

"Christine!" he mouthed, throwing his arms around me so hard and fast, we fell to the ground, with me landing on top of him. "Baby . . . baby, are you all right?" he asked, crying. His eyes were extremely blood-shot and swollen. It looked like he had not shaved or combed his hair since the day I disappeared.

My head felt so heavy, I could barely move it, but somehow I managed to nod. "I'll be fine," I assured him. "Will you take me home," I whimpered.

"Oh, baby, I thought I'd never see you again. Did they hurt you?"

"I'm fine, J.R. They didn't hurt me. I just want to go home," I sobbed, my head on his shoulder. We rose and stumbled to his SUV. With his hand shaking like a leaf, Jesse Ray opened the door on the front pas-senger's side and tucked me in, buckling my seat belt. Then he got in, but he didn't start the motor right away. He looked at me for a few moments; then he broke down and cried like a baby. He shook so hard, I thought he was having a seizure. I managed to wrap my arm around his shoulder. "It's going to be all right," I said, hoping that it would be.

"I never ever thought I'd have to deal with something like this," he managed between sobs. I wiped tears from his face with the palm of my hand. "I don't know what I would have done if they'd . . . if I'd never got you back."

"Jesse Ray, they said if you called the cops or told anybody else about this, they'd be back," I whispered, still wiping tears off his face. "They said they'd kill me for sure."

"Baby, you don't have to worry about anything like that happening. I swear to God you don't. I will make sure of that," Jesse Ray said, grab-bing me in his arms and squeezing me so hard, I couldn't breathe.

"What did you tell your family?" I asked, my face pressed against his chest.

"I told them that your mama was sick and you had to go stay with her for a while. I told Jeanette and Nita the same thing."

"Nobody but us ever has to know about this?" I asked. Jesse Ray sniffed and wiped his nose with a tissue he fished out of the glove box.

"Christine, the only thing I care about is that I got you back and that you are all right. I don't care about revenge or getting the money back or anything. I love you." Jesse Ray hugged me again. This time I had to pry his arms from around me.

"Uh, they were waiting for me when I came out of the beauty shop. They had been watching me for days, they said." I volunteered that piece of information before Jesse Ray asked.

He sniffed and cleared his throat. He blew his nose before he spoke again. "Baby, did you recognize them? How many were there?"

"Uh, there were two of them, and I had never seen them before. They kept me blindfolded most of the time. And, when they didn't, they had on ski masks." I closed my eyes and shook my head.

"If I could get my hands on those black bastards, I'd kill them!" Jesse Ray hollered, slapping the dashboard with his fist.

"Uh, and that's another thing . . . They were white," I said.

"Two *white* dudes snatched you?" Jesse Ray asked, with a surprised look on his face. "Hmmm. I could have sworn that the one that called me was a black dude. He sounded so much like my brother, Harvey, I thought it was him. . . ."

"The one that called you used a black accent to throw you off. I'm positive that those guys were white," I insisted.

"White devils!" Jesse Ray roared, slapping the dashboard again.

"Uh . . . I . . . I need some clean clothes before I go home. I don't want anybody to see me looking like this. Especially Adele."

"You don't have to worry about Adele anymore. They moved two days ago into that new development in West Oakland," Jesse Ray told me. "I told you I was working on getting them out of our house."

"That's nice," I said in a hoarse voice. And, before I could ask my next question, Jesse Ray answered it for me.

"I've interviewed two nurses. The one I am going to offer the job to is with Mama right now, as we speak. A sister from the islands."

"I'm sorry about all this, J.R. I didn't want it to happen." I *was* sorry about what happened. I regretted the whole thing now. I couldn't think of anything as bad as being double-crossed by somebody I trusted to make me feel as humble as I felt at this moment. I didn't know how, but I knew that some day I had to make this up to Jesse Ray.

"Baby, I want to take you to the hospital to have you checked out," Jesse Ray told me.

"What for? I told you I was all right. They didn't rape me or anything like that. I would tell you if they did," I wailed. "Can't we just go home, where I can take a long, hot bath, and get some rest?"

"Christine, you have been through a traumatic situation. You need to talk to somebody who knows how to deal with these kinds of things."

"Jesse Ray, what will we tell them? We can't tell them I was kidnapped," I yelled, frightened. "What will we tell them?"

"They don't have to know what really happened. We can say you got mugged or assaulted on the street."

I shook my head. "I'm fine. All I need is a hot bath and some clean clothes. And a glass of wine wouldn't hurt." I managed a smile, and then I leaned over and kissed Jesse Ray so hard, he squirmed. "Baby, just take me home."

And that's exactly what he did.

CHAPTER 60

It was amazing how well my in-laws had cleaned the house before they moved out. They had left nothing behind that indicated that they had even lived with us.

I didn't dive into a hot bubble bath when I got home. I was so drained, tired, and angry about what Wade had done to me that all I could manage to do was fall into bed. I didn't even take the time to stop and check in on Miss Rosetta or meet the Jamaican nurse that Jesse Ray was going to hire.

I had so much on my mind, I didn't expect to sleep much that night. As angry as I was about what Wade and Jason had done to me, I was more concerned about them telling the wrong person and implicating me. I was pretty confident that Jesse Ray would not go to the authorities or even tell his closest friends or family. Somehow I did manage to fall asleep. I didn't wake up until noon the next day.

Jesse Ray was sitting on the side of the bed, with a smile on his face. "I just put on a pot of coffee," he told me, brushing hair off my face. "I can fix you something to eat, or I can send out for something."

"How come you're not at work?" I croaked, attempting to rise.

"I haven't been back since . . . since I delivered the . . . ransom. Mel is holding down the fort until I return. He thinks I've got some type of infection," Jesse Ray said in a stiff voice.

"Jesse Ray, please tell me again that you won't ever tell anybody about this. I don't want to drag the cops into this, and I don't want those white dudes to come after us," I whispered. "We might not be so lucky the next time. . . ."

"As far as I am concerned, this never happened. If it would make you feel better, we can move. We can move out of this city, this state. We can even move to Canada if you want to. I've been thinking about opening up a store in Vancouver, anyway."

"We can talk about all that later. I just want to get my bearings back. If Jeanette or Nita calls, or anybody else, I don't feel like talking. Tell them that I caught whatever it is you got," I said, faking a cough. It wasn't really necessary for me to play sick. I really did feel like shit.

Jesse Ray nodded. "Let me get you some coffee." He left the room and closed the door behind him. I suddenly felt more paranoid than I'd ever felt before in my life. Not knowing what Wade was up to was a frightening thought. He had tapes of our conversations plotting our crime. He even had Polaroids of himself and me in some extremely explicit poses. What if he decided he wanted even more of Jesse Ray's money and wanted me to help him get it? Would he use the tapes and the Polaroids to force me into another crime? Just thinking about all the possibilities was making me dizzy. I curled up like a snail and cried like I'd never cried before in my life.

When I couldn't manage to squeeze out any more tears, I turned over and faced the large window where I used to enjoy the view of the Bay and the San Francisco skyline. I could even see the famous Golden Gate Bridge from that same window. The curtains were open, and the hot sun made my eyes burn. I turned in the other direction because I was too weak to get out of bed and close the curtains.

I flipped over on my back and stared at the ceiling, wondering if I'd have to trade all of this for a cell in some dank women's prison. I didn't even hear the door open and Jesse Ray padding across the floor. What he said next hit me like a ton of bricks.

"Wade Fisher is dead," Jesse Ray told me.

There was a profound jolt. My first thought was that we were having an earthquake, or I was experiencing a scene straight out of *The Exorcist*, because my bed shook so violently for a split second, I almost rolled off of it. I sat bolt upright.

"What did you say?" My voice was so heavy and hoarse, I could barely get the words out.

"Wade Fisher is dead," Jesse Ray repeated. There was a blank look on his face as he stood in the middle of our bedroom floor, holding a tray with two cups of coffee on it. "The biggest wannabe star I ever met."

"What are you talking about?" I let out a breath that was so strong, it could have blown Jesse Ray down if he had been close enough.

"You remember that punk from the old neighborhood who was always going around talking about how he was going to be in the movies? He was a dead ringer for that rock star. Uh, what's his name? Lenny Kravitz," Jesse Ray said, snapping his fingers. "Thought he was God's gift to women. Wade, not Lenny. But then again, Lenny probably thinks the same thing. And, women can be such fools when it comes to men like that." I didn't like the tone of Jesse Ray's voice or what he'd just said. It almost sounded like he was jealous.

He dipped his head and gave me a mysterious look. "And, don't tell me, you don't remember Wade Fisher, because males, especially young males, like to brag. Especially back in those days, when we were kids. Wade told everybody in Berkeley how he'd busted your cherry on your thirteenth birthday. . . ." Jesse Ray leaned over the bed, handing me one of the cups of coffee. "But, like I told you before, what you did before we got together is your business. Watch out, baby. This coffee's hot." My hands were shaking so hard, I spilled most of it on them and my lap. And, as hot as it was, I didn't even feel it.

"How . . . how did Wade die?" I asked, my lips quivering. The top of my head felt like somebody had sliced it open. I recalled how nervous Wade had been standing near that mortuary the last time he called up Jesse Ray. "Bad karma," he'd said. I prayed that Wade's betrayal would be the only bad karma I'd have to face.

"It's all over the news, on every channel," Jesse Ray said, wiping coffee off my hands with his fingers. He was acting too calm to know as much as I thought he did. I sat there staring into his eyes, trying to read his thoughts. "Some neighbors called the cops after they heard gunshots inside his mama's house. The paper thinks it was drug related because the guy that shot Wade had a rap sheet as long as a mule's dick."

"Jason Mack," I mouthed. It took me a moment to realize that I was talking out loud.

Jesse Ray's body got stiff, and he gave me a puzzled look. "Yes. But . . . but how did you know?"

"Uh, they used to be running buddies, and I heard that they did some burglaries together," I said. "They were real close," I added. "You said they think it was drug related?"

"The cops arrived before Jason made it out of the house. Apparently, he hung around after he'd shot Wade and tore the place up, looking for Wade's stash. Cocaine, no doubt. When the cops tried to get Jason to surrender, he came out blasting. And that was the last thing he did in this life."

"Did the cops find any drugs or anything else? Maybe Jason was looking for money."

"Well, whatever he was looking for, he didn't find. And, even if he did, it won't do him any good now. Baby, drink your coffee before it gets cold."

"Oh," I croaked, sipping coffee I couldn't even taste, because I was in such a state of shock.

"I'm anxious for you to meet Daisy," Jesse Ray said in a cheerful voice that I knew was forced. He strolled across the floor and opened the curtains even wider. The pain that the sun caused to my eyes was nothing compared to the pain in my head.

In addition to everything else that I had to worry about, now I had to worry about Wade's mother, the cops finding those tapes of me planning my own kidnapping, those Polaroids of my naked ass grinning into a camera, and a million dollars of my husband's hard-earned money.

Even dead, Wade was still "fucking" me.

CHAPTER 61

I crawled out of bed like a lizard around two that afternoon. I slid to the floor and stood in the same spot for at least five minutes, trying to sort out my thoughts. I took a quick shower and wrapped myself up in a bathrobe. Compared to the bleak bathroom in the motel that I'd been holed up in for the past few days, my bathroom looked and felt like something in a palace. But I didn't feel like anybody's princess or queen. I still felt like hell, physically and mentally. One of the nagging things at the front of mind was, where do I go from here?

I started sweating and crying, standing there in my bathrobe. Bile rose in my throat, and I had to lean over the commode to vomit. With the snot that ran out of my nose, the sweat, the tears, and the puke on my face, I was such a nasty mess that I had to take another shower. After I dried myself off, I let the lid down on the toilet; then I sat there and cried some more.

"Hey. You all right in there?" Jesse Ray asked, gently tapping on the door. I didn't have my watch with me, and there was no clock in the bathroom, so I didn't know how long I'd been in there. I was sorry that I hadn't locked the door. Before I could respond, Jesse Ray eased the door open. "Baby, it's going to be all right." He leaned over me, patting my back with one hand, rubbing my shoulder with the other. "Now pull yourself together, and come say hi to Mama."

Jesse Ray wiped my face with a towel and led me back into our bedroom. He put lotion on my hands, face, and legs, like he'd seen me do almost every morning since we'd been married. Then he dressed me. He didn't just snatch another bathrobe out of my closet or the first thing he got his hands on. He took his time and went through all my drawers, selecting my underwear and one of the many loose-fitting dresses that I liked to wear around the house. He even pulled my hair back, braided it, wound it, and secured it to the nape of my neck with hairpins. "Now," he said, with a broad smile, smoothing down the sides of my dress after he'd slid me into it feet first.

"I'm fine," I insisted, with a smile, when he attempted to lead me downstairs by the hand. I didn't want to look at myself in the mirror. I didn't want to see my eyes. They were aching and itching, and I knew that from all the crying I'd just done, they were red and swollen, too. But the real reason I didn't want to look into my own eyes was because I didn't want to see what I really was. I didn't want to look at my lying, evil eyes. I couldn't face the reality of what I'd done. I managed to smile at my husband again, anyway.

"I'm fine, baby," I said again, pushing his hand away. I slid my feet into the fuzzy pink bedroom slippers I kept on the floor by the side of the bed. I was so wobbly, I started walking like I had a big stick stuck up my ass. Somehow I managed to make it downstairs without Jesse Ray holding me up, but he walked so close behind me, I could feel his breath on the back of my neck.

It was nice to see that Miss Rosetta was doing all right. Well, not exactly all right, but as well as could be expected. She was no better and no worse. She just stared up at me from the bed that had become her prison and blinked. Then a few large tears oozed out of the corners of her eyes.

I was happy to meet Daisy Meekes, the buxom, middle-aged nurse that Jesse Ray had hired. Not only had she already cleaned and fed Miss Rosetta, but she had also done things for the old woman that I had not even considered when the chore was on my shoulders. She had permed and styled what little bit of hair Miss Rosetta had left on her head. But what really brought tears to my eyes was the fact that she had put make-up on Miss Rosetta's face. She had slapped on too much powder and the wrong shade of lipstick, just like Miss Rosetta used to do it.

It pleased me to hear that Daisy had already moved into the room that nasty-ass Odell had occupied. It pleased me even more to hear

that Jesse Ray had replaced the mattress that that boy had mastur-
bated into day and night. Not only had Daisy agreed to take care of
Miss Rosetta 24-7, she was also going to help with the cooking and
housekeeping. I was not surprised to hear that she was the one who
had cleaned up all of the rooms that my in-laws had vacated.

"I'm here to make de day easier for you," she told me in her charm-
ing Jamaican accent, shaking my hand so hard, I thought it was going
to fall off. "You look like you need to get a lot of much-needed rest."
Lady, you don't know the half of it, I thought to myself, forcing myself to
smile. I liked Daisy right away. She reminded me of a younger version
of Miss Odessa.

"I'd appreciate that," I told her. Jesse Ray stood a few feet behind
me. "I think I just want to rest today," I said, turning to face him. I declined Daisy's offer to fix me something to eat. Now that I knew that
my house was back under my control, I wanted to go back into hiding.
I had to be alone because I still had some very serious issues to work
through.

"Nita and Jeanette wanted to come by, but I told them to wait until
they hear from you," Jesse Ray told me, steering me back toward the
stairs that led to our bedroom. "They said that if they don't hear from
you by tomorrow, they'll stop by. They wanted to know if you wanted
to go to that funeral with them."

"What funeral?" I gasped, sitting back down on the side of our bed.
I slid off my house shoes and was working the zipper on the back of
my dress.

"That Wade's funeral," Jesse Ray said, with an exasperated wave of
his hand. "I didn't know they knew him, too."

My body froze. Just hearing Jesse Ray mention Wade's name almost
turned me to stone. "They . . . they got to know his mama through
me," I stammered. "You know, almost everybody in Berkeley eventually got to know Miss Louise, the way she got around." I paused and
offered a fake laugh. "She's probably borrowed money from everybody she knows at one time or another. When I was in school, she
used to borrow my lunch money to buy make-up. That old sister
makes Harvey and Adele and her bunch look like amateurs when it
comes to borrowing money." I let out another fake laugh.

"I don't like to speak ill of the dead, but from what I heard about
that Wade, he wasn't living right anyhow. I'm sorry he ended up
dead, but he had it coming. I'm just glad you didn't get more in-

volved with him than you did during your teens. He could have ruined your youth." Jesse Ray shook his head. "Anyway, if you want to go
to the funeral to pay your respects to Wade's mama, I'll go with you."

"I'm not going," I said quickly. Wade was the last person on the
planet I wanted to see again, dead or alive. He had caused me enough
pain to last me the rest of my life. And it wasn't over yet.

"That's fine with me, but we will send flowers. And, if you want to
pay Miss Louise a brief visit, let me know."

"I . . . I will," I managed.

"You can sleep as long as you want to. I don't want you to worry
about anything anymore today. You've been through a lot."

"Where did you drop the ransom money off?" I asked. I had stepped
out of my dress and was now back in bed, with the covers pulled up to
my chin.

Jesse Ray gave me a slight frown at first. "That's not important.
What is important is that they got what they wanted, and I got what I
wanted." He smiled. His eyes looked tired and sad. "I would have given
them every penny I've got to my name to get you back."

Then my eyes started filling up with tears, which I couldn't hold
back. "Jesse Ray, I am so sorry about all this," I sobbed.

"You don't have to keep telling me that. This was not your fault," he
said, sitting down on the side of the bed.

"And you won't call the cops? You won't tell anybody about any of
this? Ever?" I asked.

"You don't have to keep asking me that. I've told you and told you
that as far as I am concerned, this never happened. Now, you get some
more rest." Jesse Ray glanced at his watch. "I'm going to make a few
calls."

"Are you going to work?"

"Not for a while," he told me. "I think you need me more than that
video store does."

CHAPTER 62

I finally called up Jeanette that Monday, hoping I'd get her voice mail. I had purposely waited to call her at work because I knew that she was usually too busy to talk. A few minutes before I'd dialed Jeanette's number, I'd left a message on Nita's voice mail, telling her that I was doing fine and that I'd arrange a get-together with her and Jeanette in a few days. For the first time since I'd met Jeanette, I was disappointed to hear her voice. She answered on the first ring.

"Girl, we have been worried sick about you! Hold on. Let me get rid of this other call," she said before I could respond. I held my breath for a few moments, hoping that Jeanette wouldn't return. I was tempted to just hang up, but before I could do that, she was back on the line. "Are you all right? Is there anything I can do for you?"

"I'm fine . . . I guess," I rasped.

"You are the healthiest woman I know. I've never even known you to have a cold, let alone a bug that shuts you down for so many days. Did you see a doctor?"

"Uh, yeah. Dr. Fine. He gave me some pills and a shot. And he told me to sleep as much as I could. This thing is real contagious, so I'd better stay away from everybody for a while." I coughed and let out a few moans and groans.

"Well, you still could have called to let me know what was going on, anyway. I can't catch whatever it is you've got through the telephone.

I couldn't get much of anything out of that man of yours. I even showed up at your house the same day Adele and her gang were moving out. I wanted to see if you needed anything. Chicken soup, something to read."

"Like I said, what I have is too contagious. I told Jesse Ray, and Dr. Fine told him, too, not to let anybody near me."

"Was that why your in-laws moved out so suddenly?" Jeanette asked, with a cackle. "They were throwing their shit into Mel's old van like it was contagious, too." I was glad to hear Jeanette laugh. Then she got serious. "I didn't know Wade, but I went to his funeral," she told me, her voice cracking. "I ran into his mama at the beauty shop the day before the funeral, and she . . . she had everybody on the premises in tears."

"Oh," was all I could say.

"I'm glad you'd stopped fooling around with him. Whatever it was that got him killed, you might have got caught up in, too."

"I know," I said. "Uh, will you call Nita and tell her we talked? I'm so weak, all I want to do is sleep right now."

"You take care of yourself, and if there is anything I can do, just let me know," Jeanette told me. "I'm having lunch with Nita today, and I'll tell her we talked."

Nita called me up a little after nine that night. I had moved from my bed to the living-room sofa downstairs. Jesse Ray was in the bathroom and Daisy was busy getting Miss Rosetta ready for bed when the phone rang. I grabbed it on the third ring. As soon as I realized it was Nita, I faked a coughing fit. I was hacking so hard, my throat hurt, and then I really did have to cough.

"Christine, I just called to hear your voice, but I can tell that you are not up to talking. You go and get your rest. I'll call you or come by in a few days," Nita said in a gentle voice. As much as I loved my dear friend, I was glad when she hung up.

Jesse Ray heard me all the way from the bathroom, so when he came into the living room, he handed me a tall glass of iced water. I practically snatched it out of his hand and put it up to my lips so I wouldn't have to talk.

"I thought you'd like to know that Adele and the twins are not speaking to me," Jesse Ray said, with a mild chuckle. "Adele called me a stingy bastard when I refused to help her pay her American Express bill this month."

I almost choked on my water. With my mouth hanging open, I set the glass on the coffee table and swung my feet to the floor. "What about all the money you've already given to her? What about the money you paid for them to get into their new apartment?" I asked.

Jesse Ray shook his head and shrugged his shoulders. "I know better now," he said. "I told her, and I told Mel and the kids, that they are welcome to come visit Mama whenever they want to. And, they are still welcome in my house, but it'll be a *long* time before they get any more of my money. It's going to be awkward with Mel working for me now, but . . ." Jesse Ray paused and looked away. He sniffed and rubbed the side of his head before he finished saying what he had to say. "You're all I need now. Other than Mama, you are the only person who ever really appreciated my generosity. That's why I was willing to pay whatever it took to get you back."

I couldn't bring myself to look at his face. My own face was burning with shame.

"Uh, I need to go to the Department of Motor Vehicles to get a new driver's license," I said, steering the conversation in another unpleasant direction. "They took my purse," I mumbled.

"I figured they would. Right after I got that first call, I cancelled your credit cards," Jesse Ray told me. Before he could say anything more, the telephone rang again. He grabbed it on the first ring. The stunned look that crossed his face as he gazed at me made me so nervous, I held my breath.

"One moment please," he said to the caller, looking at me now with both his eyebrows raised. "It's your mama," he whispered.

I gasped and gave him an incredulous look. I had been married to Jesse Ray for over twelve years, and this was the first time my mother had called our house.

"Do you want to take the call?" he asked, still whispering.

I don't know how long I just sat there glancing from his face to the telephone. I don't even remember what I said, if anything. But the next thing I knew, the telephone was in my hand.

"Mama?" I croaked.

"Christine, are you all right? Your daddy and I have been worried about you. We've both had some very bad premonitions . . . about you. I woke up one morning with a feeling of darkness and evil all around you. Daddy felt it, too," Mama told me. It had been so long since I'd heard her voice on a telephone that I almost didn't recognize it. She sounded like a stranger.

"Mama . . . Mama, I was a little sick this week, but I'm all right now," I managed. "Mama, are you and Daddy all right?"

"We get by, like always. You know we are survivors," she added.

"Me, too," I said, still stunned to be hearing from her. "Where is Daddy?"

"He's out on an errand for that fishy Fisher woman down the street. Since that boy of hers, Wade, got himself killed, she's been in a tizzy."

"Uh-huh. I heard about him getting killed. When you see Miss Louise, please give her my condolences," I offered.

"I will do that, Christine. I hope you will continue to do well," Mama said, with a heavy sigh. "I hope I didn't disturb you. . . ."

"Mama, you didn't disturb me. I am glad you called. And, you are welcome to come to the house anytime you want to. You and Daddy both," I insisted. It pleased me to see Jesse Ray nod.

"Good-bye, Christine." Mama hung up before I could say another word to her.

"Jesse Ray, can you drop me off at my mama's house?" I asked, already up and getting back into my clothes.

"Christine, why don't you take it easy for a few more days? You don't look too good, and I don't want you to fall apart in front of your mama and daddy. You don't want them to start asking you a lot of nosy questions now, do you?"

"Jesse Ray, Mama said she and Daddy have both been having bad premonitions about me. They are worried about me. I have to go over there so that they can see that I'm all right."

Jesse Ray shook his head. "Baby, wait at least one more day. That's all I'm asking. I will go with you."

"I will not wait one more day. And you will not go with me. This is something that I have to deal with on my own," I said, rushing into the bathroom. "Give me the extra set of keys to my Lexus," I ordered over my shoulder.

Half an hour after my mother had called me up, I was speeding down our street, driving like I was on a speedway. But when I spotted a scowling cop behind me in his cruiser in my rearview mirror when I stopped at a red light, I got so nervous, I pulled to the side of the street and stopped until he passed. I wanted to stay as far away from the cops as I could for as long as I could. Getting a speeding ticket was the least of my concerns when it came to the police. I was more concerned about them finding out about my involvement with Wade.

CHAPTER 63

Ihad retained two sets of keys to the apartment that my parents still lived in. One set had disappeared along with my driver's license, and the other items in my missing purse. The other set was on my spare-key ring, the one that Jesse Ray had so reluctantly given to me.

I didn't even have to use the keys when I arrived at the address on Prince Street. Daddy was looking out the front window when I parked.

"Christine?" he mouthed. "What the devil are you doing here?" he asked as soon as I reached the door. And then he did something that stunned me even more than Mama's telephone call. He rushed up to me and gave me a hug. "Mother and I have had some very bad feelings about you. You look okay, but are you?"

It had taken over thirty years for me to hear some serious words of concern about me from one of my parents.

I nodded my head so hard, it felt like it was going to roll off my shoulders. "Mama called me. I just wanted to come over . . . so that I could see you. And so you could see me," I said, my voice cracking like ice.

Even after Mama's telephone call and my unplanned and hasty visit, once I got inside and they both saw that I was physically all right, I realized that things had not changed that much. Within minutes, it felt like I'd walked into a stranger's home. Daddy became aloof, and Mama became distant.

"Mama, I am glad you called," I said, touching my mother's cold hand. "I hope you call again, and I hope I see you and Daddy more often."

Mama's face looked like it was going to turn to stone when she smiled. "I hope so, too," she said, with a yawn. "It's late now." She stood up and started moving toward the door. Then I remembered something that Miss Odessa had told me many years ago. She had told me things about my parents that I didn't know. She'd also told me that if I wanted to know more about them, all I needed to do was ask. So I did.

"Mama, how come you and Daddy never loved me?" I asked.

Mama froze, with her hand on the doorknob, and gave me the most frightened look I'd ever seen on another person's face.

"I know you never really wanted me, and I know you almost died giving birth to me, but what did I do to make you feel the way you do about me?" I asked. I had made up my mind that I was not going to leave until I got some answers. Just then, Daddy shuffled back into the room, plopping down on the sofa, where he'd already laid out his blankets and pillows. It amazed me to see that he still slept on the couch, especially knowing that my old room was empty now.

"Your daddy, Reuben, needs his rest, and from the looks of the dark circles around your eyes, you do, too," Mama responded, opening the door. I looked over Mama's shoulder as I backed out. There was a hopeless look on Daddy's face.

"I'll be back tomorrow night," I assured them. And, I did return the next night and the next night. It took a lot of effort on my part, but it eventually paid off. The strange story about my parent's background finally began to unfold about a week later, after I'd made six clumsy visits.

As usual, Mama took the lead, while Daddy remained in the living room, on the sofa. I sat across from her at the kitchen table. A pot of oxtail stew sat simmering on the stove.

Staring at her hands, she started talking in a slow, controlled voice, like she was reading cue cards. "People had very little where we come from, but we had each other. We all looked out for one another because . . . because we loved each other. It didn't matter if one was blood or not. We shared our love. The soldiers would raid out village . . . and they were soldiers from hell. They killed the strongest men; they raped the females. Even the baby girls and the blind old ladies.

My family and your father's family, we were lucky ones. For years, the soldiers left our families alone. Then things changed, all in one day. Reuben and I knew we wanted to be together, and we were as often as we could. One day, when Reuben and I were supposed to be working in the fields, we went to the woods instead. We returned just in time to see what was left of the village after the soldiers had raided it again."

Mama stopped for a moment and wiped tears from her eyes. "Everything and everybody was gone. Destroyed by machetes, bullets, and fire. My sister Carmen had just had a baby girl a week ago. We arrived in time to see the soldiers toss the baby in the air and shoot her as Carmen lay on the ground in flames. Reuben and I ran back into the woods, and we kept running. We ran for years. We didn't stop until we made it to this country, with the clothes on our backs. We were afraid then; we are still afraid.

"Reuben used to be good with words. He met people, he talked to people, and he got the information we needed. He married an American woman so he could get the citizenship. I married an American man, whose first name I can't even remember. But it allowed us to stay in this country. The memories we manage to hold on to are not good ones. But we forced ourselves to forget a lot because it was too painful." Mama paused again. Then she looked at me, with tears streaming down her face. "We even forgot how to love," she whispered.

"Don't you at least love Daddy? Doesn't he love you?" I didn't know what else to say. It was hard to absorb what I'd just heard because it didn't make a whole lot of sense to me. "How can a person forget how to love?" I wanted to know. "I am your own flesh and blood."

"We lost everything and everyone we loved. We were afraid to let it happen again. I have a different kind of affection for your father. It is all I have left to give."

"Oh." I dropped my head for a few moments. "And nothing left for me," I managed. I rose to leave, but my mother grabbed my hand and pulled me back to my seat.

"Christine, things can change. I know that now. Your daddy knows that now. I know because I couldn't stop myself from calling you," Mama said. "And, I will call again. . . ."

"I will, too, Mama," I said. Just as we rose from the table, I looked toward the door. Daddy stood there, with his head bowed. When he glanced up and saw me looking at him, he returned his attention to the floor. Just as I was about to leave, Mama came around the table and wrapped her arms around me. A few moments later, I felt Daddy's arms embrace me from behind. The group hug lasted at least two minutes. Nothing was said, and it was not necessary now. At least not at this moment. I reluctantly pulled away, and then I left.

They say that when one door closes, another one opens. That's what it felt like. I knew that my marriage was coming to an end. But I had a very hopeful feeling about resuming a relationship, a healthy one this time, with the parents I hardly knew.

"What do you mean you're leaving your husband?" Nita asked as soon as she entered my house three days later.

Jesse Ray had finally returned to work. And, true to her word, Adele had stopped speaking to her brother. We had run into her and the twins at the mall a few times, but each time they'd ignored us. She refused to even enter or call the video store that Jesse Ray still allowed Mel to manage. Instead, when she needed to talk to Mel, she'd have one of the twins call the store and tell him to call her. Harvey and his lady friend had moved to Chinatown in San Francisco and rarely called or visited. I didn't ask, and Jesse Ray didn't volunteer the information, but I was certain that Harvey had changed his MO because Jesse Ray had cut off his credit, too. But none of that mattered anymore. I knew it was time for me to make a drastic change, too.

"Your man is finally doing everything you want him to do," Nita added. "What more could you ask for?"

"I've got to get away from Jesse Ray," I admitted. "He's trying hard to make things work, and I appreciate him doing that, but I just can't stay with him any longer. The wounds that his family opened up on me are still too fresh." I needed to heal from my wounds. Especially the ones I'd inflicted.

"How are you going to live? Where are you going to live?"

"My mother wants me to move back in with her and Daddy until I figure out what I want to do," I said, with a smile so broad, it made my face ache. Yes, it was true. My mother, the woman who had rejected me all my life, had invited me to move back into my old room so we could "sort things out starting from scratch."

And, at this point I felt that it was the best move I could make.

"I hope things work out for you, ma'am," Daisy said as she helped me pack and load my things into the SUV that Jesse Ray had just bought for me. I'd sold my other car because it contained too many memories of Wade. His scent had permeated the interior. At least, it seemed that way to me. I'd only driven it three times since I'd returned home. "Mr. Thurman will be hurt and surprised when he returns home this evening," she added, with a sad look on her face.

"I'll only be across town," I told her, returning to the living room to give Miss Rosetta a long hug and tell her how much I'd appreciated her kindness. Her flat eyes didn't even respond to my gesture. She didn't even blink.

Nita followed me in her car to my parent's apartment so she could help me unload my belongings. I was glad that both my parents had chosen to go to work that day. I wanted to be by myself again.

CHAPTER 64

An hour after Nita left, Jesse Ray called me up on the new cellular phone he'd purchased for me two days earlier.

"Christine, what the hell are you doing? I called the house to invite you to lunch, and Daisy tells me you've moved back in with your folks? How in the hell are we going to work things out with you over there and me over here?" he asked in a frantic voice. "I'm on my way over there!"

"And the only way you'll get in is if you break in," I warned. "I don't want to see you."

"What are you saying? Are you telling me that after all that's happened—my spending another fortune to get you a new vehicle, too—you are leaving me, *anyway*?"

"I need some time to myself," I explained. "I can't think straight in your house."

"*My* house? It's your house just as much as it is mine."

"Now it is. All those times when I tried to talk to you about the way things were going, you kept reminding me that everything was yours," I said.

"Look, you are talking foolishness. Now let me get off this telephone so I can come over there and talk to you face-to-face."

"I don't want to see your face," I revealed. "I just told you, I need to be by myself. I need to work on my relationship with my parents."

"But you don't need to work on your relationship with your husband? Is that how it's going to be?"

"J.R., I still love you, but I don't think . . . I don't think I'm *in love* with you anymore," I admitted.

"What do you want to do, Christine? Do you want a divorce?"

"The only thing I know that I want right now is to be away from you so I can think."

"When will I see you again?"

"I don't know."

"Can I call you in a few days?"

"Yes." I hung up so he couldn't say anything else.

That evening I sat down to dinner with my parents, but they were just as uncomfortable as I was. But they were trying to piece our fractured relationship together, and so was I. The day before, Daddy had confided in me how much he was looking forward to retiring. That didn't mean much to me until he told me that one of the things his retirement would mean was that he could spend more time with me.

And, no matter who I talked to, or what we talked about, the conversations always got around to Wade's mother. I had not paid Miss Louise the visit that I had been meaning to pay her, but it was always good to hear about her. I was glad to hear that she was in good health and still working. She had gotten through her grief intact.

A month after I left Jesse Ray, he called me up one day and caught me in a good mood. I had just enjoyed dinner with my parents at Giovanni's for the first time. Daddy had shared some of the few pleasant things that he could remember about his childhood. He'd raised a goat by himself. He'd taught himself how to swim when he was just five years old. Mama had seemed as fascinated by Daddy's stories as I did. In fact, she had regaled me with a few of her own, laughing like a schoolgirl when she told me about the time a chicken chased her into the woods and pecked her on her legs.

Jesse Ray's telephone call couldn't have come at a better time, because I honestly did want to see him.

"Christine, can we get together tomorrow for a few drinks?" he asked, sounding as shy and meek as a schoolboy. I could hear the desperation in his voice. Other than visiting a few bars with Jeanette and Nita, I had done no socializing. And, getting back into the dating game was the furthest thing from my mind. After Wade and Jesse Ray, I wasn't sure I ever wanted to make love to another man again. But I knew that was an unrealistic notion. When Jesse Ray called, I felt that I was ready to go back in that direction, but one step at a time.

"Okay," I said, with a sigh. "You can pick me up tomorrow around noon."

Even with Jesse Ray, the conversation often ended up being about Miss Louise. After we'd chitchatted about Miss Rosetta's health, which was no better, and about the rest of his family ignoring him, Jesse Ray's tone took a disturbing turn. "Miss Louise is finally living the life she always wanted," he started, toying with the stirrer in his rum and Coke. We were seated at a corner table in a secluded little bar in downtown San Francisco.

"I guess she's finally gotten over what happened to her son," I volunteered.

"She just bought a new condo, and she's driving around in a brand-new Cadillac," Jesse Ray reported.

I gave him a thoughtful look and blinked as I considered this piece of information. "Miss Louise always lived beyond her means," I reminded. "She finally stopped borrowing from Daddy. As a matter of fact, she paid him back all she owed him, with interest. I guess she must have had a real good insurance policy on Wade."

Jesse Ray shook his head. "Not a dime. That's the problem with so many black folks. They don't plan for the important things, like funeral costs."

"How would you know?"

"Baby, I didn't want you to ever know this, but Mel told me that Miss Louise got some church to raise money to bury Wade. Even I pitched in a few bucks anonymously," Jesse Ray said, looking embarrassed. His words seemed to float above my head. I almost swallowed my tongue just thinking about what he'd just told me. Not only had my lover beat my husband out of a million dollars, but my husband helped pay for him to be laid to rest. It was too incredible to believe. If I'd seen this drama in a movie, I'd have walked out.

"That still doesn't mean she didn't have insurance on Wade. Maybe the insurance company didn't pay off right away, and that's why she had to get help with his funeral expenses. She came into some money somehow. She's paying people back that she's been owing for years. She just bought a new condo, a new car, new designer clothes. She must have won the lottery or . . . or . . ." I couldn't finish my sentence.

"I doubt that. That bigmouthed woman would have told everybody on the planet." Jesse Ray leaned across the table and started talking in a low voice. "Rumors are floating around town that Wade must have had some drug money stashed away in Miss Louise's house, which she stumbled across when she started cleaning out Wade's room. And, it had to be quite a pile for her to be spending the way she's been spending."

Like a million dollars! That was the only other explanation! Miss Louise had somehow gotten her greedy hands on the million-dollar ransom that Jesse Ray had paid Wade to get me back. That woman had to be in hog heaven now—even though she'd lost her precious only child. That explained why the police never found any money. Now it all made sense. After Wade had double-crossed me, Jason had attempted to double-cross him. But Wade had hidden the money, and that had to be why Jason had shot him.

As far as Wade having tapes of my conversations with him, he had never proved that to me. That hadn't made sense when he told it to me, and it didn't make any sense now. Wade had no reason to tape our conversations at the time. How could he have known in advance that I'd strike up a telephone conversation with him about him helping me plan a phony kidnapping? Wade had never been that clever. Yes, he had taken a few Polaroids of me in the Marriott Hotel, but all that proved was that we'd had a relationship. And everybody already knew about that. The pictures didn't reveal a date, so I could have posed for Wade's camera long before I married Jesse Ray. Wade had said himself how young I looked in the pictures.

"Does that big smile on your face mean yes?" Jesse Ray asked, squeezing my hand. My mind had been so far away that I had not heard what he'd asked.

"Yes for what?" I suddenly felt warm all over because now I had some answers. I had no proof, but I finally had some peace of mind.

"I just asked you if we could try to work on things. I want you to come on back home, baby," Jesse Ray said, squeezing my hand again. "We'll move anywhere you want to move. I think that would help."

"I don't want to leave Berkeley," I said. "My parents are getting old, and they are going to need me now more than ever. I want to be here for them."

"Oh. I guess that means you won't be coming home with me today?

We won't be starting over? We can even start over from scratch. A few innocent dates, just like when we first got together. I didn't pressure you for anything more then, and I won't do it this time."

I shook my head. "I won't be coming home with you today." I looked around the bar because for the first time I wanted everybody in it to see the glow on my face. Then I looked at Jesse Ray. "But maybe we can start over . . . *from scratch.*" It was a new beginning for me, my parents, and Jesse Ray.

"I'd like that, Christine," he said, getting teary-eyed.

I had just as many tears in my eyes. "I'd like that, too," I told him. And I meant it.

DELIVER ME FROM EVIL

MARY MONROE

ABOUT THIS GUIDE

The suggested questions are intended to
enhance your group's reading of
DELIVER ME FROM EVIL
by Mary Monroe.

DISCUSSION QUESTIONS

1. Christine's husband, J.R., spent more time at his job than he did at home, but she knew what he was like before she married him. Was she unrealistic to expect him to change for her?

2. Christine received very little attention and affection from her parents. Do you think that this was the reason she was so desperate for attention from the men in her life?

3. J.R. gave "loans" to his greedy relatives for one "emergency" after another. When Christine found out that these emergencies included shopping sprees, gambling excursions, cruises, and trips to Disneyland, she tried to put a stop to it. Since J.R. had been giving in to his relatives' financial demands long before he married Christine and it didn't seem to bother him, should Christine have not interfered?

4. When J.R.'s mother had her stroke and had to be cared for like a baby, Christine didn't hesitate to become her caretaker because the old woman had always been nice to her. It was only after the rest of the in-laws moved into her house and got "too busy" to help Christine care for Miss Rosetta that Christine decided she'd had enough. Do you think that you would have tolerated your in-laws' actions for as long as Christine did?

5. When Christine's former lover, Wade, returned to town, out of frustration she eagerly resumed a sexual relationship with him. Wade used Christine for whatever he could get, and she used him. Do you think that they had any real feelings for each other?

6. When Christine discovered VHS copies of some of the pornographic movies that Wade had starred in, should she have told him—so that he would have stopped lying about his "successful" career in Hollywood?

7. Because of the pre-nuptial agreement that Christine signed, she would get next to nothing if she divorced J.R.. If you were

in a similar situation, would you consider something as extreme as a bogus kidnapping and ransom demand so you could get paid?

8. In addition to the in-law problems that Christine had to live with, J.R. didn't tell her until after they were married that he couldn't have children. Did he cause her enough grief to justify her kidnapping scam?

9. Wade didn't agree to help Christine arrange her "kidnapping" because he was a compassionate man. He did it because he was greedy. He didn't just want a portion of the million dollar ransom, he wanted it all. Do you think that the love of money was so powerful that it brought out the worst in Wade, or was he just bad to the bone anyway?

10. Did you have any sympathy for Christine when her plan backfired? Were you surprised when Wade turned on her?

11. Were you glad that Wade's plan backfired, too? Jason Mack, the accomplice that Wade had recruited was just as greedy as Wade. Were you as surprised as Christine was when she heard that Jason had shot and killed Wade to get the ransom money?

12. When the police shot and killed Jason, there was no mention in the news report of the money he'd killed Wade for. Christine was on pins and needles wondering what had happened to the ransom until Wade's mother, Miss Louise, started spending money all over town. Were you glad that the money ended up with Wade's cash-strapped mother and not Christine?

13. When Christine returned home from her kidnapping ordeal, J.R. kicked his trifling relatives out of his house, and he promised Christine that he would put her ahead of his family and his job. Christine had committed a crime and gotten away with it. But it was J.R.'s actions that had pushed her over the edge. Do you feel that their marriage was worth saving?

Catch a special sneak preview of Mary Monroe's
SHE HAD IT COMING
Available in hardcover in September 2008
wherever books are sold!

CHAPTER 1

People often tell me that when it comes to picking friends, I "sure know how to pick 'em."

I saw my best friend kill her vicious stepfather on the night of our senior prom. Our boyfriends—mine would later end up in prison for life without the possibility of parole for rape and murder—who had reluctantly agreed to be our prom dates, were relieved when I called them up and told them we had to cancel due to Valerie's "sudden illness." While our classmates were dancing the night away and plotting to do everything we had been told not to do after the prom, I was helping Valerie Proctor hide a dead body in her backyard beneath a lopsided fig tree.

Ezekiel "Zeke" Proctor's violent death had come as no surprise to me. The first question that had entered my mind during the crime was, "Valerie, what took you so long?" It happened sixteen years ago but it's still fresh on my mind, and I know it will be until the day I die, too.

Mr. Zeke had been a fairly good neighbor as far back as I could re-member. When he wasn't too drunk or in a bad mood, he would haul old people and single mothers who didn't have transportation around in his car. He would borrow money, dole it out to people who needed it, and he never asked to be repaid. He would do yard work and other maintenance favors for little or no money. And when he was in a good mood, which was rare, he would host a backyard cook-out and invite everybody on our block. However, those events usually ended when he got too drunk and paranoid and decided that every-body was "out to get him."

When that happened, barbequed ribs, links, and chicken wings ended up on the ground, or stuck to somebody's hair that he'd thrown it at. People had to hop away from the backyard to avoid step-ping on glasses that he had broken on purpose. There had not been any cookouts since the time he got mad and shot off his gun in the air because he thought one of the handsome young male guests was plot-ting to steal his wife. In addition to those lovely social events, he'd also been the stepfather and husband from hell.

Valerie's mother, Miss Naomi, bruised and bleeding like a stuck pig herself after the last beating that she'd survived a few minutes before the killing, had also witnessed Mr. Zeke's demise. Like a zombie, she had stood and watched her daughter commit the granddaddy of crimes. Had things turned out differently, Miss Naomi would have been the dead body on the floor that night, because this time her hus-band had gone too far. He had attempted to strangle her to death. She had his handprints on her neck, and broken blood vessels in the whites of her eyes to prove it.

To this day I don't like to think of what I'd witnessed as a murder, per se. If that wasn't a slam dunk case of self defense, I didn't know what was. But Valerie and her mother didn't see things that way. They didn't call the cops like they'd done so many times in the past. That had done no good. If anything, it had only made matters worse. Each time after the cops left, Miss Naomi got another beating. They also didn't call the good preacher, Reverend Carter, who had told them time and time again, year after year, that: "Brother Zeke can't help hisself; he's confused," and to be "patient and wait because things like this will work out somehow if y'all turn this over to God." Well, they'd tried that, too, and God had not intervened.

"None of those motherfuckers helped us when we needed it, now we don't need their help," Valerie's mother said, grinding her teeth as she gave her husband's corpse one final kick in his side. She at-tempted to calm her nerves by drinking Vodka straight out of the same bottle that he had been nursing from all day like a hungry baby.

Miss Naomi and Valerie buried Mr. Zeke's vile body in the backyard of the house that Miss Naomi owned on Baylor Street. It was the most attractive residence on the block; not the kind of place that you would expect to host such a gruesome crime. People we all knew got killed in the crack houses in South Central and other rough parts of L.A., not in our quiet little neighborhood in houses like Miss Naomi's. Directly across the street was the Baylor Street Mt. Zion Baptist church, of which almost everybody on the block attended at some time. Even the late Mr. Zeke . . .

The scene of the crime was a two story white stucco with a two-car garage and a wraparound front porch that was often cluttered with toys and neighborhood kids like me. The front lawn was spacious and well-cared for. A bright white picket fence surrounded the entire front lawn like a hounds-tooth necklace. Behind the house, as with all the other houses on the block, was a high, dark fence that hid the backyard, as well as Valerie's crime.

Miss Naomi's house looked like one of those family friendly homes on those unrealistic television sitcoms. But because of Valerie's step-father's frequent violence, the house was anything but family friendly. He had turned it into a war zone over the years. Valerie's baby brother, Binkie, referred to it as Beirut because Mr. Zeke attacked every member of the family on a regular basis, including Valerie's decrepit grand-father, Paw Paw, and even one-eyed Pete, the family dog.

Even though there was blood in every room in that house, that didn't stop me from making it my second home. Over the years I had learned how to get out of the "line of fire" in time to avoid injury whenever Mr. Zeke broke loose.

It was because Valerie was my oldest and dearest friend and Miss Naomi my surrogate mother that this house was the only other place in this part of L.A. where I felt welcome and comfortable. When I went to visit, I didn't even knock, or announce my arrival. I came and went as casually as I did in my own house, two doors down.

I had innocently walked into the house and witnessed Valerie's crime that night. As soon as I realized what was happening, I threw up all over the pale pink dress that had cost me a month's worth of my babysitting money. I continued to vomit as I watched Valerie and her long-suffering mother drag the body across the kitchen floor to the backyard so casually you'd have thought it was a mop.

Before they reached the gaping hole in the ground that had several little mounds of dirt piled up around it like little pyramids, they stumbled and dropped the corpse. There was a thud and then a weak, hissing sound from the body that made me think of a dying serpent. Somebody let out a long, loud, rhythmic fart. I could smell it from where I stood in the door like a prison guard. And it was fiercely potent. I couldn't tell if it had come from Valerie, her mother, or if it was the last gas to ooze from the asshole of the dead man. It could have even been from me, but I was such a wreck, I couldn't even tell. I squeezed my nostrils and then I froze from my face to the soles of my feet.

I held my breath as Valerie stumbled and fell on top of one of the mounds of dirt. Miss Naomi, breathing hard and loud, fell on top of Mr. Zeke's corpse. One of us screamed. I didn't realize it was me until Valerie scolded me. "Dolores, shut the fuck up and help us," she hollered, swiveling her head from one side to the other, looking around. Why, I didn't know. With the tall dark fence protecting the backyard like a fort, none of our neighbors could see her. "We need to get him in this hole *now*," she said, huffing and puffing. I couldn't believe that this was the same girl that Reverend Carter had baptized less than a week ago in the church across the street from the scene of her crime.

CHAPTER 2

The Los Angeles experience was like something out of a movie. Literally. Things just didn't happen in L.A. Even things that most cities took for granted. Being that this was where Hollywood was located, even night didn't just happen in L.A. It made an *entrance* the same way Gloria Swanson did in that old movie *Sunset Boulevard.* Just like the demented character that she had so brilliantly portrayed, this particular night was *ready for its close-up.* And I was right smack dab in the middle of it. I was not the star, but in a way I had a strong supporting role. It was not where I wanted to be. But I was, and now I had to deal with it.

Even in the dim light, I could see that the hairdo Valerie had spent a hundred dollars on was ruined. Her usually glorious mane, matted with dirt and saturated with sweat, looked like a sheep's ass. With every move she made, the long curls that she was so proud of flopped about her face like limp vines. She leaped up from the ground, pulling her mother up by the hand. They then continued to slide Mr. Zeke into his final resting place. Well, it was final as long as some busybody didn't dig him up.

"Lo, you need to hold that goddamned flashlight straight," Valerie informed me, speaking in a voice I hardly recognized. There was a desperate look in her eyes that I had never seen before. But, unfortunately for me, it was a look that I would see again in our future. And, I would be her victim . . .

I was temporarily unable to speak. I moved my mouth, my tongue, and my lips, but nothing came out. All I could do was stand there in that same spot in the doorway leading from the kitchen to the backyard, trying to hold that fucking flashlight in place. Even with the porch light on, and the beam from the flashlight in my hands, everything seemed so dark; including my beautiful light pink dress. And nothing seemed real. Things didn't look the way they did in the movies that night. Even Dracula was considerate enough to observe the basic rules of etiquette. His deadly bites were always neat. I always thought that with crimes such as this one, the perpetrator was supposed to wrap the victim's body in a sheet or a blanket or a garbage bag. Why, I never knew or bothered to ask. Until this night.

"Aren't y'all supposed to wrap him up in something?" I asked in a trembling voice. It seemed almost disrespectful not to include a shroud. I even snatched a towel off the kitchen counter and held it up, waving it, hoping they would at least wrap up his head and cover his eyes. But Valerie and her mother ignored me. Mr. Zeke went into the ground with just the clothes on his back. Almost every single inch of the white shirt he'd died in had turned red with his blood.

Valerie and Miss Naomi put together didn't weigh as much as that loathsome body that they had dropped into a hole that had already been dug. I don't know how I managed to stand there holding the flashlight that Valerie had shoved into my hands. Both of my hands were shaking hard. I had to use both to hold the flashlight in place, so she and her mother could see what they were doing.

Mr. Zeke had dug the grave himself the day before, and told Valerie's mother that she'd be in it by the weekend. No, he had promised her. Ironically, he'd dug it long and deep enough to accommodate his six foot four, two hundred and seventy pound frame.

The murder weapon, a butcher knife that could have passed for a sword if it had been any longer, was on the kitchen table with half of the blade missing. I'd find out later that the missing part of the blade had been buried with Mr. Zeke, still planted in his chest like a spike. This was a horrible way for a horrible man to die, and for some reason I felt unbearably sad. Despite everything he was and had done, he was still somebody's son. Having never known my blood relatives, family had a special meaning to me.

There was a large pot of turnip greens simmering on a back burner on the stove in Miss Naomi's kitchen. The smell of the greens, seasoned with smoked turkey necks, per my request, filled the air. She knew how much I loved me some serious soul food and had assured me that there would be plenty left for me and Valerie to share with our dates after the prom.

The blood on the floor was so thick it looked like you could dip it up with a spoon. There was a large puddle in front of the sink that covered the floor like an area rug, and a wide trail that looked like a thick red snake that led to the door. The spot in front of the stove was where Mr. Zeke had issued his last threat, and breathed his last breath. Pete, the dingy black mutt that Valerie and I had rescued from the street, had already started slipping and sliding across the floor, lapping up blood like he was at a hog trough. Pete stared up at me with his one remaining eye. Mr. Zeke's blood was dripping from his tongue, whiskers, nose, and paws.

Besides Valerie and her mother, who died from natural causes herself three years later, and Valerie's one-eyed dog, I was the only other individual who knew what had happened to Mr. Zeke. That night, I promised Valerie that I would carry her secret with me to my grave. And one thing I knew how to do was to keep a promise. I decided that that was the reason Valerie told me so much of her business.

I had kept that promise for sixteen years. And it had not been that hard for me to do. I knew that my knowledge of the crime, and not reporting it, put me somewhere in the vicinity of the guilt. Since Valerie never talked about Mr. Zeke's murder after that night, I didn't know if she had shared her secret with anybody else. And I didn't want to know.

Even though I knew that Valerie's mouth was one of the biggest things on her body, I shared secrets with her, too. A lot of people did. When I shared something with Valerie it was usually something petty; something that a lot of our friends already knew anyway, or would hear from me eventually. But not this time.

Not only was Valerie Proctor my best friend and former roommate she was one of the most popular bartenders I knew, because her ears were even bigger than her mouth. She was the one person I knew who'd be more than a little interested in my confession, and the only person who would have any sympathy for me. But even before I spilled the beans, I had to ask myself, "Should I be telling this woman my business?" I didn't even have to think about my answer. I had to tell somebody. This was a load I could no longer carry by myself. Besides, what were best friends for?

"Now what's so important you had to drag me away from the comfort of my own place of business, and a possible date with one of the hottest men on the planet this side of Denzel? And it better be good," Valerie warned, her voice half serious, her eyes wide with curiosity. "Girl, I've been itching to hear some juicy news all week. I want to hear some news that is going to make my ears ring."

"Well, I've got some . . ." I said, speaking with hesitation. "And, it's real juicy . . . I think."

"Who about? Paris Hilton? Nicole Richie? Lindsey Lohan? Beyoncé? Will Smith? Star Jones? Big-mouthed Rosie O'Donnell?" Valerie served drinks to a lot of celebrities who visited Paw Paw's, the bar she owned in West Hollywood. And it was profitable for her in more ways than one. A lot of the things she heard from the famous and not so famous patrons had ended up on the pages of the tabloids. She was well paid by her media contacts, even for something as petty as one of the Lakers leaving a five dollar tip on a hundred dollar tab. "Who? Who?" she said, sounding like an owl. And the way her eyes were stretched open, she looked like one, too.

"Uh . . . me."

Valerie reared back in her seat so far her neck looked like it belonged on a goose. "*You?*" From the expression on her face, there was nothing I could have said that would have disappointed her more. She let out a disgusted sigh and rolled her eyes. "Shit," she mouthed.

"Uh-huh," I muttered. "Me."

"Oh. Whatever, whatever," Valerie said with an exasperated shrug. "Well, what did *you* do; mow somebody down with your Honda, and flee the scene?"

I shook my head. "Valerie, I need to talk to you about something I've done. But you have to promise me that you won't ever tell anybody. I . . . I can't keep this to myself any longer," I said, speaking in a low voice. "This is serious. Real serious."

I was glad to see that Valerie seemed more interested now. She held her breath and stared at me for a moment. "Please don't tell me you've got some fatal disease," she squeaked, her eyes full of tears and her lips quivering. "I don't know what I'd do without you!"

I shook my head again. "I'm not going to die," I assured her.

"All right then. I'm listening," she replied, letting out a loud sigh of relief.